Heartstones
by
Kate Glanville

Published by Accent Press Ltd 2014

ISBN 9781783755103

Chapter One

Phoebe looked down on the rain-shrouded mourners. She was too far from the grave to make out the cleric's words; the only noise she could hear was the rhythmic sound of wheels on wet tarmac coming from the flyover behind the cemetery wall.

Her long red hair whipped against her freckled cheeks in the wind and the heels of the unfamiliar shoes were sinking into the sodden turf; mud began to ooze inside, they would no doubt be ruined. Phoebe hoped Nola wouldn't be too annoyed. She wrapped the thin, black jacket around her tiny frame. It was at least four sizes too big; Nola had shoved it at her when Phoebe arrived at her house earlier on.

'Here, you'd better borrow my work jacket, you can't possibly go to a funeral in your old parka, and take off those awful boots and I'll get you my patent shoes.'

Phoebe had reluctantly shrugged on the jacket and put on the shoes. Her sister had looked her up and down with arms folded across a suit that strained at all the seams, 'You could have at least have done something with that mane of hair of yours and put some make-up on. You look terrible, and you really need to get more meat on your bones. No wonder you haven't had a boyfriend for years.'

As the wind and rain increased Phoebe shivered and Nola's words echoed in her head. She wished for the thousandth time that she could tell someone the truth

Below her she could just make out the crow-like figure

1

of Sandra – black coat flapping around her gym-honed figure, ash-blonde hair scraped tightly back, her expression agonised. Phoebe thought her role as grieving widow could have won an Oscar; there was no doubting that she was the star of the show. Beside Sandra stood the twins, their small white faces stark against their funeral clothes; a lump rose in Phoebe's throat at the sight of the two little girls. She knew how they would be feeling; lost, confused, frightened. She had felt the same, standing, shivering beside her sister all those years before. Phoebe wanted to scoop them up and take them away, wasn't it bad enough that their father had died? They shouldn't have to witness him being lowered into the cold, dark ground.

Suddenly, Sandra covered her face with her hands and turned away from the open grave. She seemed to crumple into the line of mourners behind her; their inky forms enclosed her in a cocoon of black umbrellas and supportive embraces until she had completely disappeared.

In the distance Phoebe could see the large figure of her sister Nola detaching herself from Steve's side and moving to join the others until she too was absorbed by the tight group.

Phoebe stood very still. Around her people had started moving, walking up the hill, slowly at first, then hurrying as the ground levelled out. Their waiting cars would take them to the brightly lit function room of the local pub where, as they dried out and filled themselves with sandwiches and tea and pints of beer, they'd go over and over it all again – almost relishing the tragic set of circumstances that had led to David's death.

Victoria Leach touched Phoebe's arm with a bony, blue-veined hand.

'You're soaking,' Victoria said. 'Didn't you bring an umbrella, foolish girl?' Phoebe didn't reply. She had taught in the classroom next door to Victoria's for over three years, but she had never managed to get over the

2

feeling that the older woman thought of her as just another silly pupil rather than a fellow teacher and colleague. Phoebe looked at Victoria's lips – two thin lines of orange lipstick. They were moving; she was talking but Phoebe couldn't hear the words, only a gushing sound, like water filling up her head, blocking out the world around her. Suddenly words burst through again.

'It's such a shame we couldn't have had a bit of sunshine to see him off,' Victoria sounded almost cheerful. 'This wet weather makes it all seem even worse.'

Even worse? Phoebe wanted to scream the words back at her. *How could it be even worse?* But she remained silent, not trusting herself to speak. Victoria began to move away.

'Are you coming to The Kings Arms?' she called. Phoebe shook her head. Victoria stopped. 'You could at least come for half an hour. To show a bit of respect. He was the headmaster, Phoebe.'

'I can't believe you couldn't even be bothered to come to the pub afterwards.' Nola filled the kettle in Phoebe's tiny kitchen. 'I don't think poor Sandra was in a fit state to notice who was there, but, all the same, you could have made the effort.' Nola searched through Phoebe's cupboards for tea bags, white jeans stretched tight over her thighs as she crouched down on the wooden floor. 'Don't forget that he gave you your job, though probably with a hefty prod from Sandra.' Phoebe sat at the table, still in her pyjamas and dressing gown, her unbrushed hair a mass of auburn tangles. She stared mutely at her sister.

'Honestly, Phoebe, when did you last go shopping?' Nola stood up. 'No wonder you're so skinny.' She looked disdainfully around the cramped kitchen. 'I don't know why I'm thinking of making tea anyway, all your mugs need washing up and I suspect you haven't a drop of milk in the fridge. I know you're domestically challenged but this is worse than usual. Are you ill?'

Phoebe realised she had been unconsciously twisting at the cuff of her dressing gown so tightly her wrist hurt. When she released it she saw an indented ring of red left on her skin. She thought of the bracelet David had given her for her birthday – a thin string of silver links interspersed with red glass hearts.

Nola sat down at the table and her ample chest spilled out in front of her like a shelf. Phoebe looked down at her own small breasts beneath her dressing gown and remembered how the bitchy girls at school used to call her Flat Phoebe. She'd once gone home in tears but Nola had simply told her to stuff some socks in her bra and stop being such a drip.

Nola let out a sigh and ran her hands through her messy blonde bob.

'Poor David, I can't stop thinking about him.'

For the first time Phoebe could see that her sister's dark brown roots contained a scattering of grey. She kept noticing little things like this, tiny, inconsequential things that grabbed her attention for a few seconds, offering brief respite from the painful thoughts until a deluge of misery engulfed her again.

Nola reached into her handbag and brought out two packets of M&Ms. She pushed one towards Phoebe.

'My secret stash of bribes for the children. When all else fails, throw chocolate at them.' She ripped the shiny brown packet apart and Phoebe noticed the tiny broken veins on her sister's plump, pink cheeks. 'The diet can start again tomorrow. Steve thinks I've gone to the gym; he's taken the kids swimming. I just couldn't face the gym, it's bad enough having to exercise without everyone asking questions, *'How is Sandra? How are the girls? How are they coping?'* Honestly! How do people think Sandra is? She's lost her husband; she's devastated, in pieces. I can't see how she'll ever recover from this.'

Phoebe thought of the rows that David had told her about, the plate of macaroni cheese he said had hit his back as he walked out the door to go to the last governors' meeting, the wine bottle smashed against the kitchen wall, his cold and lonely nights in the spare bedroom, the empty silences at mealtimes – was that what Sandra would miss? Or did she feel regret? Guilt? Phoebe had noticed the way Sandra flirted with the teachers' husbands at staff get-togethers, she'd seen the way she danced with Steve at his and Nola's last New Year's Eve party. *You make me feel like dancing, romancing* ... Sandra had sung along loudly with the Nolans while shimmying around a delighted-looking Steve. What did she feel now? Phoebe wondered if Sandra had the throbbing pain in her chest. Had she lost all sense of taste and touch? Did she have to remind herself to keep breathing, to keep taking breaths when everything inside her longed to give up?

'Are you not eating these?' Nola picked up the unopened packet of M&Ms still lying on the table between them. Phoebe managed to shake her head before Nola opened it and poured half the contents into her palm. 'Sandra and David were together for *so* long,' she said through a mouthful of chocolate. 'Do you remember that first time she brought him to visit us? They were on their way to the airport, off to spend the summer travelling round India – I was so jealous, she seemed to have it all, gorgeous boyfriend, university, the chance to travel to somewhere so much more exotic than a caravan park in Tenby.' Nola poured the rest of the chocolates directly into her mouth. 'I was eight months pregnant with Amy, felt like a whale – I had no idea I'd still be feeling like that twelve years later.' She pulled her cardigan tightly over her stomach.

'We had a barbecue,' said Phoebe quietly. 'You thought Steve was going to set the hedge on fire.'

'That's right,' Nola laughed. 'We'd only just moved in,

the garden was awful; overgrown and full of piles of builder's rubble. I'm surprised you remember; I'd have thought you'd have been moping about in your bedroom taping the Top 40 or something. Steve was in charge of the cooking, he put on a terrible PVC apron with a bra and frilly knickers printed on the front – I was so embarrassed. I can still see him now, wielding flaming sausages, pretending to be some sort of fire eater, assuring us they were cooked when really they were stone cold in the middle.' Nola smiled. 'David was so funny; he told us stories about his tent getting washed away by rain at the Glastonbury Festival. He did some trick I can't quite remember – something circusy, I think he'd done a circus workshop on his gap year in Australia. Was it plate-spinning?'

Juggling, it had been juggling. The images of that summer evening were still vivid in Phoebe's mind. She had been fifteen and wearing her baggy camouflage jeans. David had juggled with Steve's barbecue tongs, fish-slice, and fork – stainless steel flashing against the empty blue expanse of sky. Steve had tried not to look upstaged and ended up looking grumpy. Phoebe thought that David was the most wonderful human being she had ever seen.

'Life's too short to get tied down,' he had said as he helped her wash the dishes later on. *'You've got to grab each day and live it to the full, see the world, meet people, experience as much as you can.'* He'd pushed back his mane of sun-streaked hair and Phoebe had looked at the tattoo around his bicep and the bright white shark's tooth necklace around his neck and wondered what it would be like to wake up beside him in a muddy field in Glastonbury.

'I can't get the image of those poor little girls out of my head.' Nola had heaved herself up and was running hot water into the sink, swirling Fairy liquid into a froth of bubbles before starting to wash the pile of dirty mugs and

6

glasses. 'Did you see them at the funeral? Did you see the twins?' She turned to look at Phoebe. 'They're not much older than you were when the accident happened. You were too young to remember but I'll never forget how it felt.'

Phoebe closed her eyes; she could see her ten-year-old self standing beside Nola. Her wild red curls had been pulled into two tight plaits by unfamiliar hands and she had felt hot and uncomfortable in a borrowed black coat. Her eyes flew open at the memory of the three wooden coffins disappearing one by one into the ground.

'Don't forget you're baby-sitting for us tonight.' Nola was drying her hands on a tea towel covered with two hundred happy faces; it had been Phoebe's idea to get the tea towels printed, every child in the school drew a self portrait and there had been a competition to draw pictures of the staff. It had raised over £1,000. David had told her she was fantastic. 'If you don't feel well enough then Amy and Ruben could come round here, watch telly with you.' Nola was using the tea towel to rub at a stain on her cardigan. 'Tell you what; we'll bring round fish and chips when we drop them off. You look like you need feeding up.'

'Honestly, Nola, you know I love seeing Amy and Ruben but I don't think I can manage ...'

Nola put the crumpled tea towel on the table and sat back down on the chair.

'Don't worry, you don't have to have a whole portion, I'll have a bit of yours – it'll stop me stuffing my face in the restaurant.'

Phoebe reached for the tea towel and slowly spread it out in front of her. She found her own face, drawn by Hannah Jewson aged nine and three-quarters. The little girl had depicted Phoebe's hair as a mass of tiny ringlets and dotted her cheeks with so many spots she looked as though she had measles rather than freckles. David was at the centre of the tea towel, of course. The portrait had been drawn by Samuel Elson, Year Two – he given David a gigantic tie, spiky hair, and a big wobbly smile. Phoebe touched his damp, linen face and wondered what Nola would say if she told her.

Chapter Two

Days blurred into one another. For the first few weeks Phoebe managed to make it into work most days – it was as though the reality of the situation took some time for her to understand. It took at least two months to realise that David really wasn't ever going to come breezing back into the staff room with his cheerful smile, let alone come bounding up the stairs to her flat.

The Christmas holidays were awful – empty days without a class of five-year-olds to distract her. On Christmas Day Phoebe dragged herself and a bag full of badly wrapped presents round to Nola and Steve's. Nola drank too much Buck's Fizz and argued with Steve about the turkey, while Amy and Ruben could hardly be prised away from their new DS games. Everyone forgot about the plum pudding in the microwave.

Sandra and the girls came round in the evening and they all squeezed on to Nola's leather three-piece to watch a BBC comedy special in silence. Halfway through one of the girls climbed on to Phoebe's lap and Phoebe had to blink back her tears as she whispered *my Dad used to laugh at this show*. Later Phoebe let her tears fall unchecked as she ran home through the freezing night.

Phoebe was only vaguely aware of the New Year seeping in and by the time she returned to school it became harder and harder to go through the motions of her day. On Valentine's Day she gave up and simply stayed in the flat. By the following Monday Phoebe barely had the strength to crawl from her bed to call in sick again.

'We can't keep finding supply teachers to cover for you, Phoebe,' said Victoria Leach, who was now the Acting Head. 'We've all had this nasty flu bug but everyone else has managed to get in after a day or two.'

Sometimes Phoebe set off for school in the morning, feeling slightly better, manoeuvring her ancient Morris Minor out into the rush-hour traffic only to find herself unable to drive more than a few metres, her vision dangerously blurred by tears, her legs incapable of working the pedals. Often she would leave the car, parked haphazardly against the curb, and walk and walk and walk, until her feet stung from so many miles of hard pavement and her head ached from lack of food and water. Then she would go back to bed.

'You're going to lose your job if you carry on like this,' said Nola, opening the curtains and picking up the jeans and jumper that lay on the floor where Phoebe had discarded them the afternoon before.

From where she lay Phoebe focused on the heart stone mobile. It hung from the curtain pole against the window. Thirteen stones worn into perfect heart shapes by the sea – tied with fuse wire and suspended from beach-bleached sticks by thin lines of black cotton.

Nola reached up and opened the top of the window. The heart stones gently tapped against the glass. 'When are you going to grow up and get rid of all this eco-hippy rubbish?' Nola said, giving them a push so that the tapping became a clatter.

'Why do you have those funny stones hanging up?' David had said to her the day before he died. Phoebe lay with her cheek nestled against his chest. She breathed in the clean citrus smell of his skin mixed with the wine they were drinking. She relished his warmth against her body.

'They're special stones,' she mumbled, wishing she could fall asleep.

10

'Did you find them in India?'

'No.'

'Thailand?' She shook her head.

'Australia?'

'I found them in Ireland, on the beach with my granny.'

'I always forget that you're really Irish.' David twisted a long curl of her auburn hair around his finger. 'My little Celtic colleen.' He pulled.

'Ow! That hurt.' Phoebe tweaked his chest hair in return and David caught her wrist. Briefly they wrestled until Phoebe freed herself and fell back on the pillows laughing. After a few seconds she wriggled back into his arms. 'I'm only half Irish and anyway my dad was Anglo-Irish, not a Celt. I hope that doesn't destroy any of your fantasies.' David didn't answer and they lay in a silence broken only by the distant sounds of the evening rush hour. Phoebe thought about the broad, red-headed man who had been her father. Her memories of him were hazy but she felt sure he had actually been much more Celtic-looking than his long-limbed, handsome-featured mother.

'Are you asleep?' David asked, giving her a little prod.

'No,' she replied and slowly started to kiss the smooth muscles of his chest, working her way up towards his lips. She felt him lift his arm and knew he was looking at his watch.

'I'd better go,' he said.

Phoebe stopped kissing him and sighed.

'Soon, Phoebe, very soon,' he said, reading her mind. 'I've decided that I'm going to tell Sandra after Christmas.' He sat up and drained his glass of wine.

Phoebe had hardly dared to breathe. She reached up and traced the tattoo around his arm; the skin still brown from his half-term holiday in Tenerife; she thought about the pictures she'd seen on Facebook – David and Sandra and the girls, running through waves, laughing in a restaurant. Sandra had posted them, *Fab Times,* she had written. *It was hell,* David had said on their return.

'What about the girls?' Phoebe's voice was a whisper. 'I thought you'd said you couldn't put them through a divorce.'

David had found his boxer shorts at the end of the bed and he began to pull them on. He turned and stroked her cheek. 'It will be hard at first but they'll get used to it.' He tucked a stray strand of hair behind her ear. 'Anyway the girls adore you and when they see how happy we are, they'll be happy too.'

'But …'

He put his fingers on her lips, 'I love you, Phoebe Brennan, and I want to be with you for ever.'

Now for ever wasn't going to happen and Sandra would never know he'd planned to leave her. She got to be the grieving widow while Phoebe was just an acquaintance, a colleague, the little sister of a family friend.

'It's not like you to be ill like this,' said Nola. 'You need to see a doctor. I'll make you an appointment when I get into work.' She started smoothing the bedspread. 'Maybe you're depressed, though goodness knows what you've got to be depressed about; you should try living with Steve and two self-centred kids – and if you only knew the sort of abuse I get from patients at the surgery – then you'd have something to be depressed about.'

'Nola,' Phoebe shifted her head against the pillows. 'Can I tell you something?' She didn't look at her sister. She could see the trees outside the window; already plump buds were pushing their way out of the skeletal branches. She could hardly bear to think of the season changing, the world carrying on without him in it. She took a deep breath in. 'It's about David.'

Nola sat down heavily on the edge of the bed and took a crunched-up tissue from inside her cardigan sleeve. 'Let's not talk about him, you'll set me off crying again,' she wiped her nose. 'I'm seeing Sandra most days at the moment. I think she's still in shock, poor thing, she doesn't sleep, she's lost weight. She's hardly able to do the shopping and get meals for the girls.'

'I just need talk to you about something that happened, something that was going on.' Phoebe could feel her heart beginning to beat faster.

'I think if Steve died I'd just get on and cope, I'd be sad, upset for the kids, but I would carry on. But Sandra, she loved David so much, adored him. They adored each other.'

'Nola ...'

'Poor Sandra, last month she told me she thought she might be pregnant.'

Phoebe felt as if ice-cold water was suddenly pouring through her veins.

'Pregnant?' Her voice came out a whisper.

'She wasn't, it must just have been the trauma. I thought that it would be a relief – the last thing she needs is another child with no father – but she was heartbroken. She wanted to be pregnant, to have another little piece of him, a new life they had created together.'

Phoebe couldn't bear to think of them creating a new life together. David said he spent most nights sleeping in the spare room, that all affection was long gone, how could Sandra possibly have thought she was pregnant? Phoebe's head spun, the trees outside the window blurred.

'Apparently they often talked about having another child,' went on Nola. 'Sandra said he'd always wanted a son.'

Phoebe felt her stomach contract and she knew she would be sick. She quickly threw the covers from her bed and rushed into the bathroom.

Nola crouched down beside her and rubbed her back as Phoebe retched into the toilet; days of not eating meant that nothing much came up.

'Oh, Phee, you really are ill. I'll get you an emergency

appointment – Dr Riddick, not a locum; that's one of the perks of being the receptionist.'

Phoebe sat back against the radiator and wiped her mouth with a tissue offered by Nola.

'No, don't,' she said. 'I'll be all right.'

Nola felt Phoebe's forehead as if she was still the little girl that Nola had had to care for. 'If you're not better by Monday afternoon I'm getting you an evening appointment.' She stood up. 'I'll ring you, OK? I'd better get back, Ruben's got a judo tournament and Amy's threatening to dye her hair pink with food colouring.'

At the doorway Nola turned. 'Was there something you wanted to tell me?'

'It doesn't matter,' Phoebe said.

Phoebe heard the bang of the door and then, half a minute later, the distant thud of the main front door downstairs. Almost with relief, she lay down on the bathroom floor and let hot tears flow over her face and onto the ceramic tiles. She couldn't bear to think of David and Sandra talking about having another baby, planning the future, making love; while all the time David had been making love to her, talking to her about exactly the same things. He had told Phoebe that one day, when they were together, when he and Sandra were divorced, they would have children – as many children as Phoebe wanted. They'd even had a conversation about names; how could he ever have wanted more children with Sandra?

The thought of it hurt Phoebe like a physical blow and she drew her legs up to her stomach as if in self-defence. Then, suddenly, she realised the truth. Sandra had been making it up, lying, pretending she might be pregnant to get more sympathy, making up the story about David wanting another baby to add to the pathos of her husband's death.

Phoebe relaxed a little. David hadn't lied to her; he would have left Sandra, he'd been just about to leave her.

She pressed her hands against her stinging eyes. If only the driver hadn't used the brake as she skidded on the black ice outside the school. If only David hadn't been shepherding the Year Four children across the road at the time. If only David was still alive.

After a long time Phoebe went back to bed and let herself sink into memories of the past – the only thing that brought her any comfort.

Phoebe thought about the second time she had met David, many years after the barbecue on that hot summer day in the overgrown garden. This time it was winter, she had just returned from Thailand. Back at Nola and Steve's, permanently cold, sharing her old bedroom with Amy; she felt uncomfortable, in the way, itching to get on a plane and leave again, she wasn't even sure why she had come back to Britain.

She sat shivering, in multiple layers of clothing, in front of Steve's computer, trying to find out how to get a job teaching English in Japan.

'Planning your escape already?' a voice said and Phoebe turned to find David standing beside her. Ten years had passed and this time his hair was short and he wore a suit and tie. The tie had pictures of Bugs Bunny printed on it and even though it had been loosened to reveal an unbuttoned collar and a tiny patch of chest hair, he looked ridiculously conventional. Phoebe stared at him, surprised at the transformation, though his face was just as handsome as before, his intense blue eyes making her feel like an awkward teenager again. She forced herself to swivel on the office chair and face him.

'I'm grabbing the day, just as you advised.'

David raised an eyebrow in a question.

'Don't you remember, *live life to the full*, it's what you told me to do, *see the world, meet people*.'

David grinned down at her. 'Did I say that? I'm flattered that you remember.'

Phoebe felt her cheeks flush. Through the wall she could hear Sandra talking to Nola and the shrill shrieks of the twins up above in Amy's bedroom – probably going through her rucksack, pulling out her bikini tops and denim shorts.

'It was a long time ago,' David continued. 'Though I do remember that you looked like the kind of girl who was longing for an adventure, and from what Nola tells us you've certainly been having one. How long were you travelling?'

'Too long – according to Nola – and I can just imagine the things my sister has been telling you about me. She thinks I've been wasting my time and wasting my education. She says it's time to settle down and get a proper job.' Phoebe made a face.

'Didn't you do something quite arty at college?'

'Illustration.'

'That's right, I remember. I heard you were good.'

Phoebe shrugged. 'What about you? Still living your life to the full?'

'Well,' David began slowly, 'I'm sure you know that Sandra and I got married and that we've got twin girls. We moved back here to be closer to Sandra's parents and now I'm headteacher of the local primary school.' He paused as one of the twins let out a squeal above him. 'I think that just about sums up the last decade for me. Is that enough information for you?'

'I suppose I thought you'd do something more ...'

'Exiting?'

Phoebe found it hard to drag her gaze away from his. She smiled. 'I just never expected to see you in a suit and comedy tie.'

'Don't knock what you don't know. I did the travelling thing too, followed the trails, smoked the hashish, did the bungee jumps, but I'd say that becoming a father and a teacher has been the biggest adventure by far.'

Phoebe rolled her eyes and they both burst out laughing. 'That sounded really corny, didn't it?' said David.

'Just a bit,' replied Phoebe. David leant against the study wall and ran his hands through his neatly cut hair.

'You're right. Life hasn't exactly been what I was planning when I last saw you. Sandra got pregnant, I needed a job, we needed a house, teaching was the easiest and quickest option; living life to the full was suddenly on hold.'

'Are you happy?'

'Are you?'

'I'm free. I can do whatever I want, go wherever I want.'

'Run away wherever, whenever you want,' said David.

'I'm not running away.'

'Then maybe you should try sticking around for once?'

There was a thud from up above, followed by the clatter of Amy coming down the stairs. 'Auntie Sandra, the twins are fighting again.'

Phoebe and David both looked upwards. They could hear the high-pitched bickering of little girls. There was another thud, then silence followed by a long, loud wail.

'Behave,' Sandra bellowed from the kitchen.

Phoebe looked at David.

'Maybe you're jealous,' she said.

'Jealous? Of what?'

'Of me travelling, taking off whenever I want.' She paused and gave him a sideways glance. 'Living your dream.'

David shrugged. 'I'm just saying you could stay here and give it a chance. Get a job doing something that really interests you.'

'You sound like a schoolteacher.'

'I am a schoolteacher.'

They both laughed again. At last Phoebe could see the

free-spirited young man she'd met at her sister's barbecue. She remembered the tattoo; beneath the suit and shirt it must still be there. Phoebe stopped laughing and turned back to the website she'd been looking at.

David crouched down beside her and looked at the computer screen. 'Can I just make one more suggestion without being accused of being a *teacher*?' His hand made a move towards the mouse.

'OK,' Phoebe could hear the drone of Sandra's voice talking to Nola; she tried to block it out and watched David click through Google to a different site.

'PGCE,' he said, highlighting the word on the screen. 'Teacher training. You could be a teacher, a primary school teacher.'

'Like you?'

'Yes, though the *comedy tie* is discretionary. Nola says you've been working in an orphanage in Bangkok so you must like children and if you're thinking of teaching English then you can't think teachers are all bad.'

'I'm not sure; I really need to get away from here before Nola drives me completely crazy; she still treats me like a badly behaved teenager.'

'So? Move out, get a flat, get the qualifications, try it for a while. You can always use it to teach somewhere else – Africa, South America. You don't have to stay in this country if you really can't bear it.'

'Where would I do it? Where would I train?'

'With me.' He smiled at her. 'You can do it in my school. There's a teaching post coming up next term and if you've already got a degree you can train on the job, get paid, get a place of your own.'

Phoebe was quiet for a little while. 'Why should I take your advice?'

'Didn't you take it before?' He took his hand away from the mouse to let Phoebe click on the *how to apply* link. His fingers brushed hers. Phoebe thought of all the years she'd spent aching for him, all the boyfriends she'd compared to him, all the boyfriends she'd found wanting.

'Here you are! I wondered where you'd got to,' Sandra stood in the doorway, her arms folded tight across her chest. 'The girls and I are ready to go now.'

David got up and smiled brightly at his wife. As he followed her out of the room he turned back to Phoebe. 'Think about it. It could be the start of something really good.'

Three years later, Phoebe lay on her bed looking up at a crack in the ceiling. David had been right; it had been good, so good that life without him seemed really bad. Outside a dusky gloom indicated the evening. Phoebe knew she should put on the light but couldn't make her arm lift up to click on the switch beside the bed.

Some time later she woke up with a jolt in the dark room. She had been dreaming, dreaming about David. They were in a boat, sailing on clear, turquoise water. David had the blue shirt on that had been Phoebe's favourite and he was steering, a huge ship's wheel in his hands, much too big for the little sailing boat. Phoebe sat beside him making tissue paper flowers, twisting the bright sheets together into blousy rainbow rosettes. A gust of wind blew, lifting them from her lap, up into the air and then down over the side. Phoebe watched them drift away leaving streaks of colour as they dissolved into the water. David leant over to kiss her but the rail she had been leaning against seemed to melt away and she was falling, waiting to hit the water. It seemed a long way down the water: much further than she had expected; and then she realised she was flying and David had become a tiny speck beneath her. Was he waving at her? She tried to shout. She woke up.

Scrabbling for the light switch, she sat up. The dream had seemed so real; now the small pale room around her seemed flimsy and imagined. Maybe everything had been a dream – the last three years working with David, secretly loving David, longing for him to turn around and notice her. The last miraculous six months since he had told her that he loved her too; maybe she had made it up.

She looked around her for something to make it real, some piece of proof, some sign of their time together. They had always been so careful, hiding any evidence. No clothes left behind, no extra toothbrush, no razor, the second glass quickly washed up and put away. He was nowhere in the flat, the space was solely hers. Phoebe scrambled from the bed, suddenly desperate. She pulled open drawers and dragged boxes from under cupboards. Letters, photographs, presents; she piled them in the middle of her bedroom floor. It didn't seem enough.

Slowly she picked each object up: the silver bracelet he had given her for her birthday, a gold and black box that had contained chocolates, a torn-out page from an exercise book (*see you later, will bring Chinese XXX*), the Bugs Bunny tie that David gave her on the day she qualified as a teacher, a champagne cork, a note on headed school notepaper *(Sandra is at her mother's with the girls. Come to the house after parents' evening X)*, a dried red rose, a photograph (David and Phoebe, arms around each other, flushed with wine and sun in a restaurant on Jersey – a snatched weekend together, a bogus conference for David, the longest time they ever spent together, two full nights, two mornings, it had been heaven – it seemed so long ago.) There were a few other things: small gifts and trinkets, scrawled notes and a copy of *Jane Eyre* that David had given her after he discovered that she'd never read it – inside the cover he had written *To my very own little orphan, from Mr Rochester X.* She still hadn't got round to reading it.

Phoebe leant the photograph against the wall and arranged the other objects neatly around it, fanning outwards, like a shrine. She sat back on her heels; chin cupped in her hands and stared at it all as though if she looked at everything long enough there might be an answer, a resolution to her pain.

Outside the sky had turned from night-time black to soft dawn grey. Phoebe tilted her head and realised she had been still for a very long time, crouching, hunched, animal-like. She got up stiffly. The air felt thick, she couldn't breathe; the misery was suffocating.

She found herself pulling on the jeans and jumper that Nola had folded neatly the previous morning, slipping her feet into socks and then the chunky biker boots that David had always hated. She urgently fumbled with the zip of one boot, cursing as it jammed half way up, left it flapping open, grabbed her parka, and headed for the door.

In less than a minute she was out of the building, into the car, and away down the road with no clear sense of where she was going. She drove until she realised two hours had passed. Thick rivulets of rain-streaked the glass in front of her, making it hard to see. She put on the windscreen wipers and noticed her petrol light glowing an alarming orange on the dashboard. Phoebe found a petrol station in the process of opening up for the day. When the tank was full, she paid, bought a packet of peanuts – the first food she'd bought for days – and drove home through heavy rain.

From the outside her flat still looked asleep; the crooked curtains drawn and sad. The rain had worn itself into a misty drizzle. Phoebe sat in the car, reluctant to go inside, and slowly ate the packet of peanuts. How could she get through another day in there?

She looked back up at the window of her flat. The smooth glass still reflected the shapes of twisted branches but she realised something had changed: the curtains were no longer drawn, the cream lining no longer visible against the panes, only the long thin line of heart stones against a dark interior. The curtains were open; someone had opened them.

Standing on the worn grey landing carpet, Phoebe put her key in the latch. Her hand shook slightly as she tried to convince herself she must be wrong about the curtains. She opened her door. A movement, a noise, she jumped.

'Hello?' No answer. Her heart quickened and tentatively she moved forward into the little hallway. Her bedroom door was slightly ajar; she was sure she had left it closed. Her heart thumped; she desperately looked around for an implement, an object to protect herself with. She couldn't find anything within her reach; if she could make it to the kitchen she could find a knife, even a saucepan. A sudden image of David flashed though her mind and she remembered she had no reason left to care about protecting herself, no reason for self-defence – what was the point? She walked towards the bedroom door and pushed it, expecting a masked and hooded figure to lunge at her.

'Nola!'

In front of her Nola knelt on the bare wooden boards, her pink mac speckled by rain, her hair glistening with droplets of drizzle; a blue-lidded Tupperware box beside her. As Nola looked up Phoebe realised with horror that she had been staring at the little group of objects against the wall. Then Phoebe saw the photograph in her hand. 'Nola,' she said again, quietly this time, barely a whisper. Nola turned and looked at her; Phoebe couldn't read her face – bewilderment, anger, disappointment?

'I made chocolate brownies for Sandra's girls.' Nola spoke slowly. 'I thought you might like some as well.' She nodded towards the Tupperware box. 'You always used to like them, do you remember? Mum used to make them when we came home from school? I assumed, when you didn't answer the door that you were still ill. I used my spare key …' Nola stopped and looked at the picture in her hands. 'But you were out and then I saw …' She stopped and gestured to the group of objects and flicked the edge of the photograph with her fingers.

'I tried to tell you ...' Phoebe began to explain but the words refused to come.

'To tell me what?' Nola flashed an angry look up at her sister. 'To tell me that you'd been having some sordid little affair with my best friend's husband?'

Phoebe closed her eyes, wishing it was all another dream. She opened them; Nola was still there.

Phoebe took a deep breath. 'It wasn't sordid.'

'Just an affair then? My God, Phoebe, how could you? Sandra is practically family. She's like another sister to us.'

'No she's not,' Phoebe felt indignation welling up inside her. 'Not to me anyway.'

'She's my oldest friend; you've known her since you were born. Sandra is very fond of you. If only she knew what you'd actually been up to.' Nola heaved herself up from the floor, steadying herself with one hand on the chest of drawers. 'What was it? Because he gave you a job in his school, because he gave you a chance, an opportunity to earn a proper income for once? You thought you'd just have him as well, as part of the package? Or were you just playing with him, a bit of an extra thrill, did you get a kick out of knowing he belonged to Sandra?'

'I loved him.'

'Do know what love is, Phoebe? When have you ever had a meaningful relationship?'

'I do know what love is, I know when it feels like you're just meant to be with someone no matter what. That's how it felt with David.'

'For God's sake, Phoebe, get real. You're not in some Mills and Boon novel, you know.' Nola shook her head and stared back down at the picture in her hand. 'Where did I go wrong with you? I tried my best and now I don't know why I wasted so much time trying to bring you up

23

after Mum and Dad died.'

'Nola!' Phoebe felt hot tears stinging in her eyes. 'Please stop.' But Nola went on.

'I should have sat my exams and taken that place at medical school. I could have had you put in care you know, that's what they wanted, all those social workers. They said I'd never cope with bringing up a ten-year-old but I gave up everything to do it.'

'You didn't have to give everything up, you didn't give up Steve. You married Steve.'

Nola sank down onto the bed and bowed her head. Her silence was worse than her angry words. Phoebe moved towards her and touched her shoulder. 'Don't!' Nola flinched away, pulling her mac around her defensively.

After a few seconds Nola turned to look at Phoebe, her face suddenly vicious. 'How could you have been doing such a horrible, disgusting, deceitful thing? After everything Sandra and her parents did for us after the accident: they took us in, gave us a roof to live under when there was no one else; no rich relatives appeared to adopt us, you know, no fairy god-parents flew in to take us away, we were on our own – proper little orphans. What will Sandra's parents think now? What would *our* parents think if they were still alive? They'd be so disappointed with you Phoebe, so upset – and Granny would have been too.'

Instantly they all appeared in Phoebe's head; her mother, pink-cheeked and sensible, always waiting with hot chocolate and flapjacks when they came home from school, eager to hear about their days, proudly pinning Phoebe's drawings to the cork tiles on the kitchen wall; her father, usually lost in a day dream, his handsome face, sun tanned from working outdoors, hair like Phoebe's own, wild red curls never quite contained by monthly haircuts from his wife. And lastly her granny; tall and graceful, white hair loosely coiled at her neck, draped in scarves and multi-coloured layers of linen and silk, except for when she was making pots – then she wore a faded smock and a wide-brimmed yellow hat. How Phoebe wished they were all still there. Still alive for her to disappoint. Tears poured down her cheeks and she didn't bother to wipe them away.

'Go on. Have a good cry,' Nola's voice grew louder. 'It won't do any good, don't think I'm going to feel sorry for you. I suppose you think you've a right to grieve for David, is that why you've been moping around the flat for weeks?' She paused and stood up as if to leave and then went on, 'How am I ever going to look at Sandra again? I feel guilty and I haven't even done anything! Sandra must never know what you did; she must never know that you seduced her husband.'

'I didn't seduce him; it was David that made the first move. He told me how unhappy he was with Sandra, how horrible she could be to him. He said he thought she had other men ...'

'Stop!' Nola's hand shot out like a policeman stopping traffic. 'You're lying, they had a wonderful marriage.' Nola moved towards the door. 'I can't bear to be with you any more. You make me feel sick, Phoebe; I don't want to see you, I don't want to be with you. I wouldn't ever be able to trust you with Steve – you'll probably be after him next, if you haven't had him already.'

'Stop it, Nola. That's a horrible thing to say.'

Nola didn't stop. 'Goodness knows what you were up to when Steve used to help you with your homework and I was trying to deal with stinking nappies and cracked nipples and getting babies off to sleep.'

She looked down at the picture of Phoebe and David that she still held and, using both hands, crumpled it up into a small tight ball. Phoebe gasped.

'No, please don't!'

Nola threw it at her, hard; it missed and bounced onto

the floorboards and rolled under the chest of drawers. Phoebe knelt down to retrieve it and when she stood up the room was empty, Nola had gone.

Phoebe unrolled the scrunched-up photograph and tried to flatten the crumpled paper; thick creases zigzagged the image, fragmenting the smiles, cutting across the shining eyes. She touched David's distorted face; he seemed like a stranger, she could barely recollect his voice. She tried to remember things he'd said to her, words of affection, little jokes, intimate endearments – nothing came to her. Even the memories had died.

She lay down on the bed, still in her coat and boots. She wanted the world to end, life to stop. She wanted to die. What was the point of going on? No David, no parents, now Nola would never want to see her again, she was all alone. She tried to work out how many paracetamol tablets she had in the kitchen cupboard – probably not enough. Could you kill yourself with echinacea and evening primrose? She didn't even have the energy to swallow tablets. She'd only make a mess of it and end up still alive but terminally ill, making her even more of a burden on Nola. She wondered if she could just will herself to die. In Australia she had heard that Aborigines could just lie down and let death overcome them. If only it was that easy. Her eyes closed but thoughts raced around her head as if her brain was desperately trying to override her aching heart.

If she couldn't die, maybe she could leave, pack up and just walk away. That's what she would have done in the past; if things got hard she got up and left. Ran away, as David would have said. She had a bit of money, but not much, not enough to get her very far in a hurry.

Think, Phoebe, think. Where could she go? Where had she been happiest in her life? When had she ever been truly happy?

Paddling in a pebbly stream – the memory began to

slowly develop, like a Polaroid in her mind; *hazy, purple mountains, flat sea, warm rocks on a beach of silver sand* – she couldn't quite remember where it was. *Whitewashed walls, a bright blue door, soft rain dampening her itchy Aran jumper,* she scratched her neck as though she could still feel it. *Red and purple fuchsia in a chipped brown jug, hot chocolate beside a peaty fire, her grandmother bent over a whirling lump of clay.*

Phoebe opened her eyes. The boathouse at Carraigmore! She hadn't thought of it for years, but she and Nola must still own that boathouse by the sea in Ireland. Along with a legacy of a few thousand pounds (Phoebe's had been mostly spent on her travels, Nola's went towards the deposit for her and Steve's first house) her grandmother, Anna, had left the two girls the small stone boathouse that had been her home and pottery studio in the last years of her life, with the stipulation in her will that it was not to be sold. It must still be there, thought Phoebe, though Nola hadn't mentioned it for a long time. Phoebe could remember her sister's annoyance that they couldn't sell it when she wanted money for a kitchen extension and Irish property prices were at their highest – but that had been years ago.

Phoebe stared at the ceiling, a hundred memories flooding back: sitting on the slipway to the sea – the rough concrete hot against her legs; picking at paint blisters on a window frame; watching her grandmother sitting at a potter's wheel, lost in the rotations of the clay; eating biscuits in a big armchair, staring out at crashing waves; lying on her grandmother's wrought-iron bed – her back stinging from too much sun; the slightly acrid smell of the gas kiln mixed with the smell of the sea; the beach with its pearly shells and long swathes of seaweed; the two boys from the Castle. Phoebe had forgotten their names but not their white blond hair or their ability to dive, sleek and smooth as gannets, from the black rock at high tide. And all the time the Castle up above them; impossibly romantic with its gothic façade and creeper-covered turrets, drawing her grandmother's wistful gaze, luring Phoebe and Nola up the lane to peer through wrought-iron gates that they were never allowed to walk through.

Phoebe wondered if the boathouse was still standing. Maybe it had fallen down, been swept away by winter storms or maybe it had simply collapsed into the sand for lack of love or care. Even if it was still there it must be in pretty bad condition, not fit to live in, surely.

Suddenly she had to know if it still existed. Phoebe sat up. How long had it been since anyone had lived there? How long since they'd picked her grandmother up from the airport on that bright blue morning? Fifteen years? More? She stood up, determined to leave as soon as possible, get a ferry, buy a map, and she would drive her little Morris Minor until she found it. As she began searching in the cupboard for her rucksack she was already imagining the blissful isolation of the west of Ireland.

Chapter Three

Phoebe didn't take much with her; she dumped bags of clothes and books and ornaments outside the various charity shops along the high street – her life so far in a series of bunched-up black bin liners.

A letter to her landlord, a letter to the school, a letter to Nola that she ripped up at the last moment and threw into the dustbin along with the string of heart stones as she walked out of the flat for the last time.

She swung the battered rucksack into the back of her car. The rucksack contained a jumble of scrunched-up clothes and the few items that she'd thought worth keeping: the notes from David, the creased photograph, the copy of *Jane Eyre*, a sketchbook, pencils, a small, round, green-glazed, jar – a present long ago from her grandmother, a selection of drawings done for her by Amy and Ruben over the years and the details of a savings account which contained the last of her inheritance.

With a pang of sadness she remembered it was Ruben's birthday the following weekend. Phoebe had promised him she'd go to his party at Laser Quest. The previous year she had led a team of eight- and nine-year-olds to victory over Steve and Ruben's side; Ruben had been determined to be on Phoebe's team this year. Phoebe wondered if she should stay till after the party. She thought of Nola's angry face and doubted that she would be on the guest list any more. Instead she went down to the corner shop and bought a brightly coloured rocket-shaped card. She put a twenty-pound note inside and added a brief message:

Hope that Laser Quest is a blast – go get 'em space boy!
Love you loads, Aunty Phee x.
p.s. give your sister a big hug from me – go on, give her
the hug, she's not that bad!!

Just as she was about to slip the key through the front
door, Phoebe realised she had forgotten the school tea
towel. It had slipped behind the kitchen radiator; she had
to use a wooden spoon to poke it out, the linen creased and
cardboard-hard. Phoebe's heart lurched; she'd miss the
children, miss her class. She stopped, staring round the
empty flat. Was she doing the right thing? Should she at
least go back to school until the end of term? Then she
remembered the letter she'd already posted and winced at
the thought of Victoria Leach's reaction when she
discovered that Phoebe had left without giving notice.
There would be no going back.

The ferry was old. The smell of petrol and clanking of
chains on the car deck immediately took her back to her
childhood: nausea mixed with the excitement of the
coming holiday, her father hurrying them up the stairs
towards the lounges, the rush to get four seats in a row, she
and Nola waiting for the duty-free shop to open so that
they could try all the perfumes before sea sickness made
the smells repugnant and they returned to cuddle into their
parents for the rest of the journey. The memories filled
Phoebe with sadness; if they had known then how little
time they would have together, would she have hugged
them harder, held them for longer? If she had known what
would happen to David would she have forced him to
leave Sandra, to spend every waking hour with her? Tears
threatened and she blinked them back.

The boat began to move and Phoebe went outside

despite the biting cold. Leaning against the rail, she watched the Welsh coast slip into the gloom and wished she hadn't left her coat in the car.

Shivering, she looked down at the steely sea and wondered if Nola had even realised she had gone. Two days and there had been no message from her, no attempt to get in touch. But despite her sister's silence every gust of salty wind seemed full of Nola's condemnation, whipping around her as she stood on the deck.

Phoebe closed her eyes and tried to let thoughts of David fill her mind instead.

'Are you not frozen?' The voice made Phoebe jump, her eyes sprung open. She saw an old man standing no more than a foot away; his lined face looked concerned. 'I didn't mean to startle you,' he had an Irish accent. He took a packet of cigarettes from the pocket his coat and offered her one.

Phoebe shook her head.

'Sensible girl.' He smiled and cupped his hands around the cigarette as he lit it. Phoebe wished he would go away.

'Holiday or business or going home?' The man blew out a long stream of smoke that was instantly whisked away by the wind.

Phoebe didn't feel much like talking; in fact she wasn't sure if she'd spoken to anyone since Nola left her flat. She shrugged and looked back down into the water.

A few minutes passed. Phoebe could still feel him looking at her.

'If there's one thing my many years on this earth has taught me,' the old man finally said, 'it's that nothing's ever as bad as it seems.' Then he moved away to talk to someone else.

Phoebe tried to rekindle her thoughts of David but the man had interrupted her memories and made her feel annoyed. She looked up at the seagulls wheeling overhead. If only she could escape into the air and fly away from

31

mundane conversations with strangers, fly away from the unbearable banality of life. That was what she would do in Carraigmore, find the solitude and isolation she longed for. She would walk; lots of long walks on the beach and on the headland, she would read *Jane Eyre*, and she would draw. She would draw every day.

She closed her eyes again and thought of the first time David had made love to her six months before. He'd asked her to stay after school to talk about a difficult pupil in her class. Afterwards he'd insisted that she shouldn't wait for the bus in the rain, insisted on giving her a lift even though he lived on the other side of town; outside her flat she'd been just about to get out of the car when he'd kissed her, melting her resolve to ignore the way she'd felt about him for almost half her life. Later he had picked up the sketchbook beside her bed and flicked through it.

'You're very good.'

'These days it's just doodling.' Phoebe pulled the sheet around her shoulders, suddenly feeling exposed. 'I haven't done much real drawing since I finished college.

David examined a pen-and-ink study of a vase of tulips; he traced it with his fingers and Phoebe tried not to notice the wedding ring that glinted in the light cast by the bedside lamp. 'This is beautiful,' he said. He looked at her and she found herself hypnotised by the intensity of his eyes. 'Don't give up. You have a real talent.' He put down the sketchbook and drew her closer to him until there was no room for guilt or doubt or thoughts of drawing.

Standing staring at the churning sea, Phoebe trembled at the memory of David's touch but this was quickly followed by a cold wave of disquiet. Was Nola right? Had what she had with David really been a disgusting and deceitful thing? A sordid affair? Her hair blew across her eyes, temporarily blinding her as she shook her head. No, they had been drawn together by real love, a union of minds not just of bodies, they had been meant to be together. Phoebe felt in the pocket of her jeans and found the bracelet David had given her. She caressed it like a string of rosary beads, stroking each heart-shaped charm as it passed through her fingers. '*He loved me, he loved me.*' She would not let Nola's cruel words spoil something that had been so precious. She pressed the bracelet to her lips; the glass hearts were cold.

A misty rain began to fall and the familiar memories came back to her like the recollections of a horror film you wish you'd never been to see. Phoebe turned around and searched for the old man who'd tried to talk to her earlier, she needed a distraction. The man was heading for the sliding doors; they opened and he disappeared. Soon it would be too late. Phoebe clutched at thoughts of David but they were disappearing too; she tried desperately to recollect the meals they'd shared – he once had told her she made the best cheese on toast he'd ever tasted, he used to bring her pink Cava. What did they do when they'd been in Jersey? Surely the whole time wasn't spent in bed? Phoebe remembered being in the airport shop with him, looking at the bookshelves – the only time he'd held her hand in public. Her frantic attempts at diversion failed and suddenly she was in an airport shop with Nola many years before. The memories appeared in her head like cine film flickering on a screen.

Polos or Refreshers? Her hand dithered between the two cylindrical packets. Nola stood beside her, tall and seventeen, her flat stomach exposed beneath a pale pink crop top, Levi 501s hanging low on narrow teenage hips. Or maybe just chewing-gum like Nola?

'*Come on, girls,' her father shouted from the concourse outside. 'They've just announced that the plane from Cork has landed. Granny will be here any minute.*'

Then Phoebe was sitting in the car with Granny wedged tight beside her, Granny's skirt was rough against her leg, the satisfying fizz of dissolving sweets was on her tongue. Nola, on the other side of Granny, listened to her Walkman and chewed her gum. Her father, driving, fiddled with the radio, looking for the cricket, his mop of curls hanging down, obscuring his face.

'Chicken pie for supper,' her mother turned from the front passenger seat and smiled at her mother-in-law.

'Oooo, my favourite,' Granny replied and then she leant over and whispered to Phoebe, only to Phoebe, 'I've got something wonderful to tell you all later.' And then there was a thud and a lurch and the spinning; like being on a waltzer at the bank holiday fair. Phoebe wasn't frightened; 'It's just a funfair ride' she told herself, as the car spun round and round, metal crunching on unseen objects, pebbles of glass showering on top of her. Then the realisation that she wasn't wedged in by Granny any more; the pressure against her thigh was gone, Granny was gone, the seat beside her was empty.

Then she was standing on a verge strewn with wild flowers; tall daisies swaying in the smoky breeze, the taste of Refreshers still on her tongue. Nola's face was blank but Phoebe could hear her teeth chattering even though the siren sounds were getting louder.

'Don't look back,' a stranger repeated over and over. 'Don't look back.' Instead Phoebe looked down at her hands and was horrified to see them oozing little pearls of blood. 'Mummy,' she called and turned and then she screamed and then there were no more memories until she was standing beside Nola in the graveyard, miserable and frightened in the awful coat.

Chapter Four

As Phoebe drove away from Rosslare, the flat khaki landscape and utilitarian industrial parks made her wonder if Ireland had been the right place to escape to after all. Where were the stone-walled craggy fields and thatched white cottages of her memory? Where were the sheep and donkeys and statues of the Virgin Mary? Had it all been devoured by the Celtic Tiger? Or maybe they were not true childhood memories at all, but images from films and books – an Ireland of fiction and fantasy that had never really existed.

This post-boom landscape seemed inhospitable and unwelcoming. For miles Phoebe didn't see a living person. Her battered Morris Minor passed cars and lorries on the dual carriageway, but the constant movement of their windscreen wipers obscured the drivers until she wondered if she could be the only human being on the sodden island.

As she headed west the landscape softened and began to undulate a little. Industrial estates were replaced with a succession of small grey towns. The road narrowed, edged with hedges threatening to burst out in green; here and there a snatch of sea, a wooded hillside, ivy-covered walls obscuring country estates, hens pottering on the grassy verge. A man in a flat tweed cap wobbled on a bicycle as he waved to a woman in her garden. Phoebe laughed out loud as she realised he was followed by a donkey, trotting obediently behind him, attached to his handlebars with a rope.

Past Cork the rain stopped, the clouds parted to reveal a setting sun, and Phoebe's heart began to lift. The towns grew prettier; brightly painted shops and houses were strung along the road, even the churches were wedding-cake colours; pink or white or virgin blue. The landscape grew mountainous, the roads grew smaller, twisting sharply around rocky outcrops and climbing steeply up hills before dropping with a gear-defying plummet down the other side. The patchwork of green fields seemed to be stitched together with dry-stone walls or hedges raked by ocean winds.

The sea was always to her left, breakers crashing against high cliffs or rolling onto beaches on an incoming tide. She saw a surfer riding the first spring waves and in the distance little dots of fishing boats bobbed on the horizon.

For a few moments she let herself believe that David was with her, that they were setting out on holiday together in the car he used to call her Miss Marple-mobile, chatting about the journey, admiring the view; soon she would show him her childhood haunts and walk with him along the beach at Carraigmore.

The sudden shriek of a car horn and a screech of tyres made Phoebe realise that she had drifted on to the wrong side of the road. A 4x4 had had to swerve to avoid her and as she glanced in panic at her rear-view mirror she could see a man's hand gesticulating out of its window. Taking a deep breath she determined to banish all thoughts of David until she arrived.

At last, in fading light, Phoebe saw a sign to Carraigmore which led her off the main road and down a narrow, pot-holed lane. She passed a caravan park next to a small estate of holiday homes, flat-fronted and neatly thatched – a large sign read: 'Sea View, Traditional Cosy Irish Cottages, with authentic turf-burning stoves'. Out of season they looked cold and empty and Phoebe reckoned the only view you'd get of the sea would be from the roof.

'Welcome to Carraigmore, we like a cautious driver', was positioned outside a surprisingly large and modern-looking primary school and adjacent medical centre, and from there an orderly line of fir-hedged bungalows led into the village, each garden neater than the last.

Nothing looked familiar to Phoebe until she saw the magnolia tree. Thick white buds adorned the bare branches like candles on an elaborate candelabra. It stood in the garden of an imposing Victorian villa. Phoebe was pretty sure that this was where her grandparents had lived when her grandfather had been alive. Then it had been the surgery, now it had two entrance ways and looked as though the large house had been divided.

Phoebe drove slowly on, a vague sense of anxiety growing. In her memory Carraigmore had been a bigger place and she'd been certain she'd find a hotel or a B&B without any trouble – now she wasn't so sure. A string of pretty cottages, washed in different colours, preceded a parade of shops: Murphy's Butchers, Molly's Hair Hut, Carraigmore general store, Rainbow's End Gifts, Fibber Flannigan's Pub. The street seemed deserted, no sign of life at all. Phoebe drove on towards the grey smudge of sea at the bottom of the hill.

She passed the cottage where they used to stay when Phoebe was a child. The boathouse had been too small to accommodate them so every year they'd book into the Black Rock B&B. Whitewashed with a slated wall at its sea end to protect against the Atlantic weather, it looked just as it had when Phoebe had last seen it, except the fuchsia hedge was gone and the front garden had been tarmacked to accommodate an expensive-looking Range Rover. There was no B&B sign now, only a plastic triangle in the window saying that it was part of Carraigmore's neighbourhood watch scheme. The old schoolhouse next door also provided a backdrop to a large

4x4, and the flicker of a television set through a long arched window suggested its conversion to a family home. Next to that the grey stone Protestant church now wore a sign advertising its own conversion to Carraigmore's Art and Craft Centre.

It was nearly dark – too dark to go down to the beach and look for the boathouse. Spots of rain started to speckle the windscreen. Phoebe turned back up the street and parked outside Fibber Flannigan's. The pub looked very quiet, no one going in or out, heavy curtains drawn at the windows making it impossible to see if any lights were on. Getting out of the car she noticed a flaking board leaning up on the wall: 'Food and drink available here. Voted Best Pub in Carraigmore; Kerry Farmer's Gazette 1996.' Phoebe glanced up and down the deserted street. It seemed to be the only pub in Carraigmore. Maybe the landlord could tell her if there was a place to stay nearby. Cautiously she pulled the heavy wooden door, half expecting the pub to be locked up on a cold, mid-week evening in March. The door opened and Phoebe braced herself for all eyes instantly to turn in her direction, all conversation to stop at the appearance of a stranger.

Instead Phoebe's eyes widened as she took in the scene in front of her. The bar was packed – people squeezed tightly into every available space, men and women pressed shoulder to shoulder, some even standing on chairs and tables, several perched on a long bar at the back, all eyes focused, intently, not on her, but on one wall. The room was silent, as if a collective breath had been taken and was being held. A fog of smoke lent a ghostly effect to the scene (the smoking ban obviously hadn't made it so far west). Phoebe stared, her hand still holding open the door, she had never seen so many people make so little noise. Then suddenly a huge cheer filled the room, people jumped up from tables to hug each other, sloshing pints of beer in excited toasts, the line of men and women perched on the bar stood up on it and started an impromptu conga and a young boy standing on a bench began banging on an Irish drum. Phoebe was pulled over the threshold of the door and found herself hoisted off the ground by a pair of thick hairy arms and kissed roughly on the lips.

'One to twenty-three, one to twenty-three! Can you believe it?' the heavily bearded protagonist shouted into her startled face, before releasing her and repeating his performance all over again with another woman on his other side.

The crowd started up a slow melodic chant of 'Carraigmore, Carraigmore', swaying as one huge mass, making it impossible for Phoebe to move forward towards the bar.

'What's going on?' she asked a girl wedged in beside her.

'Carraigmore 1-23, Kilcummin 1-12. Isn't it fantastic!' The girl raised her arms into the air and started to chant along with everyone else, 'Carraigmore, Carraigmore'. The chant turned into a song, someone started playing an accompanying flute; Phoebe thought they were singing a traditional Gaelic lament until she realised it was Robbie Williams's 'Angels'. She noticed a huge television screen practically filling up one wall of the bar, burly men were wandering around against a bright green pitch, pulling off their shirts and punching each other with manly camaraderie.

'Is it a rugby match?' she shouted to an elderly man sitting hunch-backed on a stool to one side of her.

'It's football, of course,' he shouted back, then he peered at her. 'You're not local, are you?' It was a statement rather than a question. 'This is *the* football not your English girl-guide stuff – Gaelic football, the true national game of Ireland, as played by Brian Boru himself!'

'Oh,' said Phoebe nonplussed, but before she could ask

any more the man had stood up and, standing surprisingly straight, began loudly to sing.

'Sinne Fianna Fáil
A tá fé gheall ag Éirinn …'

Though Phoebe hadn't a clue what the words meant she recognised the tune from hearing her father sing it long ago – the Irish National Anthem. Within seconds 'Angels' petered out and the whole room was standing upright, fervently joining in with the old man.

Phoebe used the opportunity to squeeze through the crowd to get to the bar.

When she finally made it through the throng she looked up and down the space behind the counter but the only face she could see was her own reflection staring out of an etched mirror advertising Power's Whiskey. Disturbed by her dishevelled appearance, Phoebe turned her gaze to a large collection of old tin advertising signs for Guinness and Harp larger; she had a feeling that they had been on the walls for decades rather than having been put up recently for fashionably retro effect.

Suddenly she noticed a pair of eyes peering up at her from between the pump-handles.

'What can I get you, miss?' the tiny figure asked.

Phoebe looked down at the girl in front of her. Surely she was no more than nine years old. In her arms she held a squirming Jack Russell as though it were a baby; it gave one last frantic wriggle and escaped to the floor. 'We're all out of white wine,' the little girl continued, 'but we've a special on double shots tonight and a free packet of smoky bacon crisps with every gin and tonic.' Then she leant across the bar until her feet were off the floor and whispered conspiratorially, 'The crisps are past their sell-by date, but only by a few weeks.'

'Thank you for telling me,' Phoebe whispered back as

she lowered her head towards the girl. 'I just wondered if your mum or dad was around.'

'My mum's dead and my dad's depressed,' the little girl was still whispering. 'I like your hair.' She reached out and pushed her finger inside one of Phoebe's long curls.

'Leave the lady's hair alone, Honey.' A woman with a foreign accent appeared beside the child, a sleek dark bob framing high cheekbones and full red lips. 'I'll serve her. You put the glasses away.' The little girl slid back down to the floor, giving the woman a cheerful smile before disappearing to the other end of the bar. 'Good girl.' The woman turned back to Phoebe. Her voice was thick but silky smooth, like melted toffee; Phoebe wondered if she was Polish. 'Slovakia.' The woman said as though she'd read Phoebe's mind. 'Everyone always think I am Polish.' She smiled at Phoebe and pushed back her glossy hair with long fingernails decorated with tiny twinkling stars. Phoebe wondered what such a woman was doing behind a bar in a small-town Irish pub; she looked like the sort of woman Phoebe always wanted to be, tall and elegant and glamorous instead of small and chaotically unkempt. 'You bring the good luck with you tonight,' the woman went on. 'Carraigmore has not beaten Kilcummin for over thirty years.'

'They're all certainly very happy.'

'We are all happy tonight. What can I get you?'

The national anthem came to a rousing finale and there was a sudden surge towards the bar. Phoebe felt herself being crushed by the rowdy crowd behind her.

'Hey, you guys, there must not be pushing,' shouted the woman behind the bar, her accent getting thicker with her exasperation. 'First is come, first is served, and right now it is this lady.' The calling and pushing grew even louder, the woman's requests for quiet ignored. Suddenly a high-pitched screech brought the room to total silence. The little girl stood on top of the bar, a silver whistle in her hand.

'Thank you, Honey,' the woman said smiling at the little girl. 'Now please get down and go and tell Fibber and Mrs Flannigan to come and serve this bad-behaving lot.'

'I don't want a drink, thank you,' Phoebe said as the woman returned her attention to her. 'I just wondered if there is a place to stay in Carraigmore, a hotel, or B&B, or somewhere like that.'

A stocky, badger-haired man appeared, his muscular arms already pulling pints in response to orders from the desperate throng.

'There's nowhere like that round here,' he said. 'Your best bet's over twenty miles away, and I'm not sure if they'll be open till the season starts.' Though his expression was serious, blue eyes twinkled in his ruddy face. 'Katrina, can you get three Heinekens for Rory O'Brian over there and a Galway Hooker for Tommy Kean?' He winked at Phoebe. 'That's a pale ale to the uninitiated.'

'Of course, Fibber, three Heinekens and Tommy's Hooker coming up,' the beautiful woman leant across the handpumps and kissed Fibber's cheek. He stopped pulling the pint in his hand and smiled back at her with such affection that Phoebe had to look away. As she did so she found herself being scrutinised by another woman now serving at the other end of the bar, a much older woman with tight grey curls, thick make-up, and a cascade of diamante hanging from each ear. She stared at Phoebe but didn't return her smile.

Phoebe turned around to leave the pub, prepared for a long night of searching for a place to stay.

'You can stay here,' Phoebe turned back to the bar; the offer was from Katrina but Fibber was nodding eagerly beside her. Phoebe started to protest.

'Yes, why don't you stay here?' Fibber said. 'It's late and cold and we have a spare room upstairs. You're very welcome to it.' He called over to the older woman. 'Isn't she, Ma?'

'What about the child?' the older woman called back. 'Isn't she staying here tonight?' Her narrow eyes now focused on a dark stream of Guinness pouring into a pint glass in her hand, lips pursed tightly, either in concentration or irritation.

'I'll sleep in the living room,' Honey had pushed herself in between Katrina and Fibber. 'I'll put the cushions from the sofa on the floor and use your sleeping bag, Uncle Fibber, and I'll put a hot water bottle in the lady's bed and find some magazines for her to read before she goes to sleep.'

'You've got it all sorted out, haven't you?' Fibber ruffled her hair affectionately.

'It's very kind of you to offer, but I don't want to be any trouble.' Phoebe tried to politely back away. 'I'll just go back to Cork, I'm sure there're lots of places there.'

'No, you're no trouble at all, and haven't we got a great plan worked out now? Honey will enjoy camping in the living room.'

'She'll be camping nowhere,' a loud voice said. The bar had fallen silent once again as the crowd parted to make way for a tall, broad-shouldered man; the collar of his heavy coat was turned up, a wild mass of fair hair glistening from rain. He pushed in roughly beside Phoebe, making her knock her neighbour's glass; lager sloshed onto a beer mat. Phoebe looked around for someone to apologise to but all eyes were on the newcomer; his eyes were on the small girl. 'She's coming home with me.' Phoebe could smell whiskey on his breath and see at least three days' stubble on his chin.

'But Daddy, I want to …'

'Get your coat, Honey,' the man interrupted her. 'The car's outside.'

Honey looked up anxiously at Katrina and Fibber. The grey-haired older woman marched up from the other end of the bar and put her arm around Honey's shoulder.

Fibber leaned forward and spoke quietly into the man's unshaven face. 'I think you should leave, Theo,' he said, pronouncing each word slowly. 'You're not safe to drive, I won't let the child go with you in the car.'

The man lowered his own voice and glared at Fibber. 'You have no right to tell me what I can and can't do with my own daughter.'

The whole pub seemed to be straining to hear the conversation; no one spoke, no one moved.

'Honey is my niece,' Fibber said. 'She comes here of her own accord, she wants to be with me and Katrina and her grandmother. The poor kid has no life up at that house. You can't look after her; and till you sort yourself out you aren't fit to look after your dog, let alone the child.'

'How dare you, Fibber Flannigan! One of these days I'll take you outside and I won't be held responsible for what I'll do. Honey, I said get your coat, we're getting out of this place; a bar is no place for a little girl.'

'At least the drinking doesn't start round here until lunchtime.' Fibber's voice was barely a whisper, but Theo slammed his hand down on the bar with such force that Phoebe jumped in fright and several more drinks sloshed their contents onto the counter.

'That's enough now, Theo.' Old Mrs Flannigan held a phone in her hand. 'If I make just one call to the Guards to say you're driving under the influence, Sergeant Jackson will be here in a flash and you'll lose your licence for good this time.' Theo looked as though he might jump over the bar and throttle the old woman, but instead he turned around and started to walk out of the pub.

'Just think about how Maeve would feel if she could see the state you've let yourself get into,' Fibber addressed the man's retreating back. 'It would break her heart, God rest her soul.' Theo stopped in the middle of the room. Phoebe waited for him to turn around and come back to haul Fibber over the counter for a full-blown fight but instead he headed for the door and disappeared into the night.

The silence continued for a few seconds before the clamouring at the bar resumed.

'There are never the boring moments in Carraigmore,' said Katrina to Phoebe with a smile.

'*Never a dull moment*,' corrected Fibber, then added, 'not with Theo the way he is now. Sorry, Honey, I know he's your dad but he's not the man he used to be at all.'

'He's just sad.' Honey sounded years older than she looked.

'Time for bed sweetheart,' said Mrs Flannigan. 'School tomorrow.' Honey gave a groan.

'Ah, you know you'll love it when you get there,' said Fibber. 'I know you have a secret crush on Mr O'Brian.'

'Yuk, no I don't.' Honey made a face. 'He's mean and he looks like an old frog – in fact all the teachers I've ever seen look like old frogs.'

'I'm a teacher,' said Phoebe with amusement. 'Do I look like an old frog?'

Honey looked surprised, 'No, you look like a princess, not like a teacher at all.'

'Maybe the teacher-princess here could come and give Mr O'Brian a kiss and he might turn into a handsome prince,' Fibber winked. Honey shuddered.

'I bet he'd still have breath like old potatoes and get cross with me for getting nought out of ten in my spelling test.'

'Bed!' ordered Mrs Flannigan, giving Honey a gentle prod with the ice tongs. Honey blew them all a kiss and waved good night.

''Night Uncle Fibber, 'night Katrina, 'night 'night Grandma, good-night Teacher-Princess.'

'I'll be up to tuck you in a minute,' called her grandmother, smiling the first smile Phoebe had seen her give that night.

'Right,' shouted Fibber setting up a microphone stand. 'Who's for a spot of karaoke?'

The opening bars to "Dancing Queen" blared out across the room, and three large women, Carraigmore T-shirts stretched tight across their breasts, sprang up from their seats to stand on a small stage in front of the television. They swayed ample hips and started to sing along with the music, stumbling over the words that sailed across the screen.

'I am sure by now you are needing a drink,' Katrina shouted to Phoebe above the noise. 'What will you have?' Phoebe suddenly felt overwhelmingly tired and the thought of a drink was appealing. Maybe she would accept their offer of a bed for the night.

'I'll have a gin and tonic, but can I pass on the out-of-date crisps?'

Katrina smiled. 'Honey is too honest. Fibber told her "do not mention the date on the crisps."'

'Is that why he's called "Fibber"?' asked Phoebe.

Katrina burst out laughing, 'I think this lady wants to know if you are a liar,' she playfully poked the big man beside her with a long fingernail.

'No,' replied Fibber, busy pulling pints, 'I'm as honest as a mirror buffed with vinegar, that's the truth. But I do come from a long line of Fibbers. Fibber Flannigan the fifth I am, my mother was married to Fibber Flannigan the fourth, my granny was married to the third, his father was the second – you get the idea I'm sure, and all of them as true and straight as they come – well, maybe my old dad was a bit prone to distorting the specifics when it came to the ladies, but that's all in the past.' He winked again at Phoebe.

'And have they always had this pub?' she asked.

'There's been a Fibber Flannigan's Pub in Carraigmore since Michael Collins sat on his mother's knee.' Fibber replied. 'There's nothing gone on in this town that the Flannigans haven't known about for over a hundred years – isn't that right Ma?'

Old Mrs Flannigan stopped pouring coke on top of a shot of vodka and leant her solid body against the counter.

'That's right.' She answered her son but all the while she stared at Phoebe.

'Here is your gin, Phoebe,' Katrina handed her a cool glass and Phoebe found herself drinking it down too fast. Her head spun a little; maybe she should have had the crisps.

'What can I get you, Béarla cailín deas?' asked the elderly man who'd sung the national anthem; he was so stooped that Phoebe had to bend to hear his cracked and wavering voice. 'That means *pretty English girl*,' he continued. 'You're in the Gaeltacht now you know? Another gin is it?' Before Phoebe had time to say she'd like an orange juice or ask what the Gaeltacht was, she found that anther glass of gin had magically appeared in front of her.

The old man raised his own glass of whiskey to her and shuffled back to his seat. Phoebe took a sip of her fresh drink, hoisted herself onto a high barstool, and watched the boy with the Celtic drum accompanying a young girl singing an Adele song on the karaoke. Soon the whole pub was joining in with the singing, and as Phoebe finished her third gin and Fibber was up at the microphone giving a rendition of 'Always on My Mind', she found herself swaying in time to the music and singing along to the chorus.

An hour later, more gin, the rousing strains of "The Irish Rover" and several encouraging locals, had lured Phoebe off her stool to partake in a whirling dance of interchanging partners that left her laughing and breathless in the middle of the small space cleared for dancing. This was followed by much enthusiastic stomping and clapping to "Come on Eileen" and then a lively display of accompanying actions to a *Grease* medley. Phoebe collapsed back onto her stool as a wizened woman with no teeth stepped up to the microphone and began sweetly to sing 'The Rose of Tralee'. Phoebe turned to Fibber behind the bar and declared, with only the merest hint of a slur, that the people of Carraigmore were the most wonderful people in the world and that she loved them all.

Chapter Five

The painful throbbing in her head broke through a tangle of dreams. A team of muscle-bound Gaelic football players had been serenading her with "Super Trouper" until David appeared and started to dance the samba dressed from head to toe in luminous green. With great difficulty Phoebe opened one eye. For a moment she wasn't sure where she was. A pale morning light filled the unfamiliar room; she could see orange floral curtains complementing a floral duvet, floral pillowcases, and floral walls. The patterns hurt.

Phoebe closed her eye again. Memories of the night before came back in blurry snatches; the several gin and tonics that had led to a double whiskey, and then Fibber's special Carraigmore cocktails – she hated to think what had been in them. She had had quite a few and then – oh no, please no! Phoebe buried her face in her pillow, trying to suffocate the recollection – had she really sung karaoke "Wind Beneath My Wings" and, even worse, "How Am I Supposed To Live Without You"? Had she really started to cry in front of all those strangers and then been sick in that poor boy's Celtic drum? She had a vague recollection of being put to bed by Katrina and a very grumpy Mrs Flannigan. She could remember little of the bedtime scenario, but the fact that she was still in her clothes suggested that she'd either passed out pretty quickly or struggled so much they couldn't get her undressed.

Phoebe groaned; she couldn't possibly stay here now;

she'd have to leave Carraigmore before anyone saw her. She would have to leave Ireland. It had been a ridiculous idea to come anyway; what was there for her here, just a pile of old stones by the cold, grey sea? She'd drive to the nearest airport and get a flight as far away as possible. She would take a vow of silence in some remote Indian Ashram or lose herself travelling across the Gobi desert, or at least go somewhere where drinking was prohibited. She tried to sit up but her head felt as though it was made of lead, her neck too feeble to support it. Gently she eased herself back down onto the pillow and was immediately overcome by a wave of nausea. She'd leave her escape for a few more minutes.

'Good morning, Phoebe,' Katrina was standing at the end of the bed with a tray. Bright sunshine poured in through the opened curtains, Phoebe realised she must have gone to sleep again. 'Feeling better?'

Phoebe tried to speak; only a cracked croak emerged from her dry mouth.

'Tea and paracetamol,' said Katrina, putting a mug and two tablets down on the bedside table. 'And when you've had that you must eat.' She put a plate beside the mug. 'Soda bread and raspberry jam. I bake the bread myself, this morning. It will make you better.' She sat down on the bed and picked up Phoebe's hand, examining it in her own. 'You are very thin, are you sick?

'Only when I mix my drinks,' croaked Phoebe weakly.

'Fibber's cocktails are strong; I should have told you to be taking care.' Katrina's silky Eastern European accent sounded soothing to Phoebe's aching head.

'I'm so embarrassed,' whispered Phoebe.

'You weren't the only one who was a little – what is it that you say in English? Bad for wear? But you were very sad last night. You were crying when we try to get you into bed. All the time you were saying, "David, David, I miss David". He is your man? Have you had row? Split

50

up?'

'No.'

'Then do you want me to phone him and tell him where you are?'

'No, no,' Phoebe moaned. 'You can't phone him.'

'But he could chat with you, cheer you up.'

'He hasn't got a phone.'

Katrina shook her head in surprise, her glossy bob swung against her cheeks. 'No mobile? No work number? There must be some way you can be getting hold of him.'

Phoebe sighed, she hadn't wanted anyone to know, she hadn't wanted anyone to feel sorry for her, but since she had managed to reveal her broken heart to the whole town within a few hours of arriving, what did it matter?

'He's dead.'

'Oh! You poor thing,' Katrina leant down and stroked Phoebe's hair. Phoebe started to cry. 'You know him long time?' Katrina asked, taking Phoebe's hand again.

'I met him when I was fifteen.'

'Was he your husband?'

Phoebe thought about explaining that he had actually been someone else's husband but found herself nodding her aching head instead.

It was nearly midday by the time Phoebe managed to drag on some fresh clothes and make it down the stairs. In the kitchen she found Katrina sitting at the table; a round of rolled-out pastry lay beside her while two big iron pots emitted delicious smells from the Rayburn. Despite her hangover Phoebe was suddenly starving.

Katrina didn't hear Phoebe; she was reading, completely absorbed in the thin sheet of paper that she held between her manicured hands. She sniffed and picking up a tea towel wiped her eyes. Mascara smudged down her cheek.

'Are you all right?' Phoebe asked. Katrina jumped.

'Oh, Phoebe, you give me fright out of my skin,' she quickly folded the letter and slipped it into the pocket of her apron.

'Sorry,' said Phoebe. 'Are you sure you're OK?' Katrina smiled broadly and stood up.

'Yes of course, I am as OK as the rain. Did you eat the bread and jam?' Phoebe shook her head. 'You must eat, I have told you this. You will feel better if you eat.' Still smiling, she hustled Phoebe into a windsor chair at one end of the table and pushed a crocheted cushion behind her back. After a few seconds a steaming bowl of soup appeared in front of her and another plate of soda bread, spread thick with yellow butter. 'Good for the morning afterwards – it will help your head, and after soup you must have stew.' Katrina gave the second pot a stir and sniffed its contents. 'Mmmm. Is good I think.'

'What are you making with the pastry?' asked Phoebe between mouthfuls of the comforting soup.

Katrina nodded to a bundle of rhubarb sticks at the end of the table, 'Rhubarb and almond pie. I will serve it with some honey and ginger ice cream for the lunch-time customers.'

'I didn't expect food like this in Carraigmore,' Phoebe said, wondering how Katrina managed to cook with those incredible fingernails; now the glittering stars had gone and each nail was painted with a leopard-skin effect.

Katrina effortlessly lifted the thin pastry and draped it over a pie dish, gently pushing it down into the base with her knuckle, easing it up the fluted sides. 'I am a good cook. I learn it from my mother.'

'In Slovakia?'

Katrina nodded and Phoebe noticed that her expression was suddenly sad again.

'What brought you here in the first place?' Phoebe asked after a little while.

Katrina started to trim pastry from the edge of the pie

dish.

'Maeve's funeral.' She didn't elaborate and Phoebe let the silence linger, not wanting to press her. Katrina looked deep in thought as she slowly turned the dish around, then she looked up. 'When she die I come all the way from Dublin to say goodbye to my friend.' She gathered up the pastry off-cuts and threw them at the feet of the Jack Russell, sitting pressed against the warmth of the Rayburn. 'It is very sad but at the end of the days there was some good because I found Fibber and now I am happy.'

'Who was Maeve?' Phoebe asked, surprised to find she felt curious about the lives of the people in Fibber Flannigan's pub, it had been weeks since anything had roused her interest.

Katrina pricked the pie-case with a fork, slid it into the oven, and leant back against the Rayburn. 'She was so much, is hard to say. When I meet her I was living in a bedsit in Dun Laoghaire and she and her husband and her little girl are living in the house next door.'

'So she was your neighbour?' asked Phoebe.

'Yes, she was my neighbour but she was also very good friend – and also she was Mrs Flannigan's daughter, Fibber's sister, Honey's mother, and Theo –you remember Theo from last night?' she did a brief impression of an angry figure stomping their feet. 'She was Theo's wife.'

'He seemed very upset,' said Phoebe.

Katrina didn't respond but turned her back to ladle out the stew onto a plate.

'Honey seems like a lovely little girl.' Phoebe smiled up at Katrina as she placed the plate in front of her and handed her a fork. 'She must have been through a tough time.'

Katrina sighed and sat down next to Phoebe. 'Yes. But Theo can't see that Honey is hurting too. He can only feel about himself. I think he does that thing that some unhappy people do – how is that how you say it? – Taking bath in his sad feelings?'

Phoebe thought for a few seconds, 'Wallowing in his own misery?'

'Yes that is it, he is always wallowing.' Katrina wiped her floury hands on the tea towel. 'But you must know how it is he feels, how it is to grieve for the person that you love. It must have been hard times for you when your husband died.'

Phoebe pushed the stew around the plate, her appetite suddenly gone.

Katrina picked up a stick of rhubarb and began to chop it into little pieces. 'So tell me, Phoebe, what has brought *you* to Carraigmore?'

Phoebe shrugged. 'Oh you know, half the world wants to come and find their Irish roots don't they?'

'But Carraigmore in March? Is not best time to see this place, you know?'

'It felt like the best time to me.'

Katrina stopped chopping and looked at Phoebe. 'Maybe you think walking on the windy beach will mend your heart? That will not work you know – to start with no one will leave you alone, everyone will want to know who you are, why you here,' she laughed, showing off a beautiful set of teeth. 'They will want to know what is favourite TV show, what you like for breakfast, where you buy your underwears. In Carraigmore finding other people's businesses is nearly as big a sport as is the football.'

'If you really want to know, my grandmother was from Carraigmore. I used to come here as a little girl to visit her and I wanted to see the beach again.' Phoebe took a small mouthful of stew, and then another as her taste buds came alive. 'Wow, this stew is amazing, what's in it?'

'Pheasant and red wine and my secret ingredient.'

'What's that?'

'Like I say, is secret. But tonight you must taste my

Thai green curry, it is also very good.'

'Oh, I'm not staying that long – especially after last night. I'll be gone after I've had a quick look around.'

Katrina looked disappointed. 'That is shame, especially as I am thinking you have to talk to Fibber's mother, she must have known your grandmother; she has known everybody who ever live here.'

'I don't think she likes me.'

'Why do you say that?'

'She gave me some very dirty looks last night and that was before I got sick all over her pub.'

'Mrs Flannigan is a good woman but sometimes she can seem hard. Since Maeve died she too has been very sad. She is like a lemon.'

'Bitter? Sour?'

Katrina nodded. 'Yes, just like that. But I like her, she is letting me live here with Fibber, she is giving me this job at the pub, good pay. Underneath her bitter, sour lemon she is kind.' Katrina lowered her voice. 'Also, Fibber he tell me this, Mrs Flannigan's mother was not right up here,' Katrina tapped her head with a long finger nail. 'She was, I think, a little mad, and also when Mrs Flannigan was a schoolgirl the teachers always beat her because she couldn't learn to read and write.'

'Poor Mrs Flannigan.' Phoebe stared out of the window on to an overgrown back garden. She thought about the class of children she had left behind in England. She couldn't imagine ever thinking it would be a good idea to beat them. She felt guilty that she hadn't had a chance to tell them she was leaving. Maybe she should just go back to England, face up to Nola, ask Mrs Leach for her job back before she found another Year One teacher to take her place.

'Katrina!' The shout came from another room.

Katrina chopped the final stick of rhubarb and stood up. 'I must go and help Fibber in the bar. There will many be wanting the hairs of the dog today.' Katrina took off the apron and hung it on a hook. Phoebe noticed that she took the letter from the apron pocket and slipped it into the back pocket of her skin-tight jeans. With a wave to Phoebe Katrina went through an adjoining door into the bar, and as the door slowly closed, Phoebe caught a glimpse of Fibber wiping away the smudged mascara on her cheek.

Chapter Six

Phoebe shivered as she stepped out onto the blustery high street. It felt bitterly cold despite the bright sunlight of the day. Delving into her coat pocket she drew out a dark brown bobble hat. She pulled it down on her aching head and thought of David. He used to tease her when she wore the hat on yard-duty at school: *You look like you're wearing a tea-cosy!*

As she headed down the high street towards the sea she could hear the high-pitched shrieks of children playing in the Carraigmore school playground behind her. A buzzer sounded, the shrieking stopped, and Phoebe imagined the small boys and girls lining up to file back into the building for afternoon lessons. She thought of her own class doing just the same in England. She hoped it wouldn't be too late to get her job back.

'Hi, Phoebe,' a heavily tattooed man shouted from the open window of a van. 'How's the hangover today?'

Before Phoebe could even feel surprised that a complete stranger knew her name, *and* that she had a hangover, a middle-aged woman with a tartan shopping bag called out.

'Beautiful singing, Phoebe. It brought a tear to my eye.'

'Did you have a good night, Phoebe?' from an elderly, flat-capped man sitting outside the butchers.

'Hiya, Phoebe! Enjoying the Irish climate?'

'Hello, Pheebs, how are you doing?'

'Nice hat, Phoebe! How's the head?'

She continued being hailed by people down the length of the street until Phoebe wondered if there had been anyone in Carraigmore who hadn't been in Fibber Flannigan's the night before. Though she had little recollection of the evening, she seemed to have made quite an impression. She would definitely leave as soon as possible; she had managed to embarrass herself in front of an entire village.

By the time she reached the end of the high street, Phoebe had decided to forget the boathouse, turn around, get in her car, and drive away, but a gang of young men were suddenly coming towards her. In padded check shirts and dusty boots they looked like builders – they were bound to have been in Fibber's the night before. Rather than wait to see what they had to say she veered into the Carraigmore Art and Craft Centre.

Inside, Phoebe looked around the vast interior of the converted church. It was very beige; beige mugs and bowls, beige wool, beige linen, beige watercolours on beige walls, a few shamrock-decorated things for tourists. After a quick glance round she headed for the door but found that the young men had taken up residence on a bench outside. They were unwrapping pies, cracking open cans of Coke, lighting cigarettes, and evidently preparing themselves for a lunch break. Phoebe went back inside; at least the woman behind the till didn't look like she would have been in Fibber Flannigan's, being small and mousy with a pale brown bowl of hair and a knitted waistcoat the colour of a cow-pat. She was sorting through a pile of greetings cards, pricing each one with a hand-written sticky label and only briefly glanced at Phoebe before returning to her task.

Phoebe moved around the room looking at the shamrock-embroidered handkerchiefs and the tea towels printed with traditional Irish recipes. A flock of toy sheep had been herded into a neat straight line on a shelf. She picked one up and wondered if Amy and Ruben were too old for cuddly toys – probably. Anyway she doubted that Nola would let her children accept any more gifts from their wanton aunt. Phoebe replaced the sheep and fought back threatening tears. She turned around to find herself in front of a display of tweed deerstalkers. If David had been alive she would have bought him one so that they could have both had a funny hat to wear. In the past this would have made her laugh but now a wave of sadness seemed to engulf her, and she moved away from the hats to stare at a shelf of surprisingly beautiful pottery.

The pottery looked out of place amongst the rest of the stock. She wondered who had made it and felt suddenly compelled to touch the blood-red glaze that dripped down the side of a vase. The woman behind the till let out a little cough and Phoebe's hand sprang away from the vase like a naughty child caught touching a bowl of sweets.

Instead she looked at a display of postcards, gently spinning the rotating stand. She was sure she'd bought the one of a little red-haired girl and donkey when she had been a child, and the view of Carraigmore beach on a busy summer day had a distinctly 1970s feel to it. Phoebe kept spinning, wondering if she should send a card to Nola to let her know she was still alive. No, Phoebe decided firmly, if Nola wanted to know how she was she could get in touch herself.

She gave the display a final spin and was just about to turn away when she noticed the postcard. Unlike the others it was a painting, powerful brush strokes depicting a dark and angry sea, thick streaks of grey and swirling blues, white waves crashing onto a thin strip of umber sand. A single smudge of red suggested a figure walking on the beach, battling against the stormy weather, all alone in the full force of nature's elements. Something about the image appealed to Phoebe. She picked it up, drawn to the wildness of the ocean and the determination of the lonely figure. She couldn't decide if the image signified hope or some kind of hopeless despair. She turned it over, *W.M. Flynn, Carraigmore, 1994.*

'Can I help you?' The voice made Phoebe jump.

She looked up to find the mousy woman hovering beside her.

'Just looking, thank you,' Phoebe craned forward to glance through a window to see if the builders were still sitting on the bench. They were. She peered intently at the postcard so that she didn't have to make conversation with the mouse.

'One of Ireland's greatest landscape painters,' the mouse said over her shoulder. 'Do you know his work?' Phoebe moved to put the postcard back but something changed her mind.

'No,' she said.

'He manages to imbue each simple brush stroke with such force and energy; I find his paintings quite invigorating.' The mouse leant forward to touch the card and gave a little shiver.

'I'll take it,' Phoebe held out the card towards the woman who beckoned to her to follow her to the till. After she had taken Phoebe's money and slowly and carefully recorded the sale in an exercise book and written out a receipt, the mouse placed the card in a candy-striped paper bag and handed it to Phoebe.

'May I ask what brings you to Carraigmore?'

I used to come here to visit my grandmother when I was a child. I wanted to see the village again and find my grandmother's house.'

'Have you found it?'

'Not yet,' replied Phoebe. 'She lived down by the beach, in the boathouse.'

'Do you mean the pottery studio?'

'Yes, that's right. She was a potter.'

'Anna Brennan!' The mouse gasped and her little pink

60

fingers flew to her chest in excitement. 'You're Anna Brennan's granddaughter?' Phoebe nodded (as much as her residual hangover would allow.) 'Oh, I adore her pots, I'd love to own one but I think they're rather out of my price range now.'

'Did you know her?'

'I'm a recent blow-in from Dublin so I'm afraid I didn't, but I'd very much have liked to. She was such a talented potter, wonderfully fluid forms and lovely celadon glazes. How exciting to meet you. Are you a potter too?'

Phoebe shook her head.

'I have a picture of her work here,' the mouse scuttled away and returned with a large book – *Irish Studio Pottery*. 'It was printed to go with an exhibition at a Dublin museum many years ago.' With some difficulty, owing to the book's size and weight, the little woman began flicking through the pages.

'Here we are,' she said holding up a double-page spread in front of Phoebe's face. Phoebe took a step back and saw a photograph of eight cylindrical lidded jars of varying heights and sea green shades, each one inscribed with swirling linear decorations. 'Just look at that depth of colour she achieved,' the woman said. 'The subtle changes from duck egg to turquoise, and then look at that deep green, and the quality of line in that incised decoration,' the woman paused and took a breath before almost whispering, 'exquisite.'

Phoebe thought they were beautiful but she liked the little pot she had better; it had *love from Granny* on the bottom and it had been filled with sherbet pips. Nola had dropped her own pot on Boxing Day, trying to winkle out the last pip from the bottom with a pencil. Phoebe could still see the green shards lying on the quarry tile floor, Nola hadn't cared; she had a New Year's Eve party to go to and a bottle of Pomagne cider to smuggle out of the house. Phoebe wondered what had happened to the

61

collection of her grandmother's ceramics that had lined the kitchen's dresser shelves: the wide blue fruit bowl on the table, the vase her mother used to fill with tulips in the spring. Where did all that pottery go?

'And, of course, it was in Nigeria that she met the great English potter Michael Cardew.' Phoebe hadn't realised that the mousy woman was still talking; she forced herself to look interested. 'She worked with him in his famous pottery in Abuja and he taught her a huge amount, got her throwing and interested in shape and form, but it was when she came back here that she developed these lovely glazes and really began to make a name for herself in Ireland.' The woman touched Phoebe's arm. 'I'm sorry, I'm waffling on, I'm sure you know all this already.' Phoebe didn't know any of it; she knew her grandmother had made pots but nothing of why, where, or how she started or how well known she might have been. 'It was a tragedy that she died the way she did.'

Phoebe nodded and looked away.

Through a huge arched window she could see the backs of the builders retreating down the hill.

'I must go now,' she said. 'I want to leave Carraigmore before it gets dark and I haven't been down to the beach yet.'

'So soon?' the little woman sighed. 'Why don't you stay around longer? I'm sure there are lots of people in town who remember your grandmother and would love to meet you.'

'No, I think I've been here long enough.

The woman peered at Phoebe through a straw-like fringe and patted her arm again.

'If you're embarrassed about last night, don't be,' she said gently. Phoebe could feel her face reddening. 'We were all well away after that victory for Carraigmore. Your singing was lovely, but if you feel badly about the mess you made of young Tommy Gibson's bodhrán we have a

62

very fine collection of traditional Celtic drums for sale.'

Chapter Seven

The road narrowed as it dipped towards the sea. Phoebe soon found herself walking down the winding lane that led towards the beach. Memories swept over her with every step; she could hear Nola running ahead shouting 'Come on, last one in is a loser,' and her father behind them, grappling with the body boards, calling, 'Say hello to Granny first.'

Her mother would have been beside him, one hand in his, the other carrying a basket filled with crisps and biscuits from the general store, contributions to the lunch of soup and bread her grandmother would have made in her ancient Baby Belling cooker.

Phoebe had to consciously prepare herself for the fact that her grandmother wouldn't be there as she turned the corner. She wouldn't be standing outside the boathouse in her denim smock; she wouldn't be wearing her yellow hat or waving a clay-covered hand. The boathouse might not be there either, and if it was it would surely look very different from the romantic little building that Phoebe remembered.

She closed her eyes and took a deep breath – a few more steps around the corner and she'd be there. *One, two, three.* She opened her eyes and there it was, right in front of her. Not crumbling, not falling down or ramshackle but neat and white with pale blue paint on the doors and windows and a weed-free brick path leading to the door. Terracotta plant pots were grouped around the walls;

daffodil shoots poking up through rich, dark soil. Phoebe could remember the apple tree her grandmother had planted and the pebbly stream that trickled through the garden on to the beach; how many hours had Phoebe spent sitting beside that stream as a child, floating buttercup petals down it or poking at caddis flies in their knobbly cocoons?

Everything looked immaculate; no one would ever think it had been unused and neglected for over sixteen years. As she approached Phoebe wondered if someone could be living there. Maybe no one realised that it actually belonged to Phoebe and Nola. Phoebe stopped a few yards away from the boathouse door, reluctant to go too near as though she might be intruding. Instead she looked out across the beach.

A long stretch of empty sand glittered in the afternoon sun, and the mountains of the opposite peninsula looked like pyramids against the sky. Phoebe could see white breakers crashing against distant cliffs and up above her a sea gull wheeled and cried out in the wind.

The tide was far out, exposing a large black rock sitting on the beach like a monolith. It looked almost artificial, as if someone had placed it there: an ancient, man-made monument paying homage to the waves.

The stream cut its way across the sand, widening as it approached the sea, rivulets fanning out like veins before being integrated with the foaming water. Phoebe remembered building dams across the stream to make paddling pools. As a child she'd made sandcastles, collected shells, flown kites, and played cricket on the beach but had never stopped to think how beautiful it was.

Something caught Phoebe's eye. A movement beside the rock, something quick and darting; too fast to focus on, in an instant it had vanished.

Phoebe turned away and walked towards the boathouse, feeling certain that someone must be using it. She felt slightly indignant, had it been made into a holiday home?

The front of the building had two huge sliding wooden doors running across its width, left over from the times when boats would have been stored inside. Phoebe stood on tip toes and peered through a window in one of the doors, expecting to see a neatly arranged living room or modern kitchen where the boats and then her grandmother's studio would once have been. Instead she saw her grandmother's large gas kiln, still standing, top heavy on its thin metal legs in one corner. In front of it a long wood workbench looked dusty with pale grey smears, a large yellow sponge still in the middle of the bench as if a cleaning job had been interrupted. An old tin can holding pottery tools sat on one side of the bench, a stack of books on the other, while underneath it bags of clay were wrapped in clear plastic, neatly piled up like building blocks. Phoebe craned her neck, trying to see more through the glass. She could just see the edge of her grandmother's potter's wheel and Phoebe remembered how, on fine days, her grandmother liked to open up the doors and throw her pots with the sea and beach and mountains spread out in front of her, pausing every now and then to gaze at the view.

Everything looked just as Phoebe remembered. If it hadn't been for the freshly painted walls and woodwork and the neatly planted bulbs Phoebe would have thought it hadn't been touched since the day her grandmother left to visit her son and his family in England.

Phoebe walked around down the little path to the side entrance and tried the door, assuming it would be locked. Instead it opened easily. She paused and called *Hello* – no answer. She called twice more and stepped over the threshold into the silent room. A surge of hot, dry, dusty air engulfed her. Phoebe moved towards the source of the heat, it was coming from the kiln. She recognised its contented hum, as a little girl she'd often fallen asleep to the sound as it drifted through the floorboards above. A digital display on the wall showed that it was heating up, already nine hundred degrees inside its thickly insulated walls. What could be in it? Who had turned it on?

Phoebe looked around. On a windowsill a chipped brown jug was filled with catkins, beside it a straight row of jam jars neatly labelled: copper, cobalt, rutile, manganese.

Phoebe saw a tower of plastic containers in one corner. She read their scrawled labels and recognised her grandmother's handwriting: *Green Glaze, Deep Turquoise, Marine Blue*.

Walking over to the workbench Phoebe touched the sponge. It was wet; a thin stream of muddy water seeped out of it and dripped onto the painted concrete floor. She looked down and noticed the dusty footprints. They led to a flight of steep wooden stairs; Phoebe hesitated at the bottom, called out *Hello* once more, and started to climb.

The air was hotter upstairs and thicker, it made Phoebe want to cough. At the top she stopped and scanned the room, half expecting to find someone there. It looked empty. She stepped up from the top step onto a wooden boarded floor. She started; something had moved, there was a figure standing in front of her, as still as she was and staring straight at her, Phoebe took a step backwards and the figure stepped back too. With relief Phoebe realised it was her own figure reflected in an overly large mirror on the opposite wall, its ornately carved frame looked much too grand for the simple surroundings.

Looking around her everything looked very much as Phoebe remembered, though smaller. The single wrought-iron bed covered with a faded patchwork quilt, the bedside table, the red and white rag rug on the floor, the chest of drawers and next to that a Lloyd Loom chair. The floral-covered armchair was still beside the window overlooking the sea, and in one corner the Baby Belling sat on top of a makeshift workbench, a gingham curtain screening off a cupboard underneath it. Next to the workbench was a white enamel sink and an ancient immersion boiler that had provided water for washing and cooking. A small pot-bellied stove squatted in the facing corner, the wicker basket beside it still half-filled with logs and kindling. It had been a simple home for Anna Brennan but after twenty-five years living in a corrugated-tin hut in Africa she always claimed that it was all she needed. By the time she had come back to Carraigmore her priorities lay with clay and glaze and having enough space to have her wheel and kiln, rather than with the material trappings of a conventional home.

Phoebe smiled when she saw Anna's yellow straw hat hanging from a row of pegs on the wall; it hung alongside brightly coloured coats and shawls, and Phoebe recognised her grandmother's potter's smock. She pulled open a drawer in the chest of drawers and the smell of L'Air du Temps hit her like a punch from the past. The drawer was full of neatly folded silk scarves and jumpers, the drawer beneath a medley of shirts and skirts. Phoebe closed the drawers and looked around her, nothing had been touched. It was as though the room were quietly waiting for her grandmother to come home from her trip, neat and tidy just as Anna must have left it on the fateful day she left for England. Phoebe ran her finger along the top of the chest of drawers, expecting to leave a trail in years of accumulated dust but there was no dust, her finger left no mark at all. She walked over to the window and touched the sill, again no dust. But there were digestive biscuits; they spilled out across the windowsill from a crumpled, nearly empty packet. A little pile of biscuit crumbs had been carefully pushed into a pointed tower beside an opened can of 7Up. Phoebe picked up the can and shook it slightly; its remaining contents gave a gentle fizz.

As she put it back down she noticed an open book lying

face-down on the seat of the armchair and a selection of coloured pastel crayons strewn across the faded upholstery. Phoebe picked up the book, admiring its dark green leather binding and the embossed gold pattern down the spine. She turned it over to where it had been left open; on one side a lined and yellowing page was covered in neatly, looping writing and on the other someone had drawn a picture, obliterating the words. Colours filled the page: a long line of pale grey and then deep blue, and then a row of smudged purple, another line of hazy blue, a small round yellow sun at the top and an intensely coloured large black dome in the middle of the scene. It looked like a child's drawing – a child's drawing of Carraigmore beach. Phoebe thought it was beautiful, despite its simplicity it had surprising depth and perspective. She looked out of the window: the view looked just the same as the picture, the tide far out, the bright sun straight ahead – as though it had only just been finished, capturing that very moment in time.

Phoebe glanced at the writing on the facing page.

September 21st, 1948. She looked back at the picture. She felt sure it hadn't been done as long ago as that. Going back to the text she started to read.

I saw him walking on the beach again today. I watched him from the upstairs window of the boathouse, through a little circle that I've rubbed in the dirt. He walks with such purpose on the sand, his dark hair blowing in the wind, his hands deep in the pockets of his jacket. I watch him and he watches the sea – we are both transfixed.

I wonder is it wrong to find a man beautiful rather than handsome? I am sure it is not, but I do know that it must be wrong to find a man beautiful on the day your father has been buried.

Something made Phoebe's eyes jerk up from the page. A

noise, a noise outside. She peered out of the window but could see nothing. She shuddered, suddenly feeling trapped in the stifling upstairs room. She wanted to get outside into the cold air.

Hurrying down the wooden stairs she stopped abruptly at the bottom and stared – she couldn't believe she hadn't noticed them before. Rows and rows of pots lined long shelves beside the door. There were so many – mostly bowls but there were also jugs and jars, and vases as big and round as bowling balls. All were unfired, with the marks of the thrower's fingers still visible on the clay. They looked like a grey army lined up for battle. Phoebe reached out and touched a vase, it felt damp and soft; her fingertip left a faintly swirling print, she tried to rub it away but made it worse – the mark became a dent and then a hole.

There was a scuffling noise outside. Heart thumping she flung open the door and looked out. A shadow flashed across the path ahead of her. Blinking in the bright outdoor light she heard footsteps on the paving stones and caught a flash of something pale. Feeling braver she ran towards the slipway in time to see a small figure running across the beach. Phoebe followed across the sand and nearly caught up with the little girl just as she reached the big black rock.

'Honey!' she shouted as the child started to scramble upwards over the barnacle-encrusted stone, 'Honey, stop! I only want to talk to you, I just want to ask you about the boathouse.' Honey looked down at her from above; perched on all fours, hair blowing wild in the wind, she looked like a little animal. Her anxious eyes glanced towards the cliffs as if searching for something or someone. She looked trapped.

'It's all right,' called Phoebe. 'I'm not going to tell anyone you're not at school.' Honey sat down on a high ledge and pursed her lips. 'Did you do the drawing?' continued Phoebe from below. 'It's lovely; it looks just like the beach.'

Honey's face twisted and she looked like she was going to cry. 'It's rubbish!' she shouted back.

'No it's not,' Phoebe started to climb the rock towards her, trying to find a foothold in between the shallow pools and clumps of seaweed. 'It's not rubbish at all.'

'Yes it is. I can't draw – I'm too messy and Mr O'Brian told me I'm the worst colourer-inner he's ever had in his class!'

When Phoebe reached her she saw the tears beginning to slide down Honey's face. The little girl quickly wiped them away with her sleeve but more were flowing. Phoebe sat down a few inches from her. Honey covered her face with her hands.

'Your colouring looks great to me,' said Phoebe gently.

'No it's not,' Honey's muffled voice replied. 'It's bad. Just like my writing and my reading. I can't do it and Mr O'Brian says I'm stupid and rubbish and naughty and he hates me – and I hate him and his boring old school.'

'Does Mr O'Brian really say those things to you?'

Honey didn't answer for a while but then said, 'No, but I got nought out of ten for my spelling test this morning and he said *Not nought again, Honey!* and everybody laughed.'

'And you ran away from school?'

'Yes, I climbed over the wall at lunch time but my dad mustn't know.' Honey lifted up her face and looked imploringly into Phoebe's eyes. 'Please don't tell my dad or Grandma or Uncle Fibber or Katrina. I don't want them to be cross.'

Phoebe smiled at Honey.

'Maybe you should talk to your dad if you're not happy at school. He could have a chat with Mr O'Brian.'

'No!' Honey sounded vehement.

'But your dad wouldn't want you to be unhappy.' Honey said nothing and stuck out her bottom lip. Phoebe persevered. 'He'll want to help you. Maybe your dad will do some extra homework with you.' Honey shrugged.

'He's always staring out of the window or making pots,' she paused. 'Or drinking whiskey.'

'Are those his pots in the boathouse?' Phoebe asked.

'Yes. I'm not supposed to go in there, but I like to go upstairs and draw.'

'It's cosy up there, isn't it?' said Phoebe.

'I like it when the kiln's on,' Honey looked more cheerful. 'I like watching the waves when it's stormy and I'm all warm and dry. It's warmer in there than at home; it's freezing up there.' Phoebe saw the child's eyes flick up towards the cliff and for the first time Phoebe made herself look up too. Even though she knew what she would see she couldn't help the feeling of surprise. It looked smaller than Phoebe remembered – a perfect miniature fortress, straight out of the pages of a children's story book. Granite grey, it seemed to grow out of a tangle of wintry bushes and trees. Virginia creeper wove its way up the turreted towers, along the crenulated battlements and around the gothic arched widows and Phoebe remembered how, in autumn, the whole building turned a fiery red.

She stared, now she'd looked at it she couldn't seem able to drag her eyes away. The Castle – her grandmother's one great passion, apart from clay. Anna Brennan had never seemed able to let it go, returning to Carraigmore from Africa to be close to it, persuading its owner to sell her the boathouse so that she could live and work in the shadow of her childhood home. Repeatedly she told her granddaughters its story, imbuing them with her own passion for the magnificent house. It had once been a monastery, one of the towers was part of the original building but the house itself had been a Georgian addition – the gothic fantasy of a wealthy Anglo-Irish aristocrat who had won the ruined tower and the surrounding land in a game of cards. His descendants had

73

enjoyed his prize for generations.

Phoebe had a sudden memory of her grandmother standing on the beach, staring up at the house, shielding her eyes from the sun.

Phoebe always thought it strange that Anna, who in many ways hated rank and wealth and material concerns, should be so in thrall to her aristocratic roots. But looking up at the Castle, Phoebe could imagine the sentimental pull that extraordinary house must have had on her.

As a child Phoebe would lie awake at night in the little rosy bedroom in the B&B telling stories about the Castle, making it a place of magic, an enchanted fairy castle that she and Nola were princesses of. Nola, lying next to her, would tell her to shut up, but Phoebe once heard Nola tell the white-haired boys on the beach that it was her rightful home, not theirs.

'Do you live there?' Phoebe asked Honey.

Honey nodded, 'Do you think it's spooky?'

'No, I think it's beautiful.'

'The children at school say it's haunted and that I'm weird because I haven't got a mum and I live in a castle.'

'I bet they're jealous of you. Do you know, I wanted to live in your house when I was a little girl?'

Honey looked up at her, surprised, and was about to say something when they were both startled by an angry shout.

'What the hell do you think you're doing with my daughter?'

Phoebe looked down to see a man standing on the sand below them. She recognised him at once. Theo looked up, tall and broad shouldered with a chiselled face flushed red either from the wind or whiskey, or from his temper. A black Labrador stood beside him, barking up at the two figures on the rock.

'Did you hear me?' Theo shouted again. 'What are you doing with my daughter? She's meant to be at school.' Phoebe could only just hear his voice against the barking and the waves that crashed along the shore.

'Come on,' Phoebe said to Honey. 'I think we'd better go down and see your dad.' Carefully she started to climb down the rock, putting out her hand to help Honey, who followed reluctantly behind her.

At the bottom she stood in front of the irate man, Honey's hand still holding on to hers. The dog growled and Phoebe felt a momentary flash of alarm. Theo bellowed at his dog to shut up and then bellowed at Phoebe.

'Let go of my child at once.'

'It's all right, calm down,' Phoebe tried to loosen Honey's hand but the little girl held on tight. 'Please don't shout.'

'Don't tell me how to behave.' He still looked furious but at least he had lowered the tone of his voice. Honey released Phoebe's hand and he picked up the small girl and held her tightly. 'Sorry, Sweetheart, I didn't mean to be cross. It's just that I've been so worried and Mr O'Brian is probably on the phone to Sergeant Jackson right now, getting him to round up all the Guards in Kerry to form a search party. What on earth did you think you were doing – disappearing like that?' Honey looked unhappily up at him through her long blonde hair, and then she threw her arms around his neck.

'Sorry, Daddy, I'm so sorry. Please don't be cross with Phoebe.'

Theo looked at Phoebe. She could see his body relaxing, his fury subsiding with the relief of having found his daughter. She noticed that he had shaved since last night; he looked less dishevelled, apparently sober. The dog had also calmed down and was sniffing around the lower ledges of the rock.

'Who are you?' Theo sounded suspicious.

'She's a teacher,' said Honey wriggling out of her father's arms.

'What? You took her out of school? Are you a supply teacher?' Theo put one hand proprietarily on Honey's shoulder while with his other hand he dialled a number on a phone.

'No, I'm not Honey's ...' Phoebe began.

'I can't believe it,' Theo interrupted her, the phone at his ear as he waited for it to be answered. 'Did you take her out of school? Why didn't Mr O'Brian know that Honey was with you?'

'I'm not ...'

'Hello. It's Theo Casson here.' The phone had evidently been answered. 'Could you tell Mr O'Brian that I've found Honey? She was on the beach with one of your teachers and I really think it's shocking that you don't even know when a member of staff has taken a child out of school.'

'You don't understand,' Phoebe tried. Theo turned his back and took a few paces away from her; the rest of his conversation disappeared into the noise of the sea. She just could make out, 'I really feel I'll have to make a formal complaint.' And then, 'You have a duty of care for my child.'

'Daddy,' Honey ran up to her father and tugged at his jacket. 'Phoebe's not a teacher at my school,' she shouted above the waves. Theo looked down at her.

'I'm going to have to go,' he said into the phone. 'Just let Mr O'Brian know she's safe.' He stormed back towards Phoebe. 'What is going on? Did you entice her out of school? I have a good mind to have you arrested.' He started dialling on his phone again.

'No, Daddy.' Honey was crying now. 'Please don't. Phoebe didn't take me. I ran away from school.'

Theo stopped dialling and looked from the small child to Phoebe and back again.

'What were you doing with her then?' he asked Honey. Honey looked silently down at the sand. He looked back to

76

Phoebe,

'I found her on the beach,' said Phoebe deciding not to mention that either she or Honey had been in the boathouse. 'I had already met her at Fibber Flannigan's. I was the woman you pushed past at the bar last night, but you probably don't remember.' Theo looked at her blankly and Phoebe wondered if he remembered the night before at all. 'Honey and I were just having a chat about school.'

'Did it not occur to you that school was where a little girl should be at this time of day?'

'Yes. I know. But she was upset, I couldn't just …'

Theo interrupted, 'You could at least have found out where she lived.'

'I did, but …'

'Did you not think that people would be worried about her? As a teacher do you not …'

This time it was Phoebe who interrupted. 'Maybe you should ask your daughter why she ran away, listen to her, and try to help her, instead of getting angry with me.'

'Who do you think you are?' Theo pushed his hands through his unkempt hair, the colour in his face rising again. 'I've had enough of people telling me what I should and shouldn't do with my own child.' He took a step towards Phoebe and angrily pointed his finger at her, 'You have no idea what I've been through.'

'Stop it, stop it.' Honey had her hands pressed over her ears. 'Stop shouting!'

Theo immediately squatted down beside his daughter and took her hands in his. 'It's all right darling. You're safe with me now.' He stood back up and glared at Phoebe. 'Come on, Honey, let's go home.' He began steering her up the beach followed by the dog. Honey looked back at Phoebe over her shoulder and Phoebe raised her hand to say goodbye. Honey tried to wave but Theo took her hand in his and held on tightly to it as they started to walk up the cliff path towards the Castle.

Phoebe watched them go and realised she was breathing heavily, in and out almost in rhythm with the sea as waves of fury washed over her. How dare Theo speak to her like that? She thought of running after him to make him listen to her but she knew that would just have continued the argument and upset Honey again. She took one very big breath and started to trudge back to the boathouse. As she approached the little blue door she felt another wave of fury; how dare Theo use her grandmother's studio and equipment to make his pots, she was the one who should be calling the Guards to report a trespasser.

Once back inside the little room Phoebe warmed her cold hands in front of the kiln. She remembered doing the same thing as a child after swimming in the freezing sea; jostling for the warmest spot with Nola. *Shove over, squirt* Nola would have said, probably issuing a hefty prod to Phoebe's ribs with her elbow. What would Nola make of her behaviour since she'd come to Carraigmore? Drunken exhibitionism, vomiting in public, weeping and emotional displays, and now being threatened with the police by a stranger on the beach. Phoebe felt sure that Nola would say it was just the sort of behaviour she expected.

Suddenly Phoebe felt extremely tired, her hangover had subsided but the confrontation with Theo seemed to have drained her of all remaining energy. She climbed the set of wooden stairs and, after moving the book and pencils from the seat, flopped down onto the armchair. She sat very still and looked out across the sea. She dozed for a little while and when she woke up she noticed that the black rock threw a long shadow across the sand and an incoming tide was beginning to slap around its craggy base.

A gang of small boys ran across the beach laughing as they chased a football, trying to keep it from rolling into the waves. It must be past home time at the school, Phoebe thought. She ought to get back to the pub, pick up her bags, get in the car, and leave Carraigmore. She rubbed her eyes, where could she go next? She wished she didn't feel so tired.

Her thoughts drifted to Honey; she hoped Theo hadn't been too cross with her. Phoebe leant forward and picked up a biscuit from the windowsill and at the same time remembered the diary entry in the notebook Honey had been drawing in. Phoebe picked up the book and noticed the faded writing on the marbled inside cover, *Anna Shaw*. Slowly munching the digestive she began to flick through the pages of loopy handwriting to find the page that she'd been reading before.

Mother looks grey, like a ghost, even with her make-up on. After Father's funeral she gathered us together in the drawing room and told us that all the money has gone and the Castle can no longer be our home – it belongs to the bank in Dublin now.

We were all quiet until Richard said that Father took the coward's way out, and then Mother slapped his face and said that anyone can have an accident with a shotgun. Then she slapped his face again and started screaming until Mrs Reilly came running from the kitchen, and Mother stopped screaming and said that everything was quite all right and ...

At that point Honey's bright picture covered the next page and it was impossible to read the writing underneath. Phoebe turned the page over.

September 22nd, 1948

Richard and George are going to Canada. I have begged them to let me go with them but they keep telling me I am too young – at Christmas I will be nineteen, they are still only twenty-two. I must go to England with Mother, Aunt

Margaret has agreed to let us live with her. They still have rationing in England and I'm sure everywhere will be bomb sites, and Aunt Margaret is a snob and Elizabeth is even worse – she has always treated me like the poor relation, goodness knows what she'll be like now that I really am.

I looked on a map to find where Cheltenham is and it couldn't be further from the sea. What will I do without the waves and rocks and sand, what will I do without the Castle?

I was walking Razzle on the beach when I saw that man again. He saw me looking at him and stared back at me. We leave in three days; I will never see him again.

September 23rd, 1948

Everyone in the village knows we have no money now. The postman told Mrs Reilly that he doubted she'd be seeing any more wages from us, and she put on her coat and left before she'd finished cooking dinner, the new Spong mincer in her bag, in lieu of outstanding debts she said. I tried to finish cooking the meal myself but I let the gammon pot boil dry and burned the meat. Mother pushed her plate away and it fell onto the floor. When I went to clear it up she told me to leave it for the bailiffs to clean.

Dr Brennan has visited Mother every day since Father died; he stopped me in the hall and told me her nerves are very bad. He's a kind man as I'm sure he knows he'll never get his bills paid.

September 24th, 1948

We leave tomorrow; Mr Flannigan will take us in his cart to the station at dawn. I packed what clothes I could into my old school trunk and I have spent the day wandering around the house, touching the walls, trying to take pictures with my mind so that I will never forget. I loved Father very much but I will never forgive him for what he has done to us.

I don't think Mother will ever recover, sometimes I think she is going to go quite mad. She made George build a big bonfire and she threw on all the family portraits, she said she wasn't going to let the bailiff's men get their hands on our ancestors. Then she threw in all Father's books and his rare map collection and boxes and boxes of letters. I took Razzle for one last walk along the cliffs and you could see the tower of smoke for miles.

After dinner I heard gunshots; George and Richard were shooting Father's dogs so that they will not starve when we've gone. I have Razzle with me here in my room; he'll come with me no matter what.

When we get to Holyhead we have to say goodbye to George and Richard. They go to Liverpool to board a ship for Canada while we make our way down to Cheltenham. I don't know what I'll do without them. It all just feels too awful.

Richard says if Father hadn't killed himself he would have gone to prison. Despite everything he did I miss him terribly.

September 25th, 1948

I cannot quite take in what's happened. I am sitting in a spare bedroom in Dr Brennan's house; I feel like I've been here for years but I know it is only just past one o'clock. An hour ago the housekeeper, Mrs Smythe, brought me up a bowl of soup but I could not eat it. She kept telling me that I should be grateful that the doctor wants me after everything that's happened. I started to cry and she left me alone again. At least I still have Razzle, he is curled up in the corner on my coat but everyone else is gone.

Mr Flannigan came before dawn as planned. He was

loading up the cart with our luggage when Dr Brennan arrived in his car, I thought he'd come to give Mother more pills but then I heard Mother tell Mr Flannigan to put my trunk in the back of Dr Brennan's car, and when I asked her why she told me Dr Brennan had offered to look after me, and that it would all be for the best. Dr Brennan kept telling me to calm myself, and opened the passenger door, and he and Mother had me inside the car before I could comprehend what was happening.

I can't remember what I said but I know that I was crying, begging Mother to let me go with her, and Mother started shouting at me as if she didn't care that Mr Flannigan was there. George passed Razzle to me through the window, the poor little thing was whining dreadfully. I heard Mr Flannigan tell Richard he thought it was a very bad affair to leave me with the doctor. Richard said it was none of Mr Flannigan's business and I was sure that he and George had known about this plan for days, and that Mother has always planned to leave me here with Dr Brennan. Aunt Margaret has never liked me, though apart from being Father's daughter I've never understood why. Now I'm sure she only agreed to take Mother in if she came without me. I have a terrible feeling that the words 'look after' mean marriage, and though Dr Brennan is a pleasant man the very thought of it makes me shudder. I once heard Mrs Reilly say he was the handsomest bachelor in the village but he is so old, at least forty, and no one seems to have wanted to marry him before.

There will be much talk in Flannigan's pub tonight.

Phoebe let the notebook fall into her lap. She'd always imagined a great love affair between the village GP and her grandmother, the impoverished young girl from the Big House. But this sounded more like a hideous arrangement forced on to Anna by her unhinged mother. She rubbed her eyes and wondered why the local doctor would have wanted to marry a girl whose family were destitute and immersed in scandal?

Looking around her, Phoebe realised that the light was fading fast. Outside the beach looked gloomy, the tide right up, the rock half-sunk into the sea. She needed to find another place to stay; making the long drive to Cork to find a cheap hotel was all she could think of doing tonight.

She looked down at the diary still in her hand and wondered if she could take it with her, she longed to know what happened to Anna next but Honey obviously used it for a sketchbook. After a few moments she slipped it into her coat pocket; she would post it back to Honey when she'd finished reading.

Phoebe made her way down the dark stairs and left the boathouse. As she started the climb up the lane she realised that hours had passed and she hadn't thought of David at all.

Chapter Eight

'She's back!' Phoebe heard Fibber's shout as she walked in through the door, but when she looked around there was no one in the bar.

Katrina emerged from the kitchen wiping her hands on her apron and calling out in her rich European accent,

'Phoebe, you have come back to us at last. We begin to wonder if you have left for good just when we are needing you so much.'

'Sorry if you've been worried,' said Phoebe. 'I lost track of time. I'll just go and get my bag, and then I'd better get going.'

'No, no,' Katrina came out from behind the counter and took Phoebe's arm. 'We need you to help us here tonight.'

'I can't, I've got to go.'

Katrina steered her towards the kitchen door. 'Please stay; it will be all hell here by seven o'clock.'

'Why?' asked Phoebe, looking behind her at the empty pub. 'What's going to happen?'

'It will be the boys. They are coming.'

Phoebe looked nonplussed. 'The boys?'

Katrina threw her hands up in exasperation, 'You tell her Fibber; the curry it will never cook itself.' Katrina vanished into the steaming kitchen leaving Phoebe seemingly alone.

'I'm at your feet,' a voice said. Phoebe looked down and saw Fibber, crouched down, sorting through boxes of crisps under the counter, the big man straightened up and grinned. 'I'm getting rid of the out-of-date ones once and for all.'

'Who are "the boys"?' asked Phoebe.

'It's the football team, they're all coming in this evening and the whole town will be in to celebrate.'

'I thought that's what the town did last night.'

Fibber grinned and opened up a bag of onion rings. 'Now we have to toast the team themselves – didn't they do us proud?' He pushed a selection of bags towards Phoebe. 'Bacon bits, cheese balls, or good old ready-salted. Can I tempt you?' she shook her head.

'I'd better leave before everyone arrives, I don't want to be in your way.'

'We have something we want to ask you,' Fibber said through a mouthful of crisps. 'Would you stay another night and help us out behind the bar? My mother has taken to her bed with one of her "heads", and we were out looking for Honey when Katrina should have been preparing the fancy curry that she's doing as a special tonight. I just don't know how we're going to manage when the hordes arrive. Please, Phoebe.' He fluttered his pale eyelashes; Phoebe laughed. 'We're desperate. I'll even crack open a brand new box of fancy crisps for you, I have sweet chilli down in the cellar.'

'Hand-cooked?' joked Phoebe.

'By specially trained leprechauns.'

Phoebe considered Fibber's offer for a few moments; could she face the residents of Carraigmore again? What did she really care, after tonight she'd never have to see them again and the thought of driving for miles in the dark suddenly seemed daunting.

'My bar skills are a bit rusty,' she said. 'I haven't worked in a pub since I was back-packing around Australia years ago.'

'They say it's like riding a bike,' Fibber scrunched up his empty crisp packet and flicked it neatly into an open bin. 'You never forget how to pull a good pint.'

'I warn you, my pint-pulling was always on the wobbly side.'

'As long as you can keep the drinks coming we'll be happy; no one will be looking for fancy pictures on top of the Guinness tonight.'

Phoebe smiled and took her coat off. 'OK. In exchange for another night in your spare room I'll help you out.'

Four hours later Phoebe staggered into the kitchen and slumped down at the table.

'They have you worn out, I think,' Katrina was scrubbing out a huge steel cooking pot in the sink.

'It's been non-stop,' said Phoebe, her chin resting in her hands. 'This is the first lull we've had all night.'

'Carraigmore likes to party, yes?'

'You can say that again,' said Phoebe. 'Those footballers are insatiable, they just keep downing pint after pint.'

'Fibber told me it is you that keeps them round the bar. Like bees around the heather he says.' Katrina smiled at Phoebe and Phoebe felt herself blush. 'Don't worry, he has told them you are grieving for your husband, you will not be interested in their big muscles and hairy chests.'

Phoebe had forgotten she'd told Katrina David was her husband, it felt somehow comforting to hear him described as that. 'I don't think they've listened to Fibber,' she said. 'I've already had three offers of a date, a proposition of marriage, and one just came straight out and asked me to go home with him tonight – he said not to worry, he had put clean sheets on his bed on Saturday!'

Katrina laughed. 'That sounds like Brian Nolan, always not shy to come forward if you know what I mean. Did he have curly hair and ears like this?' She pushed at her own ears so that they stuck out; Phoebe nodded. Katrina made a face. 'I wouldn't trust him about his sheets. You ask him which Saturday – I bet it was one before Christmas.'

'I don't care when he changed his sheets,' Phoebe said. 'I have no intention of ever going home with Brian Nolan.'

'Did you find out about your grandmother today?' Katrina asked as she started to unload the dishwasher.

Phoebe paused; it had been so hectic all evening that she had almost forgotten what had happened earlier that day.

'I found the little studio where my grandmother used to live. It's by the beach, the boathouse, do you know it?'

'You mean Theo's studio?'

'No!' Phoebe straightened up, indignant. 'It's mine. My grandmother left it to me and my sister when she died.'

Katrina made a sucking noise through her perfectly white teeth, 'Oh dear. I think that Theo hopes that no one will ever come back to claim that place.'

'Well, it actually belongs to me.'

'But you are leaving here tomorrow?'

Phoebe shifted in her seat as she remembered she was meant to be thinking of somewhere else to go. 'Yes,' she said. 'I'll go in the morning.' Katrina said nothing for a while as she stacked towers of white crockery into a big pine cupboard.

Then she said, 'It is a shame you can't talk to Mrs Flannigan about your grandmother. She must have known her because she always tidies the little path and plants the flowers around the boathouse and makes Fibber paint the walls and doors every year. She say she likes to keep it nice for Mrs Brennan's memory.'

'Was she a good friend of hers?'

Katrina shrugged, 'I don't know; you ask her.'

'How long has Theo lived here?' asked Phoebe, changing the subject; she didn't want to have to get into a conversation with the ill-tempered Mrs Flannigan – she already felt relief that she hadn't had to face her all that day.

'Theo, he come back two years ago, but he grew up

here as a boy.'

'In Carraigmore?'

'Yes, where he lives with Honey now, in the big house on the cliff. It look like a castle. You can see it from the beach.'

'He grew up in the Castle?' The image of the white-haired children on the beach flashed into Phoebe's mind: two wild boys trying their best to impress an impassive Nola with daring diving displays from the black rock. 'His father was the film director?'

'Film director, yes,' Katrina said. 'Very famous. He won an Oscar, I think.' Phoebe could remember the middle-aged man in a panama hat strolling along the sand with a beautiful young wife. He had never noticed the little girl who watched his golden sons and coveted his home. 'He left the big house to Theo in his will,' Katrina continued. 'Maeve she had dream to set up fancy hotel at the Castle. Theo had dream to come back to make pots and let Honey grow up like him – happy on the beach and running around in the green Irish fields. But as soon as they come back Maeve become very ill, and before any dreams were made true she died.' Katrina sighed. 'It was sad. It has made us all sad, but Theo most of all. He is unhappy man.'

'He is also very rude,' said Phoebe. 'I've been miserable since David died but I wouldn't speak to someone the way that he spoke to me on the beach today.'

'You meet with him?'

Phoebe started to tell Katrina what had happened on the beach when Fibber's head appeared round the door.

'Phoebe, your fans are asking if you'll do a turn on the karaoke again. Molly Mackey from the Hair Hut wants to know if you'll sing "Did you Ever Know That You're my Hero" and dedicate it to her husband? He's just fixed a leaky shower head on her basin after eleven years of promising to sort it out.'

Phoebe buried her face in her hands. 'But Fibber, I was so drunk last night. I don't usually sing – in fact, I think, the last time I'd sung in public I was six years old and in a school production of *The Wizard of Oz*.'

'Grand, can you sing "Somewhere Over the Rainbow" for us?'

'I was a munchkin, not Dorothy.'

'Ah go on; say you'll give us a song and I'll make you one of my cocktails – extra strong; it'll loosen you up in no time.'

'NO!' exclaimed Phoebe. 'Definitely no more cocktails for me, thank you.'

'Come on, Phoebe,' Katrina was taking off her apron. 'I will sing with you. Do you know 'Islands in the Stream'?' Phoebe grimaced. Katrina grinned, 'I think you do. That is my favourite song. We do that first.'

'You have a lovely singing voice.' The man said as Phoebe pulled the final pints at 'last orders'.

'That's kind of you to say,' she said concentrating hard on the golden stream of lager she was pouring. All night she'd fended off a variety of propositions usually starting with just such a compliment followed by an offer of a trip to the nearest night club or something rather more bawdy and immediate.

'What year group do you teach?'

Surprised, Phoebe looked up and found herself facing a clean-shaven face with a pleasant smile and dark eyes fringed with eyelashes she would have paid good money to have herself. The gel-styled quiff and neat checked shirt implied an interest in grooming and personal hygiene far greater than most of the men who had tried to chat her up that night.

'Year One,' she said. 'Five- and six-year-olds.'

'That's a nice age, isn't it? Before they get too cocky. I taught that age group in my training but I'm very happy now with my Class Fours. They're just beginning to take a real interest in the world around them.'

'You're a teacher?'

'Yes, I teach here, in Carraigmore, which is great because my parents have a farm up on the moor and I can live with them while I save up for my next big trip – I've seven peaks left that I want to conquer – the big E being one of them of course but that costs a fair bit.'

'Big E?'

'Everest – I'm looking for sponsorship but with the dodgy economic climate and everything it's hard to find, so in the meantime I'm trying to fund it myself, which is why I still live at home and I train on the cliffs below the farm. I also love to surf and Carraigmore beach can have waves as big as houses. You know, you have the most fantastic hair, is it a perm? And the colour is wild as well.'

'I like your hair too. Very rock and roll.'

The man grinned, little dimples forming on each side of his cheeks. 'Can I get you a drink?'

Phoebe hadn't had a drink all night, but suddenly a gin and tonic seemed appealing. She poured it out and raised her glass to the man to thank him.

He raised his own glass back, 'Sláinte!' He smiled at her. 'That's Irish for *To your health*.'

'I know,' said Phoebe. 'My father was Irish, he always said that when he had a drink, even if it was only a weak Ribena.'

The man laughed. 'Good for him. My name's Rory by the way. Rory O'Brian.'

'Mr O'Brian!'

'Well, you can call me that if you like.'

'I mean are you Mr O'Brian? Mr O'Brian from Carraigmore school?'

'Yes.'

'Honey's teacher?'

'Honey Casson?' Phoebe nodded. 'She's in my class.'

Phoebe had to try to re-evaluate the picture she had

formed in her mind of Mr O'Brian – a wizened craggy face, mean eyes looking over half-rimmed glasses, and a stern expression. This Mr O'Brian didn't look like that at all.

Phoebe served a waiting customer and turned back to Mr O'Brian. 'I met Honey today.'

'She's a nice girl,' said Rory.

Phoebe leant against the bar and lowered her voice. 'She seems lovely, but rather sad.'

Rory sighed and ran his fingers over the top of his quiff. 'She ran away from school today.'

Phoebe nodded. 'Yes, I know.'

'She vanished at lunch time,' continued Rory, 'I was demented with worry, I had everybody out looking, I had already called the Guards when her father called to say he'd found her on the beach with some weird woman.'

'That was me,' said Phoebe indignantly – who had called her weird?

Rory laughed. 'I know it was you, I'm only teasing. Apart from your crazy perm you're obviously not really weird at all.'

'I bumped into Honey by chance but her father practically accused me of stealing her from school!'

'The man has a reputation for letting his temper run away with him lately. He's already torn a strip off me for letting Honey run away again. Honestly, who'd be a teacher! You get very little thanks and an awful lot of stress from the parents – thank goodness for the children; sometimes I think they're more grown-up than the adults!'

Phoebe smiled and started to pour a pint for Molly from the Hair Hut's husband, 'I know what you mean, but it's a rewarding job.'

Rory grinned and took a sip of his drink. 'It certainly is, especially when you're faced with a challenge.'

'You mean like Honey and her learning difficulties.'

'Honey doesn't have learning difficulties.'

Phoebe stopped pulling the pint mid-flow. 'Don't you think she has literacy problems?'

'No, I don't think so. Why do you say that?'

'She implied that she feels like a failure at school.'

Rory looked incredulous. 'You think I would make one of my pupils feel bad about herself?'

'No, I'm just saying that maybe she needs more help.'

'What about the pint I need?' said Molly's husband, indicating the glass in Phoebe's hand.

'What do you mean?' asked Rory.

'If you ask me Honey has dyslexia.' Phoebe passed the glass to Molly's husband, forgetting that it was only half full. 'She needs some special attention.'

Rory seemed to visibly bristle. 'And if you were asking me I'd tell you that I try to give her extra time, I read with her as often as I can, we go over and over the alphabet and one day she'll be grand and I'll think we're getting there and the next she's all over the place, unable even to keep her eye on the line we're reading.'

'It sounds like classic dyslexia.'

'I don't want to put a label on the poor kid after everything she's been through.'

'But you can't just ignore the situation. I did a two-day course that stressed that dyslexic children need a lot of support and understanding in the classroom; they need a teacher who doesn't make them feel as though they're failing and who understands their difficulties.'

'Your difficulties seem to be understanding the difference between a half and a whole pint.' Molly's husband waved his glass in Phoebe's face.

Beside him Rory stiffened. 'Thanks for the advice; you're certainly doing a grand job of making me feel like I'm failing.' He raised his own glass to his lips and sank the rest of his pint quickly. 'I'd best be heading home before I decide to jack my job in completely.'

'I didn't mean to criticise your teaching methods,' said

Phoebe. 'I just think that Honey might need more help.'

'Yes, I've got the message, but I've known Honey since she was five and, with all respect to you and your two-day course, you've only been here since last night.' He picked up his jacket and shrugged it on. 'I'm sure I'll be seeing you around.'

'I give up,' said Molly's husband as Fibber called out time. 'Half a pint will do me fine.'

Phoebe picked up Rory's empty glass. 'I'll be leaving tomorrow.'

'Great,' said Rory. He started to walk away but then turned around. 'Are you really Anna Brennan's granddaughter?'

'Yes I am.'

Rory stared at her for a few seconds. 'You're not much like her, are you?' He turned again and headed for the door.

'I'm sorry if I've offended you, Rory,' Phoebe called, but he either didn't hear or didn't want to respond. 'And by the way, it's not a perm.' The door slammed shut.

'Have you been upsetting the locals?' Fibber approached her with a tray of empty glasses. 'He's a fine man, a good teacher.'

Phoebe sighed. 'I'm sure he is.' She picked up a tray herself and started working her way down the bar, picking up the empty glasses and gathering the sodden bar towels.

'You were grand tonight. Your pint-pulling was a joy to behold.'

'Thanks,' Phoebe said flatly. The conversation with Rory had left her feeling strangely disconcerted; she had only been trying to help. She seemed to be doing a great job of aggravating the men in Honey's life.

'You've too many glasses on that tray, girl.' Fingers glittering with gold and diamond rings deftly gathered up a clutch of glasses and deposited them onto another tray.

Phoebe looked up to find Mrs Flannigan standing

beside her in a padded housecoat. 'And those bar towels go straight in the bucket, you're dripping slops everywhere.'

'Phoebe's done a great job here tonight, Ma,' Fibber said, producing the bucket from under the bar and dumping the towelling mats into it himself. 'We'd have been lost without her.'

'I'm sure you would have managed,' said Mrs Flannigan tersely. Phoebe tried not to gape at the old lady's ingratitude. In an effort to placate her Phoebe asked if her migraine was better.

'It's on the wane,' replied Mrs Flannigan without looking at Phoebe.

'My poor mother's a martyr to her head,' Fibber said cheerfully. 'Hey, Ma, you'll never guess what Katrina told me. Young Phoebe here is Anna Brennan's granddaughter.'

'You don't need to tell me, son, I knew who she was as soon as she walked in the bar.' Mrs Flannigan looked at Phoebe, steely eyes staring straight at her face. 'You have a look of him.'

'Who?' asked Phoebe.

'Your grandfather.'

'Was he your doctor?' Phoebe asked. 'Did you know him?'

'Dr Brennan was my doctor,' Mrs Flannigan's tone was brusque.

'I never knew him,' Phoebe persevered. 'I wish I had. I think I must get my love of travelling from him.' Mrs Flannigan was silent. 'And you must have known my grandmother when she came back from Africa.' Mrs Flannigan leant against the counter, crossed her arms across her considerable chest and stared out across the bar as if in deep thought.

'I knew your grandmother better than you'll ever know,' she said eventually, though her words were so quiet that Phoebe wondered if she'd meant to speak them out loud.

'She was a fine friend to you, wasn't she, Ma?' Fibber smiled benignly at his mother. 'She was very good to you when my Da ran off with his woman from Roscommon.'

Mrs Flannigan gave a snort and muttered, '"Woman" is too good a word for that home-wrecking little floozy.' She picked up a cloth and started vigorously to wipe the dark wood counter.

'It was a tragedy your grandmother died the way she did,' continued Fibber. 'And your poor parents too. It shook us all. Everyone was so sad to think of two little girls left alone like that.' Fibber poured a dish of peanuts back into a large glass jar. 'Cars can be the very instruments of the devil himself.'

Phoebe thought about David; Fibber was right about cars, they had destroyed everyone she had ever loved. They were all silent for a while; the clink of empty glasses and the clatter of Katrina unloading the dishwasher again in the kitchen were the only sounds. Fibber crossed the room to dismantle the Karaoke microphones. Mrs Flannigan seemed to have become fixated on the counter-wiping.

'What did you mean?' asked Phoebe suddenly, Mrs Flannigan stopped wiping and looked at her with a puzzled expression.

'You said you knew my grandmother better than I'd ever know.'

'I don't think I said that,' the older woman replied curtly.

'Yes, I'm sure you –'

'Fibber,' interrupted Mrs Flannigan, shouting across the room. 'Have you counted tonight's takings yet?'

'No, Ma, not yet.'

'Well do it now and come up and tell me what we made. I'm off to my room; I can feel my head coming on again.' She turned to Phoebe. 'I sleep in on a Saturday. You'll be gone when I get up?'

As Mrs Flannigan disappeared through the door Phoebe couldn't help but feel her parting words had been an instruction rather than a question.

Chapter Nine

At last Phoebe fell into bed, her feet were throbbing from standing all night, her arms aching from pulling pints. In the darkness she lay back on the floral-patterned pillow and expected to fall asleep immediately. Though her body felt exhausted, her mind whirred with images of the residents of Carraigmore: the affable Fibber and Katrina, the inexplicably hostile Mrs Flannigan, the mousey woman in the gallery, Rory O'Brian and Honey and Honey's angry father. Two days ago she hadn't known them at all and now they had all made enough of an impression on her, good and bad, to keep her from sleep. She forced herself to think of David but her new acquaintances seemed to be pushing him to the back of her mind.

Beneath the scratchy nylon sheets she repeatedly turned over then back, until after what seemed like hours she reached out for the bedside lamp (a white china flower girl surmounted with an apricot pleated shade) and turned it on. Downstairs she heard a clock strike three, outside a gale was getting up, battering at her window and whining through the cracks in the panes. It was no good; she'd never get to sleep now. Throwing back her covers Phoebe slid out of bed. She needed a distraction.

Crouching, cold, and on the floor, she rummaged through her rucksack searching for *Jane Eyre*, but as her hand felt the book's soft pages amongst the jumble of clothes she knew she wouldn't be able to concentrate on

99

Charlotte Brontë's story; there was another story she wanted to read now. She stood up and saw her coat where she had left it, casually thrown over an upholstered stool. Searching in the pocket she found the diary and climbed back into bed, leafing through it until she came to the last page she had read. She re-read it and started on the next, immediately plunged into the awfulness of her grandmother's situation: fatherless, penniless, abandoned by her mother to live with an unfamiliar older man.

October 4th

Dr Brennan has given me tablets which I think make me sleep. I have trouble knowing day from night and dreams from reality except that sometimes I am back in the Castle, sitting in my bedroom or gazing at the sea from the battlements – then I am back in this room and I know I must have been asleep. Once I stood at the window and saw Father walking across the garden towards the ice house. I could see the shotgun at his side and I banged on the glass to make him stop, but when he turned around there was nothing, just a gaping hole where his face should have been. Then Dr Brennan shook me awake and told me I'd been screaming; he was wearing a green plaid dressing gown and I knew it must be night.

October 7th

I woke up and found Mrs Smythe's daughter Della in my room this afternoon. She was playing with Razzle, tickling his stomach and making him stand up and beg for bits of bacon. She's a pretty girl, small and fair, with a figure much more developed than my own – though I would only put her age at around fifteen. When she saw that I was awake she offered me an iced caramel from a paper bag, and for the first time in days I felt hungry. I ate one and it stuck to my teeth but its sweetness was a comfort. Della showed me a tiny pearly shell that she had found on the beach and then she asked if she could brush my hair. I let her, and it felt so nice that I began to cry and she put her arms around me and soothed me as if I were much younger than her. Mrs Smythe came in and scolded her for letting a sponge cake in the oven burn.

October 8th

I cannot think what I should do; I cannot think at all, my mind is full of fog.

October 9th

Shall I try to leave? I could walk out any time, I don't think Dr Brennan would try to stop me, he hasn't mentioned marriage and now I wonder if I've been mistaken. Maybe Mother left me with him because he is a doctor and I am as unbalanced as Father and need professional looking after. Am I going mad? I'm certainly confused and I can't make plans that make any sense. I thought of going to London; an English woman once came up to me at the Dublin Horse Show, she said I had the looks to be a fashion mannequin. She said she knew Norman Hartnell and would get me an interview – Mother pulled me away before she could give me her name: 'Only common girls are mannequins'. I have a vague idea to go to Dublin and get a job in a department store but I have no money for the train.

October 10th

Dr Brennan had a letter from Mother today; he read it out to me at breakfast. The weather in Cheltenham has been beautiful, the trees much prettier colours than they ever turn in Carraigmore. Mother and Aunt Margaret have been to London to see the new Dior collection. They had tea in Fortnum's and Aunt Margaret had a fitting for a winter coat. Mother said she saw a lot of bombsites from the train and hopes that I am well. She also sent a cutting from the London Evening Standard of Cousin Elizabeth at the Queen Charlotte Ball; underneath she had written 'She looked like a princess'. I thought she looked like a horse.

October 14th

I am becoming used to the routine now. Every evening Dr Brennan and I eat dinner in the dining room where a stuffed fox in a glass case stares at me and puts me off my food. When Mrs Smyth clears the plates she always asks if my food is to be wasted, and I nod and feel like a small child reprimanded in the nursery for not eating tea.

October 15th

Tonight, after Mrs Smythe had cleared the plates, Dr. Brennan cleared his throat, in that odd way he has, and said he had something very serious to discuss. I tried not to –

Phoebe turned the page only to find another of Honey's drawings filling both sides, thick oil pastel obliterating the writing underneath. At first Phoebe thought it was an abstract pattern but as she studied it she realised it was some kind of beast, a dragon, dark green, with wings and claws and a long forked tail. It was an extraordinary creature, big, much too big; it crouched, head low, back hunched up, as though the page was its cramped cage, confining it, imprisoning it, preventing it from spreading out its wings. It gazed sad-eyed at Phoebe and she wondered what inner demons could have driven an eight-year-old girl to create such a poignant image.

Squinting in the dim light thrown by the bedside lamp, Phoebe found she could just make out the last sentence at the bottom of the page – as though Anna was struggling to keep telling her story from the past, trying to emerge through the thick layer of crayon.

I asked him why he wanted to marry me. 'I find myself in need of a wife,' he replied. Phoebe turned the page, *'and you have always seemed an agreeable girl and now you are in need of a home.' As a proposal of marriage it hardly had the ardour of the love stories I used to read under the blankets at school and I wondered if I was supposed to be flattered by being described as 'agreeable'.*

Suddenly I found myself standing up and shouting that if he was that desperate why didn't he just marry Mrs Smythe. He asked me to sit down and for some reason I obeyed him. Then he said, pronouncing each word slowly as though to a small child, 'I can assure you, I have no designs on Mrs Smythe.' He took a deep breath and explained that he was going to send a monthly allowance to my mother to help her in England, and that she has already sent a suit for me to wear at the wedding – a present from Aunt Margaret. I had to hold on to the edge of the table to stop myself from throwing plates and smashing glasses. I feel as though my mother has sold me to this man.

I tried to keep calm. I told him I would need to consider his proposal and he asked if I could think of any alternative arrangements for my future. When I didn't answer he got up and walked around the table to come and briefly stroke the top of my head as though I was one of his spaniels.

Later in my room I felt so sleepy I lay down on the bed in all my clothes. Mrs Smythe came in and undressed me as though I were a child; she pulled my cotton nightdress over my head and tucked the bedclothes around me. She said, 'You could do much worse than Dr Brennan,' and I wondered whether he had talked to her about marrying me or if she had been listening at the door. Then I slept for a long time.

I am writing this early in the morning. I know it should be a Saturday but the bell is ringing for Sunday Mass and I have a feeling that I have slept through a whole day.

I sit with Razzle curled up on my lap and look out of the window. I watch a line of people walking towards the sound of the bells and I realise that I have no choice. Dr Brennan is not a bad man, he was kind when I had measles, but he is not the sort of man I ever would have wanted as my husband. I am trapped, as trapped as the dead fox in the dining room.

October 25th

It is done.

We went to St. Michael's today and the Reverend Watkins married us.

The suit was hideous, cream crepe and shapeless. The skirt slipped down on my hips but Mrs Smythe put a safety pin at the waist to keep it up. The suit came with a little pill-box hat with a spray of flowers and a netted veil, obviously Mother's choice. It does not suit me at all, but I don't care one bit. As we left for the church Della came running down the path with a bunch of chrysanthemums for me to carry, and then Dr Brennan took my arm and we set off down the High Street as though we were simply going for a stroll in the autumn sunshine.

As we passed, people stopped and took off their hats and wished us well, and I wished the street would swallow me up and I could disappear. I tried not to meet their eyes but I could see the pity in them for the girl who used to be

104

from the Castle, the girl whose father stole money and then shot himself, and whose family abandoned her, as well as respect for the good doctor who is so kind as to take her on.

I realised that though I have lived here all my life I don't know most of the people in the village. I recognise some faces but we did not mix with them, we had our own set – our own friends – we did not need to mix with the locals – though none of those 'old friends' were at Father's funeral and none of them would want anything to do with me now.

When we reached St Michael's Reverend Watkins was waiting with his wife. The last time I saw Mrs Watkins it was at the parish tea party held in the Castle garden in July when Mother had drifted about in a new dress from Paris and the good ladies of the Church of Ireland complimented her on the roses and Mrs Reilly's Victoria Sponge.

Mr Watkins and his wife both looked awkward as they ushered us inside the empty church. I hardly remember the ceremony; Mrs Watkins was one witness and Mr Nuttall the solicitor the other. At the end Dr Brennan's lips brushed mine and they felt dry. I tried very hard not to cry.

When we got back to the house Mrs Smythe had laid out tea. We sat in the drawing room while Della served us meat paste sandwiches and rock cakes on lace doilies. We drank sweet sherry (which I hate) and talked about the weather.

Later Mrs Watkins took me to one side and asked me if my mother had explained things to me about being a wife, and when I said she had Mrs Watkins said, 'Very good,' and went to find her husband to tell him it was time to go. I knew what she had meant, and of course Mother has never explained anything to me at all, but there were always girls at school who knew, and I have a sort of an idea about what will happen though I shudder at the thought.

After dinner Dr Brennan told me that I must learn to call him Gordon.

I keep touching the thin gold band he pushed onto my finger; it feels uncomfortable.

I assume that he will visit me here, in this room, tonight. I am sitting, writing in bed, waiting with Razzle curled up by my feet. I don't know if I'm shivering with cold or fear.

Phoebe closed the book, that entry had been on the very last page, written on the inside of the hardback cover. Anna had kept writing as far as she possibly could until there was nowhere else to go. Now Phoebe would never know what happened on her grandmother's wedding night – maybe she didn't want to know.

She thought about Anna, the beautiful, confident, middle-aged woman who had always talked of her husband with such affection. Nothing seemed to fit.

All Phoebe knew about her grandfather was that he had done wonderful work in Nigeria, establishing hospitals and clinics in remote rural areas, helping thousands of people before he died from a severe attack of Yellow Fever. Phoebe remembered that her father's heroic stories about their grandfather had made Nola want to become a doctor herself.

She wondered if this Gordon Brennan in the diary and the man her grandmother had been married to for over twenty years could be the same. She wished she could talk to Nola about it; ask her if she remembered anything else about their grandfather. Phoebe wriggled down under the covers for warmth, the floral patterns on the walls danced around her in the pale orange gloom.

Maybe she would go home tomorrow, try to sort things out with Nola, tell her what she'd found out about Anna and Gordon. Surely Nola would forgive her if she realised how much Phoebe had really loved David. After all she

106

and Nola were sisters; Nola would always put that first wouldn't she? Phoebe's eyes felt heavy and started to close. Placing the diary on the bedside table she switched off the light and finally slept.

Chapter Ten

'Hello.'

Phoebe opened her eyes to find Honey sitting at the end of her bed. There was a smell of burning in the air, Phoebe sniffed. It smelled like toast. She pulled herself up on to her elbows.

'Here's your breakfast,' Honey indicated a small tray on the bedside table. 'Sorry about the toast. No one else is up and I'm not allowed to use electric things without a grown-up, so I did it on top of the Rayburn. I think I left it there too long. I've put loads of jam on top so you can't really see the black bits.'

'What about the coffee?' asked Phoebe. 'Did you make that on top of the Rayburn too?'

Honey shook her head, 'No, I just used the water from the tap – it's very hot in the mornings.' Phoebe glanced at the mug; little flecks of un-dissolved coffee granules floated on the pale beige surface. She picked up the mug and took a tiny sip.

'Delicious!'

Honey beamed. 'Really?'

Phoebe nodded and forced herself to take another sip. 'How are you this morning?'

Honey shrugged and started tracing the patterns of stitching on the quilt with her finger.

Phoebe bit a corner of the charred toast; it immediately broke into brittle pieces falling, jam side down, onto her pyjama top. Honey sprang up and took a large handful of tissues from a box on the windowsill.

'Your spotty pyjamas are all messy now.'

'Don't worry,' Phoebe mopped ineffectually at the sticky smears with the tissues. 'I need to do some washing anyway.'

'I'll show you where the washing machine is. I'm sure Grandma won't mind.'

Phoebe suspected that Mrs Flannigan would mind very much.

'I'll find a launderette somewhere.'

'But there isn't a launderette in Carraigmore.'

'I'm leaving this morning so I'll –'

'No!' Honey's face crumpled in distress. 'I don't want you to go. Please stay here.'

Phoebe reached out and took Honey's hand in hers. 'I can't stay here; I think I need to go home, back to England.' Honey bit her lip.

'You will come back won't you?'

Phoebe smiled. 'Of course I will, maybe I'll bring my sister and my niece and nephew.' That seemed like wishful thinking but at least Honey looked happier. The little girl sat down on the bed again.

'Soon?'

'I'll try.'

'How old are your niece and nephew?'

'My niece is twelve, getting a bit teenagery if you know what I mean – she wears her Superdry coat at all times and finds grown ups *SO* embarrassing.'

Honey nodded as though she knew all about teenagers.

'But my nephew is only a bit older than you; very handsome and fantastic at karate.' Phoebe realised it was Ruben's birthday and felt a pang of sadness. 'He looks like an angel.'

Honey made a face. 'But he's a boy.'

Phoebe laughed. 'Well, he can't help that. He's a boy who looks like an angel.'

Honey shook her head. 'Weird. Aren't you going to finish your coffee?'

'Oh, yes, I'd quite forgotten about it.' Bracing herself to take another tepid mouthful she reached towards the bedside table for the mug and suddenly saw the diary. She picked it up and offered it to Honey.

'I have to give this back to you. I borrowed it yesterday because I wanted to read it but I can see you've been using it to draw some lovely pictures in.'

'You can keep it,' Honey said. 'I've got more at the boathouse.'

Phoebe sat up straighter. 'More of books like these?'

'Yes.'

'With writing in them?'

'Yes.'

'Like this?' Phoebe opened up the notebook and showed her a page of her grandmother's writing.

'Yes, just like that, lots of funny, loopy letters.'

'Can you show me?' Phoebe was already swinging her legs out of the bed, picking up her jumper and jeans from the floor, searching for clean knickers in her bag.

'OK,' said Honey with a cheerful smile.

Outside dark clouds were scudding away towards the Atlantic, leaving behind damp pavements and a fresh smell in the chilly air.

'That was a big storm last night,' said Honey as she and Phoebe walked briskly down the High Street. 'I couldn't sleep because of the rain and wind.'

The shops were still closed though there were some signs of the village emerging from its slumber. Mr Murphy the butcher adjusted his green and red plastic foliage in the window prior to displaying his chops and sausages, The General Store had already rolled up its metal shutters and Molly Mackey from the Hair Hut was poking at her stripy awning with a broom to get the rainwater off. She turned and waved. Phoebe waved back but Honey pulled her on.

They only stopped briefly for Honey to show Phoebe a small carved dragon in the window of Rainbow's End Gifts.

'I love dragons,' she said, gazing at the polished jade statue mounted on a crystal rock. 'I wish I was a dragon.'

'What would you do if you were?' asked Phoebe.

'I'd breathe fire all over Mr O'Brian so that he could never make me read to him again.' She breathed all over the window in front of her making a little foggy circle on the glass. 'Like that!'

Phoebe laughed. 'I met Mr O'Brian last night. I don't think he deserves to have fire breathed all over him.'

Honey grunted and set off down the road again so quickly that Phoebe had to run to catch her up.

'Look!' said Honey as they rounded the bend in the little path leading down on to the beach. She pointed at the shoreline below them and Phoebe could see that it was edged with a thick brown line as though someone had drawn along the last waves of high tide with a broad marker pen.

'What is it?'

'Seaweed of course. Loads and loads of seaweed. It came in with the storm.' She jumped off the path onto the sand. Phoebe watched her as she picked up one end of an enormous strand and pulled it with her across the beach.

'It looks like a dragon's tail,' called Phoebe, and Honey laughed and started to run faster, making the seaweed swish behind her.

As Phoebe got closer she could see that the seaweed lay in great shining mounds, different sorts: thick, thin, flat, wavy, green, brown, amber – some were very red.

Honey picked up another piece, yellow and whip like; she coiled it round and round to make a spiral on the sand.

'We could make a picture?' Phoebe suggested.

'I know. Let's make a whole dragon over here,' Honey was already pulling several slimy strands towards the black rock. She draped the seaweed over a low humped promontory so that it resembled the back of some sort of exotically striped reptile, and along the middle she placed a wavy length of amber weed that extended on the sand to form an undulating tail.

Phoebe looked at her watch and tried to work out what time the ferry from Rosslare might leave.

'Can you help me?' Honey was trying to pull a huge piece of root-bound seaweed from the tangled heap. 'This is going to be his head.' Phoebe walked towards her and together they heaved until the slippery stalk suddenly slid free, causing Phoebe to lose her balance and sit down hard on the wet sand. Honey laughed but put out her hand to help her up.

'You'll have a soggy bottom now.'

Phoebe put on her most pompous voice. 'Artists always have to suffer to make great works of art.'

'Do you think that man who painted all those sunflowers had wet knickers?'

'Which man?'

'That van man. Mr O'Brian told us about him. He only had one ear.'

'Van Gogh.'

'Yes, that's him; we had to paint a vase of sunflowers just like his; it was fun.'

'So you do some nice things with Mr O'Brian?'

Honey shrugged her narrow shoulders and started heaving the great brown stem towards the body of the dragon.

'That looks wonderful,' said Phoebe, standing back to admire the seaweed creature that looked as though it was crawling menacingly up the sand. Its elongated neck gave way to a vicious-looking head with white pebbles for eyes and bright red seaweed coming from its mouth in a veiny facsimile of fire.

'He looks really scary.' Honey walked around the

dragon with a satisfied smile.

'What about a name for him?' said Phoebe. 'You could write it in the sand.' She handed Honey a sea-bleached piece of driftwood to use as a tool.

'You do it,' Honey looked reluctant.

'OK.' Phoebe crouched down and wrote 'Daisy May' in swirling letters. 'Daisy May suits him, don't you think?'

Honey's long blonde hair swung around her face as she shook her head vehemently. 'That's not a scary name at all!'

'All right, let me have another go,' Phoebe crossed out 'Daisy May' and wrote 'Scamp'. 'There, that's just right for a dragon.' She stood up and started to walk towards the boathouse.

Behind her she could hear Honey slowly reading out the letters, finally putting them together to make out the word. 'Scamp!' She ran after Phoebe shouting, 'That's a dog's name; my dragon's not going to be called Scamp.'

Phoebe walked back towards the little girl. 'You do it then, if you think you've got a better name for him,' she handed her the stick, 'though I really can't imagine anything that would be better than Scamp.'

Honey took the stick and very slowly started to write. Her letters were huge and wobbly, her face fixed in an expression of concentration. At last she stood back, her hands on her hips.

'Now that's what I call a scary name!'

Phoebe read the child's words out loud, 'Dlub curblu?'

'No!' Honey underlined the name as though to make it clearer. 'It says "Blood Curdler".'

'Oh, I see now.' In her mind Phoebe read it out phonetically and reversed the jumbled letters – suddenly it made perfect sense. 'That's a terrifying name, fantastic for a dragon – I'd never have thought of that.'

'I know,' Honey pranced in front of her making dragon-like expressions. 'I can't believe you wanted to call him Daisy May or Scamp.'

'Honey?' Phoebe crouched down beside the sand writing and beckoned for Honey to come closer. 'Do you want me to show you a way to remember which way round your *b*s and *d*s go?' Honey backed away, her whole body seeming to stiffen.

'I knew you were going to tell me I spelled it wrong, you're just like Mr O'Brian.' She threw the stick on the ground.

'I just want to show you something that helped some of the children in my class to get their letters the right way round,' Phoebe said gently. 'Reading and writing can be very difficult and sometimes we need to use little tricks to get it right. Watch this.' Phoebe held up the index finger on each hand and then curled her thumb to touch her second finger. 'Now can you see I've made the letters *b* and *d*,' Reluctantly Honey nodded. 'If you imagine an *e* in the middle what word have we made?' Honey was sullenly silent but continued to watch her. '*B,e,d*-bed,' went on Phoebe. 'If you ever want to check you've got your *b* and *d* the right way round just think bed and do that with your fingers. Do you want to have a go?' Slowly Honey raised her own hands and with her fingers formed the letters.

'What are you two up to?' the voice made Honey's face fall. Phoebe looked up to see Rory O'Brian standing beside them in very short shorts and a T-shirt emblazoned with *Mountaineering Rocks*. He bent over, his hands on his knees and took a series of deep breaths; sweat glistened on his skin, his quiff slightly drooped to one side. He had evidently been running.

'Are you having a spelling lesson?' he asked after a short pause. Phoebe wondered if she were imagining the irritation in his voice.

'I'm just showing Honey a trick to get her *b*s and *d*s the right way round.'

'We have a trick at school, don't we Honey?' said

Rory. Honey glowered at her teacher. 'Have you told Phoebe about the bat and the drumstick? No? We've got picture cards with a cricket bat and a ball that look like a *B* and a drumstick hitting a small round drum to make a *D* shape. You have the cards on the wall by your desk, don't you, Honey?' He straightened up and started doing some stretching exercises, lunging from left to right – it made Phoebe feel slightly giddy. 'It really helps you doesn't it?'

'I like Phoebe's way better,' said Honey petulantly.

'Mr O'Brian's way sounds good too,' said Phoebe quickly. She looked at Rory. 'I'm sorry if I sounded critical of your teaching last night, it's none of my business.'

The dimples appeared on Rory's cheeks. 'I'm sorry I got so huffy.'

They smiled at each other, then Rory suddenly jumped theatrically back as though he'd had a fright. 'Don't look now girls but there seems to be a rather large dragon behind you; shall we make a run for it or shall we stay and put up a fight?' He preformed a nimble little boxing move in front of the seaweed-strewn rock. Phoebe smiled but Honey continued with her straight-faced scowl. Rory stopped boxing. 'It was certainly some storm last night. I wish it had been in the daytime; I would have loved to surf the rollers that brought all this seaweed in.'

'You seem quite the action man round here,' Phoebe said. She hadn't meant to sound derisive but a sudden flush on Rory's face suggested she had embarrassed him. 'I mean, I can see you're very fit.' That sounded worse.

'I'd better go,' he said. 'I don't want my muscles to seize up and my father needs help on the farm before lunch. You're leaving today aren't you, Phoebe?'

'Yes, soon,' Phoebe replied. 'There's just something that I want to look at first.'

'Well, come back and see us again, won't you. I can tell you're a big hit with Honey.' He smiled at Honey and

Phoebe saw a kindness in his eyes that the little girl certainly seemed to be oblivious to. He waved at them both and took off down the beach, turning once to wave again.

'I don't think Mr O'Brian is quite the ogre you make him out to be,' Phoebe said, taking Honey's hand in hers and leading her up the beach.

Honey made a face. 'I just don't like teachers – apart from you. Why can't you be my teacher? You could stay here and have Mr O'Brian's job.'

Phoebe laughed and was about to explain why this wouldn't be possible, for so many reasons, when a movement on the cliff above them caught her eye. Looking up she saw a figure standing outlined against the sky. Phoebe sensed it was staring at her, watching her progress up the beach with Honey. She put her hand to her eyes to try to see who it was, but the early morning sun was too bright to make out anything but a dark silhouette.

'Is that your father on the cliff?' she asked Honey.

'No,' Honey replied without looking up. 'He's never out of bed before lunchtime when he's been drinking.'

'Was he drinking last night?'

'After I had gone to bed he started on the whiskey. I told you I couldn't sleep because of the storm; I came downstairs and I heard him crying. I went back to bed before he saw me.' She disengaged her hand from Phoebe's and suddenly ran on ahead. 'Hey!' she called back. 'Look at the stream, it's like waterfall.' The little stream that usually babbled beside the boathouse and trickled on to the beach was now a small torrent pouring down the slope of the cliff behind the building and gouging out a mini canyon on the sand.

'It must have been all that rain last night,' said Phoebe jumping up onto the concrete slipway to avoid getting her feet wet. A dog barked and she looked up at the cliff-top again; the figure was nowhere to be seen.

Chapter Eleven

November 6th

It is so cold today. Mrs Smythe laid a fire in the dining room but I couldn't help but shiver over my oxtail soup. Gordon called for Della and asked her to fetch a jumper for me, but when I explained I only had the one I was wearing he said I must go to Mrs O'Leary's shop and buy as many new jumpers and cardigans as I need. He also asked me if I need a new coat and do I want stouter shoes for walking on the beach?

Thankfully he still shows no intention of ever visiting my room at night.

November 19th

I took Razzle for a walk on the beach but when the sleet started I went into the boathouse to shelter for a little while. Someone had been there. Razzle found a scrunched-up paper bag and he made short work of the half-eaten sandwich inside. There was also a smell of cigarette smoke, cigarettes like the ones Old John the gardener used to smoke. I feel upset, it is my own special place and now some other person has sat by the cracked window looking at my view.

November 25th

I knocked over the milk jug this morning, it smashed across the quarry tiles as I tried to make a cup of tea for Reverend Watkins's wife. She called by with fruit scones and village gossip. Mrs Smythe was out on errands and Gordon was with his patients, so for the first time I was on my own to play the hostess and what a mess I made of it. Poor Della is ill but she came running from her bed when she heard the crash of the fallen jug.

She found a week-old newspaper for me to wrap the shards in and that is when I saw it – an advert in the Irish Times *for the sale of the Castle by auction next month. I sat down at the kitchen table and wept. Della put her arms around me though I'm sure she thought I'd gone quite mad.*

Eventually Mrs Watkins came to see what had happened to her cup of tea. I couldn't bear to show her what I'd found in the newspaper and her concern for me made me cry all the more. She told me that women in a certain condition could get very tearful and smiled knowingly and patted my hand; I'm sure half the ladies of the Carraigmore Church Guild will be knitting shawls and booties by now.

November 26th

I went to Mrs O'Leary's Ladies Outfitters after lunch and was surprised to find Della behind the counter. She told me proudly that Mrs O'Leary says she has an eye for clothes. Mrs O'Leary is right, Della found a bright red coat that fitted me perfectly and a pretty fair-isle cardigan that Della said brought out my eyes. I also chose a pea-green knitted hat that Della didn't like and I'm sure Mother would say looks awful, but I just want it to keep my head warm when I take Razzle for his walks.

November 27th

120

I christened the coat and the pea-green hat by wearing them down to the beach with Razzle. I wanted to see if they could stop the piercing wind from driving me home sooner than I'd like.

As I walked I tried not to look at the Castle, I can't bear to think that in three weeks time it will belong to someone else; whenever I do look up at it I think I see sadness on the grey façade, like a child that has been abandoned and can't understand why.

I walked to the end of the beach and looked out across the sea. I could feel the empty windows of my old home boring into my back like eyes. As I retraced my steps I looked down at the sand, I wouldn't let my gaze be dragged up to the house no matter how much I longed to stare at it. That's why I didn't notice the man until I was almost on top of him.

He leant against the black rock, sketching a fishing boat rolling on the waves. In his dark grey jacket and black trousers he seemed to merge into the rock face.

After months of watching from a distance he was suddenly so close that I could see his hair was the colour of conkers and that he was younger than I'd imagined, not much older than myself. A box of coloured pastels spilled around his feet and no sooner had I apologised for nearly walking into him than Razzle stole a crimson crayon and chewed it up, foaming red around his mouth. I apologised again and the man smiled at me and told me that he didn't have much need for the crimson any more. His direct gaze seemed to search my face for a response but I could think of nothing clever enough to say so I called Razzle, who now looked like a circus clown, and walked away. I wish I hadn't been wearing the hat.

'And there's this one at the back too,' Honey stretched her arm far underneath the floorboard to pull out yet another leather book. She added it to the teetering pile beside her then sat back on her heels. 'That's the last one.'

Phoebe dragged her attention away from the diary in her hand to look at the others; there were eight in all. 'I wonder why my grandmother hid them under the floor like that. However did you find them?'

'I could tell the board was loose because it rocks when you walk on it,' she placed the floor board back in place and stood on as though she were on a surf board, 'Watch! It goes back and forwards like this.'

'You look like Mr O'Brian riding his rollers!'

Honey laughed and pretended to fall off with an exaggerated wail of anguish. Suddenly she threw herself onto the armchair and draped herself over the arm so that her hair hung down onto the floor. From her upside down position she looked at Phoebe, 'Under the floor is the best place to put my crisps and biscuits,' she whispered loudly, 'I don't want my dad to know I come up here so I have to hide them.'

'Good idea,' Phoebe whispered back. 'Did you find anything else under there?'

Honey stopped whispering, 'Only some old crayons.' She pulled herself upright and handed Phoebe the box of crayons that she had been using to draw her pictures in the diaries. *Superior Artist's Quality Oil Pastels, 2/6d.* The faded label was torn and peeling. Phoebe lifted the wooden lid and stared at the array of multi-coloured pastels, some worn down to stumps, some hardly used at all. 'No red?' she asked and when Honey shook her head Phoebe thought of Razzle with his scarlet muzzle. Phoebe squatted down and picked up another of the leather-bound books. Flicking through it she saw the writing looked rounder, neater, and more immature. She found a date at the front, 1946: two years earlier. Anna would have been sixteen, oblivious to the heartbreak that was to come.

June 10th, 1946

Hare for dinner again – George and Richard are obsessed with shooting them on the moor this summer – but afterwards we had meringues just how I like them, crisp outside and chewy in the middle – well done Mrs Reilly!

Father is home, at last, from England, and Mother is overjoyed because he bought her a new hat from Bond Street with purple feathers and a spotted veil. She went to Patricia Fitzgerald's bridge party to show it off to all her friends.

Father took me for a walk along the beach and I told him that I think Mother's hat is hideous and he winked at me and said he knew it was just the sort of thing that Mother likes; then he reached into his pocket and brought out a silver fountain pen with my name engraved along the side. I am writing with it now – Father always knows what I will like best. He's told me I can have one of Old John's puppies when his terrier bitch gives birth next month – a puppy just for me, not to live outside with Father's hunting dogs but to be mine alone no matter how much Mother protests. If it is a girl I will call her Opal after my birthstone, if it is a boy I will call him Razzle after the horse Father won on in the Derby when he was away.

June 14th, 1946

A dull, dull day. Father has taken Richard and George shooting in Kildare and I have been forced to sit and take tea with Enid Norton and her turtle-necked son Nigel. The Honourable Nigel is twenty-one with a face full of spots, ears like saucers, and all he talks about is salmon fishing. For some reason he has asked me to a dinner-dance in Dublin next month and Mother says I must go because Nigel is in line to inherit from his second cousin, who is related through marriage to the Earl of Cavan. I heard her telling Father 'It would be a very suitable match.'

Aunt Margaret has written to say that Cousin Elizabeth

is to be presented at Court and Mother is desperate that I should be too. I really can't bear the idea of being paraded around all those London balls and tea parties like a prize heifer on market day. I'm too tall for the layers of chiffon and lace Mother will want to squeeze me into, and I'm bound to topple over when I curtsey to the King. Besides, I think it would be inappropriate after all those poor people have died in the war in England; and the last thing I want is to do is spend the summer away from the Castle and the beach and Father and my new little dog.

What the hell are you doing here?' The voice made Phoebe up look from Anna's diary with a start. She saw his reflection in the mirror first – Theo Casson standing at the top of the stairs looking furious, yet again.

'We didn't touch your pots,' Honey said quickly.

'Well someone has, there's a bloody big hole in one I threw yesterday,' Theo glared at Phoebe as she turned around to face him. 'I thought I told you to keep away from my daughter – and this is private property that you're trespassing on.'

'I think you should know that this is my property and *you* are the one who is trespassing.'

Theo's face flushed. 'And I think *you* should know that this building is on part of my land.'

'Really?'

Phoebe thought she saw a flash of uncertainty in his eyes, a slight hesitation before he spoke again, 'What do you mean *your property*? Do you know who I am?'

'Oh yes, I know you; you used to dive off the black rock on the beach when the tide was in. I remember one day one of you lost your swimming trunks in the sea and had to run up the beach stark naked.'

Theo looked astonished.

'That was you, Daddy, wasn't it? Uncle Oliver told me.' Honey giggled. 'He said the whole beach was full of

124

people on holiday and you had no clothes on and that your face was the colour of a tomato and they could all see your ...'

'All right Honey, that's enough of what Uncle Oliver told you,' though his voice was stern he ruffled Honey's hair. He stared at Phoebe. 'How do you know about that?'

'I was there, sitting on the slipway, waiting for my grandmother to finish making a pot.'

Theo stared at her as though trying to recall her face. 'Nola?'

Phoebe laughed. 'No, I was the annoying little sister, Phoebe; you and your brother were too busy showing off to Nola to notice me.'

Theo looked flustered. 'I remember Nola; she had long blonde hair and skinny legs. My brother Oliver fancied her like mad; he was always hanging about the beach when she came over from England.'

'You fancied Nola too if I remember rightly. Didn't you once have a fight over her?'

Honey's eyes widened.

'Did you really fight with Uncle Oliver?'

Theo looked down at Honey. 'We were always fighting, that's what brothers do.' He turned back to Phoebe. 'How is Nola?'

'Still blonde, but not such skinny legs these days. She's married with two kids and working as a doctor's receptionist.'

Theo ran a hand down his unshaven face. 'I knew that Anna left her studio to her granddaughters, but I doubted you would bother coming back to claim it after all this time.'

'Well, I'm back now.' Phoebe folded her arms.

'I shouldn't have spoken to you like that.'

He looked apologetic, his blue eyes crinkling at the corners, his tired face suddenly made handsome by a smile.

'No, you shouldn't.' Phoebe relaxed her stance a little but kept her arms defiantly crossed. 'And you shouldn't be using my grandmother's studio for your own work. Who's paying the bills? Am I going to find I suddenly owe hundreds to the electricity and water companies?'

'No! I pay the bills.' Theo sat down on the bed and let his hands drop between his knees, as he looked up at her. 'To tell you the truth,' he said. 'I've only just started to use this place. When we first moved back to the Castle I was full of plans to set up my pottery in the old stable block.' He stared down at the floor and was silent for a while. He sighed. 'And then events rather overtook us.' Honey sat down beside him and he put his arm around her. 'When I looked in here I was amazed to find it all just as Anna had left it, with her clay and tools and everything just like it used to be. Maeve's mother had been looking after it for years, cleaning it, painting the outside. I never really understood what her attachment to it was but it seemed the ideal place for me to start again. Maeve's mother said it would be fine, gave me a key. She said that Anna would have liked it to be used for making pots again.'

'Did you know my grandmother?'

'Oh yes, when I was a boy I spent hours in the studio with Anna. She was generous with her knowledge and time and very talented.' He smiled. 'She had large hands, I always remember them, extraordinarily big for such an elegant woman, she seemed to be able to use them to make the clay do exactly what she wanted it to do. It was because of her that I wanted to become a potter. It's been comforting to be in here again, to work at Anna's wheel, to be surrounded by her things.'

'I think I saw your work in the craft centre in the village, it stood out amongst all that tourist tat.'

Theo laughed, 'Don't let Sally O'Connell hear you calling it tat; she's very proud of her shop and her sales of my work have kept me and Honey in baked beans and

126

biscuits for the last month.' And whiskey, thought Phoebe; but she didn't say it. 'She's waiting for more stock,' continued Theo. 'That's what's in the kiln. I came to see if the it was cool enough to open but unfortunately it's still much too hot.' He nodded towards the pile of books on the floor. 'What are those?'

'Just some notebooks of my grandmother's.'

'To do with her work?'

'No, just writing she did as a girl; stuff about living at the Castle.' Phoebe felt reluctant to say too much.

'She had very fond memories of the Castle,' said Theo. 'When I was a boy I used to ask her to come and look round, to tell me if it had changed much.'

'And did she?'

Theo shook his head, 'I think she wanted to remember it as it had been. My father was on his third wife by that time; all those different women had wanted to make their own mark on it so she was right, it wouldn't have been the same at all. My own mother was American, en-suite bathrooms and central heating were her contributions – though she still called the place a draughty old pile of rubble.'

Honey giggled, 'I bet she didn't like all the cobwebs and the leaky roof and broken windows.'

Theo smiled down at his daughter. 'It wasn't quite so run down in those days.'

'As children Nola and I longed to see inside,' said Phoebe.

'You can see it now!' cried Honey. She turned to her father. 'Shall I show Phoebe round the house?'

Theo looked uncertain. 'I expect Phoebe has things to do.'

'Please.' Honey's large blue eyes looked imploringly up at Phoebe. 'Come and see the Castle.'

Phoebe hesitated. It was just too tempting; something to tell Nola if she'd ever talk to her again. 'Oh OK, just a quick look round.'

Theo stood up. 'You'll have to take us as you find us; I haven't had a chance to tidy up today.'

Chapter Twelve

They took a short cut along a narrow path, climbing steeply through the trees. Honey chattered non-stop; pointing out the first celandines and the holes where foxes lived and the place where she was sure she'd found a dragon's footprint. Theo's black dog panted beside them as they walked. Every now and then the dog ran on ahead and Theo would call *Poncho* and the dog would return obediently to his master's side.

The clouds had cleared to reveal a high, blue sky; all around them fat buds and uncoiled ferns hinted at the coming spring. Phoebe took a deep breath and savoured the smell of damp soil mixed with the sea air; the sun felt warm on her cheeks and her duffle coat a little hot.

Suddenly they emerged from the woods and were standing in front of the grey façade of the house. It rose majestically in front of Phoebe and seemed so much bigger than it looked from the beach. Phoebe gazed upwards. Two round towers flanked the central building and gothic arches outlined windows that seemed so randomly arranged that it was hard to tell how many floors there were. Mottled yellow lichen created patterns on the stonework, and ivy and Virginia creeper suckers wove their way around the carvings that adorned the front. Centuries of Atlantic weather had worn the carvings but it was still possible to make out the remnants of a row of gargoyles and the vestige of a coat of arms. Beneath a turreted portico, stone steps led up to an arched doorway with a heavy double oak door.

Honey pirouetted in front of them on the weed-strewn gravel. She stopped abruptly and looked at Phoebe. 'We only live in a bit of it; we can't afford to live in the rest because we're poor.' She started to spin again.

Theo looked up at his home. 'We tend to live in the kitchen and a few rooms above it but we've made it through two winters and I think we're getting used to the cold now, aren't we, Honey?'

Honey stopped spinning and ran up the steps, ignoring the question. 'This is the door we don't use,' she said and danced down the steps. 'But this is the one we do.' She disappeared around the corner. Phoebe and Theo followed her. At a half-glazed door Theo gestured to Poncho to wait and ushered Phoebe inside.

Phoebe stopped and stared around the cold and cavernous room. Centuries of use had left layers of kitchen history that would have been treasure-trove to the social historian had it not been for the mess.

Every surface was covered in clutter; half-unpacked supermarket bags spilled out across the filthy work surfaces – jostling for space with dirty crockery, over-flowing ash trays, piles of newspapers, letters, and Honey's school books. Jumpers and coats lay in jumbled mounds with muddy dog blankets. Discarded Wellington boots and shoes were heaped up at the door beside an overflowing box of empty bottles.

Phoebe took a few steps into the room; the floor felt both sticky and gritty. Looking down she saw worn slate flagstones covered with a layer of mud and sand and goodness knows what else. In the middle of the room Honey was desperately trying to tidy up a large pine table; so many bottles, cartons, mugs, and dirty plates were strewn across it that she was making little impression.

Theo pushed past Phoebe to swiftly remove several empty glasses; he put them in a Belfast sink piled high

130

with pots and pans.

'I'm afraid it's all a bit of a mess.' He didn't look at Phoebe but walked over to a fireplace to throw a piece of driftwood onto the dimly glowing ashes; he threw another into the fire-box of an ancient Aga. 'Tea or coffee?' Something about the stiffness in his stance made Phoebe wonder if he regretted asking her back to the house.

'Tea please.' Phoebe took another gritty step across the floor.

'I'll get out the milk.' Honey opened the door of a large, double-fronted fridge that hummed in one corner, a period piece in its own right, 1970s maybe? Phoebe decided it had probably been installed by Theo's American mother along with the central heating. Apart from the fridge little attempt had been made to bring the kitchen into the twentieth century, let alone the twenty-first. Looking up she saw a row of huge black hooks set into a wooden beam; this was where the meat would have hung in her grandmother's day.

Theo set a kettle on the Aga; water splashed onto the hotplate with a hiss and a cloud of steam.

'Come and see the rest of the house,' said Honey, pulling at Phoebe's hand as though to distract her from looking around the chaotic room. 'The kettle always takes ages to boil.'

'Do you mind if I look round, Theo?' asked Phoebe.

'Do whatever you like.' Theo looked over his shoulder at her; she thought she saw a flash of defiance in his eyes, challenging her to criticise his home, then he turned away again and began to stoke the fire.

'This way.' Honey was already dragging Phoebe through a wooden door that opened on to a steep spiral staircase. 'This is the way the servants brought the food upstairs in the old-fashioned days.' Her voice echoed around the circular walls.

The stairs abruptly ended at another wooden door and a

thick carpet muffled Phoebe's steps as she stepped into a very different room. Phoebe gazed around. It was beautiful and, unlike the kitchen, devoid of any clutter – in fact devoid of anything but a long dark mahogany dining table that looked as if it could easily have seated twenty people. The pale pink walls were a patchwork of darker pink squares and rectangles where paintings must once have hung. Sunlight poured through long un-curtained windows which looked on to the garden at the back of the house, Phoebe stared outside; a long-disused fountain rose up from a pond now full of thick green sludge instead of water, while flowerbeds which probably had once been full of roses were now a tangle of brambles and weeds. Despite the sunlight Phoebe shivered.

'We don't use this room,' said Honey. 'We use the room next door because there's a fireplace that doesn't blow back all the smoke.'

'What about the central heating?' asked Phoebe.

'Too expensive,' said Honey, beckoning to Phoebe as she opened a door.

The adjoining room was smaller and warmer, but just as beautiful. Pale yellow walls were edged in elaborate plasterwork and a glass chandelier was suspended from an intricate ceiling rose of acanthus leaves and lilies. The wall in front of her was semi-circular and must have been built into one of the towers; three long windows were set into the curve and looked out over the sea towards the mountains of the opposite peninsula. Heavy velvet drapes fell down to the floor on either side of the windows, and oriental rugs lay across a worn cream carpet. At one end of the room an assortment of sagging sofas and armchairs were gathered around a marble fireplace. The fireplace was heavily carved with what looked like little figures. As Phoebe approached it she saw that they weren't human figures but monkeys, clad in sailors' costumes; they scrambled up each side and along the front where a group

132

of four were busy playing billiards.

'I like these monkeys,' Honey stroked the smooth little white head of one of the billiard players. Phoebe felt compelled to touch one too and was surprised by the warmth of the marble beneath her fingertips.

Theo and Honey's use of the room was evident: a dusty television set sat on a low table, stacks of books were piled along one wall and clothes, dirty crockery, and newspapers were scattered around the floor along with broken toys and remnants of biscuits and apple cores; it seemed almost as chaotic as the kitchen downstairs.

'We sleep in rooms off there.' With a wave of her hand Honey indicated two narrow doors side by side, but she led Phoebe to the other side of the room and through another door. It led into a vast entrance hall. Phoebe stood on the black-and-white marble tiles and stared up the sweeping stone staircase. Light flooded in from a glass dome set into the ceiling high above them. She had a sudden image of her grandmother, running down the stairs, maybe to greet her father, maybe to be reprimanded by her mother for her haste or lack of decorum.

'Watch this!' Honey's voice echoed around the hallway as she began a display of hopscotch on the floor tiles. When she had propelled herself to the other side of the hall she opened another door and beckoned Phoebe to follow.

This room was grander than the previous ones; the plasterwork on the ceilings was even more elaborate, numerous windows looked out at the view both front and back and a huge fireplace incorporated a coat of arms into its carved decoration. Phoebe stood and stared at it; a fierce-eyed crow stood proprietarily on top of a crest and a greyhound lay elegantly along the bottom. Phoebe realised that this must be her grandmother's family crest; it seemed bizarre to have one's own coat-of-arms and she smiled at the thought of getting it made into a T-shirt for Nola's birthday present.

The room was completely empty apart from a grand piano in one corner.

'That's Uncle Oliver's,' said Honey with a wave of the hand. She didn't give Phoebe a chance to ask any questions as she took her hand and pulled her through yet another door.

Now they stood in a completely circular room. It was lined with long, glass cupboards, each one fitting perfectly into the curve of the walls.

'This is the library,' whispered Honey with a giggle. 'Look at all these books –who'd ever want to read them?'

Phoebe opened one of the cupboard doors and read the titles on the cracked leather spines. A complete set of Shakespeare, Chaucer, the Greek philosophers; she wondered if the books had been there in her grandmother's day or if they had belonged to Theo's father.

A series of smaller rooms led them back into the hallway and Honey skipped up the staircase with untiring energy. Phoebe followed and found herself being led through a warren of corridors that incorporated countless sets of small uneven steps; the middle floor seemed to be on so many different levels that it explained the higgledy-piggledy arrangement of the windows seen from the outside.

Numerous empty rooms led off the corridors. Phoebe counted at least eight bedrooms and three bathrooms of varying periods. Faded wallpaper peeled away from the cold, damp walls and Phoebe noticed cracks across the windowpanes and mould mottling the ceilings. An assortment of buckets and plastic bowls were set out in almost every room, Phoebe assumed the water they contained was rain. Honey dipped her finger into one and flicked water drops across the floor.

'They all need emptying after last night.'

Phoebe tried to imagine which had been her grandmother's bedroom. She decided that the largest, lightest room might have been a nursery where her grandmother and her brothers would no doubt have been brought up by a nanny, before being sent away to school.

Honey took her up another flight of stairs to the attic floor. Small rooms that had once been the servants' quarters were piled with boxes, furniture, and paintings.

'These are all Uncle Oliver's things. Daddy inherited the house and Uncle Oliver inherited the things inside it, but he never stays anywhere long enough to need them.'

'What does he do?' asked Phoebe.

'Oh, he goes all over the world giving piano concerts. He's famous.'

Oliver Casson – the name sounded vaguely familiar to Phoebe, she thought she'd heard him mentioned on a radio programme. 'He used to live in New York with his wife Gloria,' Honey continued, 'she looked like Barbie, but Uncle Oliver liked another lady so he married her and went to live in Hong Kong, but now he's on his own and mostly he just lives in hotels and has girlfriends.' She shook her head as if bewildered by the complications of the adult world.

A cardboard box at Phoebe's feet overflowed with black and white photographs, their sides curling in the damp. Phoebe squatted down and began sifting through the pictures; she recognised Theo's father's long jowly face and she also recognised many of the other people who appeared in the photographs with him; film stars, actors, politicians and musicians.

'What a wonderful record of your grandfather's career.'

Honey looked indifferent. 'I didn't like my grandpa much, he was always grumpy and he thought my mum was "just a pretty little floozy from the local pub, fine for kissing after a village disco but my dad should have married someone from a better family."' She said the last part of the sentence with a parrot-like intonation and a broad West-of-Ireland accent.

Phoebe looked up in surprise. 'Did your father tell you that?'

'No, I heard Uncle Fibber saying it to Katrina when they thought I wasn't there. But my grandpa was wrong. My dad shouldn't have married anyone else and I don't care what that ugly old man said anyway.'

'He thought enough of your parents to leave them this beautiful house?'

'He only left it to them because "he thought they would never be able to run it on the money Daddy made from pottery and he wanted to see it destroy them."' Again Phoebe heard the parrot-like expression in the child's voice.

'Did you hear your Uncle Fibber saying that?'

'No. I heard my mum say it to Grandma when we first came to live here. My mum said she was going to show the old goat's ghost that they were going to make a successful business out of the Castle and prove him wrong.'

'Goodness, you overhear a lot of things Honey, don't you?'

Honey pursed her lips and Phoebe thought she caught the glimmer of tears in the corner of her eyes. 'Mummy was going to make the Castle all lovely but now she's dead and the Castle is cold and dirty and Daddy says we'll have to sell it.' Honey wiped her eyes on the woollen sleeves of her jumper. Phoebe longed to wrap her arms around the tiny body and tell her that everything would be all right but she wasn't sure it would.

Phoebe stood up. 'Well, is this the end of the tour?'

Honey smiled and her face lit up. 'No! I haven't shown you the best bit yet. You have to see outside.'

Phoebe headed for the stairs, prepared for a trip around the gardens.

'Not that way,' called Honey, disappearing in the other direction, 'outside is over here.' Phoebe followed her and suddenly they were outside, standing on a lead gully that ran along the bottom of the slated roof. Crenulated battlements surrounded them and crows watched with interest from rows of tall brick chimneys. When Phoebe looked down she could see the beach, and the sea and in the distance the opposite peninsula and then the Atlantic. It all swept spectacularly in front of them as though they were flying.

'Wow,' gasped Phoebe. 'What a view!'

'You can see Carraigmore from over here,' said Honey, taking Phoebe's hand and leading her along the narrow walkway. Phoebe tried not to feel dizzy; the stone walls around the edge were at least four feet high and there was no danger of falling, but still Phoebe couldn't help but feel a little queasy while Honey seemed to relish the height and the view and the strong wind that blew her hair back from her face.

On the other side the gardens were spread out below them in a jungle of overgrown shrubs and brambles. The old stable block had trees pushing from its sagging roof, and beside it a cracked and blistered tennis court was steadily being encroached on by the undergrowth, while an empty swimming pool was lined with pale green algae.

In the distance the multi-coloured buildings of the town looked like a cluster of tiny model houses, bright against the canopy of bare trees and the rocky moorland beyond, Phoebe felt as though she could reach out and pick one up and see the tiny people going about their business inside. She said this to Honey and they spent several happy minutes pretending to pick up different shops and houses and describing what each occupier would be doing if they could really do it.

'Look, I've got a miniature Molly's Hair Hut in my hand and I can see Molly's Saturday girl giving Sally O'Connell from the craft centre a trim.'

'Here's a tiny Uncle Fibber changing a barrel,' laughed Honey, 'and here's Katrina giving him a kiss and Grandma

137

giving them a row for wasting time.'

'That sounds like Grandma Flannigan,' the voice startled them both. 'Sorry, I didn't mean to make you jump.' Theo put his arm round Honey. 'It looks like you're having fun.'

Phoebe turned around to face him, pushing back her wind-whipped hair.

'I had no idea you could actually get up here. You and your brother must have loved it as children.'

'We had a very neurotic mother and absolutely no sense of fear, so the roof was strictly out of bounds.'

'What about the time you dropped water bombs on that film star who was having tea with Grandpa on the terrace?' said Honey. 'You said that you and Uncle Oliver did that from up here.'

'We did, and you have no idea the trouble we got into, but luckily our mother was away at the time so she never found out.' Theo smiled and said in an aside to Phoebe, 'I don't think our father wanted her to know that he'd been entertaining young starlets while she was gone, so he wasn't going to tell her what we'd done.' He turned back to Honey, 'How did playing the tour guide go – do you think you could do it regularly and maybe we could charge the tourists?'

Honey considered this. 'I think we might need to get rid of the buckets of rainwater first.'

'It's a beautiful house,' said Phoebe. 'I can see why my grandmother found it hard to let it go.'

Theo took a cigarette from a packet in his pocket and lit it with some difficulty in the breeze. 'I've always loved the Castle too; unfortunately my mother wasn't so keen on its ancient architectural charms, so we only ever came here in the summer. Mostly we lived in London, a large house near Hampstead Heath – that's been inherited by my older half-sister. When he was working in the States we lived in my father's beachfront house in Malibu – that went to

138

another half-sister, and his Swiss apartment overlooking Lake Geneva was left to the twenty-three-year-old girlfriend he had spent the last year of his life with. I'm afraid that as my father's properties went, the Castle was the consolation prize. I got the house, Oliver got the contents – I think that left us in little doubt as to our father's feelings towards us both.'

Phoebe's eyes widened. 'I wouldn't mind the Castle as my consolation prize, it's so romantic.'

'You sound like Maeve,' Theo smiled. 'I used to joke with her that she only married me because of the Castle.' He leant against the stone wall and looked down at the wilderness beneath him. 'She had such plans for this place: a boutique hotel, a gallery, a fancy restaurant and flower borders worthy of coach loads of garden groupies from Dublin,'

'It would have been fantastic,' said Phoebe, immediately seeing Maeve's vision herself.

Theo shook his head and gestured at some broken roof slates at his feet. 'Look at it now, falling apart around me. The money we had from selling our house in Dublin is nearly all used up, and I just can't think how we can go on living here.' He glanced at Honey who had moved away from them to roll pebbles down the roof. 'In fact I think I'll have to put it on the market but I don't want Honey to know that yet.'

'I think she knows already.'

Theo smiled grimly. 'You can't keep anything from that child.'

'What will you do?'

Theo ran his hands through his thick hair. 'I don't know. I might go back to Dublin, or London maybe. My mother lives in Arizona with her second husband; she's invited Honey to go and live with them till I sort myself out.'

'What about Mrs Flannigan and Fibber? Couldn't she

stay with them?'

'Wouldn't it be better for a child to live on a big ranch with horses and a pool and all sorts of privileges, rather than in a small Irish pub in the back of beyond?'

Phoebe thought of what Honey had overheard Fibber saying and wondered how much of Theo's father's prejudice had rubbed off on his son. 'Why can't Honey just stay with you? Surely you could find somewhere smaller for you both to live in the village.'

Theo stubbed out his cigarette in the middle of a patch of lichen.

He sighed. 'I'm not doing a very good job of being a father at the moment. When Honey's at school she runs away, when she's not at school I don't know where she is, she disappears for hours on end or she's up at the pub hanging around in the bar. I forget meal times, I forget to wash her clothes, I never remember to check if she's brushed her teeth; Maeve would be appalled at the mess I'm making of bringing her up. Honey doesn't need a father like me.' Theo lit another cigarette and stared out across the sea.

Phoebe studied his tired face; how could he once have been that carefree boy diving from the rock and running laughing on the sand? She took a deep breath before she spoke. 'Maybe she just needs a father who doesn't get drunk every night.'

Theo turned around and a series of different expressions crossed his face. 'Talk about straight talking!' he finally said.

Phoebe leant on the wall and stared at the magnificent view. 'I know what it's like when someone you love dies. You feel like you're falling down a deep, dark hole with no hope of ever getting out, and most of the time with no desire to try to get out of it anyway.'

Theo nodded. 'That just about sums it up.'

Phoebe turned to face him. 'But don't you see? You've

got so much to try and get out of that hole for; a gorgeous little girl who desperately needs her father, an amazing house that you could fight to save, and a wonderful gift for making pots.'

'But now you've come back to reclaim my studio. How can I keep making pots?' His amused grin suggested that the question was a challenge.

'I'll do you a deal. I'll go back to England and pretend I never found you trespassing on my property as long as you stop feeling sorry for yourself.'

Theo laughed, 'You drive a hard bargain.' He paused, his eyes momentarily on hers. 'Will you come back to Carraigmore to see how I'm getting on?'

'I'll try.'

'And bring your sister Nola with you?' Theo added with a grin.

Phoebe rolled her eyes and they both laughed. A sudden icy gust of wind made Phoebe shiver.

'You're cold, let's get you that cup of tea I promised.' Theo started to lead the way to the door, calling to Honey to follow them across the roof. As she carefully went down the steps Phoebe felt her phone vibrate with an incoming text. She hoped so much it would be from Nola.

Back in the kitchen Phoebe could see that Theo had made a valiant attempt to tidy up while Honey had been showing her around; the bags of supermarket shopping had been spirited away and the newspapers and books neatly stacked in one corner. The table was now clear and the gurgling sound coming from a dishwasher suggested that the piles of dirty dishes had been dealt with. By the door the shoes and boots were neatly lined up and the overflowing box of empties had disappeared.

Theo offered Phoebe a chair, set a pale blue mug in front of her, and poured out tea from a matching teapot. He had chosen a speckled green mug for himself and lifted

Honey up to a huge dresser to choose a pale pink beaker with a band of scarlet around the top for her orange juice.

'Did you make the mugs?' asked Phoebe.

Theo nodded.

'They're beautiful.' Phoebe cradled the warm mug in her hands, feeling the ridges from where Theo's hands had coaxed in it into life on the potter's wheel. 'And the teapot is gorgeous.'

'Daddy doesn't usually bother with a teapot. Do you, Daddy?'

'I don't usually have anyone to impress,'

'You have me,' said Honey, looking at her father with her large blue eyes.

Theo smiled at Honey. 'You're right. I should try to use the teapot more often. Now, I wonder if we have any biscuits, and if we have I'll find a plate to serve them on and impress you both.'

He opened a cupboard and an avalanche of tins and packets cascaded out across the floor. Theo tried to stop it but his main objective seemed to be stopping a large bottle of Jameson's from crashing onto the slate tiles. Phoebe could see that rather than being unpacked, the plastic carrier bags had simply been shoved haphazardly behind the cupboard door. Honey sprang up to help her father tidy the mess.

As Theo and Honey now seemed engrossed in trying to stack the cupboard in a more orderly manner, Phoebe took out her phone to read the message that had been left earlier. Nola's name flashed up. Phoebe smiled; Nola never could stay angry with her for long. She touched the little picture of the envelope on the screen, she couldn't wait to reply to her sister and tell her where she was. Her eyes scanned down the message once and then, because she couldn't quite take in what Nola had written, she read it again.

Where are you? This is so typical. Don't think I care where you've run away to this time. You're on your own now, girl.

Phoebe felt as though she had been punched in the stomach, a wave of misery washed over her as she re-read the message.

'Are you all right?' Theo was sitting back down opposite her, Honey stood beside him arranging Hobnobs on an ornate glass cake stand. 'Have we overdone it with the cake stand?'

'Mummy used to put my birthday cakes on this.' Honey was making an overlapping wheel of biscuits. 'And sometimes she used it for meringues.'

'It's very pretty,' Phoebe managed to say. Honey handed her a Hobnob and automatically Phoebe took a bite; it tasted as dry as sand and she longed to spit it out, instead she washed it down with tea.

'I've got to go,' she said looking at her watch intently before realising she wasn't wearing one and had simply been staring at her jumper cuff.

'There's more tea in the teapot.' Honey lifted the lid and peered into the pot. 'Loads of it, enough for you and Daddy to have another cup.'

'I think Phoebe needs to be heading off.' He stood up. 'So you'll be back soon?' he said as Phoebe stood up and headed for the door.

'Sorry?'

'The deal?'

Blank stare.

'On the roof? About the boathouse? Coming back with Nola?'

'Oh, yes,' she stammered. 'I don't know. I'll see what's happening at the time.'

'Don't feel obliged,' Theo sounded hostile again. Phoebe hardly noticed.

He opened the door for her and Phoebe stepped out into the sunlight. She wasn't aware of Theo and Honey watching her make her way down the long drive way; she barely noticed Poncho bounding beside her, barking at her until a sharp shout from Theo turned him back.

Chapter Thirteen

You're on your own now, girl.

The phrase seemed to ricochet around her head. Phoebe barely remembered her walk back into town or the effort she had made to hold back her tears until she reached the pub. Suddenly she seemed to swim up from a murky sea of misery to find that she was sitting in Fibber Flannigan's public bar with a pair of slender, olive arms encircling her and a voice as soothing as melting caramel softly whispering into her hair.

'That's it Phoebe, let it all out, have big cry, and it will all be coming up roses for you again in no moments at all.'

Sitting up straight, Phoebe disentangled herself from Katrina's embrace and wiped her eyes on her jumper sleeve; the scratchy wool stung her skin and she began to cry again. Fibber sat down on a bar stool opposite her with a concerned expression and a box of Kleenex. He handed her a tissue and she noisily blew her nose.

'It's a terrible thing when you lose someone you love,' Fibber said with a wistful sigh. 'Life can be very cruel.'

'But time is very good at making your heart feel like it is no longer sick,' said Katrina, continuing to keep one arm around Phoebe's shoulder.

'*Time is a great healer*,' Fibber corrected.

Katrina drew Phoebe towards her again so that Phoebe's head leant against Katrina's shoulder. The warm solidity of another human body felt comforting to Phoebe, she closed her eyes and let Katrina's beautifully manicured fingers stroke her hair. 'You must have been loving your husband very much.'

Phoebe's eyes opened. Her husband? She had forgotten that Katrina thought that she was a grieving widow. Perhaps now was the time to confess, she opened her mouth to speak then stopped herself. No one had held her since David; it felt so nice, she closed her eyes again and let herself listen to Katrina's soothing voice. 'You must be hurting in your heart since he has died; I hate to think how it must be inside you. I know that when you choose to make the marriage knot with someone you are thinking it will be until you are old and he is old and you are old together, am I not correct, Phoebe?' Phoebe nodded into the warmth of Katrina's silky blouse. 'You will never be dreaming that they will be dead so soon. When they are gone it must feel like you want to be gone with them.' Phoebe nodded again. 'You will feel like you will be wishing you can end your life with knifes or ropes or medicine from the chemist, or even falling off the cliff.'

'Steady on Katrina,' said Fibber. 'You don't want to be giving the girl ideas now.'

'All I am saying is that she is feeling very sad for her dead husband and being alive will not be happy for her. But Phoebe, you will feel good again one day and maybe it will be quicker than you are imagining that it will be.' Katrina gently lifted Phoebe's head from her shoulder and taking another tissue offered by Fibber she dabbed at Phoebe's eyes. 'Now, Phoebe, what will be the ideas you will put into action today?'

'Ah yes,' said Fibber. 'You need a plan of action.'

Phoebe sniffed and gave a shrug. 'I had decided to go back to England, but now I'm not sure that there is any point. There's no one there for me now. Maybe I'll go to Cork or Dublin, see if I can get a waitressing job. I haven't got much money but maybe I can save up to travel like

I've done in the past.'

'But you must stay with us,' cried Katrina. 'You can work here and save for the travelling.' She looked encouragingly at Fibber. 'It is a good idea, do you not think, Fibber?'

'Oh yes, it's a great idea. You're a natural with the pint-pulling, and the football team would be delighted if you stuck around.'

'Don't *I* get a say in who we employ here any more?' Mrs Flannigan seemed to have silently materialised behind the bar.

'Sorry, Ma, I didn't see you there,' said Fibber with a cheerful smile. 'We were just saying wouldn't it be great if Phoebe worked with us here? The tourist season will be starting soon, we'll need to take someone on then anyway and Phoebe did a grand job last night, didn't she?'

'We usually take on someone local for the season,' Mrs Flannigan's voice was flat.

'She's Anna Brennan's granddaughter – isn't she as local as you get!'

Mrs Flannigan sniffed. 'She can't stay here; we need the room for the child.'

'Honey was fine in the living room the night before last and it's not like she stays with us every night.'

'I don't want Theo thinking we've no room for Honey with us. He'll want to whisk her off to live with that stuck-up mother of his in America, and I'll not give him any excuses to take her away from us now.'

'It's all right,' said Phoebe. 'I'm sure I can find a job somewhere else.'

'Ah no, Phoebe,' Fibber smiled at her. 'My mother's not saying you can't have a job. You're not saying that, are you, Ma?' Mrs Flannigan's crimson-painted mouth was set into a thin hard line, she didn't answer. Fibber grinned. 'That's settled then, you're on the team. I'm just about to open up; you can start now if it might help to cheer you

147

up. You'll be working four nights on and two nights off and every lunchtime except Sunday. You'll get your wages on a Saturday morning and two meals a day if you want them, which you probably will if Katrina's cooking.' Fibber stood up and clapped his hands together. 'Isn't that all grand!'

Phoebe looked at Katrina. Katrina was watching Mrs Flannigan. Mrs Flannigan was rubbing vigorously at a pint glass, lips pursed, her face flushed.

'Thank you for the offer, Fibber,' Phoebe said smiling up at Fibber's kind face. 'I'll take the job but I can't take the spare room from you. I can stay at the boathouse, the upstairs flat is really cosy – and after all it does belong to me.'

The crash made them all jump.

'Now look what you've made me do,' cried out Mrs Flannigan as she disappeared behind the bar to pick up the pieces of the broken glass. Phoebe saw Katrina and Fibber exchange glances. Fibber made a small questioning grimace, Katrina replied with a tiny shrug.

'What about Theo?' asked Fibber. 'Isn't he using the downstairs to make his pots again?'

'He can still do that,' said Phoebe. 'I'll be here a lot of the time and his kiln firings will help warm the flat up a bit.'

'I think it is a top-tip idea,' said Katrina. 'The boathouse will be perfect for your melancholy soul; it will help to heal the big crack in your heart.'

'Will you not be spooked at night?' asked Fibber. 'It's very isolated down there.'

'I'm used to living on my own,' said Phoebe, then hastily added, 'since David died, I mean.'

Why not? thought Phoebe, why not use the boathouse as a temporary home? There was no point going back to England now. In the boathouse she wouldn't have to worry about rent and the setting was just gorgeous; she imagined waking up every morning to the sound of waves crashing on the shore and smiled. Maybe Katrina was right, maybe it would help to heal the big crack in her heart.

'Have I done something to upset Mrs Flannigan?' Phoebe asked Katrina as they piled bedding and the rucksack into the back of Phoebe's Morris Minor.

'I tell you yesterday, Mrs Flannigan has had a difficult life and now she is grieving in her heart. You grieve for your husband, she grieves for her daughter. Maybe you are reminding her of Maeve, to me I see you are a little alike. Small and pretty but inside very strong.'

'I don't feel very strong right now,' said Phoebe as she failed to shut the car door against an escaping pillow.

'I can see it in you. In your middle you are sturdy as a stone.'

'I knew I shouldn't have had so much of your soda bread for lunch,' Phoebe laughed, but Katrina stood still and looked at her.

'You have hair like Maeve too, bright red, but with Maeve it was straight and she always have it up like this,' she took Phoebe's hair in her hands and deftly twisted it into a loose coil at the back of Phoebe's head. Almost immediately she dropped the hair as though it burned her hands; she stepped back.

'What is it?' asked Phoebe, surprised at Katrina's stunned expression.

Katrina shook her head, 'It is nothing, I am just being a silly one.'

'What?' Phoebe persisted.

'It is just, with your hairstyle that way, you look the same as her, the same as Maeve – it give me a shock.'

'Leaving us already?' A woman in a long tweed cape and purple beret appeared on the pavement beside them. It took a few seconds for Phoebe to recognise her as Sally O'Connell from the Art and Craft Centre.

'No, I'm staying around for a while,' replied Phoebe. 'I'm moving into the boathouse.'

'Well, that's a lovely thing,' cooed the little woman. 'An idyllic spot, tucked away from everything and everyone. Theo Casson from the Castle will be your closest neighbour; he's virtually a recluse you know. It's a shame – he's a very talented potter, well respected in Ireland and quite an international reputation too, but he's had such bad luck.' She lowered her voice. 'Did you know his wife died of cancer?' Her eyes slid to Katrina who was adding a tartan blanket to the heap of bedding on the back seat. Sally lowered her voice still further, 'Grief doesn't bring out the best in some people.' With a little gasp she put a hand on Phoebe's arm. 'I'm sorry, I was forgetting that you have recently been bereaved. Mr Murphy in the butcher's told me you'd lost your husband. My goodness, doesn't tragedy stalk you?'

'Actually I went to visit the Castle this morning,' Phoebe said with a desire to change the subject; her widowhood was obviously now common knowledge in Carraigmore.

'No!' Sally's eyes widened, Phoebe thought that if she really had been a mouse her whiskers would be twitching. 'Ooo, you lucky thing, no one gets invited in there and it's such a gorgeous house – an architectural gem, though they say he's letting it fall down around him; it needs a fortune to be spent on it. I'd love to get in for a nose around. What was it like? Didn't I once hear that your grandmother used to live there?'

'All is in the car, Phoebe,' Katrina interrupted. She came and stood beside the two women on the pavement then suddenly she rushed off calling over her shoulder, 'Do not go yet, I forget – you will be needing a kettle, Mrs Flannigan has spare under the stairs.'

'I had a little bit of news this morning.' Sally O'Connell gave a little shiver of excitement. 'I noticed in my latest *Arts Around Ireland* magazine that there's to be a retrospective of William Flynn's paintings in the National Art Gallery in the autumn.'

Phoebe looked blank. 'William Flynn?'

'You know, you bought the postcard yesterday. Don't you remember? A picture of Carraigmore beach? I told you he's one of Ireland's greatest painters? I thought you might like to see the exhibition, seeing as you were so interested in his work. In fact I thought I might organise a coach trip to see it, what with his Carraigmore connections.'

'Was he from round here?' asked Phoebe trying to be polite but wishing Katrina would hurry up; the wind blowing up the high street was cold despite the sunshine.

'He lived in the village for a while as a young man. They say it was here that he developed his passion for the sea.'

'Here is kettle and teabags and milk and some of my shortbread biscuits,' Katrina threw the kettle and a carrier bag into the car. 'We go now?'

With a brief goodbye to Sally O'Connell, Phoebe and Katrina jumped into the car and set off towards the beach.

Chapter Fourteen

Phoebe snuggled down between piles of blankets, pulled up the faded patchwork quilt, and gazed around the cosy room. She felt cocooned within its whitewashed walls, outside the waves were crashing on the beach and the rain was beating against the window pane. Inside all was warm and quiet.

She could see the big mirror at the top of the stairs; half the room seemed to be reflected in its mottled glass, creating the illusion of more space than there actually was. She had tucked the postcard of William Flynn's painting into its thick mahogany frame for lack of any way of sticking it onto the wall.

Her rucksack leant against the armchair – there hadn't been room to put any of her things into the chest of drawers, and anyway she felt reluctant to remove her grandmother's clothes. She had sifted through them as Katrina had made up the bed, holding up brightly patterned scarves and beaded skirts.

'She was hippy?' Katrina had asked as she battled with a fitted sheet on the irregular-sized mattress.

Phoebe tried to remember her grandmother more clearly. 'Just a bit alternative,' said Phoebe. 'Creative with her clothes.'

'Like you, Phoebe,'

'No, I'm just scruffy,' laughed Phoebe. 'Anna Brennan had real style.' She stood up and started taking a few things from her rucksack: her sketchbook and pencils,

Jane Eyre, her grandmother's pot and the crumpled school tea towel. She put the little green pot on top of the chest of drawers. 'Welcome home,' she whispered. Then she put the tea towel beside it, smoothing it with her hands in an attempt to flatten it out. Katrina came to stand beside her. She touched the tea towel.

'Is nice idea,' she said. 'They did that for money-raising at the school here. It was Rory O'Brian who is organising it; the children did a very funny picture of his hair.'

'This is supposed to be David.' Phoebe pointed at the grinning face.

Katrina peered at it closely, 'Very handsome,' she said, and they both laughed.

'You have photograph?' Katrina asked. 'Of your husband?'

Phoebe's heart sunk, she couldn't possibly show her the picture that had been screwed up by Nola. How could she explain the state of it?

'No, I haven't got any photographs.'

'Even no photographs of your wedding day? Nothing to have memories at all?'

Phoebe shook her head. 'They have been lost.'

'How?'

Phoebe pursed her lips and thought for a few seconds. 'In a fire.' She paused. 'At our house. Just after David died.'

Katrina's hand flew to her mouth, 'You have dead husband and a fire! Is tragic!'

Phoebe couldn't look at Katrina; the blatant lie had made her stomach twist with shame. She closed her eyes and turned away. Suddenly she was being pulled backwards and found herself in Katrina's warm embrace once more. Katrina stroked her hair. 'You poor, poor thing. Do not weep; we will look after you now in Carraigmore.'

Afterwards they went back to Fibber's for beef stew and an easy shift behind the bar in an almost empty pub. Mrs Flannigan's 'head' had her confined to her bed again but despite being short-staffed Fibber had encouraged Phoebe to leave early, 'Katrina and I will just have to cope if there's a mad influx after *CSI*.'

Driving down the sandy lane in the dark, Phoebe felt excited about the first night in her new home. Like a child with a new den, she couldn't wait to try it out, to see how it felt to actually live there.

Lying in bed she opened the first page of *Jane Eyre* and tried to read but she couldn't concentrate, couldn't help stopping to look around the room. She gave up and put the book down. She was about to turn off the lamp when she noticed a single slim drawer in the table beside the bed. From her prostrate position Phoebe pulled the drawer open and slid her hand inside. Her fingers felt an assortment of unseen objects. Curious, she pushed herself up on to one elbow and started to rummage through the contents – an odd collection of those bits and pieces that tend to accumulate in small drawers whether they have any use or not – a tortoiseshell comb, an ancient jar of congealed hand cream, several broken pencils, a Nigerian coin, two brown bottles of pills, a single silver earring, glass beads on a broken string, the condensed amber dregs of a bottle of Chanel and, at the bottom, a greetings card – a picture of a vase of tulips. Inside a child's neatly looping hand had written *Happy Birthday Granny, with love from Nola and Mum and Dad xxxx* and underneath that, in wobbly writing, *Phoebe* and a picture of a little girl and a heart.

Phoebe sat up, pulled the drawer right out, and put it on her lap. She looked down at it for a long time. The objects were so evocative that she felt as close to her grandmother as if she had simply been downstairs.

She was about to put the drawer back when she noticed something else – a small stone, slatey grey, almost black, with a line of bright quartz crystals running through its centre like a lightning flash. Picking up the stone Phoebe closed her eyes, fingering its smooth surface. She remembered blissful afternoons with her grandmother on the beach. Looking for stones had been their special thing – just Phoebe and her grandmother, not her parents, not Nola; just the little girl and the old woman wandering the beach, scanning the pebbly high-tide line, sporadically bending down, studying, discarding, occasionally keeping. They were discerning; they weren't looking for just any stones, they didn't want round ones or long ones or craggy ones; they wanted heart stones.

Phoebe opened her eyes and looked at the stone in her palm again. They would have been very pleased with this one; it really was an almost perfect heart. The quartz crystals glistened in the electric light. Phoebe felt sure that she had never seen it before; surely she would have remembered, surely her grandmother would have let her keep it and Phoebe would have strung it up with the others that had eventually hung from the window in her flat so many years later. It would probably have been in pride of place, at the top.

She put the drawer back but not the stone. Slipping out of bed she searched through the diaries that she'd tidied into a pile on the windowsill earlier on. Finding the one she wanted she climbed back into bed and, with the stone nestling in her hand, she began to read.

December 5th

We are to host a supper party. Gordon has arranged it for next Saturday evening. We will be ten at the table; The Reverend Watkins and Mrs Watkins, Mr Delaney the schoolteacher and his drippy wife, their daughter Nancy and Mrs Delaney's second cousin's son who's come to teach the top class in the school, and Mr Nuttall the solicitor and his wife who I have never met.

Gordon thinks some company might be good for me. I can't say I am looking forward to it; I'm sure it will be deadly dull compared to the great gatherings Mother used to hold at the Castle.

I don't feel much like socialising, with the auction for the Castle being next week; I can hardly bear to think of what will happen to my home. Della tells me it is the talk of Carraigmore, with a rumour circulating that it is to be bought by a businessman from Dublin who wants to turn it into a hotel, another has it that a builder wants to pull it down to build bungalows, and yesterday she came home from the shop and said that Mrs O'Leary told her that a Hollywood film star wants to buy it.

All I know is that I have a knot in my heart and a pain deep down, so deep I can't even place it; I so miss its beautiful rooms and the gardens and the view – and what will happen to the boathouse?

December 8th

Gordon has gone to Dublin for a meeting of the Royal Academy of Medicine. He will stay the night so at least I don't have to struggle to join in with his awkward conversation over dinner, though sometimes I find myself quite interested when he talks about his medical cases. He seems to have a passion for his work. He told me last night that he used to have a practice in Howth. I wanted to ask why he left to come somewhere as small and quiet as Carraigmore but his dogs broke into the room like a gang of hoodlums; Gordon left the table to put them outside and he never returned to finish his meal.

Mother sent a postcard today. It had a picture of a Scottish piper on the front. She and Aunt Margaret are in Edinburgh staying at the North British. She writes that she has seen a lovely Norman Hartnell evening coat in Vogue

157

that will be just the thing for Christmas – she wants to ask Aunt Margaret's dressmaker to copy it when they get back to Cheltenham. At the bottom, after her name, she adds that she hopes I have settled into married life.

December 9th

Gordon has returned with a new dress for me from Brown Thomas's – russet satin with a low waist and shapeless skirt, I look like an elderly matron wearing a sack. I had to ask Della to help me do up all the tiny buttons on the back. As I stood looking in the mirror making faces of disgust she told me she had never seen anyone look so lovely who wasn't in a film – I think she was just saying that to make me feel better.

Gordon is very pleased with the way the ghastly dress looks and says I am to wear it on Saturday for the supper party.

December 10th

I asked Mrs Smythe if she wanted me to go through the menu for tomorrow night's dinner with her – this is what Mother used to do with Mrs Reilly. Mrs Smythe informed me that she had consulted Dr Brennan and he was perfectly happy with her choice of leg of lamb and suet pudding, and then she left the room without starting the fire in the drawing room that I had asked for. Over lunch Gordon told me that I do not need to bother with matters of housekeeping and catering, Mrs Smythe is perfectly capable. Well, what am I to do in this gloomy house? I am sure I will die from boredom. But at least I have Razzle to take for walks and Della comes up to my room most evenings after supper– she lies across my bed and begs me to read out the gossip from the Picturegoer *magazine. Sometimes I wonder if she's able to read herself. I cannot understand how she holds down the job at Mrs O'Leary's; I'm sure she's only employed for her pretty face and the way her full figure shows off the clothes. I miss her when she's at work.*

December 11th

I am lying on my bed still wearing the horrendous dress as I can't undo the buttons by myself. I don't want to ask Della to help because to speak to someone else might break the spell I've fallen under tonight.

The supper party started well enough with sherry and polite conversation in the drawing room. Mrs Watkins and Mrs Delaney were on their very best behaviour, perched like plump parakeets on the edges of their chairs, complaining about tea rationing while the men stood by the fire talking about the problems of the inter-party government. Mr Nuttall's wife turned out to be a beautiful woman with eyes like a cat and a dress that Mother would have adored; she made me feel even dowdier than I did already. Nancy Delaney sat beside me on the sofa wearing navy crepe and a sullen expression.

Gordon was very attentive, asking after my welfare, filling up my glass with more sherry than I really wanted. I felt awkward and too much aware that I was the object of everybody's furtive looks. I found it impossible to join in the conversation and I longed to escape.

The new teacher arrived late, just as we were sitting down to eat. There was confusion over where he was to sit and in the end he sat in Gordon's chair beside me and Gordon had to sit by Nancy. We were too many for the dining table so that everyone was squeezed together with hardly enough room to move our arms, I felt too embarrassed to look at my new neighbour and I studied the willow pattern on my plate and hoped he wouldn't be expecting scintillating conversation. After a few moments of silence he surprised me by quietly asking if my dog still had a red muzzle. I turned to look at him and the whole room seemed to shift as though I'd just stepped off a carousel. It was him, the man from the beach, the man from whom Razzle had stolen the crayon. My thoughts seemed to come to a grinding halt and once more I couldn't think of anything to say. I was relieved when Della served us with our chicken soup though my throat seemed to have seized up and I found it hard to swallow.

All through the soup and then the lamb I couldn't speak. Mr Nuttall was on my other side but I couldn't even find the words to answer his strained attempts at conversation.

As Della served the suet pudding Nancy Delaney, enlivened by sherry and claret, suddenly started to tell us about her trip to the cinema to see the latest Moira Shearer film; this set Mrs Delaney off on a tirade about the evils of going to the pictures and the ill effect it was having on the moral conduct of Ireland. Apparently watching films will lead to fornication on an unheard of scale. She had obviously had too much to drink and I think the Reverend Watkins must have thought he was relieving the situation when he changed the subject to talk about the sale of the Castle. On and on he and Mr Nuttall droned about the likelihood of it being sold to a developer, then Mrs Nuttall mentioned the hotel and Mr Nuttall said he hoped there would be a golf course and Mr Delaney said that that would be a splendid thing for Carraigmore, and then Mr Nuttall said it was an old pile that should be pulled down and there were murmurs of agreement from the others. I felt as though the whole table were enjoying speculating on the destruction of my precious home, my paradise. I must have looked upset because the man from the beach inclined his head towards mine.

'Do you miss it very much?' he said it quietly, his handsome face just inches from my own.

I nodded and moved to pick up my water glass, but as I did so I knocked the wine goblet and sent it crashing to the floor, glass and claret everywhere.

Complete silence. The whole room stopped speaking and looked at me. I leant down to try and pick up the pieces at my feet but Mrs Smythe rushed in and made a grand show of clearing it up until Gordon asked her to leave it until later. 'That's the Persian rug ruined,' she muttered under her breath as she left the room. I clenched my napkin between my hands in an agony of embarrassment. Then underneath the table I felt a hand gently taking hold of mine.

'It's all right,' he said, so quiet I almost thought I had imagined it until he said it again. 'It's all right.' I didn't look at him and I knew he wasn't looking at me and that no one would know that beneath the white damask and the dark mahogany my hand was being held by a beautiful man. And then Mrs Watkins suggested that the ladies retire to the drawing room and the man let go of my hand, and I got to my feet and I didn't see him again until he was being helped into his heavy overcoat by Della and was thanking Gordon for a very pleasant evening. Gordon said, 'Thank you for coming, Michael,' and for a brief second Michael met my eye, and then he followed the Delaneys out of the door and left me standing on the hall tiles with the certainty that nothing will ever be the same again.

A bark – a loud bark, followed by another. Phoebe looked up from the diary. Now there was another noise, the creak of a door, then the scuff of feet on rough flagstones, footsteps on the stairs, slow and heavy on the wooden treads. Phoebe couldn't move, her body frozen with fright; her eyes stared, unblinking, at a dark shadow moving up the staircase wall. She wished she'd accepted Fibber's offer and stayed in the pub's spare room, how ridiculous to think she would be safe here on her own. Her heart beat so loudly in her ears that she could no longer hear the advancing footsteps. She watched the mirror, waiting for it to reveal the intruder.

'Phoebe!' Phoebe felt flooded with relief as Theo's body appeared in the glass, bundled up in a wax jacket, hair dripping, his face glistening with rain. He addressed Phoebe's reflection as it stared back at him. 'What the bloody hell are you doing here?'

'What are *you* doing here, more like!' she said in a classic bedclothes-pulled-up-around-chin pose.

'I saw a light, and I thought boys from the village must have broken in; it's happened before. I didn't recognise the car outside, I was sure it was trespassers.'

'Well, it's just me.'

Theo looked around him at the electric fire and the kettle and the clothes spilling out of her rucksack, and then turned back to Phoebe. 'I thought you'd gone. I thought you were going back to England.'

'I changed my mind. I decided to stay around for a bit longer, maybe the whole summer.' She smiled in an attempt to defuse his obvious annoyance.

Theo ran his hands through his wet hair, 'You could have told me, saved me coming out in this dreadful weather. I think I have a right to know who's living in my studio.'

'I planned to come up to tell you tomorrow.'

'Would you? Or would you just have decided I wasn't worth the bother, like when you so rudely left this morning.'

'Rudely?' Phoebe remembered the anguish she had been feeling at the time she left the Castle. She had barely held herself together long enough to make it through the door, let alone engage in polite goodbyes.

'Yes, rudely. One minute you were going to drink a cup of tea with us and the next you were gone; you could at least have had the courtesy to say goodbye to Honey. She

162

thought you'd gone back to England for good – she was upset.'

Phoebe pushed herself up in the bed, feeling somewhat disadvantaged in her spotty pyjamas, still stained with the jam from Honey's toast that morning.

'I'm sorry if I hurt Honey, but I was upset –'

'It was just a bottle of whiskey.'

'Pardon?'

'It was only a bottle of Jameson's, not a kilo bag of heroin.'

Phoebe stared at him and tried to work out what he could be talking about.

'I saw you; when the things fell out of the cupboard and you saw the whiskey bottle your whole demeanour changed, and then you walked out with that sanctimonious look on your face.'

'My being upset had nothing to do with the whiskey. You go ahead and drink yourself into a miserable hole, it's your life, I don't care what you do with it.' She met his eyes with her own and held his gaze until he looked away.

Theo took a packet of cigarettes from his coat pocket and opened it.

'Hey,' Phoebe cried. 'I don't care if you choose to smoke yourself into a miserable hole either, but don't do it here. New boathouse rule – no smoking.'

Theo put the cigarette in his mouth and for a moment Phoebe thought he was about to light it anyway, but then he took it from his lips and put it back into the packet.

'We seem to continually get off on the wrong foot.' He said with a sigh. He looked suddenly tired.

Phoebe shrugged and hugged her knees. 'It's the initial greeting that needs work; maybe a "Hello" and a "How are you?" instead of full-on rage and indignation.' She tried a smile again.

Theo stared back at her without expression.

'I'd better get back, I left Honey sleeping.' He moved

163

to the top of the stairs then stopped and looked over his shoulder at her. '*My* boathouse rule,' he said. 'Don't touch my pots.'

Phoebe's mouth fell open, but the power of speech had abandoned her. Without another word Theo started to descend the stairs.

The door banged shut beneath her. 'Now who's not bothering to say goodbye?' Phoebe shouted into the empty room. She lay down again and tried the yoga breathing she'd learned in an ashram in Bangalore – it didn't work. She sat up again and thumped at the suddenly uncomfortable pillow; she wondered if she could evict Theo, he had loads of space to work in up at the Castle. All those empty rooms, why should he have half of her space? She flung herself back on the pummelled pillow and resisted the urge to run downstairs and poke holes in all his unfired pots. She squeezed her eyes shut. More yoga breathing: in for five out for seven, in for five out for seven. Phoebe decided to spare the pots.

Outside the storm had diminished; the rattling of the wind and the noise of rain and sea lessened. Slowly Phoebe's anger began to ebb away until, finally, she fell asleep.

Chapter Fifteen

Phoebe woke up late. The fury she had felt about Theo was diminished by the excitement of waking up so close to the sea. She pulled a jumper over her pyjamas and went outside. Standing on the slipway, a breeze blew through her sleep-tangled hair, the air smelled wonderfully salty. Phoebe yawned and stretched, arms extended to the sky, a narrow strip of stomach exposed to the cool air. Above her the sun was a bright smudge in the sky, in front of her great grey rollers crashed onto the sand. Phoebe smiled; it was all hers: the sky, the sea, the sand, the boathouse, it was her own new world. She didn't need Nola, she didn't need her job at the school, or all that clutter she had accumulated in her flat – she didn't need anything or anyone. A bubble of happiness floated up inside her and she had a huge desire to run along the sand. The thought of David broke through the bubble and she felt guilty for feeling so happy and went inside to make a cup of tea.

Ten minutes later she was back outside, a steaming mug in one hand and a lump of Theo's clay in the other.

She sat down on the slipway, her unzipped boots kicking lightly against the side. Taking a piece of clay from the main lump she began to shape it with her thumb and forefinger into a small round pot, just the way her granny had shown her many years before. Tiny shells had been thrown up by the storm and Phoebe used one to leave an impressed pattern around the outside and then, picking up a twig, drew a wavy line beneath the rim.

'That's pretty,' Phoebe had known the little girl was there even before she heard her speak; she had thought of her moments before and had somehow known that she was on her way.

Honey dropped into a crouch beside her and put her finger out to lightly touch the rim of the pot. Phoebe noticed that her nails were painted a bright scarlet and cleverly decorated with tiny black spots to make each one into a ladybird.

'Nice nails,' said Phoebe. 'Did Katrina do them for you?'

'No,' Honey spread her fingers out in front of Phoebe's eyes and wiggled them. 'Daddy did them for me yesterday.'

Phoebe raised her eyebrows. 'He's good.'

'He did my toes too.' Honey took off one baseball boot to reveal sparkling blue nails with a minute pink butterfly or daisy alternating in the centre of each. 'And then I painted his toes like rainbows.'

Phoebe tried to imagine them up there in the Castle – the big, angry man and the little girl in all that mess, painting each other's nails.

'Can I have some clay?' Honey asked, already gouging out a lump. 'I'm going to make a pot too.'

'Shall I show you how?'

'I know how.' Honey began to roll the clay between her hands. 'First you make a sausage.' Slowly the clay grew into a long rope, Honey's small pink tongue protruded between her lips with concentration. 'And then you coil it round and round and round like this.' She began to make the rope into a spiral and then after she'd made a small base she started to coil it up into a little vessel, smoothing out the sides as she went, expertly giving it shape. Phoebe watched her as she picked up a different shell and pressed it gently into the soft clay until she had two rows of pretty fans around the edge.

'It's beautiful.' Phoebe smiled at her. 'Did your dad teach you how to make coil pots like that?'

'Ages ago,' said Honey. 'When we lived in Dublin he used to take me to his studio and let me play with clay while he worked. Now he only makes his pots when I'm not there.'

'I think he'd be impressed with what you've made today. Maybe he'd let you put it in his kiln and glaze it for you.'

Honey studied the little pot in her hand, turning it around to look at it. Suddenly she squeezed it hard, her ladybird tipped fingers digging into the clay, crushing the sides, compressing it into a ball in her palm. She looked up at Phoebe's dismayed face. 'It wasn't that good,' she said and threw the ball of clay onto the beach.

'What a shame,' said Phoebe. 'I would have liked to have kept that if you didn't want it.' Honey took another piece of clay and started to roll it between her palms.

'I'm glad you're going to stay,' she said, smiling up at Phoebe.

'Did you hear that I'm going to live in the boathouse for a while?'

Honey nodded. 'My dad told me this morning. He thinks you're going to be a bloody nuisance.'

'Does he?' Phoebe couldn't help smiling.

'Look I've made a snake!' Honey wormed her long rope of clay along the slipway with a hiss.

'It looks like a big letter S from here,' said Phoebe.

'Sssssssssss for snake,' laughed Honey.

'What else begins with S?'

Honey looked at Phoebe warily, as if suspicious that she'd let herself fall into some sort of trap. She shrugged and started making the coil into another pot.

'Lots of things round here begin with S,' Phoebe continued. 'Do you like "I spy"? I'll start. I spy with my little eye something beginning with S.' Honey remained absorbed in her pot. 'I'll give you a clue – it's wet and has waves.'

Honey sighed. 'Sea,' she muttered without looking up.

'That's right, well done.'

'I'm not stupid, you know,' Honey glared at Phoebe. 'I know what begins with S; I'm not in nursery school – S for sand, S for sky, S for sun, S for seaweed, S for stupid games like "I spy" – I mean the "spy" bit, not the "I".'

'What about S for shell?'

'Shell doesn't begin with S.'

'What does it begin with then?'

Honey shrugged again. 'I don't know.'

'Come on – I'll show you,' Phoebe jumped off the slipway and picked up a stick of driftwood. 'Race you down to the sea.' They ran across the sand, both laughing as the wind blew back their hair and billowed up Honey's anorak as if she might take off into the air. They stopped at the water's edge; Honey started playing "chase" with the waves, daring them to make her feet wet.

'Listen to the sea,' said Phoebe. 'What's it saying?'

'It's saying, "You're going to get a soaking if you don't get out of my way."'

'But what sound is it using to say that? Can you hear it?'

Honey stood still and listened for a few seconds and then she laughed. 'It's saying *Shoo, shoo, shoo.*'

'That's right, sh for shoo, shoo, get away.' With her driftwood stick Phoebe wrote *sh* in the wet sand left by a retreating wave, a new wave quickly slid up to take its place and gobbled up the letters. Phoebe wrote it again and again, and again and again the sea took it away.

'I want to do it,' cried Honey, and she took the stick from Phoebe and wrote a long line of sh's along the sand, skipping sideways like a crab to avoid the waves as they took away her letters, delighted with the game. 'It's like it's eating its own words,' she laughed.

168

Phoebe smiled, the misty sky had lifted and the sun seemed to reflect its sparkle in Honey's wide blue eyes. 'Sh, sh, sh!' shouted Honey to the sea as she ran along the beach writing the letters.

'My goodness, another spelling lesson, Miss Brennan?'

Phoebe turned to the man who had appeared beside her. 'My goodness, another run on the beach, Mr O'Brian?'

Rory smiled and took a few deep breaths.

'Word on the mean streets of Carraigmore has it that you're staying around.'

Phoebe smiled at him. 'Word travels fast.'

'Oh yes, you're causing quite a stir; all the boys were raving about you at band practice last night.'

'Band practice?'

'I'm in a local band.'

'What kind?'

'Traditional music mostly, but we try to punk it up a bit – you know, a bit of Pogues, a touch of The Killers – Celtic style. We've not long been playing together. It's just a bit of fun really. I play guitar and do a share of the singing.'

Phoebe raised her eyebrows. 'A man of many talents.' Rory shrugged, although his dimples gave away the hint of a smile. 'What's the band called?'

'Na Buachaillí Trá.'

'Pardon?'

'It means "The Beach Boys" in Irish. We're all surfers you see,' Rory went on in explanation.

Phoebe tried very hard to suppress her laughter. 'Sorry, I know it's not that funny. It's just the contrast between the Californian Beach Boys singing beside blue seas and sunlit skies and a Kerry version on a freezing beach with intermittent drizzle.'

'Yeah, very funny, and we don't have those tanned West Coast girls in bikinis either; it seems our West Coast girls wear baggy jumpers with spotty pyjamas and boots

169

they can't even be bothered to do up.'

Phoebe looked down at her clothes and then back to Rory. 'I've not had time to get dressed yet!' They both turned to look at Honey who was still dancing down the beach and writing in between the waves.

'You're great with the old literacy ideas,' said Rory. 'You'll have Honey reading Dostoyevsky before we know it.'

'Are you being sarcastic?'

Rory shook his head. 'No. You seem to be a great teacher; your talent will be wasted pulling pints at Fibber's.'

'Well, maybe I could help Honey sometimes to keep my hand in. You could give me some of her reading books to get us started?'

Rory frowned. 'You'd have to ask her father.'

'Does he really need to know?' The thought of another run-in with Theo was too much for Phoebe.

'Yes, he does. I couldn't agree to anything without his permission. And *you'd* have to ask him. I'm telling you, he never listens to me when I try to talk to him about Honey.'

'OK,' said Phoebe. 'I'll go up there and see him.'

'Today?'

'Maybe tomorrow, when I've unpacked.'

'You have a lot of luggage, do you?'

Phoebe gave a small snort. 'I mean I'll talk to him when I've thought of what to say.'

'Good luck to you, he's very sensitive about his daughter. Let me know if he does agree to you helping her and then I'll be happy to go over what I've been doing in class.' Rory looked at a large watch on his wrist. 'I'd better be going, my mother will be back from Mass and I always help her cook the veg for Sunday lunch.'

'I'll let you know when I've plucked up my courage to talk to Theo.'

Rory grinned. 'You'll be seeing me tonight when you

go to work. Na Buachaillí Trá are playing at Fibber Flannigan's. I'll look forward to hearing what a karaoke queen like yourself thinks of us.' Phoebe started to protest that she had never even sung karaoke before she came to Carraigmore but Rory had already started to jog away. 'Good luck with the unpacking,' he called over his shoulder.

A few yards up the beach he stopped briefly to say something to Honey and seemed impervious to the dirty look she threw at him. With a cheery wave he set off again towards the end of the beach – where Phoebe had no doubt that he would scale the cliff, abseil down the other side, and sprint the remaining few miles to his parents' farm in record-breaking time, before serenading his mother with "Danny Boy" while peeling a ton of potatoes and whipping up the best colcannon in all of County Kerry.

Chapter Sixteen

Honey followed Phoebe back to the boathouse, happily munching her way through the bag of Katrina's shortbread as Phoebe got dressed. When Phoebe asked if her father might be worried about where she was, Honey's tone was pragmatic.

'He was still drinking whiskey at breakfast time. Now he'll be asleep.'

Flopping down on the bed she picked up the heart stone that Phoebe had found the night before.

'Can I have this?' she asked.

'No, that was my grandmother's. It's too special for me to give away but another day we'll go looking for heart stones on the beach, I promise.'

Later Phoebe and Honey drove into town in the Morris Minor. Honey pushed a rickety trolley around Carraigmore general store while Phoebe filled it with white sliced bread, Tayto crisps, Galtee cheese, red lemonade, iced caramels, and many other Irish food stuffs whose very labels suddenly transported her back to her childhood holidays. As they queued up beside the checkout she saw that Kimberley Biscuits were on a two-for-one; they'd always been her favourites, she took eight.

'You eat a lot of rubbish,' said Honey, peering into the trolley.

Phoebe tried to remember the last time she'd been in a supermarket or cooked a meal or even made herself a sandwich. She was sure she hadn't bothered shopping since David died, maybe the odd packet of toilet rolls from a garage, a box of tea-bags, but not much else. No wonder all her clothes felt as though they were falling off.

'The child is right,' said a large woman standing in front of them in the queue with two packets of Rivita, some Slim a Soup and a Mars bar. 'You've got a terrible diet for such a skinny thing. Tell me your secret, is it exercise? I went to an aerobics class once and I swea: I need a double hip-replacement now.'

'I don't usually eat like this,' replied Phoebe, suddenly rather taken aback herself by her grocery choices. 'I'm usually very healthy.'

The woman looked longingly at the contents of the trolley, 'Looks like you've well and truly fallen off the wagon today. Weight Watchers meets on a Wednesday night if you need them in a few weeks' time.'

The other shops along the high street were shut, but Phoebe and Honey happily continued their window-shopping of the previous morning until Honey smelled Katrina's Sunday roast drifting out of the pub and disappeared inside for lunch. Fibber asked Phoebe to join them, calling out from behind the bar, but Phoebe wanted to be back at the boathouse, her new sanctuary.

Once there she unpacked her groceries and stored them in the little gingham-curtained cupboard. Outside it had started to rain; dark clouds scudding in from the Atlantic to obliterate the sun. Phoebe put the light on and sat at the window, watching the changing weather and eating a satisfyingly soggy cheese sandwich.

Her eyes drifted to the pile of diaries. All day she had been resisting the desire to curl up with the next instalment; she longed to know if Anna would meet the young schoolteacher again. And why had Gordon Brennan married her in the first place? Charlotte Brontë simply could not compete.

174

The starchy sandwich had made her sleepy and, taking a packet of Kimberley biscuits from the cupboard, she climbed on to the bed and picked up the diary she had been reading the night before. Snuggling down between the covers she opened the packet and leant back against the pillows, savouring the gingery taste and the soft marshmallow filling encrusted with crunchy granulated sugar. She put the packet on the bedside table and resolved to have no more that day. Flicking through the leather-bound book she found the page she'd been reading when Theo Casson had so rudely interrupted her. As she started to read her hand reached out and took another biscuit.

December 12th

I feigned a stomach ache and Gordon went to church without me. Mrs Smythe and Della were at Mass.

As I slipped out of the house with Razzle I knew he'd be there, leaning against the black rock sketching, just like he had been before. When he saw me approach he put his sketchbook in his pocket and came to meet me. In silence we started to walk along the sand. As we reached the end of the beach we scrambled up the boulders to the cliff top, Razzle leading the way like a little goat. Michael took my hand to help me up. 'You have soft hands,' he said.

We sat down on a slab of rock, Michael lit a cigarette, and we watched the waves.

I didn't feel the cold wind or mind the drizzle that had started; I could have stayed sitting there like that for ever, hugging my knees, feeling the rough tweed of Michael's overcoat lightly brushing against my wrist every time he moved.

Eventually I forced myself to stand up; Gordon would be back from church and Mrs Smythe would have Sunday lunch waiting in the dining room.

As we walked back across the cliff I pointed out the

rock face where the puffins nest in spring and told him how my father and I once found a little mottled egg at the bottom of the cliff and how Father asked Old John to blow it and had it put into a glass box for me to keep. I wondered if the bailiffs had taken it along with everything else.

When I got back Gordon was already seated at the dining table, slabs of roast beef laid out on a plate in front of him, overcooked and grey.

As Mrs Smythe set a plate in front of me she hissed in my ear, 'Dr Brennan has been waiting,' though I can't believe he waited very long as the vegetable tureens and gravy boat still sent great clouds of steam into the cold room.

Gordon asked if the fresh air had made me feel better and I said it had. He told me I looked damp and suggested a hot bath after lunch. The doorbell rang and Mrs Smythe came in and announced that a young man was in the hall; he'd come off his horse and his wrist was in need of attention. From where I sat I could see the young man waiting, he had a look of George, baby-faced and very blond. I wonder where my brothers are now.

I ran the bath, deep and hot. As I lay back in the water I closed my eyes and thought of Michael's hair: the way it curled and fell across his beautiful brown eyes, the way that he constantly pushed it back with his long fingers. I longed to see him again, I long to see him now. 'Next Saturday,' he said. I will meet him by the black rock next Saturday – how will I bear the wait till then?

December 14th

The Castle is sold. It will not be a hotel or a golf course or pulled down. Fibber Flannigan was nearly right when he told Della a film star wanted to buy it. It is not a film star but a film director – a young Englishman who has been a big success in Hollywood. Della showed me a picture of him in the *Picturegoer;* the accompanying article said he fell in love with Ireland when he made a film in County Clare. They say his new wife will be the next Vivien Leigh.

Della is beside herself with excitement, I think she imagines that Carraigmore will suddenly be filled with glamour.

There is talk of a new roof and a swimming pool. No one knows when they will come to live there. For now I will pretend the Castle is still mine, standing on the cliff-top waiting for me to come home.

December 16th

I saw him today on the High Street, wheeling his bicycle. I was coming out of O'Leary's shop with orange wool to start a scarf for Della's Christmas present. He walked past on the other side of the street. I wanted to call his name but I didn't, and he passed on unaware that I was watching him until he turned and disappeared into the school.

December 18th

The rain lashed down, driven horizontal into my face by a fierce wind. Poor Razzle couldn't understand why I would take him out in such wild weather and kept trying to shelter against hedges until I had to carry him. Gordon had been called out to a breech birth on the moor and Mrs Smythe had gone to see her crippled sister in Kenmare. Della had a headache so she remained behind in bed. No one knew I'd gone.

Michael was waiting, not at the black rock but at the bottom of the lane. The wind was too loud for him to hear me so I beckoned for him to follow and, retrieving the key from under a stone, opened the door of the boathouse, and *led the way upstairs.*

At the top we both looked at one another and started to laugh; water streamed down his face and dripped off his upturned collar. I still held a bedraggled Razzle and I knew my hair had come unpinned, long strands sticking, wet, to my face and dripping down my neck to soak my petticoat.

Shivering, we shrugged off our sopping coats and took off our sodden shoes. Michael asked if the stove worked and I said it did and showed him the pile of driftwood I'd collected from along the tide-line. Together we rolled up strips of an old newspaper and laid the fire. Michael tried to light it with matches from his pocket but his box was damp. I found matches that I'd used before and striking one dropped it onto the pile of sticks and paper and closed the wrought-iron door. We both stood in front of the stove, our hands on top, waiting for the warmth to work its way to the surface and thaw out our frozen fingers. Eventually it grew too hot to touch and he pulled an old pile of sacks towards the stove. We had one sack each for us to sit on and Razzle came to lie at my feet, gently steaming as he dried out in the warm air.

Michael offered me a cigarette and I took one, though I haven't smoked since school. I asked him about his family and he told me that his parents have a farm in Galway, that he is one of six sons and that he has been the only one to go away. I asked him if he'd always wanted to be a teacher and he said all he'd ever wanted was to be a painter; he said it was his passion. He talked about Picasso and Chagall and then took a sketchbook out of his coat pocket and showed me the pictures he'd been doing of the sea; oil pastels in shades of grey and blue, silhouettes of the wind blown trees on the headland, craggy cliffs and crashing waves. Michael turned page after page: seascapes or rocky landscapes mostly, a few studies of fishing boats or gulls. Then he came to a picture of a girl;

a girl standing on a rocky outcrop staring out across stormy sea. She had on a red coat and a pea-green hat, a scarf blowing out behind her and her hands thrust deep into her pockets. A little wiry dog sat at her feet.

'When did you do it?' I asked.

'The day your dog ate my crayon. It was a good job he ate it after I'd done the picture.' He smiled at me. 'You were standing at the far end of the beach looking out to sea, so bright against the winter sky,' he paused. 'You looked sad.'

I was aware that our faces had become very close and I thought that he would kiss me but instead he stood up and put the book back in his pocket.

After that we talked until the light began to fade, and we put our damp coats back on and eased our feet into clammy shoes. We walked back up the lane together, Michael pushing his bike and Razzle jumping up at its wheels all the way. When we reached the village he asked if we should meet again next Saturday. I asked him if he remembered where the key was in case he got there first, and he said, 'Yes' and disappeared into the gloomy drizzle.

Small snatches of our conversation come back to me as I write this. He told me that when he was young he'd tamed a raven and taught it how to swear in Irish.

His mother wanted him to be a priest.

I think of my own mother and smile at how disapproving she would be.

December 21st

He was waiting when I got there; already upstairs, the stove lit, a little kettle singing on the top. He brought two enamel mugs out of a canvas bag along with a jar of milk, a paper twist of sugar, a spoon, and a small packet of tea. We said little and I watched him spoon the tea straight into

179

the kettle for lack of a teapot. 'I should have brought a strainer', he said.

I said, 'I don't mind leaves.

He smiled at me, 'Shall we tell our fortunes when we've finished?'

He gave me a bar of Fry's Chocolate to eat and laughed when I dipped it in my tea. He asked if that what they'd taught me to do at my fancy school.

When we'd finished our tea he took my mug out of my hands and peered into the bottom. He told me the leaves said I would meet a tall, dark handsome stranger and visit the Isle of Man. Then he peered in again and said it wasn't the Isle of Man after all, it was just a bit of melted chocolate. He laughed and I said, 'You have freckles,' and suddenly my hand was on his cheek.

'And you have a husband,' he said, and then he took my hand and held it while we sat in silence staring at the stove as though we could actually see the flames inside its cast iron casing.

He told me he's going home for Christmas; he won't be back till after the New Year.

New Year seems much too long, I feel as though we'll be different people in 1949.

He asked if he could write to me, but I thought of the letters that Mrs Smythe brought in to breakfast on a lacquered tray each morning. She would check the postmark and wonder who would write to me from Galway, she would ask Gordon who I knew there. I asked him not to write.

It was the shortest day – I couldn't stay that long.

'Shall we meet here when I come back?' he asked.

I thought of Gordon and the house that smells of antiseptic, mealtime after mealtime and every morning Mrs Smythe with that gold and crimson tray of envelopes – was this was how my life would be for ever? How could I say "No"?

As we were stepping out of the door three boys ran down the lane in front of us, we both ducked back into the shadows like guilty thieves though we had done no wrong. We stood beside the upturned boats and waited for their shouts and whooping cries to fade.

'You'd better walk home on your own,' he said. 'I'll wait and come up in a little while.' Then he wished me Happy Christmas and slipped something small and heavy into the pocket of my scarlet coat. I went to take it out but Michael caught my hand and stopped me.

'Wait,' he said. 'Look later when you're alone.' And then he leaned towards me and kissed my mouth. I can still feel it now, the pressure of his lips on mine – very gentle, very soft. The first time I have ever been kissed like that.

When I got back Gordon came out of his study and asked if I had had a pleasant walk, I nodded and started to climb the stairs. He asked if I were not taking off my coat. 'I'm cold,' I told him, and now he's worried I have caught the influenza that's started in the village and has insisted that I have my supper in bed. He will be sure that I am ill when Mrs Smythe tells him the supper tray has been left untouched. I am not ill but I certainly don't feel like I have ever felt before; I may take off into the air at any minute, fly around the room and out the window into the night. I am only kept on the ground by the gift he gave me. It weighs me down: a little pebble, black and smooth, shot through with glittering quartz and shaped by sea and weather into the most perfect heart.

As Phoebe looked up she was surprised to find that she'd eaten the entire packet of biscuits and that the light was already fading outside. She looked at the clock on her phone; she was half an hour late, Mrs Flannigan would not be impressed and her jumper was covered in crumbs. Wrenching it off she started rifling through the chest of drawers full of Anna's clothes. She pulled out a lacy shirt and slipped it on. As she checked her reflection in the large mirror she could see that the shirt was a little tight across the bust, she undid some of the buttons and hoped she didn't have too much on show. Adding her boots and coat she flew out of the door straight into the solid torso of Theo Casson.

'Hey, watch where you're going,' he growled. Phoebe looked up. He didn't look good; his face was ashen, dark circles hung in crescents under his bloodshot eyes.

'Are you all right?' asked Phoebe. 'You look terrible.'

'Thanks, and you've got crumbs in your hair.' He pushed past her through the boathouse door.

'Shall we have another go at the *Hello and how are you*'s?' she shouted after the door had slammed shut in her face. 'No? We'll give it a try next time then, maybe have a practice at home first.'

She stomped down the path, shaking out her hair with her hands. As she reached the car she realised she'd left her car keys on the chest of drawers.

Muttering about grumpy men under her breath she set off up the lane on foot.

Chapter Seventeen

As Phoebe took her place behind the bar Mrs Flannigan looked pointedly at her watch.

The pub was already filling up and the band were busy tuning their instruments on a makeshift stage in front of the big TV screen. Phoebe hadn't expected such a crowd on a Sunday night. Once more Carraigmore seemed to be out in force, from teenage girls already dressed for summer to a table full of old men so wizened they looked almost mummified as they defiantly puffed on cigarettes and pipes. She recognised the man who'd bought her the gin on her very first night; he raised his glass to her and she gave a brief wave back. Sally O'Connell was there with a paunchy-looking man with a beard and a Breton cap. Phoebe wondered if he was Sally's husband. Molly from the Hair Hut was also there, along with the large woman from the General Store (her hand deep in a packet of sweet chilli crisps) and numerous other faces that were already becoming quite familiar. She pulled pint after pint as customers poured in, and she became quite adept with the slightly faulty optic on the whiskey bottle.

From the corner of her eye she watched the band. There seemed to be a lot of musicians, Phoebe counted at least seven. All of them wore tight "Na Buachaillí Trá" emblazoned T-shirts that showed off their surf-honed bodies to good effect. She was surprised; for a small village in the back of beyond Carraigmore seemed to be blessed with a plethora of fine-looking young men, and that wasn't counting the football team who were also a good-looking bunch, if you liked the Neanderthal type.

Rory had his back to her, one foot resting on a chair, his guitar supported on his knee. He was picking out chords and chatting to a dreadlocked fiddle player and a bearded young man with soulful eyes and a hefty accordion. A man in a pork-pie hat was putting a new string on his banjo while he shared a joke with a second fiddle player. Beside him an elfin-faced boy with long blond hair and a tin whistle started chatting to a table full of nubile girls next to the stage. A tall David Beckham lookalike wandered in, his chiselled face and tight jeans briefly distracting the girls. Seemingly oblivious to the stir he had caused he picked up a bodhrán, sat on a high stool, and started absentmindedly to tap out a rhythm like a heartbeat while he waited.

After a while the second fiddle player took off a checked shirt to reveal an impressive collection of Celtic symbols tattooed down both arms. He downed a pint of Guinness and then picked up another; that pint seemed to have belonged to the first fiddle player and a brief argument ensued until Rory calmed the situation by giving the second fiddle player his own pint.

Rory came over to the bar to replace his drink. 'Nice shirt, it gives you a fantastic cleavage.' Phoebe felt herself blushing and tried to fasten up her buttons. 'What do you think of the boys?' Rory asked.

'Is the one with the beard Brian Wilson?'

'Very funny. How was the unpacking?'

'Exhausting, it took all of five minutes.'

'Rumour has it you've been spotted bulk-buying processed cheese and biscuits in the store.'

'Can't a girl do anything round here without it becoming fodder for the local gossips?'

Rory grinned. 'You'll get used to it.' As he took his pint Phoebe noticed that his quiff was more elaborately styled than before, standing almost vertically, each hair perfectly gelled into place. 'I think we're just about ready to play now,' he said and winked at her. 'You're in for a treat.'

Rory jumped back on to the low stage and adjusted the microphone down to his height. He briefly introduced the band to lively jeers from the audience.

'Our first number is dedicated to the new girl in town, Phoebe Brennan. She's been a long time away but she's back on home soil now,' and with a cheer from the crowd the band were off with an extremely fast version of "The Irish Rover", followed by "If I Should Fall from Grace with God", a few instrumental reels, "A Pair of Brown Eyes", a quick Celtic version of "Human" and then "Whiskey in the Jar".

'They are not half good, yes?' Katrina stood by Phoebe; she had to shout to be hard above the music. Phoebe nodded. 'There is nothing like a man playing with his instrument to make him look sexy.' Phoebe looked around for Fibber to correct Katrina's phraseology but he was down the other end of the bar.

Honey appeared, already dressed in her pyjamas. Phoebe bent down. 'I wondered where you were,' she said. Honey put her hands over her ears. Mrs Flannigan appeared at the little girl's side.

'It's too noisy.' Honey tugged at Mrs Flannigan's sleeve. 'Tell Mr O'Brian to be quiet, Tell him I have to wake up for school in the morning.'

'Don't worry.' Mrs Flannigan drew Honey into an embrace against her sturdy hips. 'They will be over soon, they only know a few songs.'

A frenzied version of "Boys of Killybegs" came to a boisterous end and Rory stepped up to the microphone again. 'I'm afraid this next one will be our last song for tonight as some of us have school in the morning,' there was much groaning from the audience. Mrs Flannigan gave Honey a squeeze, Honey made a face and Mrs Flannigan gave one of her rare smiles; Phoebe could suddenly see that she would once have been quite pretty. 'This is a new one we've been practising all week,' continued Rory and he moved away to lean his guitar against the wall. He walked back to the microphone and lowered his head, eyes looking down at the floor, his expression far away; after a few seconds complete silence fell around the crowded room – every one was waiting. Quietly, very quietly, the bodhrán started up a steady, single beat and then, still looking at the floor, with his voice almost a whisper, Rory started to sing.

'We'll do it all, everything on our own.'

Phoebe's heart lurched; she recognised the song immediately. Rory looked up at the crowd, his voice stronger, *'We don't need anything or anyone.'* The fiddle players joined in, softly followed by the accordion and banjo. Phoebe wanted to cry, 'If I lay here, if I just lay here would you lie with me and just forget the world.' It had been their song, "Chasing Cars" by Snow Patrol, their special song. She bit her lip and closed her eyes. David hadn't known it was their special song, she didn't know if he even knew the song at all – but on her own, in the lonely evenings and on the long weekends that they had been forced to spend apart, Phoebe would play it again and again. And sometimes, when they were together lying on the rumpled sheets of her double bed, the words would repeat themselves silently in Phoebe's mind, over and over again.

The song was building to a crescendo, Rory's voice sounded more beautiful than the original, the words more poignant: 'All that I am, all that I ever was, is here in your perfect eyes, they're all I can see.' Phoebe felt a light touch on her shoulder and opening her eyes she turned to

186

see Katrina's concerned face staring at her.

'Are you OK?' Katrina mouthed. Phoebe realised she had one hand clasped to her mouth, the other tightly gripping the edge of the bar. She put her hands down by her sides and nodded, trying to smile. Rory's voice had dropped again and, apart from the drum, the band had stopped playing. Rory softly murmured the last few lines and the drum stopped. The room remained silent for a few seconds and then erupted into loud applause and foot stamping. The nubile girls clapped their hands above their heads and the old men in the corner put their fingers to their lips and whistled loudly. The band grinned at one another and set off again with a shorter version of "The Irish Rover" and then Rory announced that that was their lot, and Fibber got up and thanked them for 'the great crack' and the bar began to empty as steadily as it had filled up. The nubile girls lingered as the band packed up their instruments. Rory came across to where Phoebe was collecting the empty glasses.

'Well, what did you think?' his eyes sparkled.

'You were great! Fantastic, almost as good as the real thing, though I do think a Celtic version of "Good Vibrations" would go down rather well.' Moving down the bar she scrunched up a crisp packet and stuffed it in a glass. Rory followed her, picked up two empty bottles and put them on her tray.

'Are you all right? You looked very sad at the end there.'

Phoebe hesitated. 'Just old memories being stirred up.'

'Pam Lynch told me you'd lost your husband recently. Liam O'Casey said it was an accident with a car and Fibber told me you'd lost everything in a house fire. It must be very hard for you.'

Phoebe wondered who Pam Lynch and Liam O'Casey were and she had to think hard to remember about the fire.

One of the boys from the band shouted something

across the room Phoebe didn't quite catch. 'You go on,' Rory called back. 'I'd better get home; I've a nature trail to plan for tomorrow.'

'Look at you, living the rock and roll lifestyle, you sap,' the second fiddle player called back, his arm already around a skinny girl with a miniscule skirt and streaky orange legs.

'Enjoy yourselves.' Rory waved at the retreating band and accompanying girls and then turned back to Phoebe. 'I'll introduce you to the boys another time. They get a bit carried away after a gig, acting like they've just played the O_2 Arena.'

'Not you though?'

Rory shook his head. 'No, I don't let playing a few songs in the local pub go to my head; it's just a bit of a laugh. My glory moment will be when I reach the top of Mount Everest.'

Fibber appeared beside them and took the tray out of Phoebe's hands. 'Do you want to get off? You look shattered.'

Phoebe nodded. She suddenly realised that she was exhausted.

'Katrina's got a big box of food to give you,' said Fibber. 'She was very concerned to hear you'd been buying a whole load of processed rubbish in the store, so she's made you some soda bread and a loaf of barmbrack, and she's given you some Cashel Blue cheese, home-cured ham, some of her tomato chutney, a jar of her raspberry jam, and the last bottle of elderflower cordial that I myself made last summer.'

'You didn't need to do that.' Phoebe felt embarrassed. 'I was just indulging in a bit of a nostalgic binge. All that processed food reminds me of my holidays here as a child.'

'Well, Ireland's moved on in culinary terms; you'll be surprised. There's a deli in the next village, plus a new

188

patisserie and oyster bar in Waterville – and don't miss the farmers' market in the hall here every Wednesday.'

Phoebe nodded deferentially.

'I'm going now, so I'll carry the box to the car for you,' said Rory.

Phoebe suddenly remembered that she'd left the car at the boathouse.

'I'll walk you back then,' said Rory. 'I was going to leave my guitar here and run home anyway, so the half a mile extra will be all the better for me.'

'Do you never run out of energy?' Phoebe asked. Rory looked at her as though the very thought was inconceivable to him.

'He's our resident bionic man.' Fibber laughed.

Thin clouds scudded across a full, bright moon as Phoebe and Rory walked down the sandy lane towards the boathouse.

Rory carried the big crisp box filled with Katrina's supplies.

He talked non-stop, regaling her with stories from his mountain-climbing adventures. He'd travelled the world almost as much as she had, but while she'd spent an awful lot of time in bars and on beaches, interspersed with the odd spot of eastern meditation and voluntary work, Rory's travelling experiences had been all about physical activity.

'Did you never even climb Mount Abu in India, that's an easy one.' Phoebe shook her head. 'You must have tried bungee jumping in New Zealand?' Again Phoebe shook her head. 'White-water rafting down the Tully River in Australia?'

'No.'

'I don't suppose you climbed Mount Kosciusko while you were in Australia either?'

'I'm afraid not.'

'Ah well, I'll just have to get you up a mountain round here. Once you try it you'll love it. Shall we give

MacGillicuddy's Reeks a go? You'll have to wear your walking boots?

Light flooded from the boathouse windows as they turned the corner.

'Looks like Theo's still working,' said Phoebe, her heart sinking.

'Will you be all right?' asked Rory. 'He's not the easiest of men to be around.'

'I may not have had much experience of extreme sports on my travels,' said Phoebe. 'But I did get a lot of experience with dealing with difficult men. I'm not going to let him drive me out of the boathouse. Anyway, he's not all bad, I saw a softer side of him yesterday and he obviously adores Honey in his own way.'

'Well, don't let him bully you. Have you asked him yet about helping Honey?'

'No, I think I'll leave it till tomorrow,' Phoebe took the box of food from Rory. Rory ran his hand across his stiffly styled hair, looking suddenly ill-at-ease.

'I feel bad,' he said, speaking uncharacteristically hesitantly, 'I feel as though I've been unenthusiastic about your attempts to help Honey with her reading and spelling. I don't want you to think I don't care about her – it's just – ' he paused.

'It's all right,' said Phoebe. 'No teacher likes other people wading in and implying they can do things better.'

'That's why we're the teacher, because we like to think we're the ones that know the answers.' Rory smiled.

'Do you want to come in for a cup of tea?' Phoebe smiled back at him. 'And as you know I have a lot of Kimberley biscuits.'

'You're all right. My mother will be waiting to hear how the gig went.'

A movement at the window caused them both to turn around. Theo's face appeared, then quickly disappeared again behind the glass.

'I'll come in with you if you want me to,' said Rory.

'Don't worry,' replied Phoebe. 'I can look after myself.' She took a step towards the door. 'Thanks for walking me back, though. Enjoy your jog home.'

'Actually I don't jog, I run,' said Rory. Phoebe tried not to laugh at his earnest expression. 'There is a difference, I could show you. You could give it a try.'

'I'm sure there is a difference, but please don't ask me to do it with you.'

'You can only pass on the running if you promise to join me up a mountain next weekend.'

'OK, you're on.'

Rory held out his hand and they shook on the agreement.

A creak from the door made Phoebe turn to see Theo silhouetted against the light.

'Is that you, Phoebe Brennan?'

'Who else would it be?' Phoebe felt unable to hide the irritation in her voice.

She quickly said goodnight to Rory. He looked concerned, reluctant to leave her. *I'm all right*, Phoebe mouthed and after a few moments he began slowly running up the lane, looking back at her, his arm raised in a farewell.

'Was that the teacher you were holding hands with just then?' Theo moved away from the door to let her past with the box.

'He just walked me home because I didn't take the car with me, and it was dark, and Katrina has given me this heavy box of food.'

'No need for explanations,' said Theo, his back already turned to her, his broad shoulders bending down to look in the kiln. 'Your life here is your own. Don't let me stop you inviting your boyfriends back, though if you have designs on Rory O'Brian let me tell you …'

'Stop! I'm letting you work here but that doesn't give

you the right to interfere with my life, and anyway I have no designs on Rory O'Brian or anyone else.'

Theo looked at her in silence for a few seconds and then turned away. She had one foot on the stairs when she saw him lift something out of the kiln. She stopped, staring at the pot he held in his gloved hands. Phoebe placed the box at her feet and moved towards the kiln as though sucked towards its warmth and contents. She immediately forgot Theo's infuriating words as she gazed into the shimmering chamber; huge jade-green bowls stood beneath turquoise vases dripping with scarlet glaze and on the highest shelf a line of mottled pale blue jugs looked as delicate as thrush's eggs.

'They're gorgeous,' Phoebe breathed.

'Yes,' Theo's voice was a whisper of relief. 'The kiln gods have been kind to me this time.' Carefully he lifted out another pot, a rounded vase – deep crimson glaze seeming to pour down its spherical sides, merging into an opaque turquoise blue. Theo examined it, cradling it in his gloved hands as though it were a newborn baby.

'Can I see?' asked Phoebe.

'Don't touch,' he warned. 'It's still very hot.'

'It's like volcanic lava flowing down the sides.'

'That's from the copper in the glaze, it turns deep red when the kiln reaches its highest temperature and takes on this viscous quality. It doesn't always work – sometimes it can just remain a sludgy grey line on the rim.'

'That must be heartbreaking.'

'Pottery can be a very cruel business.'

'The shape is beautiful.'

'It's based on an ancient Korean moon jar; they were thought to have been made to represent fertility and feminine beauty. I have to throw them in two halves and fuse them together to make the shape as round as possible.'

'What makes the gorgeous blues and greens?' asked

192

Phoebe longing to touch the opalescent surfaces of the jugs and bowls.

'Iron oxide. They're called celadon glazes, invented in ancient China thousands of years ago. In the West they called it celadon after one of Ovid's characters in *Metamorphosis*.' He looked up at her. 'If I remember rightly Phoebe appears in *Metamorphosis,* doesn't she?'

Phoebe laughed, 'Oh yes, the virgin dripping in blood – hardly a pleasant image to be associated with. Nola loved that when she found out about it in her school Latin lessons. My parents told me that they chose the name because it means radiant in ancient Greek, I'd rather think of that.'

'Radiant.' His eyes seemed to examine her face, as though seeing her for the first time.

Phoebe looked away.

'Is the celadon glaze the same as the glaze my grandmother used?' she asked after a few moments silence.

He nodded and picked up a bowl the colour of shallow sea. 'She taught me how to use it and really I've just been developing her glaze recipe ever since. But now I wonder if its time I started doing something new, developed a different glaze or style of decoration, or whether I ought to just give up altogether.'

Phoebe let her eyes wander admiringly over the contents of the kiln. 'You couldn't really stop making them could you?'

Theo didn't answer but took off the heavy kiln gloves he'd been wearing. He put them slowly on the long workbench, side by side, as though it were important that they were left neatly together.

'It's late. I've a meeting with the estate agent in the morning.'

'About putting the Castle on the market?'

Theo nodded. 'But don't say anything to anyone. I

193

don't want it to be common knowledge yet.'

'I wish you didn't have to, or I wish that I could afford to buy it from you; I'd let you and Honey stay living there of course.'

Theo smiled. 'I'm assuming you don't have the odd million Euro squirreled away somewhere.'

'I'll check in my purse, but unless I have an unclaimed lottery ticket in my pocket I think the answer's "No".'

Theo picked up his coat and shrugged it on. 'I've been thinking about what you said about Honey,' he said. 'About how she needs a father who isn't miserable and drunk all the time. I think you're right.'

Phoebe looked at his piercing eyes. Underneath the grief and anger and alcohol he was a handsome man. She tried to work out how old he must be, maybe one or two years older than Nola – late thirties, surely not much more. She smiled at him.

'Good,' she said.

'You know the bottle of Jameson's you saw in the cupboard?'

'I told you I hardly noticed it.'

'It's gone now,' he interrupted. 'I chucked it away this afternoon.'

'The whole bottle?'

'Well, if I'm honest it was the last third – but that's it now, I won't be drinking any more. It's time to move on with my life, with Honey's too.'

Theo started doing up the buttons of the jacket.

Phoebe took a deep breath. She decided that now was as good a time as any. 'I've noticed that Honey has difficulties with her reading and spelling. I wondered if you'd agree to my helping her. I've spoken to Rory, I mean Mr O'Brian, and he's willing to let me look at some of her school books and tell me what he's been doing in class with her.'

Theo stopped doing up the buttons. 'Why didn't Mr

O'Brian come to talk to me first if he had concerns about her school work?'

'Honey told me herself that she found reading and writing hard, and I noticed her spelling was quite unusual – I wondered if she might be dyslexic.'

'Dyslexic? Honey?' Theo's face darkened. 'And did Mr O'Brian agree with your no-doubt expert diagnosis?'

'I don't think he agreed with me at first, but …'

'There's nothing wrong with Honey that a better teacher couldn't deal with. That's the problem with these village schools, they don't get enough good staff.'

'I'm sure Mr O'Brian is a good teacher, but I think Honey needs …'

'The sooner I get Honey out of this bloody place the better.' Theo headed for the door. As he opened it he turned around to face Phoebe again. 'I can assure you that there is absolutely nothing wrong with my daughter, so please don't discuss her with your teacher friend any further.' Phoebe waited for the entire building to collapse as Theo slammed the door.

'Arsehole!' Phoebe shouted, surprising herself. Picking up the box of food she climbed the stairs and decided that she'd never met anyone so short-tempered; even Nola in the very depths of post-natal exhaustion and mastitis hadn't been quite so quick to fly off the handle.

Once in bed she picked up her grandmother's diary in an effort to stop Theo Casson's angry words whirling around her head. It didn't take long; in minutes she almost felt she was Anna Brennan, back in 1940s Carraigmore.

December 23rd

Each day seems endless; I find it hard to be bothered to get out of bed. Gordon has ruled out influenza but thinks I have a chill and doesn't seem to mind that it is two days since I came down to share a meal with him.

December 24th

I dragged myself downstairs today and did my best to eat burnt pork chops and grey potatoes in the dining room.

Gordon went out to see a patient after lunch and brought home a tiny, twisted Christmas tree. He placed it on the drawing room windowsill, produced a box of fairy lights and ancient baubles from the sideboard, and asked me if I would like to put on the decorations.

'It may cheer you up,' he said and walked away. For ages I stood beside the tree, staring sightlessly at its spindly branches and thinking of Michael. I noticed my reflection in the darkening window; I touched my lips and remembered his kiss.

I heard the door open and Della's reflection came to stand beside my own. She picked up the string of lights and began to untangle them.

After a short while she said, 'It's no wonder you've been ill. I saw you going out that Saturday when the rain was lashing down.' She started winding the lights around the crooked tree. I thought she would say more but she was obviously waiting for my reaction. A few more minutes passed; she finished with the lights and together we started attaching the glass balls and spirals to the branches. She had a slyness to her smile I didn't like.

'The only other person about that day was that new teacher from the school, I saw him riding his bike towards the beach.' Again I offered no response, though I could feel my heart beating so loud I felt sure that Della would hear it. 'I saw you go down the path not long after, was it the boathouse you were going to?'

I felt my cheeks flush.

'I saw you together another time too,' she went on. 'Going up on the cliff. It was ages before you came back down.'

I caught her wrist in my hand and accused her of being

Dr Brennan's spy, I told her she should be ashamed of herself, I told her to tell Dr Brennan to hire a private detective instead of using a girl barely out of school, to do his dirty work. I didn't know I could ever sound so vicious.

Della looked as though she might burst into tears, the bold young woman was suddenly a child again.

'It wasn't Dr Brennan that asked me to watch you,' she snivelled. 'I just like to see where you go, to know what you do when you go out in the day.'

I asked her to tell me exactly what she had seen.

'Nothing.' I told her I didn't believe her. 'Just you and the new teacher,' she admitted. 'walking on the beach and when you went out in the rain that day I followed you, just a little way, and I saw you going into the boathouse and that's all I've seen. I promise.'

I stared at her warily: shocked at her duplicity, shocked that someone could have been watching us. 'I'm sorry,' she said. 'I won't tell a living soul.'

I told her he was just a friend and made her promise to keep what she had seen to herself.

'I won't do anything to spoil it for you, Mrs Brennan,' Della said and pushed the plug into the electric socket. Instantly the tree was transformed into a sparkling pyramid; in the window I saw the Christmas lights reflected in her big, grey eyes.

'I think it's like a story from the films,' she whispered.

December 25th

I never imagined that Christmas day could be so dull. I think of Christmas at the Castle and the weeks of preparations leading up to it; at least two shopping trips to Dublin, Mother would have new gowns sent from London, a hamper from Fortnum's, and champagne from Berry's. Christmas dinner would be endless: soup and salmon, pâtés and tureens, and then an enormous turkey,

197

and Mrs O'Leary's wonderful plum pudding. There was always a crowd. Present-opening lasted for hours and there were special presents from Father to find, hidden in a Christmas tree so tall it towered half way up the stairwell. And there was always darling Uncle Charles.

When I was a little girl the arrival of Uncle Charles seemed as though Father Christmas himself had come to join us for the holiday. I remember that just when I would give up hope of him ever coming, he would suddenly burst into the house, fresh from the last Christmas Eve ferry, always with a new car and a new girl on his arm. We loved his card tricks and the way he knew all the latest tunes to play on the piano. Once he brought a very pretty girl with him who taught me how to tap dance, Mother didn't like her at all.

It was quieter during the war, no Uncle Charles, of course, and many of the county sons away, but still the Castle seemed to come alive at Christmas.

Christmas here could not have been more different. We had our usual breakfast followed by church, then sherry at the Nutalls' and then ham sandwiches for lunch. Gordon told me we would eat with Mrs Smythe and Della in the evening, a special Christmas tradition he informed me, as though it would be a treat.

The turkey was very dry and there was no bread sauce. Gordon poured us each a glass of claret and I remembered Michael's hand on mine at the dinner party and thought of him far away on his Galway farm. Was he enjoying his Christmas Day? I wondered about his parents and his five older brothers, as well as the aunt who he told me lives with them because she lost her sight to measles as a child. I imagined a lively Christmas table in the farmhouse kitchen, with much laughter and joking from all those boys around it. I imagined a plump and pink-cheeked mother wielding serving spoons and warmed plates as she tried to keep all her boisterous offspring in

order, and a jovial father enjoying his pipe and his sons'
tomfoolery, and the aunt smiling at the sound of high jinks,
and the smells emerging from the range.

I realised Gordon had asked me a question; he
repeated it, 'Would you like to go to the meet tomorrow?'

'The meet?' I stared at him bewildered. How could
there be a meet without my father as the Master of the
Hunt?

Gordon coughed a little awkwardly as though he
realised what I had been thinking. 'Mr Nuttall has taken
on the position of Master until a suitable landowner can
be found.'

I took a sip of wine. I couldn't imagine the hunt without
my father on Elgar or my mother on her favourite grey
mare or George and Richard looking handsome on their
stallions. I suddenly wondered where the horses were.

'We'll go down and take a look,' declared Gordon. 'It
will do you good, Anna; it's been days since you've been
out.'

During this conversation Mrs Smythe had disappeared
into the kitchen. She reappeared bearing a large cut-glass
bowl and a supercilious smile.

'I always remember that you don't like plum pudding,
Dr Brennan.' She set the trifle down in front of him. The
sugar strands were bleeding into watery rainbows across
the cream.

The trifle had a taste of soap about it, I had a feeling
that the cream was off.

Some things were nice. There were crackers and Della
made me giggle as she read out the riddles in a range of
funny voices until Mrs Smythe chastised her, 'Stop playing
the giddy goat and act your age.'

We sat beside the fire and listened to the King's speech
crackling across the Irish Sea, and afterwards Gordon
found some classical music and we played three rounds of
rummy to the strains of Strauss and Mozart. Gordon

opened a bottle of Advocaat that a patient had given him as a Christmas gift. We sipped it from green glasses that I hadn't seen before and he handed round small packages: brown pig-skin gloves for Mrs Smythe, a bottle of Miss Dior for Della, and a beautiful pearl necklace for me. He even had a little box for Razzle, who lay prostrate and snoring in front of the fire; I opened it and found a new leather collar and a name-tag with 'Razzle' engraved on one side and the surgery phone number engraved on the back.

Mother had sent me a silver compact and a china brooch – a bouquet of purple pansies. An accompanying card wished me a very happy Christmas and told me that she would spend hers 'visiting friends of Aunt Margaret in Bath. I have a new cashmere twin set to wear for the informal luncheon party and full-length black lace for the evening ball – your Aunt Margaret and I are hoping to have such fun. Elizabeth's life has been one long social whirl. She's turned down several propositions of marriage already ...' I had to resist the urge to throw the card into the fire.

I put the card back in the envelope and gave Della the scarf I'd knitted and Gordon a set of handkerchiefs that I'd embroidered with his initials. I hadn't thought to buy a gift for Mrs Smythe but I noticed that her gift tag had the message 'With season's greetings from Gordon and Anna Brennan'.

Mrs Smythe and Della retired to the kitchen to wash up, declining my offers of help. Gordon and I were left alone together and suddenly I felt very tired. I stood up and thanked him for his generous present and made to say goodnight. He stood up also. 'Wait,' he said, and when I stopped he placed his hands on both my shoulders and looked at me with eyes that seemed full of sadness.

'I know this isn't how you might have imagined your marriage, Anna,' he stroked my cheek, 'but I want you to *know that I'm really very fond of you.' For one awful moment I thought he was gong to kiss me, but instead he turned away to stoke the embers in the dying fire.*

January 4th 1949

I have lost so many days. When I look back on Boxing Day now, it seems like months ago not just nine days. I have to force myself to remember what happened to try to distinguish between the facts and the feverish dreams.

On Boxing Day morning I woke up with a dull headache and wondered if I had had too much Advocaat. I felt too embarrassed to admit a hangover to Gordon so I slipped on my tweed skirt and jumper and went down to try to attempt to eat my breakfast. Mrs Smythe had gone to see her sister for the day and had taken Della with her, so we were on our own. We ate in silence and as soon as I put down my knife and fork Gordon fetched my coat and ushered me through the door to walk down to the meet.

The High Street was full of steaming horses and people; breath fogged up the freezing air and the Flannigans manoeuvred through the crowd with trays of hot punch and sausage rolls. The dogs were barking and I couldn't make out the position of the person playing the fiddle, maybe there was more than one. Small boys zig-zagged in front of us and a tinker woman thrust something towards my face and gave a toothless grin before Gordon gently steered me away. The scene reminded me of a Brueghel painting; my head throbbed and my eyes began to hurt.

All the time I thought I might see my father, mounted on his chestnut hunter, striking in his red coat and white cravat. But instead I saw faces I hadn't seen for months, friends of Father's, Mother's cronies; some smiled at me, others turned away, no one came to talk to me, no one came to ask if I was well.

201

I lost Gordon for a little while and found a space inside the butcher's doorway. I leaned my cheek against the coolness of the tiled wall and hoped I might be able to hide there until the hunt set off. I watched the crowd going through the motions of a tradition that seemed suddenly ridiculous to me. I could no longer bear to be part of the whole repugnant scene and began to search for Gordon to take me home. In the distance I saw him talking to a man dressed in a black hunting jacket. The man took off his cap and I recognised him as the young man whom Gordon had treated for a sprained wrist a few weeks before, the man who'd looked like George. I couldn't face negotiating the crowd that separated us, so instead I gave a small boy sixpence to go and tell the doctor that his wife had gone home feeling unwell.

By the time I reached the house I realised I had a fever; my bones ached, my whole body shivered. I made it upstairs to my room and still in my clothes lay down on the bed, pulling the covers over me as I was consumed with cold and then throwing them off as I burned up with unbearable heat. I continued like this for what seemed like hours until eventually I fell into a heavy sleep.

When I woke up I expected to find it dark but the piercing sunlight shafting through the window suggested it was somewhere around midday. My mouth felt scorched, all I could think of was my need for water. Unsteadily I got out of bed and made it through the door on to the landing. I heard the front door thud and Gordon's voice and then another I didn't recognise. I slowly came downstairs, my head spinning, my hands clinging on to the banister for fear of falling. Gordon and his visitor had gone into the consulting room, I wondered if there had been an injury during the hunt that Gordon was now attending to.

I had to sit down on the bottom step for some minutes, my legs too heavy to take me onwards to the kitchen. Standing up I knew I'd never make it into the kitchen without passing out, let alone back up the stairs to bed. I needed Gordon; I needed him to help me before I collapsed onto the quarry tiles that seemed to undulate beneath my feet.

I stumbled towards the consulting room door meaning to knock but as my hand touched it the door swung slowly open, gradually revealing the interior scene. The hunting cap on Gordon's desk, the satin-lined black jacket discarded on the floor, the young man dressed in shirt sleeves, unbuttoned to his waist and Gordon, still in his outdoor coat, moving his hands across the younger man's chest as though performing some sort of examination. Suddenly the man took hold of Gordon's face and kissed him and Gordon drew him tightly into a passionate embrace. I must have gasped because they both stopped and stared at me. I think Gordon said my name but I was already backing out of the room, seized with an energy that had been completely lacking only moments before.

I ran back up the stairs, my heart racing in my ears. Within seconds the symptoms of my fever had returned and soon I was shivering and burning up again as the image of what I had seen downstairs swam in and out of tangled dreams and nightmares.

I was vaguely aware of Gordon and Mrs Smythe and, once, Della wiping my face with a damp cloth. 'There, that should make you feel better, Mrs Brennan, I'm sure it will.'

I heard Gordon telling Mrs Smythe that this time it really must be influenza.

Much later I heard the clock downstairs strike midnight. I opened my eyes and found Gordon sitting on a chair beside the bed. The bedside lamp cast shadows on his face and he held an empty whiskey tumbler in his hand. He rubbed his temples and with eyes averted to the floor asked me to forgive him. I fixed my gaze on a brown stain on the ceiling and wondered how it had got there; it looked rather like a leaping hare. Gordon promised to try harder to control his urges if only I could find it in my heart to stay with him. He took my hand in his. My throbbing mind wandered to Michael, I wished he was with me by my bed, I wished it was his hand that held mine. I wished I was anywhere but in this room with Gordon.

Days passed and the fever never seemed to lessen. I began to cough and each breath hurt my ribs.

I overheard Mrs Smythe say 'pneumonia' with self-satisfied certainty.

Gordon treated me with penicillin – a wonder drug he called it and later told me it had saved my life – but still I wheezed and coughed for days and would have cried with the pain of it if I hadn't felt so ill.

All my conscious thoughts were full of Michael, once I woke with the sound of his name still ringing round the room from my unconscious cry. I opened my eyes with a start and felt relieved to find myself alone.

Gordon was kind. He sat with me for many hours reading to me, talking to me, encouraging me to take a little water or beef tea. It cannot be denied that Gordon is a caring man no matter what else he may be. Every day he takes Razzle for a walk with his dogs and lets Razzle stay in my bedroom all night as he knows it comforts me.

Mrs Smythe performed her nursing duties efficiently and Della came in every day to brush my hair and tell me the gossip: Mr Nuttall's wife has gone to Dublin on the train and rumour has it that she's not coming back; there are workmen at the Castle – the new roof will start next week.

I am sitting up in bed leaning against a pyramid of pillows made for me by Della and writing this. At last I feel a little better. The coughing fits have lessened and the pain in my chest has almost gone, but the thought of getting out of bed makes me feel exhausted.

I think of what I saw on Boxing Day. I know now it was no fever-induced hallucination, it makes sense of everything else that's puzzled me about my husband. I think I ought to leave, get a train to Dublin like Mrs Nuttall and make a new life; but then I remember what will make me stay: my complete lack of money, my love of the Castle and now Michael.

As Phoebe turned the last page of the diary three small envelopes slipped onto the patchwork quilt. 'Anna' was written in spiky letters on each one. Phoebe opened the first and took out a sheet of paper that looked as though it had been ripped from a sketchbook.

Dear Anna,

I met Della Smythe in the high street today. I'm ashamed to say I was relieved when she told me that you had pneumonia – that explains why you didn't meet me at the boathouse as we'd planned. Then I was filled with concern. I do hope you're feeling better; Della assures me that you're on the mend. She asked me if I wanted her to take a message to you so here it is, and here is a picture to cheer you up,

Phoebe studied the small drawing of a puffin, plump and bright-eyed and coloured in with pencil crayon.

Did you like the pebble I gave you? I wish you a fast recovery,

Yours, Michael.

Phoebe put it back in the envelope and opened the second letter.

Dearest Anna,

I was so pleased when Della brought your letter to the school today. You can't imagine my relief when I read that you are feeling better. You ask about my own health and I can tell you that I am very well, though both the Delaneys have the influenza so I'm teaching the middle and the top school at the same time, which is becoming quite a riot. I am not cut out to be a teacher, if only I could paint all day and make a living from it.

You also asked about my Christmas – it was the usual madness at home, my brothers are a rowdy lot especially when they're full of drink. They teased me for being too quiet and said they think I have a sweetheart in Nancy Delaney. Let me assure you I have not. If I was quiet it was because I thought of you. I know that you are married and that I have no right to think of you at all but I do, I cannot help myself.

Please write to me again, Della says she's very happy to play the post mistress (her own words),

Michael x.

Dearest Anna,

My heart soared as I read your letter. That you should think of me is more than I could hope for. Please don't feel you have to tell me anything about your marriage; it is already clear that you're not happy. Would it cheer you up to know that you are scarcely ever out of my mind? Please get better soon, I long to see you again.

In the meantime I have had to find some distraction or I should go quite mad. Yesterday I took the early bus to Kenmare and spent half a month's wages on oils, canvas, an easel, and brushes. On my return I set up the easel in the boathouse. I intend to paint there everyday. The light beside the window is good enough and I cannot see the film director coming to claim his ramshackle shed anytime soon.

I am filled with enthusiasm and last night stayed till midnight drawing out the charcoal outline for my first painting. I want to have it finished for you to see when you are better – I will work hard and fast and hope that that will hasten your recovery.

Michael x

On the bottom he had drawn a line of seals and their pups.

I saw these on the headland yesterday.

Chapter Eighteen

The days of that first week merged into one another. Quickly rituals were created, habits formed. Each morning Phoebe woke to the pale light flooding through the curtains. If there wasn't rain she ate breakfast outside. Toasted soda bread eaten in the brackish air was a pleasure to rival the first cigarette of the day when she was younger.

After she had dressed she walked – along the beach, over the headland, across to little pebbly coves beyond. Often she took her sketchbook and would sit down on the rough grass and draw whatever she could see in front of her, and sometimes things that were simply in her head. Once she climbed the track up to the Castle and stared at its weatherworn façade, wondering what would happen to it, who would buy it. She didn't see Theo but she could see his battered Land Rover sitting on the forecourt; weeds sprang up around it, bright green dandelion leaves and the soft new shoots of brambles pushed their way through the gravel. Phoebe took out her sketchbook and started on a simple line drawing of the house, but when Poncho appeared, sniffing round the corner, she drew back into the woods and made her way down to the beach again.

Sometimes, despite what Theo had said, she helped Honey as she sat at the pub kitchen table struggling with her homework. Already she could sense the little girl's confidence growing. The day she mastered spelling the word *the* Phoebe bought her the green jade dragon from

209

Rainbow's End.

All week Theo kept away from the boathouse while she was there, though when she woke up in the morning new pots would magically have appeared, and once the kiln had been turned on, continuing to warm the building for days.

Phoebe found that she enjoyed working in Fibber Flannigan's bar. The job was undemanding and every day there was laughing – with Katrina, with Fibber, with the customers. Sometimes they made Phoebe laugh so much that tears ran down her cheeks.

There had not been much laughter with David: passion, fervour, excitement, anguish, tears of frustration and despair – but not of laughter. There hadn't been much room for female friendship either; when she wasn't teaching, Phoebe's life was all for David, whether it was being with him or longing to be with him, she hadn't needed other people. She had been careful not to reveal herself in any way to colleagues who might have become her friends from fear of being found out. Even with Nola she had put up barriers.

Now Phoebe enjoyed the warm camaraderie she found with Katrina and for the first time she could talk to someone about David, to mention him in conversation.

'David would have liked that,' or 'David would have felt the same,' or 'David and I used to say …' Phoebe found that she was actually beginning to believe that David had been her husband, beginning to imagine the house they had shared together, the holidays they took, their weekly trips to Sainsbury's, the wedding dress she wore. On her walks across the cliffs she would find herself remembering things that hadn't really happened, things that David would never have taken the risk to do – a picnic in the countryside, a trip to buy him a new suit.

The hurried sex on his way home to Sandra was replaced, in Phoebe's mind, with long leisurely afternoons of lovemaking, the furtive texts with public declarations of undying love. She found great comfort in these imaginary memories and sometimes felt upset when an actual real memory bubbled to the surface: the way he sometimes didn't turn up when they'd arranged that he'd come round; the way he constantly checked his phone.

'You have been so lucky to find a good man in your life,' Katrina said as they sat side by side chopping onions at the kitchen table. 'You will always know you had good husband, good marriage, you never will have the need to regret – and believe me I know about the regret.'

Phoebe stopped chopping and looked at Katrina. 'You never talk about any men in your life before Fibber?'

Katrina shrugged. 'What is point in raking up old times?'

'Did someone hurt you?'

Katrina shook her head vehemently. 'Like I say, is all in past.' Her eyes were suddenly full of tears but when Phoebe tried to put an arm around her she turned away. 'I hate the Irish onions, they always make me cry.'

With Fibber and the other customers talk was easy – a mix of chat about the news, the latest television programmes, reminiscences, jokes, and of course the unrelenting stream of local gossip. That first week the Castle featured large, its sale and rumours about Theo and Honey's pending departure. Phoebe could see the sadness in Fibber and Katrina's eyes, and Mrs Flannigan seemed to withdraw still further into frosty antagonism and migraine attacks.

Only for Honey did Mrs Flannigan make an effort. When the little girl wandered into the kitchen after school, Mrs Flannigan would make hot chocolate for her, and, easing her wide hips into the windsor chair, let Honey sit on her lap while she drew dragons or munched on Katrina's biscuits.

If it was busy in the bar Mrs Flannigan would rouse herself enough to come and help serve, but now she didn't bother to put her careful make-up on, let alone adorn her fingers with glittering rings. Her once elaborately coiffed helmet of hair now resembled an old Brillo pad sitting on her head.

'Is your mother all right?' Phoebe asked Fibber as he showed her how to change a barrel in the musty cellar.

'I think she's very upset at the thought of Honey leaving,' he heaved the large metal container into place. 'And she's never got over Maeve's death. She had a string of miscarriages before Maeve and I were born – she was over forty by then. Little Miracles she used to call us, though I always suspected Maeve was her favourite.' He smiled, 'But I never held it against my sister. She was an angel from day one – the very image of our Honey. I hate to say this about my own brother-in-law, but Theo is behaving like a heartless bastard. How could he even think about taking Honey away from us to live on the other side of the world? It's not as if his mother even knows Honey; I think she's only met her about three times in the poor child's life.'

'What's Theo's mother like?'

'When she lived here I used to think she was like one of those women off that telly programme, *Dynasty* was it?' Fibber was bent over, attaching the lever to the new keg; he grinned at Phoebe over his shoulder. 'Though you're probably too young to remember that one, these days she'd be more like one of those ones on *Desperate Housewives* – you know, all treadmill legs and big hair. I remember she didn't used to like the sea, she said it was too loud at night and the beach was too full of sand, and it was never warm enough in Ireland for her to use the pool – the woman couldn't wait to get back to America. I don't think she even spent much time with her own two sons. I remember her at Theo and Maeve's wedding, she could hardly bear to introduce the Flannigans to her fancy new husband; the two of them disappeared off to Dublin just as soon as the cake had been cut – there was no way they were staying for the céilidh afterwards.

'What was her husband like?' Phoebe asked.

'All Tango tan and bright white teeth; you had to put your sunglasses on just to shake his hand. He complained to my mother that the roast beef we had for the reception had been sliced too thin, treated her as though she was the waitress instead of the bride's mother.'

Fibber stood up straight and checked the beer was flowing through the tube. 'To think of poor Honey living with that couple, it breaks my heart. There now, job done.' He wiped his hands on his shirt and looked thoughtful. 'You know the thing that seems strange to me about my mother? Usually she'd be putting up a great big fight about something like this, claws out, barbed-wire tongue, but she's not doing anything; it's as though she's just resigned to it.' He scratched his brush of hair and shook his head.

At night Phoebe immersed herself in Anna and Michael's burgeoning affair. She read the diary entries slowly, savouring each page like a delicious meal. She had been infuriated to find that Honey's drawings covered much of the third diary, the thick oil crayon completely obliterating whole pages. Anna's recovery from pneumonia and the initial trysts with Michael were lost for ever beneath the child's meticulous pictures and designs. Phoebe tried to scratch through the drawings, but only succeeded in tearing the paper.

Every now and then a sentence or paragraph would tantalisingly reveal itself through the intense colouring.

He must have been waiting because the instant I turned the corner he was there, coming up the lane to meet me, both hands ...

Too soon I had to go, I'd given myself an hour and that had gone the hour before.

We are tiny figures against a bright blue sky, eternally captured in Michael's thick brush strokes on the canvas.

It has been a week since I have seen him. The rain has been relentless.

Della came back from Mass with a note from Michael slipped into her pocket at the communion rail.

He has finished two more paintings.

The builders have made a bonfire at the Castle – a great heap of things the bailiffs left behind. Michael went at night and rescued the old chintz armchair from Mother's drawing room. We have put the armchair by the boathouse window and today I sat, curled up in it with Razzle and watched him while he started another painting.

Michael appeared with a huge mirror, the whole door from the wardrobe in Father's dressing room. He leant it against the wall and standing in front of it drew me to his side. 'You are so beautiful,' he said, and I watched in the reflection while he undid the buttons on my dress.

A quarter of the way through two whole entries revealed themselves before disappearing beneath a rainbow of crayon.

March 23rd

We walked beneath a brilliant sky collecting up sea shells and then arranging them in patterns on the slipway. Michael said I had a natural eye for design and I told him

214

*that the art mistress at school had told me that my still
lifes looked as though they had been run over with a steam
roller and that I lacked artistic flair.*

*Inside the boathouse Michael showed me a new picture
he has started. The black rock is in the foreground; a crow
stands on its summit and in the distance a rusty tanker
sails against a stormy sky. It reminded me of a child's
painting, and I said I liked it but I wasn't sure that my art
mistress would have approved. Michael laughed and said
that was good; he wanted to be liberated from the
constraints of perspective and scale and truth to the
image, he had no interest in pleasing art mistresses. Then
he pulled me down onto the old bed that he has rescued
from the bonfire. It was once in the maid's room and now,
with the blankets I have taken from Mrs Smythe's linen
press, it is my favourite place in the world.*

March 26th

*My chest has worsened again and I have lain in a feverish
state for the past two days. Della brought me an envelope
from Michael and in it, not a letter, but a pencil drawing
of a scallop shell.*

Phoebe looked at the yellowing scrap of paper that Anna
had taped into her diary so long ago. The picture of the
shell was beautifully executed, the perspective and shading
perfect, creating an image which seemed almost three-
dimensional; Michael had been a skilled draughtsman as
well as an expressive painter. She smiled when she saw
what he had written underneath: *Something for the art
mistress.*

'Mrs Flannigan was a fine figure of a woman in her
youth,' the man who'd sung the Irish national anthem that
first night said to Phoebe across the bar. Phoebe had found
out his name was John Doyle, and that even though he was

215

well over eighty years old he was known as Young John Doyle to everyone in Carraigmore. 'She had a look of Hedy Lamarr about her, and a tongue like a whip when it came to the lads; she gave me a good lashing many a time just for telling her I liked her dress or the way she'd done her hair.' He laughed and then that made him cough. Phoebe put down the glass she'd been cleaning, ready to rush around to the other side of the bar to help him if he collapsed. He stopped coughing, took a deep breath, straightened himself up as much as his bent spine let him, and lit a cigarette. 'I don't know how that wastrel Flannigan fellow got her in the end, she was always very wary of the village boys, wouldn't give any of us a chance.'

'Did you know my grandmother?' Phoebe asked.

The old man nodded. 'I knew Anna Brennan when she was just a schoolgirl and I was in short trousers. She and I used to help my father pull the carrots in the vegetable patch up at the Castle; he was head gardener there for years.' He drew himself up still further, as though still proud of the position his father had held.

'Old John,' Phoebe said. 'Your father was "Old John".'

'Indeed he was. He had those gardens beautiful – a picture to look at everywhere you turned until Mr Shaw's incident with the shotgun. Your poor grandmother, she always was a Daddy's girl. They used to walk down on the beach together. He bought her one of our puppies for a present.'

'Do you remember Dr Brennan?'

'Of course I do. He was a good doctor and a fine man. It was a loss to Carraigmore when he left to go to Africa.'

'Did people think it odd that he married Anna Shaw? There was a big age gap and it must have seemed quite sudden.'

Young John frowned, the lines on his face deepening. 'I can't see that it was, at least I don't remember it seeming

216

that way. I do remember people said that he was a gentleman to take her in after all the scandal up at the Castle. The family were left with nothing you know, practically just the contents of a suitcase.' He shook his head. 'It was all a very sorry state of affairs. But you should ask Mrs Flannigan, she'd be the one to know about him.'

'Don't worry,' said Phoebe. 'I don't want to trouble her.'

'Ah no, us old ones love a bit of reminiscing. I'll ask her now.'

'Please don't.'

'It's no trouble at all,' he leant forward and shouted down the bar. 'Della, Della.'

Della?

Mrs Flannigan looked up sharply from the pint of Guinness she was pulling.

'Phoebe here was asking about Dr Brennan,' Young John called out. 'I said you'd be the one to tell her about him, what with your mother being his housekeeper in those days.'

Mrs Flannigan's eyes flashed at Phoebe then back to Young John. 'It's a long time ago,' she said. 'I've enough going on in the present to want to be bothered raking up the past.' She bent her head and finished pouring the pint. Young John shrugged and turned back to Phoebe speaking in a low whisper. 'Always was a prickly mare, acted like she was better than the rest of us. Especially when she came back from living in England.'

'She lived in England? When?'

'When she was young. She got a job as a secretary, only went for a year; she told us that the London smog was rank and that she had to come home for some fresh sea air.' He laughed and coughed again. 'I think I remember it being said that the real reason she came back was because she had never learned to read.'

Phoebe drove back to the boathouse in a daze. So Mrs Flannigan had been Della Smythe, the young girl who had lived in the same house as Anna, witnessed her unhappy marriage, carried messages between Anna and Michael, watched them as their affair developed. As Phoebe walked up the path to the boathouse she stopped – no wonder Anna and Michael had used Della to carry messages, they would have been perfectly safe to say what they liked because their go-between couldn't read what they had written.

Phoebe didn't even turn her head to look for signs of Theo that night. She ran up the stairs and searched through the pile of diaries, looking for the next instalment, searching for more clues.

Chapter Nineteen

Phoebe's mind raced in circles, she wondered just how much Mrs Flannigan remembered. Phoebe had worked in the pub for weeks now, but Mrs Flannigan had never given any indication that her connection with Anna had been more than just a brief acquaintance. For the first time since receiving Nola's awful text, Phoebe wished that she could see her sister again, she wanted to tell her about Anna's diaries, she wanted to talk it all through, to try to piece it all together.

Phoebe picked up her phone and then remembered she had no signal in the boathouse. She glanced at the time, one o'clock. She couldn't possibly go to bed now; she was wide awake and whirring with unanswered questions.

As Phoebe picked up the fourth diary a letter fell out. By now she recognised Michael's handwriting.

My darling, darling Anna,

I am so sorry that I made you sad. France is just a fantasy, I walk in the Kerry rain and imagine that in France I would be sitting in the sun discussing Expressionism with Picasso, but the truth is that I can't even speak French, and the sun only burns my skin and brings out my freckles. When you ran away from me I thought my heart would split in two. I watched you disappearing up the lane and I knew that I could never bear to be without having you in my life. When I said I'd rather be anywhere than Ireland I was wrong. All I want is you, here, now, with me in my arms. Please believe me when I say I love you more than I would ever have believed possible.

M x

With a sigh Phoebe let the letter fall onto her lap; why had David never written to her with such passionate words? Pushing the thought away Phoebe started reading again. The fourth diary had been spared Honey's creative endeavours and there were more letters from Michael pushed into the pages, mirroring Anna's fervent feelings with his own. Phoebe read until her eyes throbbed with tiredness as she scanned page after page of her grandmother's looping writing and Michael's spiky scrawl; occasionally she rubbed her temples but time seemed irrelevant, sleep hopeless, her mind became consumed with Anna and Michael's affair.

Anna spent more and more time with Michael; walking Razzle was her marvellous excuse.

Della was always ready to carry messages; she seemed captivated by the young lovers, pleading with Anna to give her details, embellishing them with her own MGM-inspired fantasies.

March 20th

After dinner Della appeared in my room with too much lipstick on and a note from Michael. She said he had been waiting for her outside the shop as she was leaving; she said that he had looked soaked through by the rain. She asked me if I loved him and I found the "Yes" forming on my lips as though I knew it so readily I didn't have to think. I had to make Della promise over and over that she won't tell a living soul.

Initially Anna and Michael spent languorous weekend afternoons in the boathouse, lying on the narrow bed, their limbs entwined but as spring approached they ventured out like bears emerging from hibernation. Anna borrowed Della's bicycle and they went to see a Neolithic dolmen on the moor. They climbed on the huge stone slab to sit and eat their sandwiches and wondered about the people who had built it all those thousands of years ago. On their next trip they came across the remains of a round tower and standing inside it looked up to see a peregrine falcon.

In a letter Michael wrote that he would never forget the bird *flying across the perfect sphere of cornflower sky.*

As the weather grew warmer they ventured further afield, cycling across the peninsula and then setting out by foot along clifftops edged with drifts of thrift and gorse. They discovered secluded coves and followed streams inland, finding pools deep enough to bathe in. In May they swam naked in a deep pool at the bottom of a waterfall. In peat-stained water, like molten gold, they gazed at each other's bodies and afterwards they made love on the mossy river bank while Razzle dozed in the warm afternoon sun.

Sometimes Anna mentioned Gordon, and Phoebe noticed it was increasingly with concern.

June 13th

Gordon looked tired at supper, his eyes are shadowed and his shoulders seem to sag beneath his new summer jacket. I asked if he were well and he said he was. I cannot help but feel affection for this poor, tormented man I have been so incongruously attached to.

It is a strange thing but instead of feeling anger I feel a warmth towards him, a compassion for his situation. The only anger I feel is for my mother; Mother must have known, or at least suspected. I'm sure her love of idle gossip would have delighted in a rumour about the village doctor, she never could resist the smell of scandal until of course it was her own stench that filled the air in Carraigmore.

At least I have Michael, I have Michael, I have Michael – I could write it over and over again.

Phoebe thought Gordon must have known, or at least suspected that his wife was having an affair. By July Anna and Michael were meeting almost every day.

Sometimes they walked in the grounds of the Castle; renovation work progressed slowly and there was no sign of the film director or any of the Hollywood glamour Della had so eagerly anticipated. At the weekends the weed-choked gardens were empty; there were no workmen or decorators to see Anna and Michael as they sought out the old rose garden or searched amongst the fast-encroaching brambles for the place where the lavender always grew. Michael asked her many questions: about her childhood, her family, and her life in the idyllic house. Anna's passion for her old home must have been evident as she recorded Michael's words to her after one particular trip around the overgrown grounds.

He said a man could get to feel quite jealous of a house. I laughed and made to kiss him but he held me at arms length, his expression serious. He seemed to study my face for some time as though I were a subject for his painting and then he asked me if I'd go with him to France. I said, 'You don't speak French' and Michael told me that I'd have to do the talking for us both.

Chapter Twenty

Phoebe's eyes sprang open. Looking out of the window she saw the dim grey light of morning and realised that she must have dropped off to sleep while reading in the armchair. The diary had slipped onto the floor; she bent to pick it up and heard a gentle humming noise beneath her. The humming turned into a loud whir. Theo!

Phoebe stood up, still half asleep. She started for the stairs, unsure why she wanted to see him; maybe she couldn't bear the hostile feeling between them any longer.

As she reached the bottom of the stairs she saw Poncho lying across the doorway; he looked at her but didn't make any attempt to move. Theo was bent over his wheel, his back to her. His hands, grey with wet slip, were deftly shaping a fast-revolving dome of clay. Phoebe watched him, mesmerised by the pot that was magically appearing. It seemed to have a life of its own, moving rhythmically, growing, then shrinking, pulsing at the slightest touch from Theo's fingers. It swelled outwards, then rose up, then swelled again. Though Phoebe couldn't see his face she could sense Theo's absolute absorption in the process. His sleeves were rolled up, the muscles in his arms tense; she could see now that it would be a vase, full-bellied and round.

The speed of the wheel gradually decreased until it stopped altogether, and Theo leaned back slightly to look at his creation. Then he spun the wheel very slowly to study the pot from all angles before taking a thin piece of wire, slicing the pot away from the wheel. and lifting it onto a shelf.

Phoebe walked down the final step into the room and Poncho barked. Theo turned and Phoebe tried to read the expression that crossed his face as he saw her: surprise, irritation but something else as well, maybe a small suggestion that he was actually pleased to see her?

'It's beautiful.' Phoebe nodded at the moon jar on the shelf.

She braced herself for some cutting comment, but instead he picked up a new ball of clay and put it down onto the wheel-head ready to start another pot. His foot pressed the control pedal at the side and the wheel began its humming rotation again. After a few seconds he stopped and turned back to Phoebe.

'Did your grandmother ever teach you how to throw?'

Phoebe shook her head. 'She used to let Nola make little bowls but she said I was too young. I've always wanted to give it a try; I nearly joined an evening class last September.' She remembered it had clashed with the evening Sandra always took the twins to see her mother, giving David and Phoebe three clear hours to spend together – too precious an opportunity to waste on pottery classes.

Theo climbed off his seat and gestured to her to sit at the wheel. 'Come on then, I'll tell you what to do.'

Phoebe hesitated; did she really want to risk making a fool of herself?

'No?' Theo said. 'Maybe another time.' He sat back down and turned his back to her.

'OK then.' Phoebe stepped forward. 'I'll have a go, but don't laugh at me if I make a total mess of it.'

'Of course you'll make a total mess of it.' He paused and smiled when he saw Phoebe's indignant expression. 'Everyone always does the first time. It takes a lot of practice; you should have seen me when I started. I think your grandmother despaired that I would ever produce anything, but something kept me persevering. Have a go; I think you'll enjoy it – after all it must be in your genes.' He handed her a heavy cotton smock. 'Here, you'd better put this on; you don't want to spoil that nice lace blouse.' Phoebe looked down and realised she still wore the clothes she'd put on for her shift in the pub the night before. Pulling the shapeless smock over her head, she thought how bizarre it was to be having a pottery lesson at dawn on a chilly Sunday morning. Theo didn't question what she was doing up and dressed at such an early hour, and she didn't ask him why he felt the need to work at night instead of during the day.

Phoebe sat down on the high seat in front of Theo's wheel. The smock was huge and she had to roll the sleeves up several times.

Theo leant against the table and began to issue instructions, 'Press the pedal gently, keep your arms down, and let your hands get a feel for the clay as it turns, relax your shoulders but keep your arms firm, keep the speed steady, start to make a small indentation with your thumb, increase the speed a bit now. Good, you're doing well, remember it's all about tension, start to raise the sides – well done, keep going.'

Phoebe's heart began to lift as a tangible shape started to appear in front of her. She smiled, a vessel, a pot – it was definitely pot-shaped. The feel of the wet clay between her hands felt wonderful, cathartic, the rotation of the wheel hypnotic. Phoebe found she was enjoying it, why had she never tried throwing a pot before? She should have gone to those evening classes.

She let her fingers pull up the sides to make it bigger, the pot swelled a little, she pushed it slightly at the top to try to make a vase, determined to prove Theo wrong. Even if it had taken *him* a long time to get the hang of it, she could do it perfectly first time. Suddenly the pot began to wobble and then distort; in seconds it was uncontrollable, refusing to answer to her touch, slip splattered over the smock as it twisted back and forth. The wheel juddered to a halt as she took her foot off the control pedal. In a second the perfect shape she'd made collapsed into flaccid lump in front of her. She stared at it and tried not to show her disappointment.

'Don't worry,' Theo said. 'It happens to the best of us. You did well for your first time.' He leant over, swiftly cut the disastrous pot away from the wheel, and threw down another ball of clay. 'I could help you this time,' he said and leant in front of her to centre the clay on the wheel. Phoebe moved to one side so as not to get in his way. His arm brushed against her shoulder and she felt him flinch, though his eyes stayed firmly fixed on the rotating wheel. Phoebe tried to move over some more, risking falling off her seat. 'Maybe you should have another go on your own,' he stepped back to his position by the table. Phoebe pressed the pedal again and placed her hands onto the soft grey clay. Almost immediately the clay began to shudder, refusing to rotate smoothly, whirling awkwardly from side to side.

'Try and keep it in the middle,' Theo instructed. 'Hold your wrists firm, don't go with it, get control, show it you're in charge – no, not like that, keep your arms at your sides.' He was standing beside her again. She tried to gain control by pressing down harder on the clay. 'No, you're losing it now. Come on, try to get it back on course, remember what I said about the tension, feel it through your body, through your core,' his hands were briefly on her shoulders. 'The pressure should be coming from up here; think tension and pressure – that's the key to throwing.' Phoebe tried as hard as she could to think tension and pressure but it had no effect on the drunkenly spinning clay. She wanted to stop but her brain seemed to refuse to communicate with her foot on the pedal; her foot pressed down harder and the clay swung ever more wildly from side to side.

'Shall I help you?' Theo was leaning over her again, his hands inches from her own, longing to rectify the mess she was making.

'OK,' she replied reluctantly. Theo placed his hands on hers, firmly guiding her, gently pushing her palms against the spinning clay, his forearms leaning against hers. His hands were large, much larger than her own. She noticed the well-defined muscles in his arms.

Suddenly the swaying motion turned into a smooth whirl and a cone shape began to appear between their conjoined hands.

'There,' Theo said. 'It's coming now.' He pushed and the clay rose up into a tower, he pressed down and it spun into a drum like cylinder. 'We need to build the tension before we can make the vessel,' he explained, pushing it up again. 'Do you see what I mean? Tension, pressure, control.'

For a second Phoebe closed her eyes, the rhythmic movement of the clay felt wonderful, Theo's hands encapsulating hers felt strong. His face was very close; she could feel his steady breath against her cheek as he concentrated on the wheel. Every now and then he added more water to keep the surface moist and little droplets of grey slip would spatter across their arms leaving a pattern of tiny dots.

'Now, let's start to push down, make an indentation with your fingers, exert a little pressure to the sides.' Phoebe watched as a vase began to climb upwards, magically appearing, smooth and perfectly round. 'Lovely,' said Theo almost inaudibly, 'just a little more and we'll be there.' He moved her hands around the pot, shaping it into a narrow-necked sphere, guiding her fingers around the clay, smoothing the surface. It appeared to be finished, but Theo went on guiding her fingers and Phoebe went on pressing on the pedal to make the wheel go round, wondering when Theo would tell her to stop.

She turned her face to look at him and at the same time his face turned to hers. His leant towards her and their lips met, he drew back and hesitated for the briefest moment then he kissed her again. Phoebe found herself responding, her foot had left the pedal, the pot had been forgotten. Theo's hands were caressing her back through the smock; drawing her towards him, he lifted the thick cotton and found her skin. A tiny groan of pleasure escape from Phoebe's lips, then suddenly Theo released her and turned away. The whole encounter had lasted less than thirty seconds.

He stood by the workbench, his back to her. 'I'm sorry.'

'It's all right.' Phoebe still sat at the wheel, she pulled down the hideous smock, wanting to take it off altogether but afraid that it would look like some attempt to seduce him further.

'I don't know what came over me.' He had picked up a small piece of natural sponge and seemed to be studying it as though trying to lose himself in its intricacies.

'I told you, it's all right.' She reached out to touch his arm, but he visibly stiffened and she withdrew her hand.

'I'd better leave,' he said, taking his coat from the end of the workbench. At the door he turned and their eyes locked for a second. Phoebe started to say something but he gave a brief command to Poncho to follow him and left.

Some time later, Phoebe climbed back up the stairs. Slowly she undressed and climbed into the narrow bed. The clock on her mobile phone said seven thirty and she could see through the window that the grey sky had cleared to a brilliant blue that in no way reflected her frame of mind.

Phoebe tried to sleep but the recollection of Theo's kiss had left her restless, unable to settle into the oblivion her exhausted body craved. Thoughts of Theo mingled with thoughts of Anna and Michael; she wondered if they had made love in the very place where she now lay, she wondered how long their happiness continued. Briefly she thought of getting up and reading the last two remaining diaries but she felt too tired; her mind began to wander between consciousness and dreams. She dreamed she found a painting of a naked Anna, thick strokes of oyster-coloured oil paint making up a languorously beautiful body. She was draped across the flower-covered armchair, and the long mirror had been placed behind her to reflect a swarthy-faced young artist, his eyes intently concentrating on the easel in front of him. In her dream Phoebe held the painting up to the window light and the figure on the chair seemed to swell a little, the hips and thighs fuller, the limbs less elongated, the whole effect more fleshy. The neat dark bob was replaced with long unruly curls; peering closer Phoebe found it was her own body lying there, and that the artist in the mirror was no longer swarthy but fair, his unshaven face as chiselled as a Grecian sculpture, his hair falling over piercing eyes. Phoebe looked again and realised it was Theo and that he was trying to say something, his lips moving on the coarse canvass. She couldn't hear him, she tried desperately but she couldn't make out the words. The face changed again, she tried to work out who the artist was now, trying to recollect the clean-shaven jaw and neatly cut brown hair: David, it was David. His voice was muffled as though coming through a thick wall, but she could hear him. *Sorry, I'm so sorry,* he was saying, *I don't know what came over me.* He repeated the words over and over again.

She woke up to find herself already sitting up in bed, her heart racing, her body clammy. It took a few seconds to recollect the dream and then a few more to remember the night before. The dream became mingled with reality and she had to force her brain to work out if the passionate

229

kiss she had shared with Theo had been part of the dream or something real that had actually happened.

She picked up her phone to check the time and realised that if she didn't hurry she'd be late for her lunchtime shift at the pub.

As she climbed into a pair of jeans and slipped on her lace blouse she wondered if she dared ask Mrs Flannigan about Anna and Michael. She was sure that Mrs Flannigan must remember something, she had been fifteen at the time, the same age Phoebe had been when she'd first met David; an impressionable age, an age when romantic books and films stayed in one's memory. Surely Mrs Flannigan would recollect something of the real-life romance she had been caught up in.

Phoebe quickly brushed her teeth and applied a quick flick of mascara to her pale eyelashes. Before she left she checked her reflection in the mirror and was horrified to see the smears of dried-up clay on her blouse. She remembered Theo's hands searching beneath the smock and an initial jolt of desire was quickly replaced with embarrassment. She wrenched the blouse off over her head without undoing the buttons and flung it behind the armchair, out of sight. Rummaging through the chest of drawers she found a long-sleeved polo-necked jumper and pulled it on, wishing she had time to shower away the large grey handprint that she noticed on her back.

Chapter Twenty-one

Mrs Flannigan was in her sitting room going through the pub's accounts with Molly from the Hair Hut's husband; he had his own accountancy practice in Caherciveen, and, as Katrina explained to Phoebe, 'He is helping every month in return for free beer.' Katrina went on gravely, 'It is a serious job and Fibber and I wait with our breaths baited as he is doing the sums.'

'Baited breaths,' called Fibber from the other end of the bar.

'Whatever,' called back Katrina. 'Anyhow, we wait with our baited breaths to see if the pub has made a profit this month. If it is "Yes" Mrs Flannigan will be happy. If "No" she will be like a bear who has been hit on the head with a big hammer.'

'Bear with a sore head,' shouted Fibber in unison with the customer he was serving.

'Surely the pub will have done well this month,' said Phoebe. 'Most nights it's been busy and some nights it's been heaving with customers – even in the middle of the week.'

Katrina smiled. 'I think that is the Phoebe effect. The customers they like you; you are nice for chatting, you are good with the pints and you are very pretty on the eye.'

Phoebe could feel herself beginning to blush.

'Katrina's right,' Fibber came over to get some ice. 'You've been the best thing for business since my beautiful Katrina agreed to work here – though to this day

231

I've never worked out why she stays.'

Katrina put her arms around his neck. 'I stay for you, you silly man.' She kissed him briefly then drew back with a peevish expression. 'But I will go if you are correcting my English any more. It is you Irish with your funny ways of talking that need to be made correct. Is this not the truth, Phoebe?' Phoebe laughed.

All three of them turned to look at Mrs Flannigan as she emerged from her lair and walked into the bar. Phoebe noticed that she had her make-up on for the first time for ages.

'Are we all right, Ma?' Fibber asked. 'Or are we headed for the debtors' prison?'

'We'll make it through another month, I'd say.' Mrs Flannigan picked up a glass and started pouring a pint of Guinness for Molly from the Hair Hut's husband. 'Though go easy on those fancy crisps you keep ordering.' She started to hum "I Could Have Danced All Night" and Fibber grinned.

'When she starts on the *My Fair Lady* tunes you know that things will be OK.'

Lunchtime was busy. The good weather meant that there were already day-trippers coming to Carraigmore to walk the cliff paths and take out dinghies and kayaks. As closing time approached, Phoebe longed to escape back to her bed. She ached all over from lack of sleep and she was struggling to stop her mind from drifting back to the way Theo's lips had felt on hers.

As she started to clean out the coffee machine a cheerful voice called out behind her. 'Get your walking boots ready, Miss Brennan. MacGillycuddy's Reeks are calling.'

Rory stood on the other side of the bar, his tight blue T-shirt was emblazoned with the words *Get High, Get Hiking*. Phoebe looked at him through weary eyes.

'Now?'

'Don't worry – you've got one night to prepare yourself, though I'd suggest an early bedtime. Ireland's highest peaks await.'

'Look, Rory.' Phoebe pulled the filter unit out and a wave of coffee granules splashed into her face. She wiped them away with a bar towel. 'Three reasons why I don't think I'm quite ready to join you on Hag's Tooth or Sheep's Scull or whatever mountain it is you have in mind. One, I'm working tonight, so an early bedtime's out of the question. Two, I don't own a pair of walking boots, and three, cleaning out this infuriating coffee machine is quite enough of a challenge for me at the moment.'

Rory looked like a disappointed puppy. 'But I thought you'd enjoy it; the views are stunning.'

'By the time I got to the top I'd be too exhausted to care what I was looking at.'

'Don't you think you could do with getting a bit of fresh air into your lungs?'

'A gentle stroll along the beach is enough for me.'

Rory thought for a moment. 'What about a cliff hike, we'll go over the headland to O'Connell's Point; there's a good bit of scrambling to be had there and it's only five miles there and back, not too far at all.' He peered over the counter at her feet. 'You'll probably be fine in those sturdy boots. I'll get my mother to make us up a few sandwiches. You'll love the views and we could always go on further if we feel like it.'

Phoebe made a face. 'Five miles and a bit of scrambling sounds more than enough for me and my sturdy boots!'

'That's a date then.' Rory rubbed his hands with satisfaction. 'I'll pick you up from the boathouse at ten o'clock.'

A date! Phoebe hadn't thought of it as a date. She liked Rory well enough, she liked him a lot, but she hadn't

233

thought of him as anything more than a friend. She felt panic mounting inside, she wasn't ready for dates.

'Rory,' she began, but he interrupted her.

'Sorry, Phoebe, but I've got to go; apparently there are some real mackers coming in at Brandon Bay. A bunch of us are going to see if we can catch some tubes; the crew's all waiting for me in the van outside and they're raring to get stoked.'

Phoebe stared at him. 'Pardon?' But he already had his back to her. At the door he turned with a cheery wave and was gone.

Katrina had appeared in order to help manipulate the coffee filter back into place, she laughed at Phoebe's baffled expression.

'Surfing,' she explained. 'He and his friends are going surfing at Brandon Bay where there are the big waves – they call them mackers – and they want to surf on the curl of the wave – that is the tubes and in the end they want to get stoked – that is to be very happy surfers.'

'Oh,' said Phoebe. 'Thanks for the translation; I thought he was talking about drugs.'

Katrina laughed again. 'Rory does not need to do drugs, he is addict to exercise I think.'

Phoebe sighed. 'I can see that. And now I've agreed to go for a five-mile walk with him tomorrow and I'm a bit worried.'

'You will be fine.' Katrina looked her up and down. 'You look in quite fit shape to me.'

'No it's not that – I'm sure I'll survive the walk. I'm just a bit worried that he's got the wrong idea and thinks it's going to be more than just a friendly hike. I think he thinks its some sort of date.'

Katrina raised one expertly plucked eyebrow. 'Really?'

'Come on girls,' Mrs Flannigan bustled up and flapped a dishcloth at them, 'you can't just stand around chatting all day, the dishes are finished, and just look at the mess you've made with that coffee machine, Phoebe – there's coffee granules half way up the wall.' She started to wipe a Guinness sign, sucking through her teeth as she mopped the brown streaks from the toucan's beak. Katrina made a face behind Mrs Flannigan's back and hastily disappeared into the kitchen. Phoebe tried to use the bar towel to mop up the mess she'd managed to make on the counter, but Mrs Flannigan whipped it out of her hands. 'You'll get stains on that.'

Mrs Flannigan turned back to the metal sign, her back to Phoebe as she rubbed vigorously and started to hum the opening bars of "On the Street Where You Live".

'Mrs Flannigan, can I ask you some questions about my grandmother?' The humming stopped abruptly but Mrs Flannigan continued to rub even though the coffee stain was long gone.

'I wanted to ask about her past,' Phoebe continued. Mrs Flannigan stiffened and stopped rubbing.

'Do you remember someone called Michael?'

'No.'

'He was a painter.' Phoebe watched the woman's face. It had become still as stone. 'He and Anna seem to have been having an affair. I've found some diaries and there are letters from Michael as well. They start when Anna and her family were still at the Castle and cover the time of her father's death, and then her marriage to Dr Brennan and then the start of her affair with Michael.'

Mrs Flannigan said nothing; she stared at Phoebe, the dishcloth tightly scrunched up in her hand.

'I don't want to upset you.' Phoebe wondered if Mrs Flannigan was about to shout at her. 'I just hoped that you might be able to tell me something more about that time or what my grandfather was like – Anna and Gordon don't seem to have had a happy marriage, and I wondered how they ended up going to Africa together and what happened to …'

235

The cloth hit the counter behind Phoebe with a dull thwack, narrowly missing her face in its trajectory. She jumped in surprise. Had Mrs Flannigan really thrown the dishcloth at her?

'I don't like to talk about the past,' Mrs Flannigan's voice was almost a hiss.

'Sorry, I just wanted to ...'

'Excuse me, but I'm not feeling well.' The old woman pushed past Phoebe and disappeared into her living room, slamming the door behind her.

'Looks like we've heard the last of the *My Fair Lady*s for today.' Fibber seemed to materialise from nowhere. He picked up the damp dishcloth from the bar. 'I hope you weren't attempting to get a free *Fibber Flannigan's* T-shirt or something.'

'No, of course not.' Phoebe felt too upset to laugh. 'All I wanted was to find out a bit more about my grandmother. I only asked your mother a few questions about when she was young and living in my grandfather's house with Anna.'

Fibber gave the bar a wipe with the cloth. 'She doesn't like to talk about the past.'

'I gathered that,' said Phoebe. 'But why?'

'Well,' Fibber pulled a thoughtful face. 'She had a hard time as a child. Her mother was a difficult woman, with her own heartaches and dark secrets,' he lowered his voice. 'The poor woman ended her days in the Cork asylum. I remember being taken to visit her when I was about as old as Honey, not long before she died. My grandmother was sitting in a chair on the veranda, tied to it to stop her wandering off. She told me that the young master from the Castle would be coming to take her home in his big car, and then she called to the nurse on duty and asked for tea to be brought to the yellow drawing room. Poor thing, her mind had completely gone.'

'That's very sad,' said Phoebe. 'But I don't understand

why your mother seems so averse to talking about my grandmother. I've found some old diaries and they seem to have been quite close when they were young.'

Fibber raised his eyebrows and opened a packet of paprika crisps; he scooped a large handful into his mouth and chewed for a little while.

'Anna Brennan and my mother were not exactly what you'd call friends but it always seemed to me that they had some sort of bond between them.' He offered Phoebe a crisp, she shook her head and Fibber poured the rest into his palm. 'When your grandmother died my mother wept for days. Inconsolable, she was – I must admit that I was quite surprised. After that she made it a weekly ritual to go down to the boathouse and give it a dust and an airing, almost as though she thought that Anna might come back. She even makes me give the outside a lick of paint every few years and weed the path.' He shrugged, finished the crisps in his hand, and threw the packet in the bin. 'I've always found it easier to get on with what my mother tells me to do and not ask too many questions.'

A soft hand slipped into Phoebe's. Phoebe looked down and found Honey standing by her side.

'When are we going to look for heart stones?' Honey's hair had been curled and caught up with a large silk rose behind one ear. Phoebe wondered who had done it for her. Katrina? Mrs Flannigan? Surely not Theo.

'How about next week sometime, maybe after school?' Phoebe said.

'How about now? Uncle Fibber, has Phoebe finished all her work today?'

Fibber looked at his watch and sucked his teeth. 'I'm not sure, we may have to keep her here a few minutes longer in case we get a coach-load of Americans doing the Ring of Kerry, you know how desperate they all are experience the crack in a genuine Irish bar.'

Honey's voice took on a pleading tone. 'Please, Uncle

Fibber. Anyway I heard you say that the Americans are as tight as badgers' arses at the moment, and not interested in shelling out any money, even for a pint of a bloody Guinness.' She batted her eyelashes at an astounded Fibber. '*Please* let Phoebe come down to the beach with me.'

Fibber pulled at his niece's new curls. 'OK you can take her away if you must, but be sure to have her back here for the evening opening-time.'

Honey giggled. 'Or will she turn into a pumpkin?'

'Oh, much worse than that. Your grandmother will sack her and she'll have to go back to England.'

Honey's hand flew to her mouth in horror. 'Granny wouldn't really sack Phoebe, would she?'

Fibber took Honey gently by the shoulders and looked into her anxious eyes. 'Don't worry, that was just a joke, it's much more likely that Phoebe will just turn into that giant pumpkin and we'll have one hell of a job getting her off the beach before the tide comes in.'

Chapter Twenty-two

A sharp cracking noise woke Phoebe from a deep sleep. Her eyes flew open and immediately squinted against the bright light of the morning. The cracking noise again; it sounded as though something had hit the window. Another crack, followed by a hail of tapping; something really was hitting the window. Phoebe jumped out of bed and pulled back the curtains. Below her she could see Rory armed with a handful of pebbles already raising his arm to throw again. She undid the catch and flung the window wide open.

'Hey! There are rules about throwing stones at people's houses you know.'

Rory grinned up at her. 'There are rules about remembering to set your alarm clock when you've arranged to meet someone for a walk.'

'I thought you said ten o'clock.'

'It's twenty past now. I've been hammering on the door for ages; I was beginning to get worried.'

Phoebe yawned. 'It can't be that late already, I feel as if I've hardly been asleep at all.' It was nearly true. After one of Fibber's karaoke lock-ins she'd spent a second night tossing and turning before eventually falling into deep slumber at dawn.

'Come on down, the fresh air will wake you up a treat and you can have one of my mother's sandwiches for breakfast.'

Phoebe withdrew back into the room and scrabbled

around for suitable clothes for wearing on a walk. She squeezed into her jeans (she would have to start to forgo Katrina's wonderful puddings for the sake of her wardrobe) and found a T-shirt and a cardigan, but realised she'd left her duffle coat in the pub. She turned to the row of pegs on the wall, and riffling through Anna's assorted jackets and shawls picked out a bright red woollen coat. She loved the colour and the old-fashioned fitted shape. Phoebe slipped it on and looked in the mirror; though it was a little long it felt comfortable, even comforting. She liked the way it flew out behind her as she ran down the stairs.

Outside Rory laughed.

'What's so funny?' she asked.

'Your coat. You look like you could be going to a wedding, not a walk on the headland, and the belt is dragging on the ground – don't you have a waterproof? Or maybe you'd be better off in a gilet on a fine day like today.'

'Well I'm sorry if I don't look like someone from a Helly Hansen catalogue!' She knotted the belt of the coat tightly and set off after Rory, who smiled at her over his shoulder.

'No, don't get me wrong, I like the coat very much. It suits you, that scarlet colour looks fabulous with your hair.' He handed her a sandwich.

They walked along the beach in silence. The air was still and green waves moved lethargically on to the compacted sand beside them.

Rory was uncharacteristically quiet. Phoebe hoped she wasn't going to be forced to decline any amorous advances on the cliff-top.

She picked at the cheese and pickle sandwich as her still sleepy mind drifted to the previous afternoon.

She and Honey had spent a long time scouring the high tide line for heart stones, but the stones eluded them, or simply weren't there to be found. Phoebe tried to change the search to shells or sea glass, but this had been met with a stubborn insistence that they keep searching for the hearts.

They had moved down the beach towards the black rock, stepping on the hard sand left by the retreating tide. Here the stones were smaller and embedded, so that they had to dig with their fingers to look at the true shape of them.

'I think I've found one!' said Honey, stooping to pick up something pale and grey. 'Oh, it's more of a triangle shape, not a heart.' And before Phoebe could see it the little girl ran down to the water's edge and threw it into the froth of the receding waves.

'Is this what you're looking for?' The sound of Theo's voice startled Phoebe. She braced herself, expecting him to reproach her for being with his daughter, but instead he held out his closed hand. As he opened it she saw the stone: nestling in his dusty palm, it was smooth and white, still glistening from the sea.

'Let me see.' Honey ran up to her father. 'Wow! How did you find it? We've been looking for hours and hours. Can I have it?'

Theo slid it into Honey's cupped hands. 'Look after it, heart stones are very precious.' His eyes briefly met Phoebe's and she looked down at the sand, kicking a promising stone at her feet that turned out to be just another triangle.

'How did you know what we were looking for, Daddy?' asked Honey.

Theo smiled. 'I remember Phoebe when she was a little girl like you. She and her grandmother used to scour the beach together, picking up stones, then discarding them; occasionally they would both shout out as though they'd found treasure. Uncle Oliver and I once asked what they were looking for and Anna told us they were searching for heart stones, and that they were very special, magical almost, bringing love to those who found them and luck to those who had been given them as gifts. Your Uncle Oliver laughed and later he teased Phoebe; called her "the Heart Stone Girl" when she walked past on her own. Sometimes I used to look for them myself, though of course I never told my brother that. When I saw you and Phoebe looking so intently at the ground I knew immediately what you were searching for.'

'I remember Oliver shouting that name at me across the beach,' Phoebe smiled. 'I wished that my grandmother hadn't told him what we were looking for.'

'Never much of a one for sentimentality, my big brother – and always on the look out for someone to make fun of.'

'He sounds a bit like Nola. She was never interested in finding heart stones; much too pragmatic to believe in the special powers of pebbles.'

'My overriding memory of Nola is of her lying stretched out on the slipway in a pink bikini and big black sunglasses as though she thought she was on the Riviera.'

'Oh yes, she didn't believe in the power of heart stones but she did have great faith in the power of the Kerry sun to give her a Mediterranean tan. She used to make me rub Hawaiian Tropic on her back – the sickly smell put me off coconuts for life.' Theo laughed and his eyes met Phoebe's own.

Honey stood between them examining the stone in her hand. She looked up at Theo. 'Did you give Mummy a heart stone?' Theo shook his head. 'You should have given one to Mummy; then she might not have died.'

Theo stared out at the sparkling sea for a few seconds before he spoke. 'Your mummy was very ill. She saw lots and lots of doctors who couldn't stop her dying; I don't think a heart stone could have helped her either.'

Honey pursed her lips. Theo crouched down beside her

and took her hands in his. 'How do you fancy spaghetti bolognese for tea tonight? Then maybe we could watch a DVD and I'll let you have another go at painting my nails. I'll even let you get the straighteners out to make me look like Justin Bibber again.'

Honey laughed. 'But you won't ever look like Justin *Bieber*, Daddy; you're too old and scruffy.' She squeezed her father's face between her fingers before giving him a hug. 'Promise you won't put onions in the bolognese sauce.'

'I promise.'

'Can Phoebe come for tea too?'

'I have to go to work,' Phoebe told Honey hurriedly. She was sure that having her to tea was the last thing Theo wanted. 'In fact I'd better go now or I'll be late.'

'Another time?' asked Honey eagerly.

Phoebe glanced at Theo, all his attention seemed to be directed out at sea.

'You look like you're in another world,' said Rory. Phoebe looked at him, surprised. She had been so lost in her recollections of the previous day that she hadn't noticed that they had begun to climb up the steep cliff path. She looked behind her and was amazed to find that they were already halfway up. In front of them Phoebe could see a track leading through yellow gorse towards the distant headland.

Phoebe stopped to try to catch her breath.

'Come on, I'll give you a hand,' Rory reached down to haul her up the final bit before the cliff path levelled out.

They carried on along the narrow track in single file. The sky was now a clear bright blue, the spring sunshine warm enough for Phoebe to undo the buttons of the coat.

The shrill cry of a bird sounded above them and they looked up to see a pair of lapwings zigzagging overhead.

'They're putting on a courtship display for us,' said

Rory, holding up his hand to shield his vision from the bright sun.

By lunchtime they were standing on top of the headland. In one direction Phoebe could see the hazy mountains of a distant peninsula, in the other she could see nothing but the flat grey ocean stretching out to Nova Scotia. She took a deep breath and let it out slowly as she admired the view.

'Come and look at this,' said Rory, beckoning to Phoebe to follow him inland a few hundred yards.

It seemed to suddenly emerge in front of them; huge slabs of rock crudely put together to make a structure that looked like a giant's dining table.

'The dolmen!' she almost ran towards the ancient burial tomb.

As Phoebe reached it she put out her hand to touch the rough grey rocks that supported the enormous capstone.

'Have you been here before?' asked Rory catching up with her.

'No, but I know two people who have.'

'Who's that then?'

Phoebe didn't answer, but in her mind she thought of Anna and Michael sitting on the great slab, eating their sandwiches so many years before.

'Let's climb on top of it and have our lunch,' she said, already hoisting herself up onto the top.

'I don't know what Heritage Ireland would have to say about you climbing on top of ancient monuments.'

'Oh come on, Rory,' Phoebe laughed. 'Live a little dangerously, or at least throw up your rucksack and let me have a sandwich. I'm starving.'

In seconds he was beside her, 'Phoebe Brennan, you're very bold, you know.'

She grinned and took a sandwich from his hand. 'Your mother makes a mean doorstep.'

'She always makes sure my father and I have three

hefty meals a day,' he laughed. 'She says you never know when there might be another Famine.'

'Is it hard to be back home again after travelling the world and being so independent?'

Rory shrugged. 'It was a little odd at first, but to be honest I needed feeding up at the time, and my parents have always been pretty easy-going. The hardest thing was getting used to Carraigmore again, building up new friendships, finding people with similar interests and hobbies.'

'It seems to me that you've done a great job at that,' Phoebe smiled through a mouthful of soft white bread. 'You've got loads of friends.'

'Yes, I've been very lucky. And now you've come to live here things are even better.'

Phoebe swallowed. This was it; the moment she'd been dreading. 'Look Rory, it's lovely that you've been so kind to me, and I really appreciate you bringing me out today, but I need you to know I'm really not ready for any thing more than friendship at the moment. I have this aching void of grief inside and I'm just ...' Phoebe stopped. Rory's large brown eyes were wide, staring at her, his eyebrows raised. Slightly disconcerted by his expression Phoebe began again. 'Its not that I don't like you, I do, I like you a lot ...' she trailed off; his mouth was hanging open now. 'Maybe if circumstances were different, maybe in time, you and I could have something, you know, maybe we could have a relationship ...'

'Stop!' Rory raised his hand and laughed. 'I think you're trying to play poker in the wrong saloon, cowgirl.'

'Sorry?'

Rory wrapped the last quarter of the sandwich he'd been eating back in tinfoil, put it in the rucksack and turned to face her. 'I don't mean to rain on your rejection speech, and I think you're a lovely girl and all that too, but you ought to know that my intentions towards you have

245

never been that way inclined.'

'Oh.' Phoebe felt her face beginning to redden.

'I'm in a relationship right now and even if I wasn't you really wouldn't be my type.'

'Oh,' Phoebe said again.

'I have a very nice partner,' Rory continued, 'a paramedic in Kenmare called Bob.'

'Oh,' Phoebe said for the third time, and then, after a pause, 'Does that mean that you're –'

'Gay?' Rory laughed. 'Yes, I think the evidence so far stacks up to that.'

'No one told me.'

'Why would they?'

'I thought everything was open for gossip in Carraigmore. I would have thought a gay primary school teacher would have been the talk of the town.'

'Why? It's no one's business but my own.'

'But I can't even buy a packet of biscuits without it going round the town like wildfire. Surely the fact that Mr O'Brian from school has a boyfriend called Bob is a far more interesting bit of tittle-tattle in a small community.'

'It's really not that interesting,' Rory said. 'And it's not as if I'm the only gay in the village.'

'Who else?!'

'Well, for a start there's Swedish Jan. You know, the man in the Breton cap who sits in the snug with Sally O'Connell.'

'I thought he was her husband!'

Rory shook his head. 'No, he's heavily involved with Tony Murphy from the butcher's, has been for years, though everybody knows that Tony had a mad fling last year with Gavin from the filling station who's about to have a civil ceremony in a Kildare golf club with some fellow from Tralee. And then there's your woman who runs the Rainbow's End Gift Shop; she's a lesbian, she has a glamorous girlfriend up in Dublin who reads the news on the telly, and then there's my friend Declan who plays the fiddle in the band, he swings both ways – and I haven't even started on the football team.'

Now Phoebe's mouth was hanging open. 'Really? The football team? Are you serious?'

'No, I'm just pulling your leg about the football team – though I do have my suspicions about a couple of them – but everything else is true, and I'm sure there're others I've forgotten to mention.'

'I'm sorry to have jumped to the wrong conclusion,' she said. 'It was just that you've been so kind that I just sort of assumed you had some sort of alternative motive.'

Rory smiled at her. 'No, I just thought you were a nice person who's obviously had a rough time and I like your company.' He paused, looking out at the misty horizon. 'You spoke about an aching void a few minutes ago,' he said after a few moments. 'I know that feeling, that terrible emptiness inside, breath-taking pain that you try to run away from but it doesn't matter how far you go it just follows you and won't let go.'

'You've lost someone too?' asked Phoebe gently, Rory nodded. 'Do you want to talk about it?'

After a long pause Rory spoke. 'His name was Owen; he described himself as being built like two scrum halves sewn together – he was big and burly and Welsh, hilariously funny and absolutely gorgeous. We met at a Celtic language convention when I was teaching in Dublin; he was a teacher too, in Aberystwyth. He taught geography and we found we shared a passion for rocks and rivers and sea and Elvis. We both loved climbing. We spent every holiday together, travelled the world in between term-time, planned our ascent of Everest, and gave the Holyhead ferry a lot of business at the weekends. We talked about marriage when they made it legal over here, we planned the day right down to our outfits: I wanted to wear gold lamé like Elvis on his 1959 album

247

cover while Owen wanted to be in black leathers like Elvis's 1968 TV appearance. We'd even found a website that could make the trousers big enough to fit around Owen's gigantic thighs! We thought we'd say our vows in Welsh and Irish. I was sure we'd spend the rest of our lives together, I had a fantasy that we'd have children one day – he'd have been a wonderful father.' Rory stopped speaking. Phoebe put her arm around him. 'I haven't been able to listen to Elvis since I lost him,' he mumbled into her shoulder.

'Was his death very sudden?' she asked gently.

Rory disengaged himself. 'Oh no, he didn't die. We had a row, a ridiculous row about which Elvis film was his best – he said *Jailhouse Rock*, I said *Blue Hawaii*. It all got very personal and then he walked out and that was the last I ever saw of Welsh Owen – though I did hear that a few months later he was spotted climbing the mountains of Patagonia with a PE teacher from the Rhondda Valley – the same trip we had planned to make for our honeymoon.'

'I'm so sorry Rory, that's really sad.'

'I know it's not the same as what you must have gone through when your husband died, but to me the pain felt as bad as any grief I could imagine. I couldn't eat, I couldn't work; in the end I came back home to Carraigmore.'

'In a way it must have felt worse because you knew that Owen was happily trekking over South American mountains with another man while your heart was breaking over here.'

Rory wiped his eyes with the back of his hand. 'It was over eighteen months ago now – I can't believe it still makes me so upset. The sad thing is that I always liked *Jailhouse Rock*, I don't know why I had to make such a stand against it.' He straightened up and gave a small smile. 'I'm trying very hard to move on. I met Ben in Kenmare at Christmastime, and apart from the inconvenient shifts that he works we're very happy. He's blond-haired, blue-eyed, slinky hips, every boy's dream I'm sure; but, you know ...' Rory studied his hands in silence for a few seconds. 'He's more interested in clubbing than climbing mountains, and I'm sure he only comes surfing because he can show off his fantastic body in a wetsuit, and he once asked me if Elvis was that fellow in the white suit in *Saturday Night Fever*!' Rory shrugged again. 'He's a nice bloke but somehow he just isn't Welsh Owen.'

Phoebe squeezed his hand. 'How do your parents feel about you being gay?'

'They've been great, though I was terrified of telling them that I'd never be inclined to marry the buck-toothed girl on the farm next door like I knew they wanted me to. In fact it was your grandmother who persuaded me to come out in the first place.'

'How did she do that?' Phoebe raised her eyebrows.

'I was seventeen, trying to pretend I was the same as all the other lads, trying to flirt with the girls but always ending up having a good chat with them at the end of the evening rather than a snog. I suppose I knew I was gay but I sort of hoped I might grow out of it.

'I had been to see your grandmother to buy one of her pots for my mother's birthday. I took ages trying to decide which one, and in the end Anna disappeared and came back with a pot of tea and two enormous slices of fruit cake; she said she always had to have tea and cake in the afternoon, a leftover from her childhood.'

Phoebe nodded, 'Yes, I remember afternoon tea was always sacrosanct.'

'It was summer,' Rory continued. 'Anna had the doors at the front of the boathouse open and we sat in the sunshine eating the cake and drinking the tea. She asked me if I had a girlfriend and I suddenly found myself telling her about a massive crush I had on the brother of the buck-toothed girl next door.'

'What did she say?'

'She told me not to be ashamed of the person I was, not to try and hide my sexuality, to be proud of it rather than afraid. I can't tell you what a relief it was to finally talk to somebody about all the things that had been worrying me for so long. She died the following year, before I ever had a chance to thank her properly for giving me the confidence to be honest with myself as well as with everyone around me. She was a wise woman, it's a shame she had to go the way she did.'

'I wish she was still here now to tell me what to do,' said Phoebe quietly.

'She could have told you that you had no worries as far as my intentions towards you are concerned.' Rory laughed, and then was serious again. 'I remember she told me that someone she once knew had been gay, and that he had ended up ruining someone else's life in his attempts to hide it. I think that was when I realised I had to be honest with my parents.'

Phoebe bit her lip, wondering if she could confide in him. 'I know who my grandmother was talking about.'

'Who?'

Phoebe leaned back on the warm stone of the dolmen, her head supported on one hand. Rory leant back too so that he was facing her, and she began to tell him Anna's story. She felt as though she was outlining the plot of a novel or a film, not the real-life events that had happened to her relative more than sixty years before. Rory listened in silence occasionally letting out a little gasp, or widening his eyes in surprise.

'Then what happened?' he asked as Phoebe reached the part where Michael had asked Anna to go to France with him.

'I don't know,' said Phoebe. 'There are only two diaries left, but when I got home last night – all ready for

250

my next instalment – they weren't where I thought I'd left them. I put the diaries I'd already read back under the floorboards, but I'd left the last two on the windowsill. I searched and searched but I couldn't find them anywhere.'

'You've got to find them!' exclaimed Rory. 'I can't wait to find out if Anna and her artist ever made it to Paris. And how did she end up living in the African bush with the gay doctor?'

'Yes, that's the really weird thing. Why did she go to Africa and why did she stay with Gordon for so long? The stories I remember being told about him made him out to be some sort of saint. My father adored him and I always imagined that Anna did too.'

'I wonder why she didn't just run away with Michael when she had the chance?'

'I'm sure the diaries hold the key. I can't have simply lost them – it's not as though the room is exactly large!'

'You don't think …?' Rory looked aghast.

Phoebe nodded.

'A theft in Carraigmore?'

Phoebe nodded again.

'Dum dum duuuummm …' Rory hummmed dramatically.

'I'm being serious. I think someone has taken them.'

'There are no burglars in Carraigmore and if there were I'm sure they'd be after your cash or that nice lace blouse of yours rather than old diaries. And how would they have got in without breaking a window or kicking down the door?'

'The key is kept under a stone in the garden – anyone could get in if they wanted to!'

'Ooooh, don't tell the Neighbourhood Watch Committee – they'll just say you were asking for a trouble. Anyway I'm sure they've just fallen down the side of the bed or something.'

'I've checked, they are not down the side of the bed!'

Rory looked at his watch.

'Well, I'd love to solve mysteries all day with you, Nancy Drew, but I have a band practice with the boys in half an hour; we're playing at Fibber's tonight. Will you be there?'

'I have a night off. I might just stay at home to catch up on my sleep.'

'That's a shame; Ben is coming and I'd love you to meet him.'

Phoebe started to pack the remains of their picnic away in Rory's rucksack and slipped the red coat back on. 'Maybe I'll try and come, just for a little while. I wouldn't want to miss the chance of seeing the ambulance-driving Adonis.'

Rory laughed. 'You can keep an eye on Swedish Jan for me. I'm afraid Jan has taken a bit of a liking to Ben. He likes to tell him risqué stories about his time in the Swedish Merchant Navy.'

'I wouldn't have thought you'd have much competition from Swedish Jan, unless Ben has a thing for bushy beards and a paunch.'

They walked back along a track that led them inland – crossing the gorse-splashed moor, the sea behind them, craggy grey outcrops on each side. They headed towards the distant spires of Carraigmore – the two churches were clearly visible between a band of trees, one at each end of the town, although now only the Catholic church remained a place of worship. The sight of the redundant Anglican spire prompted Phoebe to wonder if Sally O'Connell in the Arts and Craft Centre knew anything about Michael. Had he gone on to become a professional painter or had he simply stayed a teacher in a rural primary school?'

'Don't you think your sister might have some information?' Rory said as though he'd read her mind. 'She must remember more about your father and Anna than you do.'

'I can't ask her; we've fallen out and I don't think she wants anything more to do with me.'

'Why?' Rory looked surprised. 'I can't imagine you could have done anything that bad.'

Phoebe briefly considered telling him the truth about her relationship with David but couldn't seem to find a way to start. 'Oh, you know how families are, little things blow up into all-out war at the drop of a hat.'

'Tell me about it. My cousins haven't spoken for years because one of them won the Carraigmore Donkey Derby in 1999 and failed to split the €40 winnings with his brother who owned the champion donkey in the first place. They didn't even ask each other to their weddings years later.' Rory then went on to regale Phoebe with tales of various relatives seemingly innocent misdemeanours that had resulted in family feuds that only went on to confirm to Phoebe that her affair with a married man would be really shocking, let alone the deception in which she'd now unwittingly embroiled the entire village.

They reached the crossroads where Rory would take the road back to his parents' farm where Na Buachaillí Trá were meeting up for band practice.

'Will you be all right?' asked Rory. 'I mean with the phantom diary thief lurking around.'

Phoebe smiled, 'If they strike again I'll call you.'

'You do that and I'll slip into my Batman costume and be with you in a flash.'

'With Ben as Robin?'

'He'd look very fetching in a pair of tights!'

Phoebe laughed and gave Rory a kiss goodbye before taking the road that led through town.

Sunday afternoon sleepiness pervaded the high street, even the pub was shut, though a plume of smoke that rose from behind it suggested that Fibber might be trying to clear the overgrown yard for the summer beer garden he seemed always to be talking about. Only the Art and Craft Centre had an open door. Phoebe stepped inside.

Sally O'Connell emerged from a display of Aran jumpers. She had them artfully cascading out of piles of wicker baskets and draped across a circular table. Beside the table, a dressmaker's dummy was dressed in an Aran jumper, plus a matching waistcoat and a scarf. As Phoebe entered Sally was hanging a large St Brigid's Cross pendant around the dummy's headless neck.

'It adds that certain *je ne sais quoi* to the *ensemble*, don't you think?' Sally turned to smile at Phoebe.

'Um, yes. I'm sure the tourists will love it.'

Sally seemed happy with the response and stepped away from the display to admire it from a distance.

'I take so much pride in my displays, Phoebe. To me they are like small works of art, sculpture – or installations, to coin a more contemporary phrase.'

'Mmm,' said Phoebe thinking about Tracey Emin and wondering if a few knitted expletives hanging over it would win the great mound of knitwear the Turner Prize.

'It's my one creative outlet,' went on Sally. 'I do so envy you artistic types. I'd love to have been blessed with a talent like your grandmother's, and you yourself have been spotted several times with a sketchbook and a box of charcoal crayons.'

'Have I?'

'Why yes. Only the other day someone saw you on the cliff path drawing a sprig of candytuft, and that was a lovely little sketch you did of the view from the top of the lane down to the beach.'

Phoebe started to ask who could possibly have noticed her, as both times she was sure that she had been alone, but Sally interrupted.

'I must say red suits you better than I ever would have thought.' She touched the sleeve of Phoebe's coat. 'Did you have a nice walk with the schoolteacher up on the headland? You certainly had the weather with you. Aren't we having a wonderful spring? Now, tell me, have you decided whether you need a seat on the coach to go to see the William Flynn exhibition next November?'

'I'm sorry, I just can't think that far ahead at the moment, but I do have a question to ask you. I wondered if you know anything about a painter called Michael who lived here in the 1940s. I'm sorry I don't know his surname, but I know he was a schoolteacher in the village and he did a lot of oil paintings of the sea and beach.'

Sally started to arrange a display of books, fanning them out in a circle. She stopped. 'The only painter I've ever heard of living here at that time was William Flynn himself. He worked at the school for a year or so before leaving Ireland for France.'

'But you've never heard of a Michael?'

Sally shook her head slowly, her brows knitted in thought. 'But now that I think about it, William Flynn always signed his name William M. Flynn.'

Phoebe could feel her heart beginning to quicken. 'Could M have been for Michael? Is there any way I could find out?'

'Of course.' Sally stared, searching through her book display. 'Only last week I ordered this new book about him, it's come out prior to the exhibition.' She seemed torn between her desire to find the book and her desire to keep the circular display tidy, but at last she eased out a large hardback and laid it on top of a pile of Irish cookery books. William M. Flynn was written in white letters across a close-up of dark and swirling brushstrokes and then the title: *Portraits of the Atlantic Ocean*. Phoebe tried to steady her breathing as she began to flick through the glossy pages, starting from the back. Seascape after seascape, night and day, grey and blue and green, all executed in the same vibrant style. Some paintings

255

included tiny sailing boats or ships tossed and battered by gigantic storms, some included snatches of coast line: cliffs rising out of crashing waves, water spraying flecks of white across grey stone, the red stripes of lighthouses looming on dark horizons.

Occasionally there was a suggestion of a tumbledown cottage on a cliff edge or a herd of sheep precariously grazing on a coastal overhang. It seemed, so obviously, the west coast of Ireland. Then the painting she'd bought the post card of, the suggestion of a figure on the beach – it looked brighter in the book, more vivid. Phoebe continued on flicking backwards through the book. She noticed that the artist's earlier work appeared to have been done on the east coast of America – *Lobsterpots off Maine, Winter Storm in Cape Cod Bay* – but the very earliest pictures were set in France – *Breton Fishing Boats, Sunset Over Isle de Batz*. And then suddenly, on the first page, something different: a pastel drawing of a figure on a beach – a girl standing on a rocky promenade looking out to sea, her coat was scarlet and a little terrier sat obediently at her feet. *Girl from Carraigmore* the caption beside it read.

'You can see why they are so coveted by collectors.' Sally peered over Phoebe's shoulder, 'Such strength of line, such confidence with colour. And to think he used to live in Carraigmore, I just wish he'd done more paintings while he was here; we could have had them as framed prints, I'm sure they'd be very popular.'

Phoebe wasn't really listening. She flicked through the pages to the back to find his biography. It was all there: William Michael Flynn, born in County Galway in 1928, sixth son of a tenant farmer, also named William Flynn, trained at the National College of Art and Design. Phoebe ran her finger down the list of dates. 1948–1949, teacher in Carraigmore School. 1950, moved to Paris. Not until 1950? It had been June 1949 when he had first asked Anna to go away to France with him, why had he delayed so long? Phoebe skimmed quickly down the rest of the biography. After Paris he had spent a few years in Brittany, followed by a spell in St Ives before settling for many years on the East Coast of America, and then returning to Ireland in the early 1990s. Phoebe was surprised to see that he hadn't married till the late 1960s – a fellow artist from New York – but the marriage had been short-lived, ending in divorce. There was no reference to any children.

'I wonder if it's possible to go and visit him,' Phoebe murmured, hardly aware that she'd said it out loud.

'Oh, no, dear.' Sally still hovered at her shoulder. 'He died two years ago.'

Phoebe heard a gasp and realised it had escaped from her own mouth.

'Well, he was over eighty,' Sally continued. 'They found him in the studio of his little house in Donegal, still painting up until the very end. It was the main story on the RTE news; he was so well loved in Ireland. Of course his death pushed the prices of his paintings up sky-high.'

Only two years ago. Phoebe wished she'd found out about him sooner, she longed to talk to him about Anna, to ask him what had happened in the end. She turned to the front few pages of the book to see the sketch of the girl on the beach at Carraigmore; it had to be the drawing that Anna mentioned in the diary. Phoebe looked down at the coat she had been wearing all day, looking back at the red coat in the picture. She wondered if it could possibly be the same one.

Sally had moved away, distracted by a sheep that had fallen from its allocated shelf space onto the floor. Phoebe started to close the book but stopped. A narrow black and white photograph caught her attention. It was on the inside of the dust jacket: *Photograph of the artist, Concarneau, Brittany 1953*. Michael leant genially against a fishing

257

boat, shirtsleeves rolled up above his elbows, a cigarette smouldering in his paint-stained hands. He was smiling straight at the photographer. Phoebe felt her heart lurch at the sight of the handsome face, the intense dark eyes, the mop of curly hair; she knew this face, had kept it safe inside her memory all these years, treasuring it, hardy daring to recall it in case she wore the memory out – this was her father, her father's smile and unkempt hair, the eyes you didn't want to turn away from.

'Are you all right, Phoebe?' Sally had a hand on Phoebe's shoulder. 'You've gone quite pale; in fact you look like you've just seen a ghost.'

Chapter Twenty-three

Phoebe left the gallery and walked slowly down the road. She vaguely realised that the mid-afternoon sun had become quite warm, but she was far too deep in thought to think about taking off the coat. She wondered what Gordon Brennan had felt about bringing up another man's child. She remembered being told long ago that Anna had refused to send her son home to boarding school. Instead he had gone to the local Nigerian school, with extra tuition from a Baptist missionary that lived nearby. As a child, Phoebe had assumed it was from love of her son that Anna kept him with her, but maybe Gordon had refused to pay. Or maybe Anna really couldn't bear to be parted from the child of the man she had loved so much.

Yellow tulips had replaced the daffodils in the terracotta pots outside the boathouse; the cup-shaped flowers swayed in a warm breeze, waving in welcome as Phoebe arrived home. She opened the door ready for another search for Anna's missing diaries.

Her foot was on the first step when she saw the envelope in front of her, propped up against the fifth stair, exactly where she would see it as she started to climb up to the flat. It was decorated with a picture of a large green dragon, wings outspread, at its feet a small blonde-haired figure and a wild-haired man stood with wonky smiles and dots for eyes. A child's hand had written 'Feebee' at the top, which had then been crossed out and replaced with 'Phoebe' in an adult's slanting scrawl.

Phoebe picked it up. Opening it, she found a paper heart folded into two. It was an invitation, formally worded in glittery blue ink with the same slanting, slightly scrawling writing.

Honey and Theo Casson request the pleasure of the company of Miss Phoebe Brennan for lemonade and homemade cake on the terrace of the Castle at 4 p.m. on Sunday.

Phoebe smiled, surprised at the little burst of happiness the invitation gave her. She looked at her phone. Half past three. Her search for Anna's diaries would have to wait. She decided that the occasion called for something more than jeans and a T-shirt, and, digging in a drawer of Anna's clothes, pulled out a floral dress she hadn't noticed before. She held it up against her; it was very long – what had been probably just below the knee for her grandmother was mid-calf for Phoebe. She stripped off her clothes and slipped the dress over her head, enjoying the fluidity of the fabric against her bare skin. It needed ironing, the pattern of daisies looked scrunched, and the hem hung unevenly. Phoebe pulled out the skirt and swished it, spinning around in a full circle so that it billowed out like a bell. It was very pretty.

The dress screamed out for high-heeled strappy sandals, or maybe a wedge or a peep-toe. For Phoebe the choice was boringly easy: her clumpy biker boots, that was all she had.

She looked at herself in the huge mirror on the wall. She thought of Anna and wondered if she had put on the same dress and admired herself in the same mottled glass? Had William Michael Flynn stood beside her and told her she looked beautiful in the dress? She gave a shiver. It was suddenly too much to contemplate, as if everything she thought she knew about her past had changed, as if she had changed, had different blood swirling in her veins, making her a different person.

She picked up her phone to check the time. She'd have to hurry, she didn't want to disappoint Theo and Honey by being late. She had no iron; the creases would just have to fall out by themselves.

Snatching up a cardigan she started to descend the stairs. Midway she stopped. She turned back, lifted Anna's wide straw hat from its peg, pulled it down onto her curls and full of sudden energy ran up the lane to the Castle.

She could see the table set with tea things as she climbed the flight of stone steps leading to the terrace. A teapot, jug, and three striped mugs were gathered around the glass cake stand. On top of the stand stood a magnificent cake, golden yellow and glistening with a sugar crust.

Honey appeared through the French windows carrying a stack of plates. She saw Phoebe and immediately ran back inside. Phoebe could hear her shouting into the echoing hallway.

'She's here, Daddy. She's here.'

Minutes passed with no sign of Honey or her father. Phoebe leant against a lichen-mottled balustrade and admired the view. It was not that dissimilar from the view that she and Rory had looked at from the top of the dolmen only a few hours before: the sea, the distant mountains, the bright blue sky. Poncho ambled out of the kitchen door and came to sniff Phoebe's feet. Someone had tied a red and white scarf around his neck. Phoebe crouched down and patted his sleek black coat.

'Here she is, Daddy. Doesn't she look pretty?' Phoebe hadn't heard Theo and Honey's approach. Poncho turned to his master and Phoebe straightened up. Honey had changed into a sequined party dress and Theo was clean-shaven with a fresh white shirt and his unruly hair slicked back.

'Yes,' Theo sounded rather awkward. 'Nice dress. And the hat, it's very ...'

'No biscuit crumbs in my hair today,' Phoebe interrupted as he searched for the word.

'I knew you'd come,' said Honey slipping her hand into Phoebe's. 'Daddy said you wouldn't but I told him that you would. He didn't want to shave and he said putting on a clean shirt would be a waste of time, and I said it wouldn't be a waste of time, and making the cake definitely wouldn't be a waste of time because we could eat it even if you didn't turn up, but you have turned up.' She looked up at her father with sparkling eyes, 'So you see, Daddy, she didn't probably have better things to do after all!'

Theo pushed his hands into his trouser pockets and looked at his feet. 'I saw you walking up the beach with Rory O'Brian this morning. I expected you'd be gone all day,' he muttered.

'Daddy said I could do anything I wanted today,' went on Honey, jumping from one foot to the other with excitement. 'And I said that I wanted to have you to tea and make a lemon cake, and to eat it outside, and then I want us all to watch *Harry Potter*, and for you to stay until it's time for me to go to bed.'

Phoebe smiled down at the pretty face. 'I'm honoured.'

'Come on,' Honey was impatient to get them to sit down. 'Oh, we haven't got a knife to cut the cake. I'll go and get one and I'll see if the kettle has boiled yet, and I forgot to bring the plates back out.' She ran into the house leaving Phoebe and Theo facing each other across the wrought-iron table. Phoebe took off the hat, suddenly feeling self-conscious in it.

Theo sighed. 'When I said she could do anything she wanted I had expected her to say she fancied going swimming in Sneem or a trip to McDonald's in Killarney. You've no idea how long it took to bake that cake. There's an earlier attempt in the bin and one in the dog. I just hope our last effort tastes all right.' He ran his hand across his face as though exhausted by the whole experience.

Phoebe raised her eyebrows. 'I'm so sorry, I hope you haven't had to put yourself out too much on my account.'

'No. No, of course not.' Theo looked uncomfortable. 'I didn't mean to sound disgruntled.' Phoebe resisted the urge to say that that would make a change. 'Hosting tea parties isn't exactly my forte, I usually left that sort of thing to Maeve.' He picked up an empty mug and started absentmindedly turning it around in his hand as though thoroughly absorbed in its vertical blue-and-white-striped decoration. After a few seconds he put the mug down and seemed to study Phoebe in much he same way as he'd studied the mug. 'That dress suits you. I especially like it with those chunky boots.'

'Really?'

Theo nodded. 'And the pale blue flowers bring out the colour of your eyes.'

Phoebe smoothed the floral fabric across her knee. 'It was my grandmother's.'

'I remember her style of dress being rather more ethnically inclined. I always think of her in multi-coloured scarves and shawls, and she had one of those Indian skirts with little mirror decorations and elaborate embroidery that fascinated me as a child.'

'I think she would have worn this dress many years before you knew her, maybe even before she went to Africa.' Phoebe hesitated, toying with the idea of telling him about Anna and her affair with Michael Flynn; she was still bursting with the excitement of realising that the famous artist was her grandfather.

Theo picked up the mug again. 'This was made by Anna.'

'I thought you must have made it; like the dress it doesn't seem to be her style.'

He smiled. 'I think she was going through a bit of a creative crisis at the time, trying to break away from the heavy stoneware pots she'd learned to make in Africa. She must have made these just before she started to develop the celadon glazes. I remember how she experimented with blue and white stripes and spotty patterns using a traditional Dutch technique.'

'Delftware?' asked Phoebe.

'Yes, very like delftware – tin and cobalt glazes on earthenware or porcelain. My mother bought a set of eight mugs from her, these three are the only ones that remain.'

Phoebe picked one up as well. Turning it over she saw her grandmother's initials stamped into the unglazed foot-ring: A.B. Phoebe lightly touched the mark. When she looked back up Theo's eyes were watching her again, their colour seemed darker than usual, as vivid and intense as Anna's cobalt glaze.

She picked up another mug and tried to avoid his gaze. 'I like the blue and white, I'm sure it could be used for some lovely contemporary decorations.'

'Why don't you have a go yourself?' Theo asked. 'You could decorate that pot you threw the other day. I can mix the glazes for you and show you how to apply them,' he paused. 'And I promise I won't try to leap on you this time.'

Phoebe felt her cheeks redden. She tried to say she'd like that, meaning the pot decorating, but her voice faltered as she realised it sounded as though she were saying she'd like to be leapt on, so instead she made a comment about the weather and then a silence fell between them. Theo lit a cigarette and Phoebe studied the pattern on her dress and wished that she still smoked.

The chink of china heralded a welcome diversion. They both turned to watch Honey's progress across the terrace. The sequins on her dress glittered in the afternoon sun so that she appeared to be shimmering her way towards them like some sort of fairy child. As she got nearer they could see that a large bread-knife was slithering about precariously on top of the pile of plates she was carrying.

Honey put the plates onto the table with a clatter.

'This was the only knife I could find.' She wielded the bread knife in the air and stared hacking into the cake with a flagrant disregard for the danger of sharply corrugated blades.

'Shall I do that?' said Phoebe, taking the knife from Honey.

'And I'll go and make us all a pot of tea,' said Theo, picking up the teapot and disappearing into the house.

Any awkwardness between Theo and Phoebe was soon dispersed by Honey's constant chatter.

'I love lemon drizzle cake; I love the taste of lemons, but why can't lemon fruits be nice to eat on their own? You know, like oranges, why can't they be sweet like oranges? I'm sure if they were, the people that make the lemons would sell loads more.'

'No one makes lemons, darling,' said Theo. 'They grow on trees.'

'I *know* that. I mean the people who make the lemon trees could sell loads more of them. I'm sure it can't be that hard to make sweet lemon trees, after all they invented those sweet potatoes for people who thought that ordinary potatoes were boring. Do you want more cake, Phoebe?'

'Just another little slice. It really is delicious, well worth all the hard work you both put in.'

'Did Daddy tell you that he burnt the first one, and Poncho stole the next when it was cooling on the wire rack, and then Daddy said there was no way he was making another bloody cake for you and stomped off saying lots of words I'm not allowed to say, and I had to do this cake nearly all by myself!'

Phoebe looked at Theo. He gave a small shrug – Phoebe had to restrain a laugh.

For the rest of the afternoon they sat on the terrace and talked and drank and ate three-quarters of the cake between them, until Phoebe felt awash with tea and lemon-sponge and a cool breeze coming from the sea made her wish that she had brought the red coat.

'It's getting cold,' said Theo. 'I think it's time to go inside.' He stood up and started to clear away the plates.

'That means it's time for *Harry Potter*,' cried Honey jumping up. 'I'll go and put it on.'

'Hang on.' Theo put a restraining hand on his daughter's arm. 'Maybe Phoebe has to go, she might need to work tonight or she might need a rest after being with such a chatterbox all afternoon.'

Phoebe smiled at Honey, 'I'm not working tonight, and I don't need a rest, so if it's all right with your dad I'd love to watch *Harry Potter* with you.'

'It is all right, isn't it, Daddy?' asked Honey tugging on her fathers shirt. 'You want to watch the film with Phoebe too, don't you?'

Theo grinned down at her. 'Yes, I think that would be very nice.'

The three of them sat, squashed together, on the sofa in the room that Honey and Theo used as a living room. Poncho lay, prostrate and snoring, at their feet. The room looked much tidier than when Phoebe had seen it before, and the late afternoon sun coming through the long windows gave the yellow walls a warming, golden hue.

Honey supplied a running commentary throughout the film, she claimed to have seen it over one hundred times and was eager to tell Phoebe exactly what was about to happen in every scene.

After the film, Theo made them hot dogs which they ate while they watched the complementary DVD about how the film was made. When that was finished Honey disappeared into her bedroom, re-emerging with a box that she proudly called her beautician's kit. Theo groaned.

'It's not time for my pedicure again, is it?'

'No, don't be silly, Daddy. You've still got spotty toenails from yesterday. Today I want to paint Phoebe's fingernails.'

Phoebe tried to hide her hands. 'You can do my toenails, Honey, but not my fingers, they are much too short to do anything with.' Since David had died she'd found herself reverting to her teenage habit of biting her nails down to the quick. She saw Theo glance at them and noticed that his own nails were badly bitten too.

Honey seemed to be content with Phoebe's toenails and spent a long time delicately decorating them with little daisies to match the daisies on Phoebe's dress. Theo disappeared to wash up and returned with three steaming mugs of hot chocolate and a packet of Kimberly biscuits.

'Rumour has it they're your favourites.' He smiled at her as he opened the cellophane wrapping.

'They're my favourites too.' Honey's face was painted with a chocolaty grin. She snuggled sleepily into Phoebe's side. 'I've had a lovely day,' she sighed.

'I think it's time for bed now,' said Theo gently. 'Go and put your pyjamas on and then I'll come in and read to you. What's it to be tonight? *Pippi Longstocking* or *The Water Horse*?'

'No.' Honey sprang up, suddenly wide awake again. 'I can't go to bed; I haven't straightened Phoebe's hair yet.' She picked up the straighteners and rushed to the wall to plug them in.

'I'm sure Phoebe doesn't want all her curls made straight,' protested Theo.

'It's all right,' said Phoebe. 'She can do it if she wants to; I've never had my hair straightened. It might be fun to have a new hairstyle, if you don't mind her going to bed a bit late.'

'You're a glutton for punishment,' laughed Theo. 'But

267

as long as I don't have to have it done to me again you can keep Honey up as long as you like.' He gathered up the empty cocoa mugs and disappeared back down to the kitchen.

Phoebe sat obediently on a stool while Honey, tongue protruding through the gap in her teeth in concentration, pulled the straighteners through her hair section by section. Every now and then Phoebe touched a straightened strand; there was no mirror so all she could do was marvel at the smooth silkiness and hope she didn't look too ridiculous.

Honey stood back to admire her finished work and let out a small gasp, 'You look like my mum!'

Phoebe didn't quite know what to say, the smile she had been wearing froze on her face, she touched her hair again and remembered Katrina's face when she had put her hair up on her head, *you look like Maeve*, she'd said; she had been shocked.

'Are you finished transforming poor Phoebe yet?' Theo walked into the room and stopped. He stared at Phoebe, mouth slightly open, his eyes wide with surprise.

'Doesn't she look like Mummy?' Honey said. 'Doesn't she look like Mummy when she had her hair down in the mornings?'

Theo didn't speak, he just continued to stare.

'I'm sorry.' Phoebe stood up. 'Maybe it's time for me to leave'

Theo shook his head slightly as though coming out of a trance.

'It's all right, it's just you do look remarkably like Maeve. I hadn't seen the likeness before; I'm just a bit taken aback. For a moment I thought you were her.' He turned on the light switch. 'The room was very gloomy; I think the evening light was playing tricks.'

Honey wrapped her arms around Phoebe's waist.

'I wish you were her,' she mumbled into the silky fabric of the dress.

Theo took her gently by the arm. 'Come on, sweetheart, time for bed.'

'Will you come for tea again?' Honey's eyes were shiny with un-spilt tears.

Phoebe glanced at Theo, he nodded slightly and smiled. 'We'd like that,' he said quietly.

'Then of course I will, and maybe next time I'll help you bake the cake.'

Theo laughed. 'Please do, I don't think I can go through that experience again.'

'We'll have to remember to keep Poncho out of the kitchen!' Phoebe bent and kissed Honey lightly on the cheek.

'Wait here,' said Theo. 'I've got a present for you, when I get back.' And he took his daughter's hand in his and left Phoebe alone in the room.

She walked over to the window and looked out, wondering what Theo had to give her. The darkness outside took her by surprise; she could see her reflection in the window, without her mane of curls she hardly recognised herself at all. She tilted her head; did she really look so like Theo's dead wife? Phoebe shivered and tried to ruffle up her hair; it fell back, straight around her shoulders like a thick auburn curtain.

Phoebe set off to find a bathroom. Beneath the magnificent staircase she found a small cloakroom, fitted with an old-fashioned, high-cistern toilet and a white china sink. Turning on the brass taps she filled the sink with water, submerged her head and then dried it with a hand-towel, scrunching up her hair as she did so, trying to bring her curls back to life.

Back in the living room, Phoebe found Theo lighting a fire. She watched him from the doorway for a little while; his broad back hunched over the grate as he coaxed driftwood and old newspaper into flames. Phoebe walked up to the mantelpiece and touched one of the marble monkeys climbing up the side.

'I used to love those monkeys as a child,' Theo said as he straightened up to face her. 'Oliver and I would spend hours giving them names and making up stories about them. We once got into terrible trouble for trying to hack one off with a hammer. We had a notion they might come alive. Look, you can still see the marks we made in the marble.' Theo pointed at two large chips around a monkey's sailor hat.

'What vandals you were!' Phoebe laughed. 'You and your brother must have been a real handful.'

'It was Oliver, he continually lead me astray!'

Phoebe made a face of disbelief.

'Your curls are back,' said Theo.

Phoebe ran her fingers through her damp hair. 'It didn't feel right without them.'

'I hope I didn't upset you by saying that you looked like Maeve.'

'No, it's all right; I just hope it didn't upset Honey. She must miss her mother very much.'

Theo bent down again and prodded the fire with a poker, the driftwood crackled and the comforting smell of peat smoke drifted into the room.

'It doesn't seem to get much easier for either of us.' Theo stood up and looked at Phoebe. 'But you must know all about it. Fibber told me that you lost your husband last year.' Phoebe flinched inside – *husband*, she was getting to hate that word, she wished she'd been honest about her relationship with David from the beginning. 'Is that why you came to Carraigmore?' Theo continued, 'to get away?'

'That was one of the reasons,' said Phoebe. 'I just couldn't live in a place that held so many memories.'

Theo looked around him, 'That's how I feel about staying here. It's not just about the cost of running this place, it's all the ghosts that seem to constantly jump out at me, making me remember Maeve when all I want to do is forget her and feel better.'

'But you'll never forget her. She was your wife, you had a child together, that was more than I had with David.' Phoebe looked down at the dancing flames and wondered just how much she had had with David, it wasn't as if they'd ever made a home or had a baby. She'd always imagined that one day they'd have shared those things but lately she'd begun to wonder if that really would have happened.

'Are you all right?' Theo raised his arm as if to touch her shoulder but stopped. 'I can understand if you don't want to talk about this, it must still be very raw for you.'

'I'm all right. I think I'm learning to live with the grief, accepting it as a part of who I am now.'

'Maybe that's what I need to do, accept the pain and not run away from it.'

'Yes,' Phoebe said quietly. 'And maybe Honey needs to know it's all right to feel upset, that it's all right to feel pain and that the other people and places that she loves will still be there for her.'

'I think you're trying to tell me that moving from here would be a bad thing for her.'

Phoebe shrugged. 'That's just my opinion.'

Theo sighed. 'Even if you're right there's still the problem of lack of money; this place deserves more care than I can afford to give it. The Castle is a beautiful house but it's much too big for one lonely potter and his sad little girl.'

'There must be something you can do,' said Phoebe.

'I'm afraid there isn't. I have developers coming next week with plans to make it into a hotel – one of those luxury ones the recession doesn't seem to touch; they have a chain of them across the country. I can't turn down the kind of money they're talking about; I have to think of Honey's future as well as my own.'

Phoebe felt her heart contract; she didn't want the

271

Castle to become a hotel. It had been a home for so long: her grandmother's home, Theo's home, Honey's home, it wasn't right that it should become a part of a soulless chain catering for a stream of wealthy tourists.

'Enough of this unhappy talk,' said Theo suddenly. 'I've still got to give you your present.'

'What is it?'

Without speaking Theo disappeared through the door leading into the hallway, within seconds he was back, with something small and round cradled between his large hands. As he reached Phoebe he held it out to her.

'Here. I want you to have this.'

Phoebe gasped, 'A moon jar!'

'I took it out of the kiln last night.'

Phoebe gazed at it as she took it from him; the pot was perfectly spherical, smaller than the previous ones she'd seen, its pale blue glaze as luminous as the moon she could see through the window.

'I don't deserve this.'

'You were very kind to come today and spend so much time with us.'

'I've enjoyed it; you don't need to thank me.'

Theo looked down at the fire. 'I also want to apologise for how rude I've been at times; you didn't deserve it. This last two years I've been like an ogre taking out my bad moods on anyone who happens to cross my path. I'm sorry for the times when that's been you.' He turned his head to face her and smiled. 'You're also very kind to let me keep working in the boathouse and I know how good you've been to Honey with her school work. I've been stubborn, refusing to see that you were right; she does have problems. I realise that now, and I'd be grateful for any help you can give her.'

Phoebe smiled. 'Thank you for the apology, and my present. I'll treasure it. And of course I'll help Honey. I'm very fond of her.'

'She's very fond of you,' Theo paused, then started to say something else but stopped. Instead he took the pot out of her hands and placed it on the mantelpiece. He turned back to face her. Neither of them spoke. Phoebe noticed how the fire cast moving shadows across his face, his eyes looked almost incandescent in the half light. She felt suddenly compelled to touch his cheek; her fingers moved to trace the outline of his mouth, he caught her hand in his and very gently kissed her palm. Phoebe felt her heart beating, a flutter of awakening somewhere deep inside; as he took a step towards her Phoebe instinctively raised her face to his, her lips already anticipating his kiss.

The sound of the phone was like an alarm clock shattering a dream. Theo dropped Phoebe's hand and took a step back.

'I'll leave it,' he said but they both stood motionless listening to the ringing until it stopped. It started to ring again immediately.

'You'd better get it,' Phoebe said. The phone was on a table on the other side of the room. As Theo walked across the carpet he might as well have been walking a thousand miles away from Phoebe. She could already see the door closing, the Theo who had been about to kiss her disappearing inside.

He had his back turned as he picked up the phone, she couldn't hear what he was saying, he mostly seemed to be listening, but she had a feeling it was not good news.

Theo said goodbye and turned to Phoebe, the phone still in his hand.

'That was Katrina, its Della Flannigan. She's had a heart attack and isn't expected to survive the night.'

Chapter Twenty-four

Against all expectations Della Flannigan did last the night – and the next one and then the next one after that – but for three full days she hovered between life and death, her face ashen against the white sheets of the intensive care ward.

Fibber was a constant presence at his mother's side, holding her hand, pressing her rosary beads into her fingers, begging her not to leave him, until on the fourth night Della Flannigan opened her eyes and told him not to be such a great eejit and to leave her in peace.

Because of Mrs Flannigan's illness it was deemed inappropriate to open the pub. Katrina travelled back and forth to Tralee Hospital several times a day, fretting about Fibber – taking him her homemade biscuits, trying to coax him to eat, encouraging him to change his clothes and go out for short walks around the hospital grounds.

With time on her hands, Phoebe wandered along the beach and over the moors, sketching shells and flowers, watching the puffins flying in and out of their burrows, and thinking about Theo.

'I'll see you soon,' he'd said, but now five days had passed and she hadn't seen him. She had been up to the Castle twice, but both times it had been deserted – no sign of Theo, Honey, or the dog. She knew that they had been to visit Mrs Flannigan – Katrina had told her that, she said that Honey had been terribly upset; the hospital brought back too many memories of the time her mother spent there.

'Is hard,' Katrina said. 'What is the thing that is best? For Honey to see her granny or keep her away and she never get to say goodbye if it is the worst that happens?'

Rory came to see Phoebe on the Friday evening after he had finished at school. They scrambled up onto the cliff path and walked in the opposite direction this time. Phoebe was distracted by the hope that Theo might heave into view at any time.

They turned a corner and there was the Castle ahead of them; in the late afternoon sun it looked sedately still. The Virginia creeper sheathed the towers in brilliant green and made it look like the embodiment of a stately home. *The Americans will love it*, Phoebe thought. Looking down she could see where they'd probably want to build the golf course, and the outbuildings would be perfect for some sort of luxury spa.

The day before she'd seen a soft-top Jaguar with a Dublin number plate parked outside the general store. With sinking heart she decided that it must be the developer's car; but then an elderly couple had appeared, dressed in matching slacks and fleeces. They got in the car and drove slowly up the high street to the strains of Lonnie Donegan in a most un-developer-like fashion, and Phoebe had been relieved.

'Let's just hope that Mrs Flannigan recovers,' Phoebe realised she hadn't been listening to Rory for ages; she tried hard to concentrate on his words. 'The pub wouldn't be the same without her. She's the queen of the fierce glare and pungent put-downs but we're all very fond of her.'

'How's Honey?' Phoebe asked.

Rory shook his head, 'She hasn't been in school this week. Theo phoned to say she's too upset.'

Phoebe sighed. 'Poor Honey.'

'If Mrs Flannigan dies and Theo sells the Castle he'll have Honey over in America with his mother in no time.'

Phoebe's heart lurched at Rory's words. She knew that Theo would go back to Dublin then, or even to America himself, and suddenly she realised that couldn't bear to think of that.

'You don't seem yourself.' Rory had stopped and was studying her face. 'Are you all right?'

'Oh, I'm fine.' Phoebe forced a smile. 'Grand – as you'd say round here!' She set off again along the path, Rory hurrying to catch her up.

'Did you ever find those diaries that you'd lost?' he asked.

'No, they seem to have completely disappeared.' Phoebe had begun to think she might have imagined the extra two exercise books in the pile.

Phoebe and Rory parted at the crossroads and Phoebe walked back to the boathouse across the fields instead of through the village. She wasn't in the mood for the chats she'd be bound to have to have with every other person that walked by.

Climbing over a stile she suddenly had an urge to run as fast as she could. Buttercups and daisies brushed against her bare legs and it wasn't until she came across the ruins of an ancient church that she stopped, leaning breathless against a crumbling wall. A movement startled her; a hare darted out from behind a gravestone, golden in the sunlight, white tail flashing in the long grass. Phoebe watched it until it vanished into the bushes and then she set off again, her footsteps following the track the hare had made.

Her route skirted the Castle's land and she noticed that the rhododendron bushes had burst into a haze of pink and purple flowers; from a distance they looked unreal – tissue paper blooms glued onto the waxy leaves. Phoebe climbed over a low wall to see the flowers better and in seconds she was lost inside the Castle grounds. Disconcerted by the thickness of the undergrowth and the height of once

277

carefully planted specimen trees she wandered on, sometimes fighting her way through brambles or clumps of willow, occasionally stumbling on a path that she would follow for a while before it disappeared into the bushes.

Large patches of gunnera grew around a muddy pond; it looked like a relic of a prehistoric time. Further on she came across a brick-lined cavern built into a bank of grass. She peered into the cavern's musty depths. Something from a television history programme came into her mind. It looked like the old ice-houses that the Victorians had built in order to join in the craze for ice creams and sorbets before freezers were available. She thought of Anna's diaries and suddenly felt cold. Could this have been the ice house where her great-grandfather had taken his own life? She backed away, a twig snapped underneath her foot, and the sound ricocheted around her in the silent air. A flock of crows flew up from a nearby tree, screeching as they flapped into the sky. Phoebe turned and started to run, blindly following an overgrown path. She passed a row of dilapidated greenhouses and was relieved to see the low slate roofs of barns and outhouses up ahead and the Castle's crenellated battlements silhouetted behind them in the bright sunshine.

Hot and out of breath she burst from the undergrowth into the open space of the courtyard to find half a dozen men in ties and rolled up shirtsleeves measuring the buildings and taking pictures. Theo stood slightly apart from them, hands in his jacket pockets, his expression grim. Phoebe took a few steps back and pressed herself the wall, hoping she hadn't been seen. Edging sideways she managed to get round to the back of the barn again and push her way through brambles until she found the driveway down to the lane.

Honey sat on the slipway playing with a lump of clay. As Phoebe approached she could see that the little girl was completely absorbed in making a dragon; it was lying down, head resting on scaly front legs, expression dejected, bulging eyes half closed.

'He looks sad,' Phoebe crouched down beside Honey.

'He is sad,' said Honey rolling clay between her hands to make a long, limp tail. She didn't look up. Phoebe sat down beside her.

'And what about you, Honey? How are you?'

There was a pause, then, 'I feel like the dragon.' Phoebe put her arm around Honey's shoulder. 'Daddy is selling the Castle to those horrible men in stripy shirts, Grandma is going to die, and I really don't want to go and live with my Granny Stick in America.'

'Granny Stick?'

'That's what I call her in my head; she's skinny and wizened and hard like an old stick washed up on the beach. But don't tell Daddy I call her that will you?'

'No, of course I won't, but you know it sounds as though your Grandma Della is getting a bit better.'

Phoebe took a piece of clay from the bag Honey had at her side. She started to mould a head and then a body, legs, tail, and finally little wings.

'You've made a dragon too,' Honey smiled up at her.

'Yes, but this one is a happy dragon, who's come to cheer up your sad one,' she made her model fly though the air and land beside Honey's. Phoebe put on a silly voice, 'Can you do the dragon rumba?' Honey laughed as Phoebe moved her dragon to a made-up tune; its wing fell off and Honey laughed harder.

'Looks like you two are having fun,' a shadow fell across them and Phoebe looked up into Theo's face.

'I've never seen a dragon dance before,' he said bending down to pick up the broken wing. He gently took the dragon out of Phoebe's hand and pressed it back together again.

'Have the men gone?' Honey asked, moving her own dragon away from Poncho's inquisitive nose.

279

'Yes, thank God, they've left at last. Back to Dublin in their oversized 4x4s; no doubt back to their oversized dinners, cooked by their undersized wives.'

'Did you sell it too them?' Honey's tone was deliberately indifferent, but Phoebe could tell she was putting on a brave façade.

Theo squatted down beside her. 'No,' he sighed. 'No, I didn't sell the Castle to them – not today.'

Honey put her arms around his neck and nuzzled into him.

'Good,' she mumbled. Theo disentangled himself from her grip and held her where he could look into her huge blue eyes with clarity.

'They made me an offer, but I haven't accepted yet. But Honey, that doesn't mean we not going to sell the Castle, it just means I'm thinking about their offer for a few days and then I might ...'

Honey shrugged free of Theo's grip. 'Whatever!' she interrupted, as indifferently as a stroppy teenager.

Theo let her go and Honey scrambled to her feet. 'Katrina says I can stay the night with her and Fibber at the pub. They've got all my overnight stuff there, so can I go?'

'I had thought we could go to Killarney for a McDonalds.'

Honey shook her head. 'Katrina makes homemade burgers and potato wedgies – much more healthy than McDonalds,' she turned and set off up the lane as fast as her grubby green baseball boots would let her.

'Do you want me to take you up there?' Theo called after her.

'No,' she shouted, and broke into a sprint, disappearing around the corner in seconds.

Theo sat down next to Phoebe, '*Whatever*,' he said wearily. 'Can you believe that, she's eight years old and she says "Whatever".'

'She's upset,' said Phoebe.

Theo ran his hand through his hair and looked out at the sea. 'I have no idea what to do for the best, no idea what to do for my own daughter.' He turned to Phoebe with a face that suddenly looked exhausted. 'Do you think I should go after her?'

'No, let her go. Katrina and Fibber will cheer her up. She probably needs a break; it must have been an emotional few days for you both.'

'Going to that hospital certainly felt like a big mistake – too many bad memories stalking the corridors. And if it was hard for me goodness knows how Honey felt.' He picked up a ball of clay and threw it, hard, across the beach. Poncho, delighted with the possibility of a game, jumped down onto the sand after it. 'What to do?' Theo drew his hand slowly down his face. Phoebe longed to comfort him just as she'd longed to comfort Honey when she'd found her perched on the black rock all those weeks before.

'Is it a good offer?' she asked.

He gave a brief laugh. 'Too bloody good, unfortunately.'

'I'm sure you'll know what the right thing is to do in the end.' She tried to compose her face into an expression of impassive concern, hoping he couldn't see that inside every inch of her longed to scream *Don't do it, don't sell the Castle; don't go away, don't leave me*.

'Come on,' Theo stood up. 'I need a distraction. What about decorating that pot of yours?' He held out his hand and pulled her up, Poncho, realising that the game of fetch had not materialised, jumped back onto the slipway and followed them into the boathouse.

Initially Phoebe's mind had been a blank; she couldn't think what she wanted to paint. The soft, unfired surface seemed too pure and perfect to sully with decoration. Three carefully mixed up jars of glaze were lined up

281

beside her, their raw colour more shades of grey than cobalt blue. Theo had given her a Japanese calligraphy brush to work with; its top was as thick as Phoebe's wrist, its end as pointed as a needle.

'It was Anna's brush,' Theo said. 'It's made of real white wolf hair.'

Phoebe tried to imagine her grandmother's long fingers gripping the bamboo handle, silver bracelets clinking together as she executed her brilliant brushstrokes.

'It's the kind of brush that Buddhist monks use to practice calligraphy,' said Theo. 'They let the letters and patterns flow out from their souls to leave a statement on the surface about themselves at that particular moment.'

'How very Zen,' said Phoebe, and gave the pot a spin on the decorating wheel.

'Why don't you get your sketchbook, there might be some inspiration for you in there.'

Phoebe turned around to face him, 'How do you know I have a sketchbook?'

Theo grinned and bent down to stroke his dog's sleek head, 'Poncho and I see all sorts on our walks.' He looked at Phoebe. 'We spotted you on top of the black rock only yesterday, thoroughly absorbed in drawing something.'

'Shells,' she said. 'I was drawing a collection of shells left behind after high tide.'

'Can I see?'

Phoebe hesitated, then slipped down from the high stool to fetch the sketchbook from the flat.

Theo looked at the small black book for a long time. Phoebe grew increasingly self-conscious as she watched him studying each page intensely. Eventually he reached the end.

He looked up. 'What were you doing teaching in a primary school when you could have been making a name for yourself as an illustrator?'

Phoebe shrugged, 'I got waylaid.'

'By what?'

'By life,'

Theo raised his eyebrows, 'Tell me more.'

Phoebe laughed. 'Well, first I got waylaid by a desire to get away from my bossy big sister, and then by a desire to travel the world, and in the end I suppose I got waylaid by David.'

He didn't comment on her answer but passed the sketchbook back. 'Would it be a help if I left you to it? I'll come back in an hour – give you some space to be creative on your own.'

Phoebe agreed and as the boathouse door closed behind him she took a deep breath and tried to imagine that she was a Buddhist monk.

When Theo returned he was carrying a brown paper bag. 'Dinner,' he said placing it down on the workbench and producing two cheese rolls, two Mars bars, a can of Fanta, and a bottle of Italian white. 'The best that Carraigmore has to offer at this time of day. Only the garage was open.'

He walked across to Phoebe and looked over her shoulder.' It's good,' he said, peering at the pot. 'In fact it's very good indeed.'

Phoebe leaned back and took another look at what she'd done; she'd used the sketches of the cow parsley as inspiration for an almost fantastical plant that thrust its way up from the base of the pot, five stems fanned out into delicate seed heads, tiny dots of blue circling each one like drops of dew.

'It's so simple,' Theo had bent down to study it, pushing the wheel around to get the overall effect. 'It has a touch of the Miros about it and a bit of the 1950s.' He turned his face to hers; Phoebe was aware how close they were, she could smell wood smoke and tobacco. Theo straightened up. 'Do you want to decorate another one?' He walked over to the shelves and took down one of his large bowls. 'Imagine what you could do with this,' he said, dipping it into a vat of white glaze and then placing it in front of her.

Phoebe painted a bird: simple, bold, surrounded by stylised leaves and berries.

'You have a wonderful confidence of line,' Theo said, as he replaced the bowl with a large jug.

'Are you sure you want me to paint all over your work?' Phoebe looked at the jug and decided *shells and seaweed*.

Theo grinned, 'Yes, I'm sure.' He took down another bowl. 'Are you up for one more? Then I'll let you stop and have something to eat – I promise.'

It was dark by the time Phoebe stopped painting. Theo hadn't kept his promise and Phoebe had been happy not to remind him of it. He kept producing more and more pots until she had decorated enough to fill the kiln and Theo, keen to see the finished results, insisted that he should start a firing immediately.

Phoebe went upstairs and fetched two mismatched glasses.

'The wine's for you,' Theo said over his shoulder, pointing as he packed the pots into the kiln. 'Mine's the can of Fanta; I haven't touched a drop of alcohol for weeks now.'

'I'm impressed,' Phoebe poured wine into one glass and some of the can into the other. She took a sip of her drink and grimaced.

Theo laughed. 'As I said, the best the garage had to offer.'

They were silent for a while as Phoebe watched him finish filling the kiln. He handled the pots so carefully – gently tipping each one to wipe the excess glaze from the base, and positioning them inside the cavernous metal box with the care and concentration that one might lavish on a small child at bedtime. His hair had fallen over one eye;

pushing it back he closed the kiln door.

'That's it; they're all tucked up safely.' He flicked a switch and the kiln jolted into life with a clunk, followed by a low continuous hum. Theo took the glass that Phoebe held out to him and raised it in a toast. 'To the kiln gods – please be kind!'

'I feel so excited,' Phoebe said 'Like I used to feel the night before Christmas. I'm sure I won't be able to get to sleep for hours.'

Theo took a sip and leaned back against the table, 'Then we'll have to think of something else to pass the time.' Phoebe smiled; the exhilaration of creativity and alcohol on an empty stomach had made her light-headed, she managed to hold back a desire to giggle.

'What are you suggesting? Chess? Charades? A few games of Gin Rummy? My grandmother taught me when I was about seven years old; we used to play for very high stakes – sherbet lemons and aniseed balls.'

'The only card game I ever learned was solitaire.'

'Are you trying to make me feel sorry for you?'

Theo grinned and held her gaze for a few seconds. 'You've got a smudge of glaze on your cheek.'

Phoebe's hand went to her face. 'Where?'

Theo took a step towards her and touched the skin below her eye. 'Just there.' He moved his thumb to wipe it away. 'It's gone, just freckles now.'

'I hate my freckles; they always come out in the sun.'

'I think they suit you.' His finger travelled lightly down the bridge of her nose. 'Like the speckles on an egg.'

'Is that meant to be some sort of compliment?'

'Would you prefer it if I told you that you're beautiful?'

'I believe that's the more conventional way to compliment a woman.'

He laughed. 'You don't strike me as being the conventional type, Phoebe Brennan.'

Phoebe arched an eyebrow. 'Try me,' she said, and put down her empty glass.

Slowly his finger moved to trace the contours of her lips. 'Isn't this where we'd got to when we were interrupted the last time?'

Phoebe shook her head. 'No, I think we'd got a little bit further actually.' Phoebe leaned forward and met his mouth with hers; she closed her eyes and melted into the kiss. After a few seconds Theo pulled away; he held her at arms length.

'I can't do this.'

Phoebe stared at him.

'Why?' her heart plummeted.

There was a short pause. Theo's serious expression broke into a grin. 'Because I promised that I wouldn't try to leap on you if you came to decorate your pot.'

'Oh yes, so you did.' Phoebe feigned irritation. 'But I wouldn't call this leaping, more a gentle sort of stumble.' She reached up and let her hands slide around his neck, her fingers tangling in his hair as he drew her slowly towards him.

'I don't want you to think that this is just because you have a look of Maeve.' Theo's voice brought Phoebe round from a state of blissful semi-consciousness. He shifted his arm so that he was resting on one elbow; he looked down at her face.

Phoebe also moved; the single bed was narrow, her bare back pressed against the cool plaster of the wall. She tried to disentangle her legs from his; he stopped her by trapping her shin between his knees. 'Don't move away,' he said, 'I like the way you wrap yourself around me.'

'You make me sound like an octopus.'

He leant down and kissed her. 'Or a boa constrictor.'

Phoebe pushed him back a little. 'You really are a master of the compliments.'

He laughed and kissed her again. 'Do you know what they say about boa constrictors?'

'No?'

'You don't? And there was I hoping you could tell me, because I know very few boa constrictor facts myself.'

Phoebe put on a thoughtful expression. 'They never let you go?' she offered.

'That's good,' said Theo as his hand moved down her naked torso, lingering over the curve of waist and hip and thigh. Phoebe put her own hand over his to stop him going any further.

'Is it?' she asked.

'Is it what?'

'Is it because I have a look of Maeve?'

He moved back slightly and held her gaze for a few seconds before he answered. 'No.' He twined a ringlet of her hair around his finger. 'But I'll tell you what it is about; ever since I first laid eyes on you I haven't been able to get you out of my head.'

'Even though I made you so annoyed?'

'Annoyed? Not just annoyed – you made me furious, exasperated, sometimes absolutely livid. The last time I'd seen you you'd been a quiet little girl with ginger pigtails, collecting heart-shaped stones in a plastic bucket, and then suddenly here you are, back in Carraigmore, all grown-up with wild hair, abducting my daughter, moving into my studio, making holes in my pots, telling me what to do with my child, and on top of that you have a story just as sad as my own – so I can't wallow in being the only broken-hearted person on the beach. And then the most annoying thing of all; you also happen to be gorgeous, and you made me feel the sort of things I promised myself I would never feel again about another woman.' Theo flung himself back onto the pillow. 'Honestly, Phoebe Brennan, now that I think about it I don't know why I let you talk me into going to bed with you at all!'

Phoebe laughed. 'It was your idea to come upstairs.'

'I just thought you were going to make me a cup of tea.'

'Oh, if you'd only said that in the first place!' She clambered over him. 'I'd better put the kettle on.'

He caught her wrist and pulled her down on top of him. 'I'm happy to wait till morning for the cup of tea.'

Much later Phoebe rested her head on Theo's chest. She kissed his skin and tasted the sweet saltiness of sweat. Below them the kiln clunked and hummed while outside the early morning breakers crashed against the shore.

'What do you think they're doing now?' she murmured.

'Who?'

'The pots in the kiln.'

'Let's see,' he turned his head. 'Judging by the pale grey light between your curtains I'd say it's nearly dawn.' He paused and tapped out a calculation on her shoulder. 'Seven hours, one hundred and fifty degrees an hour, it must be nearly one thousand degrees in the kiln by now, so that means the air around them will be red with the heat and the glaze will be just beginning to melt. By the time the kiln is finished the air will be so hot it's white and the glaze will be like molten glass.'

'When can we get them out?'

'Not until this evening at the earliest.'

Phoebe groaned. 'That's ages, I'll be at work by then.'

'You're so impatient,' Theo laughed. 'I'm running out of ways to distract you.' He picked up the book beside the bed. 'I'll have to resort to reading you a story to keep you entertained.' He looked at the cover. '*Jane Eyre*, very interesting. I suppose you think of me as some sort of Mr Rochester figure, brooding away behind the battlements.'

'Hopefully not with a mad wife hidden in the attic.' As soon as Phoebe had said the words she wished that she could take them back. A hollow silence fell, even the kiln and the sea seemed to stop as though they held their breath at the awfulness of what Phoebe had just said. Phoebe looked up at Theo. 'I'm so sorry, that was tactless.'

'Don't worry about it. But I can guarantee you she's well and truly buried in the cemetery of St Brigid's church in the high street.'

'I didn't mean –'

Theo stroked her hair. 'I said, don't worry about it.' He flicked through the book. 'Is it one of your favourites?'

'To tell you the truth, I don't really even know the story. David gave it to me to read but I can never get past the first few pages.'

'You must miss him very much.' Phoebe shivered and Theo pulled the quilt over her shoulder. 'Sorry, I don't mean to pry; I'm just curious. Were you very happy together? How long were you married?'

Now was the time to tell him, now was the time to admit that she had only been the mistress, not the wife; surely after intimacy there should be honesty. Phoebe took courage from his fingers gently running up and down her back. She took a breath.

'I think I ought to – '

'You don't have to talk about him if you don't want to,' Theo interrupted. 'I know how painful it can be to remember.' He kissed the top of her head. 'We're lucky to have found each other. We've been on the same journey, we can understand what it's like to lose the person you'd promised to spend the rest of your life with.'

Phoebe bit her lip. She'd thought she wanted to spend the rest of her life with David but there had been no promises, no *forsaking all others* and the *till death us do part* was a mere act of chance. Lying in Theo's arms she tried hard to remember how she'd felt with David. Had she ever been so comfortable? So relaxed?

Phoebe didn't speak. Theo held her closer; his strong potter's arms felt warm around her and she noticed that his

289

heartbeat had seemed to find a rhythm with her own.

They lay silent for a while until Theo tilted Phoebe's chin up with one finger. 'Is that offer of a cup of tea still on?'

Chapter Twenty-five

Phoebe wished she didn't have to go to work.

As she walked up the lane she couldn't help smiling, once she even executed a small pirouette, accidentally spinning into Swedish Jan who was coming down to the beach for his mid-morning stroll.

'Are you all right?' he asked her as he helped her up from the ground.

'Absolutely wonderful,' Phoebe replied before she continued onwards up the hill. She wondered if Theo was still lying in her bed; she thought about the night before and had to force herself not to go back to join him.

Eventually, long after dawn, they had slept, and woken, and then they'd slept some more. As the bright sun poured through the window Phoebe knew she'd have to get up and go to do the lunchtime shift. Fibber had a meeting with the doctors in Tralee and Phoebe had promised Katrina that she'd help her in the pub all day.

Theo was asleep. Phoebe studied his face, his beautiful features could have been chiselled out of marble, he looked perfect, the handsomest man she'd ever seen. She kissed him lightly on the forehead and attempted to get out of bed without waking him up.

'Not so fast, Miss Brennan.' He suddenly caught her arm and pulled her towards him to kiss her neck, her shoulder, her breast, and eventually her lips.

Half an hour later she said, 'Now I really do have to go to work,' and prised herself from his arms to quickly shower and dress.

'You are looking very well this day,' Katrina handed
Phoebe another tray of glasses to put away. 'Your eyes,
they look different. They look like they are full of
sparkles.'

'Probably just hay-fever,' said Phoebe, turning to the
shelves and hoping Katrina wouldn't notice her blush.

Honey sat at the kitchen table, hulling strawberries for
a pavlova.

'Are you OK in there, Honey?' Katrina called to her
from the bar. There was a short *Yep* of a response. 'Oh
dear,' Katrina sighed and lowered her voice. 'She is a sad
girl, she has so many worries that Theo will say "Yes" to
the offer for the Castle and take her away to America.'

Phoebe's heart lurched; *she* had so many worries that
Theo would accept the offer and disappear to America.
She wondered if last night had made any difference to how
he felt – a familiar fear that she would be abandoned had
already began to seep into the pit of her stomach. Maybe
last night would hasten his departure, maybe he was
already regretting what had happened, realising that
Phoebe could never live up to his memories of the saintly
Maeve.

'My good gracious,' Katrina exclaimed. 'The time; it is
flying today. Nearly it is time to open up and I have not
got the mousaka in the oven or the towels on the line –
Mrs Flannigan would be saying it is a grand day to do the
drying and I will feel very bad if we use the tumble dryer.'

'Don't worry.' Phoebe put the last glass on the shelf.
'You sort out the mousaka and I'll hang up the washing.'

Phoebe unloaded the washing machine, dragging the
soggy mats and tea towels into a plastic basket. She felt a
slight vibration in the back pocket of her jeans – a text.

Trying to do something constructive with my day but seem only able to sit around grinning and thinking of last night. T x.

Phoebe smiled, picked up the washing basket, and started to sing.

'I hear you,' shouted Katrina from the kitchen. 'You are too happy with the joys of spring. I have suspicion.' Phoebe ignored her and stepped outside.

The contrast between the darkness of the pub and the bright sunlight of the yard made her squint as she stepped through the back door. As her eyes adjusted she picked her way through weeds that pushed up through the broken concrete. Judging by the quantity of dandelions and encroaching brambles it didn't look as though Fibber had been making much of an attempt to clear the yard on the day that Phoebe had noticed the smoke. She put down the basket and began to peg the clothes along the sagging line. As she hung up the final tea towel a small scrap of paper drifted on a gust of wind to settle in the empty basket.

Phoebe bent down and picked it up. The edges were charred as if it had been burned and the ink on it had bled from dew or rain. Phoebe recognised her grandmother's writing immediately, she could just make out the date *June 15th* on one side and the words, *we walked through miles of purple heather.* Phoebe turned the paper over *he has such wonderful plans; I can hardly bear to believe we might succeed.* The rest was too smudged to make out.

Phoebe hastily looked around and found more torn-up bits of paper – nestling in between cracks in the concrete, inside a rusty bucket, lodged in between the branches of a fuchsia hedge. She gathered up the tiny pieces, examining each one as she found it. Some were illegible but many weren't.

Gordon is in Dublin. I spent the whole day with Michael –

heaven!

He brought me a bunch of late daisies, to match the new blue dress I bought in Mrs O'Leary's sale.

Della has been so sweet; today she took my note to Michael even though her headache is very bad.

We walk beneath the falling leaves around the Castle gardens. He has a plan to ...

Despite the cold, damp weather I feel a happiness I didn't know was possible.

All Hallows Eve, not too much longer now.

... only one small suitcase ...

I felt so sick this morning I had to rush out of the room. Gordon is quite ...

The days are passing much too slowly. Della keeps me company most evenings. We plan to go to Kenmare to see a matinee tomorrow.

Phoebe's heart thumped in her chest as she searched for more. They were definitely pages from the missing diaries, but why were they torn-up and scattered, semi-scorched, around the garden?

Phoebe noticed the brazier in the corner and realised that it must have been the source of Fibber's fire. Peering inside she could see the blackened pages of some sort of book, she poked it with a nearby stick and it disintegrated into a mushy pile of ash. Phoebe stared at the remnants of Anna's diary and tried to make sense of her discovery. She had been right; someone had broken into the boathouse, been into her flat, and had stolen the diaries. And then they had tried to destroy them. Phoebe's mind whirred, who could have done it? And why? Cold water seemed to be seeping through her veins.

She stepped backwards from the metal drum, trying desperately to think of some logical explanation, trying desperately to rationalise the fear that had begun to creep into her heart. It was then that she noticed something beneath the brazier itself. She still held the stick in her hand and she used it to drag the book out.

It had been shielded from the rain and even though it looked as though most of the pages had been ripped out in some sort of frenzy a handful remained. The writing was scrawled and difficult to read as though it were written in a hurry or under stress.

December 3rd

I can't give up hope, I just can't. Why do I not hear from him? I can't stop thinking of those hours I spent standing at the crossroads, waiting for him long after I had realised he wasn't going to appear around the bend. I can still feel that rain against my cheeks, the freezing drops that drenched my clothes. What would I have done if Gordon hadn't come for me? How did Gordon know where I was? He has been so kind, even though I know that he has many worries of his own. I heard the parish priest tell Gordon that he could persuade the boy to talk and then the whole village would know what abominations were being committed under their noses.

Yesterday Gordon told me that he heard that Leviticus 18:22 was quoted during Mass. I said nothing but I understood what he was trying to tell me.

December 8th.

*I asked Della to check the post in the shop again today –
she told me to stop asking her, told me to just accept that
he didn't want me and that he wasn't coming back. I saw
her looking at my stomach, looking with disgust at the
straining of my waistband, the swelling underneath my
jumper. I have caught Mrs Smythe looking too, she
puckers her lips and once I'm sure I heard her mutter
'harlot' before she left the room. Everyone will notice
soon, I cannot button my red coat so I do not go out. Does
Gordon know? I'm sure he does, he is a doctor after all.*

December 15th

*Gordon sat me down today to tell me he is going to go
away. He says he cannot go through what he went through
in Howth; he would rather leave than face the humiliation
of being denounced in the pulpit and being hounded out of
town by people he once thought of as friends. He has
heard of a position for a doctor in Nigeria and has applied
and been offered the post.*

*He suggests I go to England, to live with Mother and
Aunt Margaret. He has offered to write, to explain that he
has decided to fulfil a lifelong vocation to work in Africa
and that in the meantime he thinks it better for me and the
child to stay in Cheltenham until he is settled – a plausible
enough story I think, but the very idea of Cheltenham fills
me with horror.*

December 16th

*Gordon is to leave on Boxing Day; he has already found a
new doctor for Carraigmore.*

*I can't sleep. Where should I go? Not to Mother, that is
for sure, and I have not heard once from either of my
brothers. But I have no reason to stay in Ireland any more;
there is nothing here for me but memories.*

December 20th

I have asked Gordon if I can go with him to Africa. I have offered to help him with his practice; I believe I would make a good nurse: I have no fear of blood or illness and I have strong, swift hands and am quick to learn. Gordon told me conditions may be tough – little better than living in a mud hut, he has been told. I don't care. Anything seems better than the dark oppression of this sanctimonious village.

December 22nd

I feel lighter, better. Beneath my gloom I see a sliver of hope for the future, a crescent moon appearing in a stormy sky. All I want now is to see my unborn child, my little piece of Michael, my memory of what we had together. I think of how in Africa the sun will shine down on my baby and it will never have to endure the cold and damp and rain.

December 24th

We are packed. I have very little that is mine, not much more than when I arrived over a year ago. I have asked Della if she will look after Razzle, she has agreed but she is so odd lately it is hard to believe that she will really care for him. For many months she was a good friend to me, now she barely meets my eye. I stopped her on the stairs and asked her to forward any letters; she nodded curtly and continued on without a word.

Mrs Smythe seems quite unbalanced, there is an agitated look about her; constantly she talks of the new doctor, the preparations for his arrival seem to completely fill her time. We have had tinned soup for three days in a row for dinner.

This afternoon I found Mrs Smythe frantically polishing the writing desk in the drawing room; tears were streaming down her face and she made no attempt to wipe them away. I touched her arm and tried to comfort her; she stopped polishing and I found a look of pure hatred directed at me. 'You people from the Castle, you are all the same – callous and hard-hearted.' She started to sing "Night and Day" by Cole Porter in an odd, high-pitched voice and continued to grind in the polish as she sang. Then she spat 'Good riddance' at me and I left the room. As I was about leave she spoke, her voice almost a whisper – 'He said that was our special song.' Her eerie singing started up again and seemed to echo round the house long after she had stopped.

December 25th

We leave tomorrow, two sinners creeping away as St Stephen's Day dawns. Will we find forgiveness in Africa? Or acceptance? I felt the baby kick today, a Christmas present after all.

'Phoebe, Phoebe,' Katrina's voice took Phoebe by surprise. 'There you are.' Katrina came into the garden, her face and hair spattered with yellow cream. 'You must come quick. There is a queue of peoples banging on the door to say it is past opening time; and my electric whisk has gone up the blink so that I must go and quick shower before I face the customers.'

She turned to hurry inside, but Phoebe put a hand on her arm to stop her. 'Who was having a fire out here last Sunday?' She nodded towards the brazier.

'It was Mrs Flannigan,' Katrina answered. 'She wanted to get rid of some old account books. She ask Fibber to start a fire for her and then she start to rip them up and put them in the flames.' She peered over Phoebe's shoulder at the remains of the diary in her hands. 'Is just old notebooks, she say they make clutter. Poor Mrs Flannigan it was when she is doing this that she collapse. Fibber found her lying on the grass.'

'So she had her heart attack while she was getting rid of the books?'

'Yes, yes, that is right, but please be hurrying, Phoebe; we don't want the customers to give up waiting.'

Lunchtime dragged, the surfers and the walkers stayed put on the beach, and apart from the initial regulars who had formed the queue outside (Young John, Swedish Jan, and Molly from the Hair Hut's husband) there were few takers for Katrina's mousaka and pavlova. Phoebe received another text from Theo,

Taking Poncho for a walk, wish that you were with me, xx

and Katrina received a phone call from Fibber.

'The doctors they say that Mrs Flannigan can come home tomorrow. Fibber, he is very happy, though his mother will be a long time travelling the route to full recovering.'

'The road to full recovery,' said Honey from her position on a high stool where she and Phoebe were busy writing out the alphabet in peanuts on the bar.

Katrina sighed. 'Not you too, Honey.'

'You don't want people to think that you're not from round here, do you?' said Honey earnestly. 'It's taken ages for people to stop teasing me about my Dublin accent, and you come from so much further away than that.' She shoved a pile of nuts across the counter, 'Come on Phoebe, it's your turn. We're on *M* now.'

Phoebe's thoughts were still distracted by her discovery of the diaries in the garden; what could possibly have been in them that made Mrs Flannigan so desperate to destroy them? What had happened to Michael? Why had he and Anna not gone to France?

'If you and my dad get married we could all stay in the Castle and I won't have to go to live with Grandma Stick.' Honey didn't look at Phoebe, instead she concentrated on forming an *N*, perfect but for the fact that it was backwards.

'What makes you think we're going to get married?' asked Phoebe in surprise.

'Because you like each other; I can tell.'

'How?'

Honey shrugged. 'Oh, you know, you go a funny red colour when you see him, and he doesn't call you a bloody nuisance any more – instead he says *I wonder what Phoebe's up to today*.' She put on a deep voice to imitate Theo's and Phoebe laughed.

'And he is shaving more often, I am noticing,' said Katrina, grinning as she poured a pint of Guinness for Swedish Jan at the other end of the bar.

'And he came in to the wife for a trim the other day,' said Molly from the Hair Hut's husband.

'I'd say he has a funny air about him – you know, the one that men get when they get a mind to be courting,' Young John called out from his seat in the corner.

'And when I passed him coming out of the boathouse this morning he was whistling,' added Swedish Jan. 'And that wasn't long after I'd met you dancing up the lane.'

Phoebe felt herself blush. Why did she ever think she'd be able to have any secrets in Carraigmore?

'So, will you marry my dad then?' Honey stared at Phoebe's face, and, glancing around, Phoebe realised that everyone was looking at her, waiting for an answer. With huge relief Phoebe heard the bar door open with its familiar creak, any distraction would be welcome, she thought. Within seconds all eyes had turned from Phoebe towards the gorgeous apparition that stood in the doorway.

Molly from the Hair Hut's husband looked as though he might collapse with lust, Young John straightened his cap and tie; even Swedish Jan had a look of admiration in his eyes. A woman had appeared – high-heeled boots, skinny legs in skinny jeans and a silk shirt unbuttoned to reveal a generous amount of cleavage.

Surveying the room from behind huge sunglasses, the woman tossed back a mane of long blonde hair and strode over to the bar. It was only when the woman had taken off her sunglasses and was standing right in front of her that Phoebe realised it was Nola.

Chapter Twenty-six

'My goodness, Nola; I hardly recognise you,' Phoebe had recovered enough to be able to speak, even though she wasn't quite ready to answer Nola's *What the bloody hell are you doing here?* question.

Nola smoothed her shirt over her astonishingly flat stomach and smiled. 'Its amazing what a loss of appetite and intensive Zumba can achieve.' Phoebe looked Nola up and down, taking in the manicured nails, white teeth, perfect make-up, and a tan that looked far too deep to have been the result of an English summer. For the first time in her adult life Phoebe felt fat and frumpy next to her sister.

'Are Steve and the children with you?' Phoebe asked.

'Steve who?' Nola tossed her mane of hair again, some of it swished against Molly from the Hair Hut's husband's face – he looked delighted and Honey was staring, open-mouthed in awe. Phoebe wondered if Nola had had hair extensions, it couldn't possibly have grown that much in the four months since she'd last seen her. 'Steve is no longer part of my life,' Nola continued. 'Apart from Friday nights when he picks up the children.'

'You've split up?' Phoebe was aware that the three men and Katrina had managed to shuffle up to her end of bar, and that they were all obviously listening to the conversation with great interest. Nola didn't seem to care.

'Split up?' spat Nola through scarlet lips. 'It was less of a split and more of a bloody big kick out of the door from me!' She banged her red-nailed-hand down on the bar as though she were giving it a slap. Phoebe noticed the men flinch.

'I'm sorry, Nola,' Phoebe said. 'I always thought you had a good marriage; I mean I know that you felt you could have achieved more career-wise, but Steve seemed like ...'

'A deceitful adulterous bastard!' interrupted Nola, 'Who thought nothing of offering comfort to my best friend by regularly –' she paused and glanced at Honey, whose eyes were saucer-wide with interest in what Nola had to say, 'by regularly giving her more attention than a married man ought to. Trying to help her over her grief he said, like he was some sort of patron saint of widowed women. I wouldn't mind but he'd been having an affair with her long before David was actually dead!'

'Oh!' Phoebe felt stunned; Sandra had been having an affair all along. Had David known about Steve and Sandra? Had Sandra known about Phoebe and David?

'Apparently it all started last summer. Steve said he was only trying to comfort Sandra when she discovered David was having an affair with the peripatetic music-teacher.'

Phoebe put a hand on the bar to steady herself. Had David really been having an affair with Debbie Richards, the buxom music teacher, fresh from college, who came to teach the juniors guitar and recorder? Phoebe couldn't believe it; at the same time as having an affair with her he'd been sleeping with Debbie Richards! A wave of something awful washed over her – something that Phoebe couldn't even identify, just a dreadful emotion or maybe several dreadful emotions all at the same time.

Nola watched her as though she knew what Phoebe was going through. Her voice softened, 'Sorry Pheebs, it seems like Sandra wasn't the only person David was cheating on.'

'But I thought that David was your fella,' said Young

John pointing an arthritic finger at Phoebe.

'What?' Nola turned to Young John.

'Hush, John,' Katrina's voice was a stage whisper. 'I am thinking there are many mans called David in England. I don't think they are talking about Phoebe's husband.'

'Phoebe's husband?' Nola was looking at Phoebe again.

'How are the children?' asked Phoebe loudly. 'They must be terribly upset.'

'Oh they're all right,' Nola gave a shrug. 'Ruben's fine as long as he's plugged into some bit of technology, and Amy is too busy shortening her school skirt and worrying who's said what on Facebook to really care.'

'So you are friend of Phoebe?' Katrina asked.

Nola snorted. 'Maybe not a friend, but I am her big sister.'

There was a prolonged chorus of *Ohhh*s from the little group of spectators, then Katrina's face broke into a smile. 'Well you are very welcome, Phoebe's sister.' She turned to Phoebe. 'You must have time off to be together. You go now, its not like we are running off our foot today.'

'Can I come with you?' asked Honey.

'No, sweetie,' Phoebe heard Katrina say as she walked into the kitchen to fetch her jacket. 'I think that Phoebe and her sister need to be on their selves for a while.'

Phoebe felt that she probably needed to be on herself for a while without anyone with her at all. Nola's revelations had sent her reeling; Debbie Richards had been like a full-on blow to her stomach. Phoebe fumbled with her jacket buttons and wondered if she should pour herself a glass of Katrina's cooking brandy.

'Are you coming, Phoebe?' Nola's voice called loudly from the bar.

With a promise to Katrina that she'd be back for the evening shift, Phoebe followed her transformed sister out of the door.

'So you're a barmaid in Fibber Flannigan's pub?' Nola put her sunglasses back on even though dark clouds now blocked out the sun. 'That must be very taxing.' Phoebe didn't answer but Nola noticed her scowl.

'What? All I'm saying is that bar work isn't very challenging, especially in a pub like Fibber Flannigan's. I remember one of that film director's sons taking me there for a drink one night. I sneaked out after you and Mum and Dad were asleep. They were having a lock-in and I got out of my under-age head on Cinzano.' Nola hooted with laughter. 'I remember the film director's son snogged me on the way home, and asked if I fancied a holiday in their place in Malibu – told me he'd introduce me to some film stars. I told him he wasn't my type – God, I was a cocky little thing back then, how did I ever end up with two sulky kids and Steve on a Lego estate in the back of beyond?' She kicked at a stone as they turned down the lane. 'Fibber Flannigan's was a real spit and sawdust place then, actually it still looks just the same.'

'Which one?'

'Pardon?'

'Which son took you?'

'Oh, I can't really remember his name, Oscar or Owen or something.'

'Oliver?'

'Oh yeah, Oliver; that was it.'

Phoebe felt relieved. 'So what brings you here?'

'What brings you, more like? I was sure you'd be off meditating in some ashram or stoned in some illegal squat in Sydney. You know, the sort of thing you usually do.'

'Nola, I did those sorts of things years ago. I've held down a respectable job as a primary school teacher since then, remember?'

Nola raised her eyebrows and said nothing. Phoebe knew that she was thinking that she only held down the primary school job because of David. She didn't want to

306

get into a fight with Nola now.

'Are we headed for the boathouse?' Nola asked.

'Yes,' said Phoebe, wondering if Theo would have unpacked the kiln yet. She would love to show Nola the pots she'd decorated, that'd show her that her art college degree hadn't been wasted.

'That's good,' Nola smiled. 'Because that's why I'm here. I've been talking to the lawyer who's handling my divorce and she says we should be able to get Granny's will revoked so that we could sell the boathouse after all these years – though of course not until my divorce is through; I don't want Steve using it as one of my assets. Anyway, I've already arranged for an estate agent in Kenmare to come over on Monday to value it.'

Phoebe was so stunned that the fury she felt inside lodged in her throat and prevented speech. How could Nola possibly think they could go against their grandmother's wishes and sell it, anyway it was Phoebe's home now? Phoebe decided to say nothing; she needed time to form her argument.

They passed the gates of the Castle and Nola stopped to peer through. 'Look at that! If only it still belonged to us all my worries would be over. I'm absolutely desperate to get hold of some money; it looks like we're going to have to sell the house. Ruben and Amy will never want to share a room and the prices of three-bed places round us is way beyond what I can mange on my receptionist's salary.'

'Where will Steve go?' asked Phoebe.

'Oh, he's all nicely tucked up with Sandra. He *says* he's happy but those twins are a real handful now and at weekends they have four kids in the house!' Nola snorted. 'Whenever I feel upset about what's happened I just think of Steve and Sandra on a Sunday morning trying to contend with four squabbling children while I can lie in bed for as long as I like. Next week is half-term and Steve's having the children for the whole seven days; I can't wait to see what sort of state he'll be in by the time I pick them up.'

'Are you spying on my house?' Phoebe's heart missed a beat as she turned to find Theo standing beside them.

'Hello,' she smiled up at him. 'Fancy meeting you here.'

He bent to kiss her but as he did so Phoebe could see his eyes had already slipped towards Nola.

'Oh Theo, this is …'

'Nola,' he cut in, saying the name slowly as though she were some delicious pudding or a fine bottle of wine.

'Theo Casson.' Nola swept her own eyes over Theo. 'Look at you, all grown-up and handsome. You're looking very well.' Phoebe stared at her sister, since when had she become such a vamp? And why did she remember Theo's name when she hadn't been able to remember Oliver's? Phoebe slipped her hand into Theo's; he gave her fingers a small squeeze.

'Phoebe didn't tell me you were coming; I must say you look very well, too.' Phoebe let go of his hand and folded her arms.

'Theo's a potter now,' she said to Nola. 'Like Granny. He's using her old studio; he does wonderful things with clay.'

'I bet he does,' Nola was almost purring. Phoebe had to resist an urge to kick her in the shin.

Theo cleared his throat as though pulling himself together. 'Phoebe's been doing some amazing painting on some of my pots and she even threw one on the wheel herself.'

'I'd love to have a go on the wheel again; maybe you could give me a refresher lesson, Theo?' Nola touched Theo's arm and Phoebe was almost sure she saw her eyelashes flutter.

Theo glanced at Phoebe. 'Um, maybe, but I'm quite busy at the moment.' Phoebe smiled.

Nola looked from Phoebe to Theo. 'Is there something …? Are you two …?'

Phoebe's irritation melted as Theo put his arm around her shoulder; they looked at each other and smiled.

'Aww, how sweet.' Nola swept back her hair, her own smile was sardonic. A large splash of rain fell on the dusty ground, followed by another and another in quick succession.

'Here it comes,' said Theo. 'This storm's been brewing all afternoon, would you two like to come in, instead of peering through the gates?' The rain had started in earnest now, and as Theo pushed open heavy gate the three of them ran towards the house for shelter.

Once inside the kitchen, Nola asked if she could use the bathroom. Theo looked momentarily at Phoebe before offering to show her where it was.

'I thought you said Nola had let herself go,' he said as he came back.

'She had.' Phoebe was sitting at the table, her head resting heavily in her hands. 'And now it appears that leaving her husband has turned her into some sort of mutant cross between a footballer's wife and Mae West.'

Theo put his hands on her shoulders, 'Do I detect sibling rivalry rearing its ugly head?'

'No, of course not,' Phoebe whipped her head round to face him. 'But what right does she think she has to turn up here with her bits of false hair and Zumba thighs to try to sell the boathouse!'

'Is that what she wants to do?'

'Yes, to raise money for a house for her to live in when her divorce comes through.'

Theo put his arms around her. 'I wouldn't worry about it, Phoebe. For one thing she may find it's harder to sell than she imagines, and secondly, once she's spent a few days here she may not want to give up her little piece of

Irish inheritance after all.'

'But what about your studio?' She felt Theo shrug. After a few minutes of silence she dared to ask the question that had played on her mind all day. 'Have you had any more thoughts about the developers' offer?'

Theo sat down beside her. He took her hand in his. 'After last night I'm not in any fit state to make decisions!' He smiled and stroked her cheek. 'All I know is that the thought of leaving you right now would be impossible, unless you came with me, of course, and as I don't know where I'm going or what I want to do I think that would be too much to ask.' Theo coiled a strand of Phoebe's hair around his finger. 'I've sent a text to the developers asking for a few weeks to think things over.' He let go of her hair and leant towards her, 'And I intend to spend those weeks as productively as I can.'

Phoebe leant towards him too, 'Productively? Tell me what you plan to do.'

'Oh, you know. A bit of this, a bit of that.' He was centimetres from her lips, 'But hopefully mostly this.' He kissed her gently.

Phoebe pulled back. 'You don't wish you'd waited twenty-four hours to scoop Nola after all those years instead?'

'There's more to being beautiful than skinny thighs and a push-up bra.'

'Are you sure?'

'Believe me, Nola was just a teenage fantasy, while you are something all the more desirable.' Then he kissed her mouth with such passion that Phoebe thought they might both fall off their chairs. The thought of making love on the slate flagstones made Phoebe's entire body tremble with longing; if only Nola hadn't turned up she and Theo could be having such a lovely afternoon.

'Sorry to interrupt?' Nola was back; Phoebe quickly disentangled herself from Theo and was mortified to find the buttons of her shirt undone. Theo however seemed not in the least embarrassed and gave Phoebe one last kiss before standing up to make a pot of tea.

'I just can't seem to keep my hands off your gorgeous sister,' he grinned at Nola as he lifted the kettle from the Aga. Nola gave a sniff and swished her hair so that it all hung over one shoulder in a most alluring manner. Phoebe watched her and wondered if she had practised doing that in front of the mirror.

'I hope you don't mind, but I took the opportunity to have a bit of a nose around.' Nola sat down at the table. 'What a fabulous house, and, to think, it used to belong to our grandmother's family, Phoebe. Have you seen the coat of arms above the fireplace? Are we posh or what!'

'I've seen it,' said Phoebe. 'I thought I'd get the design printed on a baggy T-shirt for your birthday, but I doubt you wear that sort of T-shirt now.'

Nola frowned and turned her attention to Theo. 'Do you realise there's water pouring through that glass dome above the hallway? It's made quite a lake on the marble floor.'

'Oh God, has it? That's another leak to add to the hundred others around here; I ran out of buckets long ago.' Theo emptied apples from a fruit bowl. 'I'll be back in a moment.' At the doorway to the stairs he stopped and turned to Nola. 'I don't suppose you've got half a million euro lying around to donate to the roof restoration fund, have you?'

'If I had half a million euro lying around I wouldn't be in the west of Ireland in the rain, would I? I'd be sunning it in the Bahamas in a luxury resort, drinking champagne, and having my feet rubbed by some gorgeous man.'

Theo shrugged. 'OK, I just thought it was worth checking.' He disappeared, leaving Phoebe and Nola facing each other across the wide expanse of pine.

'Well, you're a fast worker,' said Nola, pushing back

her chair and crossing legs that looked as though they were sprayed with denim rather than clothed in it. 'Though it looks as though your lord of the manor is rather on his uppers at the moment. I do hope he realises that you didn't inherit any of the family fortune.'

Phoebe contemplated her answer for a moment but the sound of her phone ringing saved her from making a decision about which enraged reply to choose.

'Hello, Phoebe,' Katrina's voice was almost drowned out by the sound of singing and laughing in the background.

'What's going on? You sound like you're in the middle of a party.'

'I am. Is Fibber, he has texted everybody in Carraigmore to say that Mrs Flannigan will be coming home tomorrow, and he is so happy he is asking them come and shindig at the pub, drinks on him, and now the whole place is full and Fibber is not back yet from Tralee.'

Phoebe looked at the time on her phone. 'But it's not even four o'clock.'

'I knows. Poor Honey is having to help me with the pint pulling, I have her standing on crate to get to the pump.'

'Isn't that illegal?'

'Oh no; Sergeant Jackson is here and he said is fine. In fact he is learning her how to make a good head on the Guinness right now.'

'Look, I'll come right now and I'll bring my sister with me. Sergeant Jackson can teach her how to make a good head on the Guinness instead.'

Phoebe put the phone back in her pocket. Nola raised her eyebrows.

'Tell me more about Sergeant Jackson?'

'Come on, you can see just how challenging it is to be a barmaid after all. I'm sure you'll get a good night's pay at the end. That should help towards the three-bedroom semi.'

'It's not going to damage my nails, is it? I've only just had them done.'

Phoebe stood up and shrugged on her jacket. 'Are you sure you actually are Nola? My sister used to say life's too short to bother with mascara, let alone painting her fingernails!'

'It turned out life was longer than I thought.'

'Well, that's the Great Flood dealt with.' Theo came back down the stairs. 'And the good news is that the rain's stopped so I don't need to worry about the fruit bowl overflowing.

He looked at Phoebe and Nola. 'Where are you two off to?'

'Phoebe has me signed up to a bar job at Fibber Flannigan's.' Nola turned to Phoebe. 'Will there be tips?'

Phoebe raised her eyebrows. 'One look at you and there'll definitely be tips, though I'd tone down the cleavage, especially if the football lads are in on the big bash. Do up a few buttons.'

'Look who's talking!' Nola pointed at Phoebe's shirt. 'You've still got some of yours undone.' She turned to Theo. 'Are you coming to this little party at the pub?'

'I'm not sure. I've got stuff to do in the studio and the kiln will soon be cool enough to open. I might come along a bit later and see if Honey wants to come home. If Fibber's having one of his shindigs I expect Honey will be upstairs with the telly all evening, getting bored.' Phoebe thought it best not to mention that at that moment his daughter was standing on a beer crate handing out free pints with the help of the local constabulary.

Chapter Twenty-seven

'Oh God, I see what you mean about my cleavage,' said Nola as she struggled with the optics – accidentally pouring a triple whiskey into a glass. 'I've never seen so many leering men packed so tightly into one place – all the attention is getting rather tedious.'

'I did warn you about the football team,' Phoebe laughed.

'I can't seem to shake off that one with the sticky-out ears, he keeps asking me back to his place, says he changed the sheets ...'

'On Saturday,' finished Phoebe. 'Goodness knows what's gone on in that bed since then, if the stories about him are to be believed.'

Nola shuddered. 'Looks like you've already nabbed the best man in Carraigmore.' She turned back to the bar with the glass of whiskey. 'There doesn't seem to be much room in there for any water,' she told the happy customer before she turned back to Phoebe. 'I spoke too soon, look what's just walked through the door. I must say he is rather cute.'

Phoebe stared through the crowds to see Rory pushing his way towards the bar with his guitar. 'He definitely won't be leering at you,' she told Nola with a smile.

'Hi, Phoebe,' Rory nodded towards Nola. 'I heard your sister had blown in. Have you seen the boys yet? Fibber's asked us to play a few songs to get the evening off to a good start, though by the look of things the good start got going hours ago.'

Fibber appeared, pink-faced and beaming. 'What a grand night it is,' he rubbed his hands together. 'And this time tomorrow me ma will be back where she belongs – thank God for those doctors in Tralee, didn't they perform miracles with her?' He spotted Rory. 'Your gang are over in the corner. Start whenever you like and make it upbeat. You know, less Snow Patrol, more Abba.'

'Abba!' Rory stared at him and shook his head.

Fibber turned to Nola, 'Thanks for helping us out, you've been great. Would you like a drink?'

'I'd love one,' Nola replied. 'I'm absolutely exhausted; it's worse than Flu Jab Saturday at the health centre where I work.'

'Flu Jab Saturday?' Fibber looked confused.

'Hundreds of geriatrics fighting it out with the asthmatics for who gets to go first in the queue.'

'Sounds like it should be a spectator sport.'

'This is much worse, I never knew that so much liquid could be consumed in such a short time, and remembering what everyone wants is really difficult.'

'I told you it was challenging,' smirked Phoebe.

'I know just what you need, Nola.' Fibber was already producing his silver shaker from beneath the bar. 'One of my special Carraigmore cocktails; that'll soon perk you up.'

'Oh no! Nola, don't,' Phoebe tried to warn her.

'That would be lovely, Fibber,' Nola ignored Phoebe. 'I *love* cocktails.'

Two hours later Nola was up on the stage singing a duet of "I Have a Dream" with Rory and his band. Phoebe continued to serve pint after pint while watching her sister and hoping she wouldn't be back to Fibber for yet another cocktail.

'Ooo, look at Britney Spears up there.' A young man

with muscles like rugby balls was standing in front of
Phoebe at the bar. His pale blond hair was meticulously
gelled into a dishevelled style. Swedish Jan pushed his
way along the bar so that he was standing beside him, a
look of puppy love on his heavily bearded face. The boy
ignored Swedish Jan and waved at Rory as the song
finished. Rory smiled and waved back.

'You wouldn't be Ben, would you?' asked Phoebe.

'How did you know?'

'Lucky guess.'

'Definitely time for a break.' Rory appeared beside
them and grinned at Phoebe. 'Your sister can really belt
them out, though I think she won't be standing upright for
that much longer, she's plastered.' He winked at Ben.
'Thanks for coming,' he said. 'I take it you've met my
friend Phoebe.'

Phoebe and Ben shook hands formally and Phoebe got
them both a drink. Katrina squeezed past her.

'I say to Fibber no more cocktails for your sister or she
will be like you when you first come here, sick like dog!'

Phoebe gave the boys – now deep in conversation with
the rest of the band – their drinks and decided to use a lull
in customers to go and search for Honey; she hadn't seen
her for some time.

She found her fast asleep upstairs in the spare bed.
Peeking underneath the duvet, Phoebe could see that she
was still wearing the clothes she'd had on all day,
including her baseball boots. Phoebe unlaced them and
eased them off her feet. Her hair had fallen across her face
and Phoebe gently pushed it back and kissed her forehead.

'Good night, sweetheart,' she whispered. It wasn't until
she was about to turn out the bedside light that she noticed
Theo standing in the doorway. He walked into the room
and took Phoebe in his arms.

Phoebe leant into his broad chest; his jacket felt damp
against her cheek. Glancing at the window she saw streaks

317

of rain pouring down the pane like tears; she looked up at Theo and hoped she'd never want to cry again.

All day she had tried not to think about David and Debbie Richards, how could she have ever been so naïve? David probably never had any intention of leaving Sandra, he had never really loved her, but suddenly she found she didn't care at all. If it had all led to this moment it had been worth it – all the heartache, all the misplaced grief.

Theo kissed her lightly on the lips and the sound of Nola's voice attempting "I Will Survive" on the karaoke came up the stairs and made them both laugh.

'I unpacked the kiln,' Theo said as they walked out on to the landing.

'And?'

'All broken, I'm afraid.'

'Oh no!' Phoebe stopped.

'I'm joking,' he grinned. 'Actually the pots look wonderful. Your designs seem to really complement my shapes.'

'I can't wait to see them.'

'I think you'll be very pleased. Would you be up for painting some more?'

'I'd love to.'

Theo kissed her again and went on kissing her for a long time.

After a while he drew back and looked at her. 'What would you think of us working together? You know, trying to sell some pots; maybe get some work in galleries, get ourselves involved in some exhibitions?'

Phoebe's eyes widened. 'But what about your own work?'

'I told you, I've been looking to change what I do, looking for a new direction, and for the first time for years I actually feel excited about the idea of making pottery.' He smiled. 'What do you say? Why don't we just give it a try?'

318

Phoebe realised she had been opening and shutting her mouth like a stunned goldfish as she listened to his proposition. She wondered if she was asleep and dreaming. 'Are you sure? Supposing no one likes my decorations, supposing I let you down? I mean, you hardly know me really.' Theo gently tucked a strand of her hair behind her ear. 'I feel as though I know you very well.' He leant forward to kiss her again. 'I trust you.'

'Pheeebeee,' Nola's alcohol-addled call reached them from below. 'Pheeebeee, come and sing a song with me.'

'Oh no.' Phoebe rolled her eyes. 'I wish I'd left her in your kitchen now, she's not ready for a Carraigmore party, especially not a party with Fibber's lethal cocktails flowing so freely.'

'Do you want me to take her home? You know when I came in she was doing some rather raunchy dancing with some bloke from the football team.'

'The one with the sticking-out ears?'

Theo nodded grimly.

'Oh God.' Phoebe started going down the stairs. 'I'd never forgive myself if she ended up between his infamous sheets.'

Nola was swaying at the bottom of the stairs, one arm draped around the banisters for support.

'Come on, little sis,' she slurred. 'Fibber says you like singing karaoke, so why don't we sing a song together?'

'No, Nola,' Phoebe protested. 'I think it's time you went to bed. Theo's offered to take you home.'

'Ooooo, has he indeed?' Nola turned to Theo. 'Well OK then, I'll just sing one more song and then you can whisk me away to your castle. You can be the errant knight and I shall be your captive princess.' She linked her arm through Theo's and gazed up at his face.

'Theo will take you back to mine,' said Phoebe firmly. 'You can sleep on the bed and I'll sleep on the floor.'

'Come up to the Castle later,' Theo mouthed. Phoebe

nodded; Nola watched them.

'You don't change do you, Phoebe,' she slurred. 'Always falling into bed with any man that asks you.' Theo looked at Phoebe and raised his eyebrows.

Phoebe gave a dry laugh and steered Nola towards the kitchen. 'Come on, you can go out the back way and Theo will take you down to the boathouse.'

'The boathouse,' said Nola wistfully. 'Did I tell you that I'm going to sell it and make lots of money? I'm going to by a big house for me and the kids and show Steve I don't need him any more.' She stopped. 'Wait! No! I'm not going to buy a house for me and the kids. Steve can have the kids and I'll buy a penthouse flat in London and a sports car and I'll get a boob job.' She pushed up her already ample cleavage and turned to Theo. 'Don't you think they'd look good bigger? Bigger and more pointy upwards, would you like that, Theo? Not like Miss Flat-as-a-Pancake over here.' She gave Phoebe a little push. 'Flat Phoebe, they used to call her at school!'

'Nola!' Phoebe could feel herself going red.

'Your sister looks perfect to me,' said Theo with a grin, obviously amused by Phoebe's embarrassment.

'That's why she can't be choosy about her men?' continued Nola. 'That's why if she can't get one herself she has to take someone else's, ones that aren't that fussed about the little tits.'

'Please, Nola.' Phoebe had her by the back door now. 'You don't know what you're saying.'

'Oh yes I do, but after what that so-called best friend Sandra did to me, I don't care what you've done to her in the past.'

Phoebe looked at Theo's bewildered expression. 'Look, on second thoughts I think I'll take Nola home myself, she's completely out of it. Fibber and Katrina will just have to cope without me'

'No, don't worry. I'll look after her, and then I'll look

320

forward to your company later on.' Theo bent and kissed her cheek.

'What Nola just said,' Phoebe anxiously searched his face for signs of suspicion, 'she doesn't know what she's talking about.'

'Don't worry about it, Phoebe. She's drunk and she's your sister. I know from having Oliver as a brother that an older sibling's speciality is undermining the younger one.'

'Thank you,' Phoebe looked up into his reassuring eyes. She dragged her gaze away. 'Time to go, Nola,' she looked around. 'Nola?' Nola wasn't beside them any more; Nola wasn't in the kitchen any more. From the bar came the sound of Molly from the Hair Hut and her husband singing a duet. Suddenly Molly's shrill harmonies were interrupted by Nola's loud voice over the microphone.

'Hello all you lovely Irish people. It's me again, I just want to tell you that I've had the best time of my life with you tonight.' As Phoebe and Theo arrived in the bar no one appeared to be taking much notice of Nola. 'You're all fantastic,' Nola shouted, a few people cheered and there was a chorus of wolf whistling from the footballer's corner.

'I'd better go and get her,' sighed Phoebe, and she opened the flap on the counter and started to push her way through the crowd.

'The time has come to leave you now,' continued Nola, dramatically gesturing with her arms, 'but before I go I'd just like to sing you one more song to thank you all for being so fabulous.'

'I think your sister thinks she's Judy Garland at Carnegie Hall,' said Rory, as Phoebe passed him.

'I was thinking more Bette Midler,' said Phoebe through gritted teeth.'

'I'm waiting for "Over the Rainbow",' sniggered Ben.

'It's a song for you, but it's also for someone very

321

special in my life, my little sister Phoebe.' Nola pointed at Phoebe who was wedged between the large woman from the general store and Swedish Jan; the crowd cheered a little louder. 'My sister and I have been through a lot lately at the hands of unscrupulous men, or, as I like to call them – bastards!'

To the sounds of surprised murmurs around her, Phoebe pushed harder; she had to get Nola off the stage.

'Now I know that being someone's mistress isn't exactly the most virtuous position to be in as a woman, especially when the married man you're sleeping with is also your boss.' Nola wobbled slightly on her high-heeled boots and giggled. 'And let's face it, it's not as if Phoebe didn't know he was a married man.' She leant towards Phoebe, who was frantically mouthing *No, No, No.* 'You can't deny it Pheebs, of course you knew, you were invited to the wedding; not that you bothered turning up.'

At that point Phoebe managed to burst through the bodies, but found her way blocked by a line of stools and tables that had been moved back for the dancing. Nola addressed the room again. 'It was a lovely wedding, very tasteful, everything taupe.' She hiccupped. 'I was chief bridesmaid and six months pregnant with my second child – looked like an upholstered sofa but I put up with that humiliation because Sandra was my oldest, bestest friend and she was getting married to the lovely David – the Brad Pitt of Basingstoke, wasn't he, Phoebe? God's gift, that's what Sandra thought, unfortunately that's what he thought and several other women too, including my little sister.' Nola had the attention of the whole room now; she swayed and steadied herself by leaning against the microphone stand. 'But I know, that like I loved my Steve, Phoebe loved David, and probably believed him when he told her he'd leave his wife and two small children just as soon as he could get the chance.' Nola paused, there was complete silence, then a crash as Phoebe knocked a stool over in her attempts to get onto the stage.

'Please shut up,' whispered Phoebe as she tried to push two circular tables apart, she was only inches from her sister now.

Nola ignored Phoebe and continued on. 'And maybe if he hadn't died in that terrible traffic accident she could have broken up his home like Sandra went on to break up mine, but he would only have ended up cheating on my sister like he had been cheating on his first wife with her,' Nola paused and the silence in the room became all the more apparent. Nola continued with her speech. 'Now there was a time when even I thought my sister deserved to be punished for her unscrupulous behaviour,' she looked straight at Phoebe now, her smile disconcertingly benign. Even though Phoebe had her back to the crowd she felt the entire room staring at her. There was no point trying to stop Nola now.

Phoebe put her face in her hands; all happiness had crumbled inside her, replaced by an avalanche of humiliation. Phoebe forced herself to look up again and saw that the microphone stand was beginning to bend as Nola leaned on it. 'But now, after what that bitch Sandra and that bastard Steve did to me I can see how naïve and stupid Phoebe was, and I'd like everyone to know that I've forgiven her,' Nola's slur was now almost undecipherable, 'and even though we shouldn't be mean about dead people I think she's better off without him, like I'm better off without my snake of a husband.'

Nola hiccupped again. 'Now the song I'd like to sing is an old favourite of mine from when I was very, very, *very* young in the 1980s, it's "Sisters Are Doin' It For Themselves".' Nola pointed at Fibber who was in charge of the Karaoke machine. 'Hit it, Mr Flannigan.' Fibber didn't move. Phoebe risked a glance behind her, in an instant she took in Katrina standing with one hand pressed to her mouth, her eyes wide, Rory's mortified grimace,

Ben's highly entertained grin and at the very back of the bar, Theo. His face like stone he stared straight at her with an expression that she could only interpret as revulsion, before turning and walking out of the door.

There was an almighty bang and when Phoebe looked back to the stage Nola was sprawled on the floor, the broken microphone stand beneath her. Fibber sprang up beside her. 'She's all right, everyone,' he announced. 'She's actually trying to sing, not quite the correct words for the first verse, but she's giving it a good try. Katrina, would you help us get her into my mother's sitting room, she can sleep it off on the sofa tonight.' He briefly looked at Phoebe and then looked away.

People began to murmur all around her; Phoebe heard odd snatches of conversation:

'And to think she told us she'd been married to him.'

'I thought she was a widow.'

'Is there a word for someone who pretends to be a dead man's wife?'

'Isn't she the dark horse?'

'She had us all deceived.'

She couldn't bear it, the door was only feet away from her and blindly she pushed through the small group that separated her from it. She heard Sally O'Connell call out her name as she passed her, but she kept going and in seconds was standing outside on the pavement, oblivious to the driving rain and the wind.

A car screeched away from the kerb beside her, she recognised the number plate: Theo's Land Rover. She longed to cry, but her tears were buried beneath a wave of misery that seemed to drench her to her very core.

She began to run. She didn't care that she'd left her jacket in the pub, she didn't care that her thin cotton blouse was soaked in seconds, or that her wet hair slapped her face with every step she took. The lights of the Land Rover grew dimmer as it disappeared down the high street.

By the time she reached the lane they'd vanished and everything was thick and black and full of rain. Phoebe stumbled on; she saw no lights in the Castle as she passed. Hope sprang inside her, maybe Theo had gone to the boathouse, maybe he'd be waiting to tell her that it didn't matter what Nola had said, it didn't matter that she'd deceived him, it didn't matter that she'd just been a mistress, the sort of woman who would think nothing of breaking up a marital home.

Phoebe tripped against the root of a tree and landed on all fours in mud and grit; for a few seconds she stayed put, motionless, her head hanging low, her hair trailing in the dirt, oblivious to the physical pain she knew she should be feeling. After a few minutes she managed to stand up and ran on again until she saw the boathouse shrouded in darkness and realised that Theo wouldn't be waiting for her with forgiveness after all.

The sound of the sea was almost deafening as she reached the door. For a few seconds she contemplated turning around and walking down onto the beach – maybe everything would be so much easier if she just kept walking across the sand into those wildly crashing waves, to let the sea swallow her up and drag her down into oblivion; let the storm-enraged Atlantic ocean put an end to her miserable life.

But something stopped her, some thin thread of determination to go on living no matter what. She turned the key in the lock, the door opened, and Phoebe turned on the light. She saw the pots immediately; they were lined up along the workbench the way Theo must have wanted her to see them when he had arranged them earlier on. Phoebe could hardly bear to look; her reluctant glance took in the deep cobalt blues and the strength of her own brush strokes and designs. They were beautiful. She looked away and started to climb the stairs.

A strong gust of wind buffeted at the window with a thud and Phoebe realised she'd been sitting on the edge of the bed for ages. She'd tried to lie down but the smell of Theo on the rumpled pillow was too painful. She reached for her phone to see the time and then remembered it was in the pocket of the jacket that she'd left at the pub.

Suddenly she sprang up and rummaging under the bed found her rucksack. Imbued with a frantic energy, she began stuffing it with the few clothes she had brought with her. She left her grandmother's clothes in the drawers, apart from the daisy dress which she used to wrap the little pot her grandmother had given her so long ago. Theo's moon jar looked lonely on its own but Phoebe didn't want reminders of what she could have had.

Her packing was over within minutes; she picked up her car keys and surveyed the chaos she was leaving behind: the untidy bed, two half-drunk mugs of tea, a plate of toast crumbs discarded by Phoebe and Theo that morning, the glasses from which they'd drunk the night before. Phoebe couldn't bring herself to tidy up, to clean it all away as though last night had never happened.

Nola was welcome to it, Phoebe thought, mess and all, let her sell the boathouse and keep the money; Phoebe never wanted to lay eyes on her sister again. She remembered that the diaries were still under the floorboards, Phoebe hesitated, wondering if she ought to take them, but decided they should stay where Anna had hidden them – it was up to Nola to find them if she was interested in their grandmother's past – which Phoebe doubted.

She stopped at the top of the stairs and looked around her one more time.

She caught a glimpse of herself in the mirror. Her bedraggled hair hung limp on her shoulders, her white shirt was mud-splattered and crumpled, blood from the cuts on her hands and knees was smeared down its front;

she looked like an extra from a horror film. She shivered and realised she was freezing cold. She put on Anna's scarlet coat, and wrapped it round herself. As Phoebe passed the bedside table an impulse made her open the drawer. She took out the heart stone and, slipping it into the coat pocket, turned out the light and started to descend the stairs.

The door slammed behind her. Phoebe pushed the key back through the letterbox; it was final now, no going back. Getting into the Morris Minor she turned on the ignition and her heart sank as the engine choked and spluttered and then died. She tried again, and this time it coughed grudgingly into life. She started to drive slowly upwards, the little windscreen wipers trying to cope with the vast quantities of rain that cascaded down the glass.

Ahead of her she could see the light glowing through the banks of rhododendron bushes. Theo must be at home. Phoebe tried to increase her speed, to make it to the top of the lane, but some inner force compelled her to stop the car at the Castle gates. She pushed open the car door, battling against the strong wind and started to walk down the drive towards the point of light. Her head low against the gale, the red coat flapping out behind her, failing to protect her from the sheets of rain, she didn't know what she was doing, didn't know what she was going to do. The light grew increasingly nearer and brighter. Phoebe knew it was coming from the kitchen.

Phoebe could see Theo through the window in the kitchen door. He sat at the kitchen table, hunched over, head in hands, looking down at a large book. Phoebe's fingers rested on the door handle, she pushed down on the handle gently then stopped. As Theo turned the pages there was no mistaking what he was looking at with such a desolate face – an album of photographs. Phoebe was too far away to see but she was certain that the album must have been of his wedding, his wedding to Maeve – sweet, wholesome, beautiful Maeve.

A sudden movement beside her made her jump, something wet brushed against her. Phoebe put out her hand and Poncho's nose nuzzled into it. She bent down and hugged him; though his coat was drenched his warmth gave her brief comfort. He licked her face.

'Goodbye Poncho,' she whispered and stood up. With a final look at the scene through the window, Phoebe turned and retraced her steps, letting the pitch-black of the night swallow her up. Behind her Poncho barked but he didn't follow. Phoebe kept on walking even when she heard Theo calling to the dog; the sound of his voice was carried to her on the wind as she ran down the drive.

Chapter Twenty-eight

Phoebe drove towards the pale band of dawn. The rain had stopped and the wind had died down. Cork was now behind her, Kerry long gone – a hundred miles of road lay between her and Theo. Phoebe tried to concentrate on the immediate future and the practicalities of her hastily thought-up plan.

1. Get to a ferry port.
2. Buy a ticket to France.
3. Get to France.
4. Keep driving.

Keep driving had become her mantra, alternating with *Don't turn back.*

Initially she had headed for Cork, where she hoped to find a ferry for France. But arriving at the dark and rain-washed terminal she had found that the ferry was long gone and the next crossing wasn't for a week. Frantically she turned the Morris Minor around and headed for Rosslare.

Somewhere around Midleton she had added *Don't cry* to her mantra, but by Dungarvan so many tears were streaming down her face that it was harder to drive than when the windscreen had been awash with rain.

A lay-by sign loomed up ahead. Phoebe took the turn and stopped the car, grateful that a bank of high beech hedge obscured her from passing cars. Her head slumped against the steering wheel and a wave of misery washed over her as she thought of all the things she'd left behind. Not just Theo, but the village and all the people in it too. She hadn't realised how much Carraigmore had worked its way into her heart; its pretty shops and houses, its beach, and all the people that she'd grown so fond of. She wondered what Fibber and Katrina must think of her now, and then remembered that they would probably be much too busy getting ready for Mrs Flannigan's return from hospital to care. Rory would care, Phoebe knew that he would be disappointed in her – as would Sally and Molly and Swedish Jan and Young John and the members of Na Buachaillí Trá and all the other locals that she had duped. If buying too many packets of biscuits in the shop had once been big news then what kind of gossip would Nola's revelations be causing now?

And Honey. Phoebe pressed her fingers against her eyes. What would Honey make of her sudden disappearance? Phoebe's heart ached at the thought of never seeing the little girl's lovely face again. Who would help her with her reading and writing? Briefly she thought of turning back, if only to say goodbye to Honey, but she doubted that Theo would let her even see his daughter now. The memory of Theo's words the night before came back to her, like a knife tearing through her body: *I trust you* – within half an hour of showing that he had no trust in her at all.

With a sigh Phoebe wiped her eyes and straightened herself up in the seat. Her future lay somewhere else now, she didn't have any ideas beyond the straight poplar-lined roads of France, but she'd done it many times in the past – upped and left and made a new life for herself. She told herself that this would be just the same as before, even though it felt much harder to see the way ahead.

Long after the sun had risen she turned the key in the ignition and prepared to drive away. Nothing happened.

330

No purr of engine, no choke, slight splutter, not even a whimper.

'Damn!' Phoebe wondered what had possessed her to want to own a vintage car. She tried the ignition again. Still nothing. *Damn, damn, damn and* (as Fibber would have said) *fecking double damn with bloody bells on!* She hit the steering wheel; it hurt her hand. For a while she stayed in the car turning the key every thirty seconds or so, willing the car to miraculously return to life. When it became apparent that all vital signs were gone she looked around her; it seemed she had managed to break down in the bleakest, most uninhabited spot in the whole of Ireland. Tears pricked her eyes again but Phoebe squeezed them away. There was only one thing to be done.

Getting out of the car she started to walk.

It was already late in the afternoon by the time Phoebe pulled into the ferry terminal car park at Rosslare. She parked the car and got out. Her legs ached; she'd walked for miles before she'd found a cottage to stop at and ask for help. The young couple at whose door she'd knocked had stared at her muddy hands, tangled hair, and tear-stained face and held their two small children close to them as though she were a mad woman. Phoebe wanted to explain she didn't always look so deranged, but she was afraid she'd only start to cry again and they'd end up having her locked up. Instead she managed to stay calm while she explained about the broken-down Morris Minor, and not having a phone, and having a ferry to catch to France. The woman shook her head and told her she'd never get a mechanic on a Sunday, but the man offered to phone his friend Sean ('he's a wonder with old bangers'). Two hours and three cups of tea later Sean had worked miracles with a lump hammer and a pair of old tights and pronounced the car as good as new. Tentatively Phoebe had set off on the road again and had been amazed to find the car still working by the time she reached the ferry port.

As she walked across the car park a huge ship loomed up above her. This was it, nearly on her way; she was sure she'd feel much better if she was in a different country.

'One way to Cherbourg,' she said to the granite-faced man behind the ticket counter.

'That will be sailing on Wednesday,' said the man.

'I mean a ticket for today.'

'No sailings to Cherbourg today. The day after tomorrow is the next crossing.'

'Tuesday! I can't wait till Tuesday. Do you have any sailings before then?'

'Roscoff at eleven thirty tonight.'

Phoebe couldn't bear the thought of hanging around waiting till the evening. 'What about that ferry?' She pointed at the ship outside the terminal building.

'That's going to Fishguard, sailing in two hours.'

Phoebe sat down in a nearby chair to think. She hadn't wanted to go back to Britain, but if she took the Fishguard ferry and then drove down to the south coast she could get to France that night.

'OK,' she said, going back to the counter and opening her purse. 'I'll have a ticket for the ferry to Fishguard.'

'Sold out,' replied the man, his previously grim mouth twitched into a smirk.

'A later ferry to Fishguard?'

'Sold out.'

'All right then, Roscoff tonight?'

'Sold out.'

Phoebe was sure he was enjoying watching her mounting frustration. She tried not to scream. 'Do you have any places on any ferries this side of Christmas?'

'One left for Cherbourg the day after tomorrow.'

'I'll take it.'

'Sorry, Madam, you'll have to come back to buy your ticket tomorrow, this ticket office has just closed.'

Still seething from her encounter with the man in the ticket office, Phoebe found a low, red-brick motel. A faded sign in the car park proclaimed it to be *Star of the East*. After checking in she closed the door of her room and sat down on the bed, trying to reconcile herself to a full day of waiting around, trying not to dwell on her unhappiness. She turned on the television. It burst into an overly orange image of a group of elderly woman doing aerobics, and then the picture suddenly contracted into a tiny dot before disappearing completely and leaving the screen blank. Phoebe tried to turn it on a few more times before picking up the ancient bedside phone and telling the girl on reception that the television didn't work.

'I'll get someone to look at it.' The girl sounded bored and Phoebe doubted that she'd bother. With a sigh of exasperation Phoebe lay down, certain that she'd never be able to sleep on the rock-hard bed, only to wake up and find that she'd slept, still fully clothed, right through the night.

The only positive thing Phoebe could think of about the day ahead was the chance to take a shower. With great relief she stepped into the shower cubicle, anticipating that the torrent of warm water might bring some comfort as well as cleanliness. As she turned the taps a thin stream of water trickled weakly from the showerhead and almost immediately turned cold. Wrapped in all the towels in the room and shivering she phoned reception to ask when the television would be mended, and added a complaint about the shower. After she had put down the phone, Phoebe sat on the edge of the bed for a long time staring at the last few chips of Honey's nail varnish on her toes. Honey would be in school by now, she thought; Phoebe hoped she wouldn't be too upset. She wondered what Theo was doing, probably finalising things with the developers, booking plane tickets, avoiding Mrs Flannigan.

Phoebe lay back and tried to convince herself that she'd

had a lucky escape. What did she want with a temperamental potter with a child, a drink problem, and a dead-wife complex? With a groan she turned over and buried her face in the pillows – she simply couldn't imagine ever wanting anything else.

Later Phoebe got dressed and headed back to the port to buy her ferry ticket. After that she wandered around the harbour, but when a fine drizzle began to fall she went back to her room and made herself a cup of tea. She picked up the remote control and tried the television again. Still broken.

The drizzle stopped and Phoebe went out for another walk, stopping at a supermarket to buy three packets of Kimberley biscuits. Back at the motel she asked the receptionist for more tea bags and milk. In the room she made another cup of tea and ate two packets of the biscuits. She lay down on the bed feeling sick.

After spending a long time staring at a brown stain on the polystyrene ceiling tiles, she got up, and searching through her rucksack found her unread copy of *Jane Eyre*. Getting under the covers this time, she started to read. Much of it made her cry. Halfway through she opened the remaining packet of biscuits. When she finished the book she realised it was getting dark outside. She put the bedside light on, stared at the brown stain some more and contemplated the relationship between Jane and Mr Rochester; what would she have done if she had been Jane Eyre? Lived in sin or run away to save her soul? She had a feeling she'd have readily agreed to the former.

The next morning a loud banging woke her from a night of terrible dreams. She'd been lost on the heather moors, cold and hungry, her long dress and petticoats billowing around her in the wind. Initially the banging had been horses' hooves thundering across the moorland road, but as Phoebe opened her eyes she remembered where she was and realised that someone was at the door.

'I've come to mend the television,' a man's voice shouted. 'Kylie on reception says that you've been having trouble.'

Phoebe got up and opened the door.

'You're a bit early, or should I say late! I have to go and catch my ferry soon. Where were you yesterday when I needed a distraction?'

'I don't work Mondays,' said a rotund man; a boiler suit threatened to pop open as it strained over his stomach. He waddled into the room and started fiddling around with a panel at the side of the television set. After a few seconds a luminous orange picture of a newsreader burst on to the screen. The man fiddled some more and the colour changed to a slightly paler apricot.

'There you are,' the man took a handkerchief from his pocket and wiped his forehead, as though he'd just finished some kind of arduous physical exercise. 'Job done.'

Phoebe shut the door behind him and started to pack her rucksack. She slid the copy of *Jane Eyre* into the drawer alongside the Gideon Bible; something for the next customer to read when the television broke down again. Phoebe looked at the screen. The newsreader was describing scenes in the Dáil the previous afternoon, arguments over the economic future of Ireland, which had ended in a stand up shouting match; resignations were now being sought. Phoebe went into the tiny bathroom and tried the shower; the water was still cold. She splashed her face at the sink and brushed her teeth. Back in the bedroom the newsreader was reporting that fifty jobs were to be lost in a Limerick biscuit factory. Phoebe pulled on her jeans and, noticing it was still drizzling outside, put on a jumper; it would be cold standing up on the deck of the ferry as she said her goodbyes to Ireland. She looked around the room and felt pretty sure she had everything. She checked under the bed and once more in the bathroom, then heaved her rucksack on to her back. The television news reporter said it was 'Eight O Five A. M.' – less than half an hour until the final time for checking in. She reached for the remote control to turn the television off, and stopped. The whole screen had suddenly filled with a picture of a little girl; Phoebe's hand flew up to her mouth as she realised that the little girl was Honey.

'Concerns are growing over the whereabouts of the granddaughter of the Oscar-winning film director Joseph Casson,' the picture changed back to the newsreader, the picture of Honey relegated to the wall behind him. 'The eight-year-old girl has been missing since Sunday afternoon in the village of Carraigmore in County Kerry. Honey Casson failed to arrive back at the home she lives in with her father *(a brief picture of the Castle filmed from the gate)* and Gardai teams and local volunteers have been scouring the surrounding countryside looking for her.' The picture changed again to a line of policemen and dogs walking across the headland, heads down, long sticks prodding at the gorse. Phoebe couldn't move. Then there was Rory, saying words about Honey being a wonderful pupil at his school. She rubbed her eyes and tried to work out if she could still be having nightmares. When she looked up at the screen the picture was back with the newsreader; Honey's picture had been replaced with one of a large black pig. 'On a lighter note,' the newsreader said. 'A farmer in Donegal has broken the record for breeding the world's largest sow.'

Phoebe still stared at the television as though Honey's picture had been permanently burned on to the screen. How could Honey have disappeared? Where could she be? A string of possibilities raced through Phoebe's mind, each one more awful than the last. Phoebe thought of Theo and imagined how frantic he must be. She knew she had to get back to Carraigmore.

Chapter Twenty-nine

Within minutes Phoebe was in the car. Kylie's surprised face watched from the window as the little Morris Minor drove away from *Star of the East* at high speed.

In Waterford Phoebe had to stop for petrol. A newspaper headline on the garage counter blazed with the words *Missing – Oscar-Winning Film Director's Granddaughter Vanishes.* Underneath was the same picture of Honey that they'd used on the news: Honey in her school uniform with a red-brick wall behind her. Phoebe had last seen the picture propped up on the dresser in the Castle kitchen with a glitter-frame surrounding it and a little calendar hanging from the bottom. Without the frame the picture seemed bleak, the brick wall almost menacing; Honey wasn't smiling, her sad eyes were looking down instead of at the camera. She looked lost.

Back on the road Phoebe didn't stop. She passed the cottage where she'd asked for help two days before, and wondered if she dared stop to ask to use their phone to at least tell Fibber and Katrina she was on her way, and find out if there was any news. But Phoebe kept on driving; she didn't want to waste the time. If Honey was still missing there must be something she could do; even if she was just out on the moors with the volunteers, surely an extra body would help. Phoebe tried to think of places Honey might go; the boathouse must have been checked and all around the Castle grounds. Phoebe thought about the weedy pond ringed with gunnera and the dilapidated green houses and the ice-house with its tragic history. Had they looked in all those places? Phoebe shivered and pushed dark thoughts into the recesses of her mind.

The journey seemed to take for ever, the route much longer than before. Phoebe put her foot down and prayed that Sean's repair to her engine would hold out. Hours passed before signs for Kenmare loomed into view. After that the road narrowed and Phoebe found herself behind a succession of tractors and hay lorries with nowhere to pass. She beeped her horn to no avail, and narrowly avoided a collision with an oncoming coach when she tried to overtake a lorry.

At last she saw the sea and knew she wasn't far away.

Carraigmore was bathed in incongruous sunshine. As Phoebe entered the village, the painted shops and houses looked too bright and cheerful, the flowers too abundant, and the buckets and spades outside the general store much too redolent of fun.

There were at least five Gardai cars and a dog-handler's van parked along the high street, as well as two television trucks and numerous unrecognisable cars. A glamorous woman, flanked by a cameraman and a youth with a large fluffy microphone, was stopping passers-by and asking questions, no doubt about Honey. Phoebe parked her car in the lane behind the pub to avoid being interviewed.

The back door stood open. As Phoebe walked through the yard she could see Katrina standing at the cooker stirring something in a pan. The usually tidy kitchen looked chaotic. Dirty mugs and half-eaten plates of sandwiches were strewn all over the table, while Ordnance Survey maps lay, spread out, across the work-surfaces. Katrina turned as Phoebe stepped through the door.

'Oh, you are back!' She threw her arms around Phoebe and squeezed her until Phoebe had to pull away to breathe. Then Katrina led her to the table, picking up a pile of waterproof coats from a chair to make space for Phoebe to sit down. Katrina sat down beside her and Phoebe saw that, for the first time since she'd met her, she wore no make-up.

'Sorry, is all mess here,' Katrina gestured around her. 'The kitchen has become the base for searching party. Never have I made so many cups of tea.'

'Tell me what's happened.'

Katrina's eyes brimmed with tears. 'I think that it is my entire fault, I should have stayed with Honey, never left her on her own upstairs.'

'Why? She's often upstairs on her own.'

'But on Sunday she is so upset and angry with Theo, I tried to calm her but my mind is on Fibber coming back from Tralee with Mrs Flannigan and also with looking after your sister who is very ill with hangover and does not remember the night before – she thinks she deserves people to be nice to her!'

'Why was Honey so upset?'

'She keep saying that she was going to make Theo change his minds.'

'Change his mind about what? About selling the Castle?'

'And I think she wanted him to change his minds about you.'

Phoebe looked at the table. 'He must have been very angry when he found out about David.'

'No, Phoebe he wasn't angry.'

'But he dashed out of the pub so fast, his face looked horrified.'

'He is stunned, yes, a bit shock, yes, but he think you would come to talk to him later on at the Castle, he said you had an arrangement to go to see him there. When you didn't come he went to look for you at the boathouse and then he find that you are left.'

'I thought he wouldn't want to see me ever again.'

Katrina's dark bob swung from side to side as she shook her head. 'No, that is not right. When he finds that you gone it is very early in the morning. Still dark. He is desperate to find you, to get you to come back, to tell you that he does not care about what Nola said. He is thinking you will go back to England, so he drive all the way to Rosslare to see if he can stop you, but you are not there.'

Phoebe put her head in her hands; why hadn't he caught up with her; his car would have been much faster than hers? Then she remembered the tall beech hedge where the car had broken down; it would have completely obscured the Morris Minor from view.

'He come back here at lunchtime and he is very sad and when Honey hears that you are gone she is very, very sad and she is sure that Theo has made you go, and she is shouting that she hates him and goes upstairs upset. I am trying to talk with her but she is crying so much she will not listen, so I put on a *Harry Potter* DVD and leave her to calm down while I am making up bed for Mrs Flannigan and giving your sister many cups of black coffee.'

'Why didn't Theo take her home at that point?'

'He is gone to look for Rory to see if he know where you might be, and then when he comes back he starts drinking whiskey, sitting here at this table, and he has phone call from the developers on his mobile. He does big sigh and says, "Why the bloody hell not", and he accepts their offer for the Castle and then he say to me that he will be taking Honey to America as soon as he can. Now we think Honey might be hearing him because when I go back upstairs to see her she is gone; and the window is open in the bathroom and we think that she climbed down from flat roof on to the old beer barrels at the back. We found this in the yard and think Honey is dropping it when she jump down.' Katrina put the small jade dragon Phoebe had given her on the table.

Phoebe closed her eyes, what a mess. She should have

gone to talk to Theo, she should have thought about how Honey would feel if she left. As usual she had just run away.

'And also she leave this upstairs,' Katrina pushed an A4 sheet across the table. The writing on it looked like it had been photocopied from a much smaller note.

i haf gon uway doo not tri to fiynd mee

'The Guards have the original,' Katrina's voice trembled, 'as evidence.'

Phoebe imagined Honey trying to work out how to spell the words and thought her heart would break. 'Have they looked everywhere?'

'They are still searching the moor and all around the Castle, but today they also have the boats.'

'Oh God.' Phoebe covered her face with her hands.

Katrina picked up a tea towel and wiped her eyes. 'They are running out of hope, I think. Theo is distraught but he is out with Fibber and nearly all the village is helping the Guards search, even your sister has been looking. We are trying to keep it from Mrs Flannigan. I have such worry that she will see Honey's picture on the news. I am trying to be acting like normal but she is asking all the time for Honey and is wondering why Fibber is out.' Katrina broke down again.

Phoebe stood up. 'I must go and help them look. This is all my fault. If only I'd never come to Carraigmore in the first place. If only I hadn't tried to pretend that David had been my husband.'

Katrina put her hand on Phoebe's arm, 'Phoebe, do not be too hard on who you are. We all have secrets we try to hide.' She glanced at the doorway and lowered her voice. 'I will tell you my secret that no one knows, not even Fibber, not even Maeve when she was alive. In Slovakia I have a little boy; well he is not so little now, he is nine

341

years old. I also have husband.'

'You're married?'

Katrina nodded. 'Yes. To a bad man. When we first meet he is kind and very handsome, rich; here I think you would say he is *good catch*. But after we are married he start to get mean, he beat me up, he broke my arm, my ribs, my fingers, he burned my face with cigarette butts.' Katrina turned her cheek and Phoebe could see a row of small red scars that were usually hidden by foundation and blusher. 'And I find out he was crook.'

'That's terrible.'

'I run away from him, I take my baby son and go to my mother far away from him in the country, but we are not having enough money even to eat so I come to Ireland to earn money to send home. I was only to be here for a year but now seven years is gone and I have not seen my son or my mother, but I know they have money for food and I write every month, and my mother writes and tells me how my little Boza is getting on.'

'And Fibber doesn't know?'

'No.' Katrina was silent for a few moments, her fingers gathered a little pile of crumbs together on the table. Phoebe noticed that her nails were broken. 'I do not want him to know I am married to a criminal, and I do not want him to think badly of me leaving my child behind for all those years.'

'But Katrina, he would understand.' Phoebe sat down again. 'He would see that you had no choice, you had to leave your violent husband and you had to make sure that your mother and your son could survive.'

'Sometimes I think I will tell him but then I do not want to risk losing him. I love him.'

'Oh Katrina, he loves you too. I'm sure he'd never think badly of you.'

Katrina's almond eyes met Phoebe's own. 'And I think that Theo he likes you very much. He does not think badly of you just because you had love for a man who was married to someone else.'

Phoebe shook her head. 'It's not going to work out with Theo. I'll never be able to live up to Maeve, I'll always feel I'm living in her shadow.'

Katrina sighed. 'Theo and Maeve; maybe it was not all perfect like you think.' She swept the little pile of crumbs into her hand. 'Life, it is not clear like a bath; mostly it is like a big muddy pond, full of dirt and slime,' she paused, 'and it gets even muddier when someone like your sister comes and stir it up with big stick.

Phoebe smiled. 'Katrina, you have a wonderful way with words.' She stood up. 'But now I must go and help with the search.'

'Will you first do something for me? It would be big help if you could sit with Mrs Flannigan while I finish cooking her the lunch. Soon it will be one o'clock and we must make sure she does not see the news.'

'Mrs Flannigan won't want to see me, I'm sure.'

'Oh yes,' Katrina stood up and went back to the stove, 'she is asking for you all the time.'

Phoebe pushed open the door of Mrs Flannigan's sitting room. She could see the old woman sitting in an armchair propped up by pillows. She looked much smaller, her face like dough, puffy and pale. Phoebe walked into the room, the little Jack Russell lay curled up on a cushion beside the fire; it lifted its head and seeing it was only Phoebe promptly lay down and went to sleep again.

'Hello, Mrs Flannigan, how are you feeling?'

Mrs Flannigan didn't answer; her eyes were fixed on the television screen, some sort of quiz show flashed with bright lights every time a contestant said a word. Phoebe sat down on the edge of the sofa, inwardly longing to be outside with the search teams. She felt sure that Honey was still alive somewhere. She had to stop herself constantly looking out of the window to see if anyone was coming up the garden path with news; she'd promised Katrina she wouldn't look too anxious.

'What are they doing?' Phoebe asked nodding to the television. She was trying to look interested, trying not to look as restless as she felt.

Mrs Flannigan remained stonily silent.

'Is it naming capital cities?'

Still silence.

'Has anyone said Helsinki yet? And what about Bratislava?'

'He had hair like yours – all those wild curls.' Mrs Flannigan's voice was croaky as if she hadn't used it for some time.

Phoebe scanned the contestants on the screen, none had curly hair. 'Who do you mean?'

'Michael Flynn.' Mrs Flannigan instantly had Phoebe's full attention. Phoebe picked up the remote control and turned off the sound on the television. Mrs Flannigan shifted slightly in her seat, dislodging the pillow from behind her head. Phoebe sprang up to put it back, but Mrs Flannigan batted her away with a veiny hand and let her head fall back so that she was looking up at the ceiling. 'I suppose you think you know all about him, don't you?'

Phoebe wondered how much she should say? She could see how frail the woman had become, and she didn't want to distress her in any way, but she longed to know what had happened all those years ago.

'I knew that my grandmother and Michael Flynn were in love.'

'In love,' Mrs Flannigan repeated the words slowly. 'Yes, I suppose that summer they seemed to be in love.'

Phoebe considered what to say next. She moved along the sofa, closer to the old woman's chair.

'And I know the truth about Dr Brennan,' Phoebe said.

Mrs Flannigan let out a snort. 'What? That he liked

young men?'

'Yes,' said Phoebe.

Mrs Flannigan's voice grew stronger, 'What a scandal that would have been if it had come out.'

'So he had to run away to Africa?'

'Yes.' Mrs Flannigan was silent for a while. She still stared up at the ceiling, as if she were watching images of the past above her, as though the ceiling were a screen. Phoebe noticed how her hand plucked at the edge of the blanket that was spread over her knees. Just when Phoebe thought she wouldn't speak again she said, 'That wicked man, that priest, he had him blackmailed.'

'For money?'

Mrs Flannigan gave a short laugh. 'It might as well have been. If he had denounced him from the pulpit like he threatened, Dr Brennan would have lost his patients and his income.' She raised her head a little and searched out Phoebe's eyes. 'You have to remember those were very narrow-minded times, not like now.' Her gaze returned to the ceiling again. 'You young people, I don't suppose you can even imagine it. Father Ryan had us all living in fear as though he were the Lord himself, passing judgement on every little misdemeanour.'

Mrs Flannigan fell silent again, the television screen still flashed in front of them.

'She was very beautiful, you know.'

'Who?' asked Phoebe.

Mrs Flannigan stopped plucking at the blanket and leaned forward just a little. 'Anna Brennan. I used to think she had a look of Olivia de Havilland; she had that kind of serenity about her. I think Dr Brennan loved her in his way, hoped she might be able to save him and hoped that he could give her some sort of home after what had happened with her father. Dr Brennan was a kind man.'

'But Anna was so young.'

'Yes.' Mrs Flannigan coughed and took a deep breath

before continuing. 'Of course she couldn't save him any more than he could keep her shut up in that dismal house. She was forever walking up and down the beach. I used to watch her; you could see that scarlet coat for miles.'

'Did you watch her when she went walking with Michael Flynn?'

Mrs Flannigan said nothing, still staring upwards as though lost deep in recollections of the past. Phoebe glanced out of the window, torn between her anxiety for Honey and her desire to find out the truth about what had happened all those years before.

She leant forward and touched the old woman's arm. 'Mrs Flannigan, I know that Dr Brennan wasn't my grandfather.' She saw the old woman's eyes flicker towards her and then close. 'I know that Anna became pregnant. I know that my real grandfather was Michael Flynn. Anna and Michael's baby was my father.'

Mrs Flannigan's eyes remained closed. 'You think you know all that, do you?'

Phoebe hesitated. 'Yes, but what I can't work out is why they didn't go away together. Why didn't Michael come to meet Anna like they'd planned?'

Mrs Flannigan sighed, opened her eyes and looked at Phoebe. She struggled to sit up straighter and her voice grew stronger, even loud. 'God knows I've worried for every waking minute since you first walked into my pub. I knew that you'd start digging up the past, raking over things that shouldn't matter any more. I prayed to the Holy Mother herself that you would go away and leave me in peace. When you said that you'd found her diaries, I thought that Anna Brennan had risen to torment me from her grave, to punish me for what I did to her.'

'Why would she want to punish you?' Phoebe asked, but Mrs Flannigan interrupted.

'Lying in that hospital bed gave me time to work out things out. I decided that I couldn't agonize any longer about what you did or didn't know. I decided that the time had come to tell you what really happened, who you really are. But then I came back and you had gone and everyone's been acting all peculiar and I haven't seen Honey at all. Something's not right. What's going on?' Mrs Flannigan stopped and took a series of deep breaths.

Phoebe put the pillow back behind her head and smoothed the blanket. 'Nothing, Mrs Flannigan, nothing's going on.' She sat back down beside her, hoping that talking about the past would at least help to distract her from the present. 'What happened between you and Anna, did you do something to upset her?'

Mrs Flannigan tried to turn around in her chair. Phoebe quickly realised that she was trying to reach a knitting bag that sat beside the sofa – a half-finished cardigan spilling from the top. Phoebe handed her the bag and Mrs Flannigan put her hand deep inside and drew out an ancient Oxo tin. She held it out to Phoebe and slumped back on the pillow. Phoebe prised the lid off and held up a key. Mrs Flannigan waved one hand towards a writing desk on the other side of the room. 'In there; there's a drawer inside the desk.'

Phoebe walked over to the writing desk and opened it. She pushed aside the clutter and revealed a row of four small drawers along the bottom. Three of them pulled out when Phoebe tried them, but one was locked. Phoebe turned the key and tried again; the drawer slid smoothly open to reveal a single envelope, yellowed with age, the ink on the address faded to grey.

Mrs Flannigan's face was turned away as though she couldn't bear to look at what Phoebe had in her hand.

'Read it,' she croaked.

Phoebe drew out the brittle piece of writing paper. '*My Darling Anna,*' she began.

'Not out loud,' Mrs Flannigan cried. 'Read it to yourself, girl. I don't want to know what it says.'

Phoebe continued to read in silence.

Please don't be too troubled if I tell you there has been a terrible accident; it is only so terrible because it means I will be unable to meet you at the crossroads as we had planned. I will be mended as soon as I have had a small operation, and then I am determined that it will not be too long before we leave for France.

I know I only came home to wish my parents and brothers goodbye but I found that my father's arthritis is very bad this winter and I tried to help as best I could around the farm. Unfortunately, (and this is the part I don't want you to worry about) I turned the tractor over in the higher field and my leg was crushed beneath the wheel – three breaks to my right fibula. I have been in hospital these last two days and the doctors think I need my leg to be set properly with an operation tomorrow morning and then I will be in here for a few days more. They promise me no ill-effects – not even a limp.

But I am afraid that France will now have to wait, maybe until the New Year.

Can you bear it? I know I am knotted up with frustration at the thought of delaying our getaway. I lie here fretting while my mother fusses and brings me fruitcake and knits me bed socks. All I want is to look into your lovely eyes and have you in my arms again. I am so angry that I misjudged the slope in the field; I have been driving that old Massey Ferguson since I was a child. My brothers have been relentless in their teasing, they say that it's such a shame that I am too soft to be a farmer and shower me with pity and commiseration. If only they could see you; then they would be the envious ones.

I miss you terribly; you are constantly on my mind. I will be back for you as soon as I can and then we'll be together always.

All my love,

Michael. X

PS: Will you write to me at the address I will put on the envelope? Please write as soon as you can.

Phoebe looked on the back of the envelope and saw an address for a farm in Galway. She carefully folded up the letter and sat back down beside Mrs Flannigan who still had her head turned so that Phoebe could not see her face.

'Mrs Flannigan?' Phoebe touched her arm again. 'Did Anna ever see this letter?'

Mrs Flannigan's head shifted slightly and very quietly she said, 'No.'

Phoebe rubbed her eyes and thought of Anna waiting at the crossroads all that time, wondering where he was and why he didn't come for her.

'I loved him,' Mrs Flannigan's voice was almost inaudible. Phoebe had to lean closer to her so that she could hear. 'I loved him just as much as Anna Brennan ever did. From the moment he first came to Carraigmore I knew I'd always love him. He looked like Errol Flynn. So handsome, nothing like the other men in Carraigmore. But then I saw him talking to Anna Brennan on the beach and I knew that I had lost him.'

'But you took their notes, delivered them back and forth, became their willing conduit, their go-between.'

Mrs Flannigan turned to Phoebe with watery eyes. 'They knew I couldn't read, they could say whatever they liked, I would never know.'

'They used you,' said Phoebe.

'I wanted to do it – it was all I *could* do. If I couldn't have Michael's love I could make myself indispensable to him, to them.' She smiled. 'It was like a film, better than a film, feeling I was playing some part. I knew it was wrong but I often followed them, watched their love grow and tried not to hate her for everything she had.'

'Did you know they were going to go away together?'

'By the late summer I knew that they were making plans.' Mrs Flannigan was silent for a while. 'It broke my heart, I became ill, a terrible migraine that lasted for weeks. I still tried to take their letters back and forth but there were fewer. They didn't seem to need me any more. By the autumn I had realised two things: one, that they would soon be leaving and, two, that Anna was carrying his child.'

'I was right then,' Phoebe said. 'About the baby.'

Mrs Flannigan ignored her, continuing on as though she were almost in a trance-like state of recollection. 'He went away one day and Anna told me that he'd gone back to Galway to say goodbye to his family and then they would be leaving. She was almost glowing with excitement; she could hardly sit still long enough to finish a meal. I couldn't bear it. When his letter came to the shop I steamed it open.' She stopped, and pressed her hand against her chest, gulping down a series of deep breaths, her complexion turning grey, then blue. 'I tried so hard to work out what it said,' she gasped.

'Are you all right?' Phoebe asked anxiously. 'Can I get you anything? Do you have tablets that you need to take?'

Mrs Flannigan shook her head and seemed to recover. After a few more seconds she carried on. 'I couldn't work out the words of course and I meant to give the letter to Anna, I really did. I put it in my cardigan pocket and would have given it to her after dinner. I went up to her room; I heard her singing, she sounded so happy. I could see through the crack in the door that she was packing. I hated her then. Why should she take him away from me, why should she be so happy when all I had to look forward to were long and empty days in Carraigmore? Even then I meant to give her the letter the next day; I'd say it had come in the afternoon post.'

'But you didn't give it to her?'

'No. I watched her that evening, leaving the house with her suitcase. Then Dr Brennan brought her back and I realised the letter must have been to tell her he couldn't meet her.'

'You could have given her the letter at that point.'

Mrs Flannigan became silent, when she spoke again her voice trembled. 'In the end the days passed and I never gave it to her. Other letters came from Galway and I burned them. I didn't even open them. I just destroyed them in the wood-burner at the back of the shop. More and more kept coming; in the end there was a letter for her every day.'

'Michael must have been desperate, wondering why Anna never got in touch. Did you not feel guilty?'

The old woman shook her head. 'Not then, not till much, much later. When I realised Anna and Dr Brennan were going to Africa I was overjoyed, it was then that I knew I'd never give her the letter or tell her about the others that had come. Anna would be gone and when Michael came back I'd be there to comfort him. Never in my wildest dreams had I imagined I would get such a chance.'

'And did he come?'

Mrs Flannigan's lips twitched into a brief smile, her voice grew stronger again. 'Oh yes, he came. It was nearly spring by that time, there had been complications with his leg but he came back. And there I was waiting for him, a foolish girl of sixteen; I thought he'd realise how much I had grown up, he'd see me in a new light, realise that I was the one he'd wanted all along.

'He came to the house, right to the house and asked for her. The new doctor had let my mother stay on to work for him, but by that time she'd already started her decline. I heard her open the door to Michael and watched from the

351

window as she shooed him down the path. She was yelling at him that Anna and Dr Brennan had gone away and that it was none of his business where they were. By the time I got outside Michael had disappeared. I knew immediately where he would go – I remember putting on a new white blouse and lipstick, slipping out the back door and running down the lane. He was there, sitting in the boathouse, too consumed with misery even to realise that I'd come up the stairs. I sat down beside him on the bed and put my arms around him, but he shouted at me to leave him alone. He might as well have slapped me in the face. I ran back home in tears but then an idea came to me, I would go back to him with whiskey and that would help him mend his broken heart. I took a bottle of the new doctor's Tullamore Dew, and hiding it beneath my coat returned to the boathouse and offered him a drink. By that time he was grateful for the comfort of alcohol and he let me stay and asked me questions, and God help me I sat there and told him a pack of lies. I told him that Anna and Gordon had always seemed very happy together, that I thought she'd realised that she didn't want to leave her husband after all and when the opportunity of a job in Africa had come up Anna had been the one to encourage Gordon to apply for it. I said she had told me that she needed to get away, that she'd told me herself that Michael had become too attached to her, too clingy. He asked me if Anna had received his letters. *Oh yes*, I said, *I gave her all the ones that came.*'

Phoebe felt like a priest on the other side of the confessional, the story was pouring out now and she wondered how she could ever absolve Mrs Flannigan for the sins she had committed against her grandparents.

'I poured myself a glass of whiskey,' Mrs Flannigan went on. 'I'd never drunk alcohol before, it burned my throat and made me cough but it gave me the courage to do what I did next.'

352

Phoebe wanted Mrs Flannigan to stop talking; she'd heard enough, she didn't want to hear any more.

Mrs Flannigan was staring straight ahead. 'I kissed him,' she said. 'I kissed him and after a while he kissed me back and I let myself believe that I really meant something to him, even though I knew that he'd had half the bottle of whiskey by then. We lay down on the bed together and I knew that what I was encouraging him to do was wrong, and at the end it was Anna's name he called out with all the passion that I had hoped he felt for me. But afterwards, while he was sleeping, I held him and told him that I loved him and tried to believe that when he woke up he would want take me away to France instead.'

'And did he?' Phoebe already knew the answer.

'No, of course not. When he woke up he dressed and said he had a boat to catch. At the top of the stairs I remember him turning back to me and saying "Sorry", and then he left me sitting on the bed, my new blouse crumpled, my lipstick smudged. I didn't see him again for forty years.'

'You saw him again? When?'

'He came here, to Carraigmore, a few weeks after Anna died. He came into the pub and I served him with a pint of Guinness; I don't think he recognised me. I must have looked very different, middle-aged, plump and wrinkled, but I would have known him anywhere. Still the same dark chocolate eyes, still all that curly hair – it had turned grey by then but it was just as thick. I couldn't speak to him; I didn't know how to begin. He seemed too wrapped up in his own thoughts, too melancholy to interrupt. When he left the pub I followed him. He stood outside the boathouse for a long time and then he walked along the beach and disappeared over the headland. I never saw him again.' Mrs Flannigan's voice was getting hoarse but she continued. 'I heard he went to live in Donegal and then, of course it was all over the news when he died. I hadn't realised he'd become so famous.'

Phoebe bit her lip. 'Do you think that Anna would have told my father he was Michael's son?'

'I don't know if Anna ever suspected he was Michael's.'

'But Dr Brennan didn't even try to consummate their marriage, and there wasn't anyone else, was there?'

Mrs Flannigan's reply was so quiet that Phoebe had to ask her to repeat it.

'Your father wasn't Anna's child.'

Phoebe stared at Mrs Flannigan. Mrs Flannigan leaned back and closed her eyes.

'Here it is, your lunch at last,' a clatter of crockery accompanied Katrina's arrival in the sitting room. She looked from Phoebe to Mrs Flannigan and back again. 'Has she been all right, she is looking so washed up and pale?' Phoebe couldn't stop staring at Mrs Flannigan. Just when she thought she'd had all her questions answered there were more.

'What do you mean?' she asked, ignoring Katrina, straining to make out what Mrs Flannigan was trying to say.

'What is she saying about?' Katrina asked. Phoebe put her finger to her lips to quieten her.

Mrs Flannigan started to speak again. 'He was Michael's child, but he wasn't Anna's.' She cleared her throat a little before she whispered, 'He was mine.'

'So you're back are you, Phoebe? Come to help the search at last?' it was Nola now who stood in the doorway, her long hair tangled, her high-heeled boots replaced with muddy wellingtons. Phoebe glanced at her briefly and then took Mrs Flannigan's papery hand in her own.

'Yours?' she asked softly. 'My father was your and Michael's child?'

'What's she talking about?' Nola stepped into the room and this time it was Katrina who had her finger to her lips.

354

'I think she is telling to Phoebe something very important.'

Nola sat down beside Phoebe on the sofa. Katrina sat beside her and the three younger women all looked at Mrs Flannigan and waited for her to speak again. In the corner the silent television still flickered and the small Jack Russell woke and turned around on his cushion before settling back down to sleep again.

Phoebe shook her head. 'I'm finding it hard to take this in; are you telling me you're our grandmother?'

Mrs Flannigan nodded.

'It must be meaning that Fibber is your uncle and that Maeve would have been being your aunt,' said Katrina.

Phoebe thought for a while, 'So that would make Honey ...'

'Honey,' Mrs Flannigan's rasping voice was almost a shout. Katrina and Phoebe turned to her and saw her wild-eyed gaze directed at the noiseless television. The whole screen was filled with Honey, *missing child in Carraigmore* going by underneath on a bulletin band.

Katrina grabbed the remote control and turned it off, but Mrs Flannigan was already struggling to get out of her chair. 'What has happened? What's happened to Honey?'

Katrina and Phoebe rushed to her side and managed to get her seated again. 'Is all right,' said Katrina. 'Is nothing happen to Honey, she is all right.'

'What's she doing on the news then? It said a child is missing in the village, is it her?'

'No,' said Katrina.

'Yes,' said Phoebe and she crouched down and took both of Mrs Flannigan's hands in hers. 'Honey has been missing since Sunday. She ran away and so far no one has found her. The Guards are looking and many people from the village, everyone is trying their best.'

Mrs Flannigan's hand was at her chest again; her face had become the colour of a bruise.

'I must get the pills,' Katrina hurried out of the room and was back in seconds, a brown bottle in her hand, desperately twisting at the lid. 'I can't undo child-proofing.' Nola took it from her and opened it. Katrina tapped out two tablets and tried to make Mrs Flannigan swallow them with a drink of water. Mrs Flannigan pushed her away, the water spilling onto the blanket.

'The mirror,' Mrs Flannigan gasped. 'In the boathouse. Have they looked behind the mirror?'

Chapter Thirty

In seconds Phoebe was running down the high street. In her mind she had the image of the full-length mirror in the flat; she'd often thought it was unusually big for the size of the room, thinking about it now Phoebe realised that it could well be as big as a door.

'Hey, Phoebe,' someone called. She turned and saw Rory on the other side of the street, he had an Ordnance Survey map around his neck that no doubt showed the area he was either about to search or had just finished.

'Tell Theo to meet me down by the boathouse,' Phoebe shouted over her shoulder. 'I'm not sure but I think I know where Honey is.'

'I'll find him.' Rory broke into a sprint and ran off in the opposite direction.

'Phoebe, wait.' Still running, Phoebe looked over her shoulder just as Nola caught up with her.

'I don't need you with me, Nola, haven't you done enough damage already?' Phoebe tried to run faster but Nola's Zumba classes seemed to have made her capable of keeping up with her sister.

'That woman,' Nola said a she jogged beside Phoebe, 'that Mrs Flannigan. What was she talking about back there? Is she really our grandmother?'

Phoebe nodded. 'I can't explain now.'

'If she is our grandmother why didn't she get in touch after the accident?'

'I don't know; I can't even think about it. I need to find

Honey.'

Nola kept pace as they left the shops and cottages behind. 'She could have come and helped us; she could have helped me instead of leaving me with a child to bring up when I was no more than a child myself. She just left us all alone and let me ruin my life.'

'What do you mean "ruin your life"?' Phoebe was panting now as they reached the top of the lane.

'I was seventeen, I had everything ahead of me: my A-levels, a place at university, a chance to become a doctor – and instead I gave all that up.'

'You gave it all up to marry Steve.'

'I gave it up to look after you. I thought marrying Steve would be the best thing to do for your sake; I wanted to make a home for you, get a job, help you get through school.'

'Have the chance to boss me around at every opportunity, put me down, make me feel like a failure.'

'I've only ever wanted to look after you Phoebe; I've only ever wanted to do the right thing.'

They'd reached the boathouse now. It looked deserted; there wasn't even anyone the beach, though Phoebe could see the cliff tops were crawling with people and a helicopter was circling round and round the headland.

'And I suppose you thought the right thing was humiliating me in front of the entire village on Saturday night.' Phoebe stopped on the path, her hands on her knees as she tried to get her breath back.

'I'm so sorry, I was drunk, I didn't know you hadn't told your new friends the truth.'

Phoebe turned away from her and tried the door. It was locked.

'Damn!'

'To be honest I think I felt a little jealous,' continued Nola. She gave the door a push herself. 'Haven't you got a key?'

'I posted the key back through the letterbox when I left. What do you mean "jealous"?'

'We'll have to try to break it down,' Nola started kicking it with her foot. 'I mean coming here, finding you with a gorgeous man and lovely friends – everybody telling me how great my little sister is. That made me feel jealous. Maybe I've always been jealous of you.'

'Have you?' Phoebe was pushing at the door with both her hands. 'This isn't budging! Why would you have ever been jealous of me?'

'You've had it all: the education, the opportunities, the chance to travel, the chance to have loads and loads of boyfriends.'

'There weren't loads and loads – you always wanted to make out I was just some sort of promiscuous dropout.' Phoebe's hands were beginning to hurt but she kept on pushing, using her knees and feet as well. 'I never could do anything right.' Her words came out in short bursts with each kick and shove. 'I didn't get as many exams as you. Art college wasn't nearly as good as medical school. Travelling was simply squandering my time and money. In your eyes I've always been a failure. God, why's this bloody door so strong?'

Nola stopped kicking and looked at Phoebe. 'But I've always thought you were wonderful! I admired the way you just got on and did your own thing, saw the world, made the most of your life while I was stuck in suburbia eating Snickers bars and ironing shirts. That's one of the reasons I was so angry about David. For the first time I thought you'd let yourself down. You deserved someone better than another woman's philandering husband.' She took a step back. 'Look, I think we're both just going to have to throw ourselves at this with everything we've got.'

Phoebe stepped back too. 'OK on the count of three: one, two, three …'

Together they charged, hitting the wooden timbers with

their shoulders at full force. With a splintering crack the door gave way and Phoebe and Nola fell inside, tumbling against each other, landing in a heap on the floor. Phoebe untangled herself from Nola and holding out a hand helped her sister up.

'I'm sorry, Phoebe,' Nola brushed down her jeans. 'I never meant to boss you around, or put you down; I've only ever wanted to do the best for you.' She looked around at the room. 'My God, it's just the same as it always was in here.' She nodded towards the row of blue and white pots still lined up on the table. 'I like those.'

'I decorated them,' said Phoebe.

'You see. Another talent that I'll never have, and you ask why I'm jealous?'

'I'm sorry.' Phoebe touched her sister's arm. 'Maybe I've never properly appreciated what you did for me after Mum and Dad died; the sacrifices you had to make. You were amazing.'

They both looked up at the sound of scuffling up above them. 'Honey!' Phoebe shouted, and she and Nola rushed up the stairs.

Phoebe stood in front of the mirror feeling along the edges of the wide mahogany frame, trying to find some catch or handle, tearing away the Michael Flynn postcard as it got in her way.

'Honey! Honey!' She called the little girl's name, again and again. She stopped as a she heard a muffled noise coming from behind her own reflection.

'Phoebe?' she heard a child's voice clearly say her name. She pulled the frame as hard as she could, first on one side and then the other.

'Help,' the voice behind the reflection said. Nola jammed the fire poker behind the frame and used it like a lever. Phoebe pulled again and suddenly the mirror swung open and she could see Honey huddled in one corner of a gloomy, narrow room. The little girl still wore the dungarees that she'd had on when Phoebe had tucked her into bed two days before, and her baseball boots were caked in mud and grass stained.

Honey didn't move; Phoebe crouched down in front of her. 'Are you all right?'

Honey nodded but tears were streaming down her face. 'I couldn't make the door open.' She gulped. 'I wanted to get out and I couldn't and I've been so frightened.'

Phoebe looked around her. There was a small skylight in the ceiling, but the branch of an oak tree grew across it and not much daylight filtered through the leaves. Some things were stacked up against the wall at one end but apart from that the room seemed empty.

'You're all right now.' Phoebe put her arms around Honey and held her tightly. When she felt the little girl tremble she asked Nola to fetch an old shawl of Anna's and wrapped it round Honey's shoulders. 'This will keep you warm; it used to be my granny's.'

Granny? Phoebe thought. She'd have to get used to the fact that Anna hadn't been her granny at all.

'I didn't mean to close the door,' said Honey, her teeth chattering. 'Grandma always tells me I mustn't let it close, but when I saw the Gardai coming from the window I ran inside and slammed it shut and then it was stuck.'

'How did you get into the boathouse in the first place?' Nola asked. 'We nearly did ourselves a serious injury trying to get in.'

'Grandma keeps another spare key under the flowerpot by the door.' Nola raised her eyes and glared at Phoebe.

'Sorry,' Phoebe shrugged, 'I never thought to look.' She turned back to Honey. 'Is this where you've been since you ran away?'

'No, first I thought I'd go to Dublin. I thought I'd get a job in a pub. I started walking but coaches kept coming and nearly running me over, and then I went on to the moor, but I got lost and frightened and I didn't want to be

361

in a pub in Dublin, I just wanted to be here. I remembered something Mr O'Brian had said at school, about the sun always setting in the sea so I followed the sunset.' She looked at Phoebe with brimming eyes. 'I'm sorry, but I ate all your biscuits and a bar of chocolate and the rest of that bottle of orange juice you'd left behind.'

'It's all right, sweetheart,' Phoebe smiled, 'I don't mind; but you must be starving now. Why don't we go and tell everyone that you're safe and get you something to eat.' She tried to gently pull Honey up but the little girl resisted.

'Is Daddy still going to sell the Castle and make me go and live with Granny Stick?'

Phoebe tried to think how to answer – she didn't want to make rash promises but she didn't want to upset Honey either.

'Thank God!' a voice cried out behind them. Phoebe looked up to see Theo bounding to the top of the stairs.

'Daddy!' Honey sprang up and ran into her father's arms. 'Phoebe found me, Phoebe let me out. I thought I was going to be in that room for ever and ever, and I'd never get to see you again.'

Theo glanced at Phoebe for a second, then all his attention was back with Honey. 'Whatever possessed you to run away like that? You've had us all worried sick.' He was out of breath, his face flushed from running.

Honey nuzzled into his shirt. 'I'm sorry,' she mumbled. 'I didn't think you'd really care; I know I'm just a nuisance to you.'

Theo sighed, crouched down and wiped her tears with his fingers. 'You could never be a nuisance, Honey. Even when half the Guards in Kerry and several television crews descend on Carraigmore because of you, I never think of you as being a nuisance. You know you're more important than anything else in my life.'

'More important than your pots?' Honey asked looking

up at him. Theo hugged her tightly.

'Much, much more important than any pots.'

Honey smiled for the first time. 'Was I really on the television?' Theo nodded. 'Did you record it?' Honey asked.

'Honey!' Theo held his daughter at arms length. 'All I've been doing for forty-eight hours is desperately searching for you. I haven't even slept, let alone recorded the news! I've been terrified that I'd never see you again.' He hugged his daughter even tighter while she whispered 'Sorry' over and over again.

Phoebe leant against the doorway and watched. She saw how tired Theo looked, his face unshaven, his shirt dirty. He seemed to have aged since she'd last seen him. He turned and looked at her, Honey still pressed against him.

'Thank you,' he said.

'You will ask her to stay now won't you, Daddy? Don't let her go away again.' Honey wriggled out of Theo's embrace and threw her arms around Phoebe's waist.

Theo smiled at Phoebe. 'My two favourite women running away from me on the same day, a man's got to be very unlucky or have done something very bad.'

'No!' protested Phoebe. 'I was the one that had done something bad.' She looked down at Honey; she didn't want to say too much in front of her.

'If you mean what your sister said, I don't care. Well, I did at the time – a bit – but not now. She should never have told everyone like that.' Nola gave a short cough, and for the first time Theo noticed she was there. He shot her a fierce look. Nola made a grimace and mouthed *Sorry*.

Phoebe bit her lip. 'You don't mind about my ...'

Theo interrupted her, 'I don't care about your past Phoebe; it's only your future that I'm interested in.'

'Good line!' Nola muttered under her breath.

'What are you talking about?' Honey looked from one

363

adult to the other.

'I'm trying to follow your advice and am asking Phoebe to stay,' said Theo.

'Why don't you just ask her properly then?' She looked up at Phoebe, her face suitably solemn. 'Are you going to stay?'

Phoebe looked at Theo and then she nodded. 'Yes, I think so.'

'Good, because it's much nicer with you here and my dad's in love with you.'

Theo and Phoebe burst out laughing. Nola rolled her eyes but couldn't help but smile.

Honey looked up at Theo. 'And what about the Castle? You can't sell it to those developing men, you just can't.'

'I think before we talk any more about the future we'd better tell the Gardai and the television crews that they can go home now.' Theo put his arm around his daughter and started to steer her towards the stairs.

'And get that food we talked about,' added Phoebe. 'And we must tell your grandma and Katrina that you're safe, poor Mrs Flannigan was in a terrible state when she saw your picture on the news, though we never would have found you without her help.'

'Honey! Am I pleased to see you!' Rory emerged at the top of the stairs.

'Did you know I've been on the television, Mr O'Brian?' Honey said proudly.

'So have I,' Rory said. Phoebe's face fell. 'Though I think it's safe to say you were the star of the show.'

'There's actually a little metal catch here.' Nola had been examining the secret door. 'But it's very well hidden by the mirror's frame.'

'Don't tell Grandma that I went in the special room.' Honey looked imploringly at Theo. Theo stroked her head and told her not to worry.

'I'm off back to the village,' said Rory. 'I'll tell

everyone you're alive and well, Honey, and give them a chance to hang out the bunting before you arrive.' He bounded down the stairs two at a time and disappeared.

'We'd better make a move now, too,' Theo said.

'Hang on.' They turned at the sound of Nola's voice coming from the hidden room. 'What are all these? There's loads of them.' She emerged with a canvas in her hands. 'I don't know much about art but I rather like these paintings.'

'They're the pictures Grandma likes to look at,' said Honey.

They all followed Nola back into the room. A pile of canvases were stacked up neatly against the far wall, each one a similar size – as wide and high as a fully spread out broadsheet.

Theo picked one up and squinted at it in the murky light.

'My God, it can't really be!'

'Really be what, Daddy?' asked Honey.

'Really be a bloody William Flynn.'

Phoebe peered over his shoulder, vaguely making out a little tossing boat almost suspended against a wall of towering waves. She felt her stomach twist in excitement. Actually to see one: the powerful brush strokes, the thick layers of oil paint, almost three-dimensional in places. No picture in a book could have prepared her for the sheer energy that seemed to exude from the painting's surface.

Theo picked up another one. 'Look, it's the black rock, you can tell, and behind it there're the mountains, and just look at that sea crashing on the beach, it looks like it's almost moving.'

'That's Grandma's favourite,' said Honey, pointing at the next one: a tiny cottage perched precariously on the edge of a cliff, a line of white washing flapping against a blackening sky.

There were eight in all. One by one they took them out

of the hidden room to look at them in the sunlight of the flat.

Theo uttered a string of expletives as he examined each one in amazement.

'Daddy, you shouldn't swear so much,' said Honey, who had grown bored and was busy eating from a box of cereal she'd found.

'I can't help it. You have no idea how bloody valuable these paintings must be.'

Theo brought out the last painting and placed it against the back of the armchair.

'That's my favourite!' cried Honey through a mouthful of crunchy-nut cornflakes.

Phoebe had been studying a painting of a tanker on a heaving horizon. She looked up and glanced at the picture on the armchair.

'Oh!' she let out a gasp. It was Anna in her scarlet coat, Razzle at her feet, both of then gazing out across a tempestuous sea. It was the painting of the sketch he'd done. Phoebe stared at it. That stormy day had been at the beginning of their journey together. So much had happened because a lonely girl and a painter had found each other on a windswept Irish beach. Sixty years of repercussions; layer upon layer of secrets had been laid down just as William Michael Flynn had layered his oil paints.

Phoebe picked the painting up and held it at arm's length, admiring it, grinning at it, feeling her heart begin to beat harder at the excitement of what they'd found.

'What's that?' Honey was pulling something from the back of the canvas. 'It looks like a letter but it's got a funny pattern round the edge. Someone's sellotaped it to the painting.'

'Careful!' cried Phoebe, but already there was a ripping sound and Honey held two pieces of an envelope in her hands. Phoebe could see it was an airmail envelope. She took the pieces from Honey and held them back together again. It was addressed to Anna in a scrawling hand that looked vaguely familiar. She examined the brightly coloured postage stamp: U.S.A., the postmark 1995.

'I can't understand how all these paintings got here?' Theo shook his head in disbelief.

'It's a long story,' Phoebe said slipping the two halves of the envelope into her pocket. Theo looked at her quizzically.

'You know?'

Phoebe nodded. 'Though now it's an even longer story than I thought, and I still don't think I know the ending.'

'Uh oh,' Honey was looking outside the window. 'Looks like the Guards and the television people have arrived.'

'I think your revelations will have to wait, Phoebe,' said Theo. 'Honey, it's time to do some explaining yourself.'

Chapter Thirty-one

The sea was as calm as the warm evening air, reflecting the sunset like a mirror; in the distance the mountains looked purple against the blush pink sky.

'It's beautiful, isn't it?' said Phoebe leaning against the battlements. 'I could look at the view from up here for ever.'

Theo came and stood behind her; he lifted up her hair and very gently kissed her neck. 'You can now,' he turned her round to face him, his arms encircling her waist. 'That was the developers on the phone, you've no idea how cross they were when I told them that the deal was off.'

'You've done the right thing for Honey, you know.'

'What about for us?'

Phoebe smiled. 'We'll see.'

Theo started to roll up Phoebe's sleeves. 'You look rather nice in my old shirt.'

'I had to put something on to come up here; I didn't want the whole village talking about a naked women standing on your roof.'

Theo drew her towards him again. 'I've just put one of Katrina's chicken pies in the oven. You can stay for dinner, can't you? Fibber and Katrina have offered to keep Honey for the night.' He nuzzled into Phoebe's neck. 'I feel like I haven't seen you properly since you came back.'

'We've just spent the entire afternoon in bed.'

'I mean to talk to,' he kissed her. 'We didn't seem to do much of that this afternoon did we?' Phoebe laughed. 'It's been so busy since everyone discovered Honey had been found: photographs for the papers, interviews, Rory's party for the school children, Fibber's endless celebrations and now there's the special céilidh tomorrow night.'

'Anyone would think Carraigmore had won the football again. Honey must feel like the Queen.'

Theo sighed, 'She's been embellishing her story so much that I think she actually believes she flew off on a dragon's back and was locked up in that room by an evil goblin. I don't know whether to get cross with her for telling lies or praise her for her imagination.'

'There seems to be a great tradition of distorting the truth in this village.'

'Especially in your family!'

'My family?' Phoebe disengaged herself from Theo's arms and turned back to the view. 'Oh yes, I keep forgetting that I'm part of Honey and the Flannigan's family. It seems weird to think I'm not related to anyone from the Castle at all.'

'Do you mind?'

'Not really, at least I have some actual relatives now. Nola's a bit disappointed; she's always been very proud her aristocratic lineage, she loved to lord it over Steve whenever he was getting on her nerves.'

Theo handed Phoebe a glass of wine. 'I thought you might like an aperitif before dinner.'

Phoebe thanked him and raised her glass. 'To the Castle.'

Theo picked up his cup of coffee. 'To us.' He leant back against the battlements, cradling the coffee mug between his hands. 'So, did you discover how your father came to be brought up by Anna and Gordon Brennan in the end? Katrina said Mrs Flannigan wouldn't settle until she'd told you and Nola the whole story.'

Phoebe nodded and took a sip of wine from her glass. 'It seems that poor Della didn't even realise she was pregnant until it was pointed out to her mother by the parish priest. In a matter of days they had her bundled off to some awful home for unmarried mothers run by nuns,' Phoebe shook her head. 'I can't even begin to tell you some of the appalling things Mrs Flannigan said had happened to her in there.'

Theo grimaced. 'Poor Della, you hear such terrible stories. Did she run away?'

'No, the day after she had given birth, she was just about to be forced to sign the baby over to a farming couple from the back of beyond when Anna appeared with papers from the priest, instructing the nuns to release Della and the baby. Mrs Flannigan said she found out later that Anna had forged the papers herself.'

'Why wasn't Anna in Africa? Where was her baby?'

'Her baby had been stillborn. Afterwards she needed a hysterectomy, so Gordon sent her back to Ireland to have the operation in Dublin – safer than a Nigerian hospital. When she was strong enough she hired a car and came back to visit Carraigmore. She found that Della was missing and somehow she managed to get Mrs Smythe to tell her where Della was.'

'So she rescued Della and took her baby in return?'

Phoebe nodded. 'That just about sums it up. After a few days in a guest house in Kinsale she gave Della a lift back to Carraigmore and took my father back to Africa.'

'Did Della tell her that Michael had come back, did she tell her the baby was his?'

'No, she said she thought Anna would be so angry that she'd take her back to the nuns, so I don't know if Anna ever knew the baby was Michael's. Della never told her.'

Theo took a sip of coffee and frowned. 'Even when Anna came back to Carraigmore all those years later? But Della must have seen her son and his family on the annual summer visit; surely that must have been hard for her, and what about when your parents and Anna died, why didn't she tell anyone you and Nola were her granddaughters?'

'She says she couldn't tell anyone, she was terrified Maeve and Fibber would find out she'd had an illegitimate child and be horrified.'

'Considering Maeve was seven months pregnant when we got married, I don't think she would have cared.'

'Was she?' Phoebe looked surprised.

Theo turned Phoebe round to face him, 'I think you've got the wrong impression about Maeve. She wasn't the perfect wife you seem to imagine she was; she had a tongue as sharp as her mother's and was as stubborn as that old bugger Fibber Flannigan Senior, over in Roscommon. She was beautiful and full of fun and energy, but she not at all easy to live with.'

Phoebe looked at him archly. 'And you were, I suppose?'

Theo gave a short laugh. 'No, I know I wasn't the perfect husband either but together we weren't a good combination. Maeve and I fought like cat and dog over everything. When we lived in our tiny house in Dublin poor Honey would have to lie in bed at night and listen to us. I know she could hear because Katrina used to complain that she could hear us from next door. We were on the verge of splitting up when my father died. Inheriting the Castle seemed a chance for us to give our marriage another go.' Theo paused and drew his hand across his face. 'Though it soon became pretty clear that the Castle was only going to drive us further apart; Maeve had so many grand plans, I just wanted to make pots. She was all for taking out big loans to renovate the place. I thought we needed to be careful. Then Maeve got diagnosed with cancer and I became consumed with guilt, all that time we'd wasted arguing; suddenly I couldn't bear to be without her. When she died I thought I would go mad, not just from grief but from remorse for something that we never actually had – a happy marriage.'

372

Phoebe touched his arm. 'I'm sorry you weren't happy together but, to be honest, I'm relieved to hear that I don't have to live up to some impossibly saintly wife. I think the strain would drive me crazy.' Theo took her hands in his.

'Let me assure you, you don't have to live up to anyone.' He kissed her. 'You are perfect just the way you are.' His hand wandered underneath the shirt and he started to undo the buttons. 'Surely no one will see us all the way up here.' Phoebe smiled and closed her eyes.

'Phoebee, Phoebee,' someone was shouting from the driveway. Phoebe clasped the shirt together and looked over the battlements to see Rory standing far below, holding up his phone in his hand. 'He's texted back,' she could just make out his voice. 'He's coming over on the Friday night ferry.'

'Fantastic,' Phoebe shouted and Rory turned around and sprinted back towards the gate, whooping as he ran.

'What was all that about?' asked Theo.

'I think Welsh Owen has forgiven him.'

'Who?'

'His long-lost love.'

'What about the paramedic?'

'He succumbed to the charms of a junior doctor. Nola and I persuaded Rory to text Welsh Owen and tell him that *Jailhouse Rock* was just as good as *Blue Hawaii*.'

'I haven't a clue what you're talking about.' Theo looked confused.

Phoebe reached up and kissed him. 'It doesn't matter; we've got far more important things to do than talk about Rory O'Brian's love life.'

ONE YEAR LATER

Phoebe walked along beach, enjoying the sun on her face and the gentle breeze. As she neared the tide line the breeze turned into a wind that whipped up her curls and made goose-bumps on her arms. She had been carrying the red coat but now she put it on and wondered how much longer she would be able to do up the buttons. Poncho padded obediently at her heels, though every few minutes a gust of wind would ruffle his fur and send him racing back and forth across the sand.

Phoebe looked up towards the Castle, it was a relief to see it without its shroud of scaffolding at last. The new roof seemed to have taken ages, but now the house had been revealed in all its splendour: the stonework cleaned, the Virginia creeper cut back to frame the new windows, and the stained-glass dome repaired so that instead of filling the hallway with rainwater it filled it with a rainbow of sparkling light. Inside the builders were still working on the water-damaged walls and floors and they were doing a wonderful restoration job on the Georgian plaster-work ceilings. It wouldn't be long before Nola would be moving into the apartment she'd had made on the second floor. Phoebe knew her sister was desperate to move out of the holiday cottage she and the children had been renting in the village. She seemed to spend most of her time picking out carpets and looking at curtain swatches and trying to persuade Amy and Ruben that Carraigmore was just as exciting a place to be a teenager in as Basingstoke. Phoebe smiled, Oliver had sent an email to Theo that morning; he was coming over yet again next month. Something was definitely going on between him and Nola; ever since they'd spent all night dancing at Phoebe and Theo's wedding Nola used any excuse to bring up his name.

Phoebe could see two figures waving from the battlements, she knew it would be Honey and Boza; they seemed to have some sort of kite that they were trying to launch in the wind. Since Boza and his grandmother had arrived from Slovakia he and Honey were rarely to be found apart. Boza quickly picked up English and his Gaelic was as good as any local child. And he was now the star of the Carraigmore under-twelves football team, much to Fibber and Katrina's delight.

Katrina's mother, Rosa, had found it more difficult than her grandson to adjust to life in a new country; with a limited grasp of the language and an aversion to the sea, it had been hard for her to settle down in Carraigmore. But she had surprised everyone by getting on with Mrs Flannigan. Maybe because of her lack of English she didn't seem to mind Mrs Flannigan's cantankerous nature and, maybe because of Rosa's smiley disposition and her vast array of floral aprons, Mrs Flannigan always seemed more cheerful in the Slovak woman's company.

Rosa seemed to be enjoying working alongside her daughter in the pub kitchen, making wonderful cakes and soups and pies. Carraigmore had recently had a write-up in the *Irish Times – Top Twenty Places to Visit in County Kerry*. Fibber Flannigan's was mentioned and Rosa's Slovakian potato dumplings were recommended by the journalist, which brought an extra flush of happiness to Rosa's plump pink cheeks.

The article had also brought the Castle Pottery its first coach-full of tourists – Kieran Kennedy's Luxury Coach Tours had deposited thirty-five members of the Ohio Ladies Circle in front of the newly converted stable block.

In seconds they were swarming everywhere, taking pictures, asking questions, and enthusing about everything, while Theo and Phoebe ran around trying to keep up with them.

A genuine Irish castle, how wonderful.
Is that tower really a thousand years old?
Isn't that view just divine?
Don't you just love the pottery?
What a charming gallery, are all the things in here really made by you?
Is it true there's a connection with William Flynn?
I can't make up my mind between the cute little jug or the vase.
Oh, I adore those blue and white bowls – I'll take ten.

Since then Kieran Kennedy's had made the Castle a regular stop on its Ring of Kerry route, and Phoebe and Theo began to think maybe they did have a viable business after all.

When she reached the black rock Phoebe stopped and leant against its sun-warmed surface. She was sheltered from the wind here, and she undid the buttons of the coat and looked out across the sea. A sailing boat slipped by in the distance. She vaguely wondered if she should produce more nautical designs but her mind soon wandered to more immediate concerns. She closed her eyes. Was this really the right time? So much was going to change; but then so much had changed already.

Phoebe still found it hard to believe that the paintings could have fetched so much. She and Nola had looked at each other in disbelief as the auctioneer at Bonham's reeled off the figures. Heads kept nodding, new phone bidders kept coming in, museums bidding against collectors, a businessman from India, galleries in China and Japan; the excitement had been built up by numerous magazine and newspaper articles and even a feature on the evening news. Phoebe's head had swum as she held on tightly to Nola's hand. Hundreds of thousands of pounds, up and up. Phoebe had been shaking at the end, and when the head of a major national gallery shook her hand and congratulated her on one of the most significant finds in contemporary Irish art, Phoebe had had to excuse herself to get fresh air before she passed out at his feet.

'Has the world gone mad, or is it me?' asked Phoebe as she and Nola drank gin in a pub off Bond Street. 'No one's meant to have any money but there's still enough around for paintings to sell for ridiculous amounts.'

Nola shrugged and took another gulp of gin. 'Don't tell me you're complaining! Like everyone keeps telling us, the whereabouts of William Flynn's early works have been a mystery for years. They were bound to have attracted a lot of attention.'

'Michael knew where they were. It seems amazing that he just told Anna to keep them.' Phoebe thought about the letter they'd found, taped to the picture of Anna and Razzle on the beach, it had been dated two months before Anna had died.

Dear Anna,

I was overjoyed to get your letter in the post this morning; I didn't dare to believe that you'd reply. As I said in my first letter, when I saw your work in that book about Irish Pottery I simply couldn't stop myself from picking up my pen – I only wish I'd known about the exhibition in Dublin, I think I was even visiting Ireland at that time.

I can imagine the boathouse it is as wonderful a place for a pottery as it was for a painting studio and I think your pots are beautiful, I wonder what your art mistress would think now!

I enjoyed hearing about your son and his family in

England, and in answer to your question no, I never seemed to get round to having any children myself.

You mentioned that you still have some of my paintings. Please keep them. Hang them on your walls – remind yourself of all those happy days we spent together, long ago.

I will be coming to Ireland in June, I wonder, would you mind if I came to visit you?

Yours, William Michael Flynn.

'I think they would have got back together.'

'You're always such a romantic, Phoebe. He was a famous artist, he probably had a string of young muses to entertain him.' Nola drained her glass. 'Do you really think he'd have wanted to rekindle an old flame?'

'I think that was what Anna wanted to tell us when we picked her up from the airport. She was going to meet the man she'd always been in love with; they were going to be reunited at last. That was the surprise she told me she had for us.' Nola stood up shaking her head, Phoebe persevered. 'But he did come, didn't he? Mrs Flannigan told me she saw him in Carraigmore after Anna died. And that painting he did of the beach, the one on the postcard – he must have done that then; and the figure walking on the sand in red – don't you think that was meant to be Anna, Anna in the coat I sometimes wear?'

Nola rolled her eyes. 'I don't know Phoebe. It all sounds like some wild flight of your imagination. What I do know is that I need another G&T; you …?' Phoebe nodded, and Nola disappeared to the bar.

Phoebe received her fourth text from Theo that morning.

Come home soon, the Castle feels too empty without you. XXX

'I still think we should have sold the painting of the girl and her dog,' said Nola as she sat back down with their drinks.

'No,' Phoebe had been adamant. 'We mustn't ever sell Anna. After all, we'd have nothing if it hadn't been for her.'

Two million each, after the auctioneer's fee and the taxes. Nola had had an immediate spending spree; new car, new clothes, a holiday with Ruben and Amy, a holiday on her own, a holiday with a man called Marcus she had met on her previous holiday, and another holiday to get over her and Marcus splitting up.

Phoebe knew immediately how she wanted to spend her money. It was all for the Castle. Even though it was no longer the ancestral legacy she'd once thought it was, it had become her home. She loved living there more than she ever could have imagined when she had been a little girl gazing through the locked gates.

The house ate up the money at a tremendous rate. Nola's investment in the second floor apartment had been a help, but Phoebe and Theo were only too aware that they had to make the pottery work as a viable business if they were really going to be able to stay.

Phoebe suddenly had a huge desire to lie down on the sand. Still leaning against the rock she closed her eyes. Was it normal to feel so sleepy in the afternoons? She'd have to ask Nola or Katrina.

She opened her eyes and realised that she must have dozed off. The wind had died down; the sea looked like a gently undulating piece of satin, reminding Phoebe of the curtains Nola had just chosen for her bedroom. Phoebe looked up at the Castle and saw that Honey and Boza's kite was high above the battlements now, tail fluttering like some magnificent medieval flag. She waved to the two children, but this time they were too engrossed in flying the kite. Suddenly she noticed a figure sitting on the slipway; a large woman dressed in purple. Phoebe put her hand up to shield the sun from her eyes and saw that it was Mrs Flannigan.

'It's not often I see you on the beach,' Phoebe said as she reached her. 'Are you out enjoying a walk in the sunshine?'

Mrs Flannigan crossed her arms, small breaths escaped through her mouth; she was evidently out of breath. 'I wouldn't say enjoying is quite the word, but my doctor says I must get more exercise so here I am getting it. I only meant to walk as far as the Castle, but I could see that red coat of Anna Brennan's from the top of the lane so I knew well enough where to find you.'

Phoebe wondered if Mrs Flannigan minded her wearing the coat; did it bring back painful memories? Even though Mrs Flannigan was her grandmother, Phoebe still found herself rather uneasy in her company, and could never think of her as anything other than *Mrs Flannigan*. Even *Della* seemed consigned to the depths of another period of Mrs Flannigan's life.

'Were you looking for me especially?' Phoebe asked. Mrs Flannigan nodded so that her long diamante earrings swung back and forth, sparkling in the sunlight. She was silent for a few minutes as she recovered from her exertions. Phoebe sat down beside her and wondered if Mrs Flannigan had brought her tablets with her – underneath her make-up her face looked very red.

The old woman began groping around in the pocket of her cardigan, tutting when all she seemed to pull out were tissues and empty sweet wrappers. Phoebe thought she was looking for her bottle of pills but instead she finally pulled out a folded square of paper and handed it to Phoebe. 'I wanted to give it to you on the morning of your wedding,

381

but there never seemed to be the time, and then I thought maybe it was all best left good and buried in the past. But lately I've been thinking that maybe you ought to see it after all.'

Phoebe looked at her quizzically. 'What is it?'

'Just read it,' she said. 'I think it might be of some interest.'

The yellowing paper crackled in Phoebe's hands. It opened out into a long official-looking document. Mrs Flannigan watched her.

Registration of Births and Deaths. Form A.

'It looks like an old birth certificate.'

Mrs Flannigan grunted. 'It is old, very old; in fact it's as old as me.'

'Is it your birth certificate?' Mrs Flannigan nodded.

The certificate was filled out in spidery black ink and Phoebe had to strain her eyes to make out the tiny writing.

Date and place of birth: 8th March, 1934, Clontarf Nursing Home, Dublin.
Name: Adelaide Mary
Sex: Female
Name and Surname and Maiden Surname of Mother: Margaret Shaw. Formerly Hickey
Name and address of Father: Charles Shaw, the Castle, Carraigmore

Phoebe drew in a sharp breath and looked at Mrs Flannigan.

Mrs Flannigan nodded. 'That's right, child, Charles Shaw was my father.'

For a few seconds Phoebe couldn't speak as she struggled to comprehend what this discovery actually meant. Charles had been Anna's wayward uncle, she remembered him being mentioned in Anna's diaries.

Phoebe shook her head and looked up at Mrs Flannigan. 'But how did your mother bear him a child?'

'The usual way,' the older woman's reply was curt.

'I mean how did they meet? Were they really married?'

Mrs Flannigan pursed her lips. 'No, they were never married. That was just a bluff for the Dublin nursing home so that my mother didn't get carted off to the nuns like I did sixteen years later. Charles Shaw never showed the slightest bit of interest in acknowledging my mother's predicament or that he had a daughter. It was the age-old story; woman falls in love with man, man gets what he wants and leaves the woman to deal with the consequences.'

'How did they know each other?'

'She was a housemaid up at the Castle.' Mrs Flannigan gave a disparaging sniff. 'At the time he was languishing in the family home waiting for his elder brother to give him enough money to resume a more exciting life in London. To Charles, Margaret Hickey was a way to pass a dull, damp Irish winter, to Margaret Hickey, Charles was the love of her life.

'It was very common in those days, those landed-gentry types almost saw it as their prerogative; a pretty servant girl was theirs for the taking,' Mrs Flannigan spoke with derision. 'When my mother told him she was expecting his baby the money was suddenly found to send him back to London and my mother found herself dismissed. It was Dr Brennan that took her in. She appeared on his doorstep with stomach pains and bleeding. He gave her a bed; looked after her until the danger of a miscarriage had passed. Then he himself took her to Dublin to work for a friend – an actor who wasn't shocked by a pregnant serving girl so long as she was prepared to turn a blind eye to the sort of late-night entertaining that would have got the man a prison sentence at the time. After I was born my mother came back to Carraigmore to work for Dr Brennan. I think, at the time, she secretly hoped Charles would come back to the village to find her.' Mrs Flannigan laughed incredulously. 'As if he ever would have; he probably didn't even remember her! The war was on in England and my mother used to listen to the news and worry he'd be killed in action as much as if she'd been his wife. In the end Charles Shaw was killed, not in action but dancing with a Wren at the Café de Paris on the night it got hit by a bomb.

'My mother was never the same. Now they'd probably say she had a breakdown or give her a condition with some complicated name, in those days she was simply suffering from her nerves. Dr Brennan was very good to her, kept her going with various pills and his support. She couldn't cope when he left for Africa and then, what with me and the baby,' Mrs Flannigan sighed, 'by the time I came back from that godforsaken laundry the new doctor had had her put in the asylum.'

'That's awful,' whispered Phoebe.

Mrs Flannigan shrugged. 'I returned to Carraigmore with nothing – I'd lost my mother, my baby, and my home – my job at O'Leary's had gone to someone who could read and write. It was no wonder I agreed to marry that old goat Fibber Flannigan when he asked me.' The old woman stopped and her watery eyes followed a passing gull across the sky until it became a speck on the horizon and vanished. 'I had eight miscarriages before Fibber and Mauve were born – each one a penance for what I had done.'

Phoebe touched her arm. 'I know it can't be easy for you, dragging up the past.' The two women were silent for a while then Mrs Flannigan sniffed and pulled her cardigan around her chest. 'I'd better get back. I've better things to be doing than sitting around chatting all afternoon, though I'm not looking forward to the steep walk back up that lane.

Phoebe tried to hand back the birth certificate. Mrs Flannigan shook her head.

'You keep it, girl. It's not as if I can read a word of it anyway.' With difficulty she eased herself down from the slipway until she was standing on the sand.

'Wait.' Phoebe jumped down beside Mrs Flannigan. 'Did Anna Brennan know that her uncle was your father?'

'Oh yes – she told me that Gordon Brennan had told her when they got to Africa. I think that's why she was so happy to take my baby; even if she never guessed that it was Michael's she knew it was part of her family.'

'Wait till I tell Nola she's a Shaw after all.' Phoebe smiled. 'She'll be so pleased.'

'And you,' asked Mrs Flannigan with unusual softness. 'Are you pleased?'

'Yes, yes I am. But isn't it strange the way that things work out? I'm actually living in my ancestral home after all.' They both looked up at the Castle. Honey and Boza and their kite had gone and the setting sun lit up the windows.

Mrs Flannigan let out a long breath. 'Some things are meant to be.'

'Come on,' said Phoebe. 'I'll walk back to the pub with you. You can lean on me if you like.' Phoebe put out her arm and Mrs Flannigan took it. Slowly they set off up the beach towards the lane with Poncho beside them. 'I'll see if Katrina will make us a cup of tea?'

'If you like.' Mrs Flannigan shrugged, then suddenly gave a little grin. 'Rosa's made her famous ginger and honey cookies. Ginger always helps if you're feeling sick.'

Phoebe wondered how she knew. Lately she felt nauseous all the time.

Mrs Flannigan stopped suddenly. 'What's that?' She kicked at something at her feet, half buried in the soft, dry sand. Phoebe pushed Poncho's inquisitive nose away and bent to pick it up. Warmed by the sun and as smooth as new-born skin, the pale pink stone had been worn into the most perfect heart Phoebe had ever seen.

She looked at Mrs Flannigan, 'You've found a heart stone, the best one ever.'

Mrs Flannigan grunted, but Phoebe could see that a smile twitched at the corners of her mouth, 'Keep it. It can be the first gift for your baby.'

'My baby?'

'The baby that you're carrying. You must be three months gone, I'd say.'

Phoebe touched her stomach; it felt flat beneath the cotton of her dress. 'How did you know? I haven't even told Theo yet.'

Mrs Flannigan had started to walk on ahead with surprising speed. She stopped and turned back to Phoebe.

'Haven't you learned yet?' She smiled and her eyes seemed nearly as glittery as her earrings. 'You can never keep a secret in Carraigmore, even if they take a lifetime to come out.'

THE END

A Perfect Home
by
Kate Glanville

Claire appears to have it all – the kind of life you read about in magazines; a beautiful cottage, three gorgeous children, a handsome husband, and her own flourishing vintage textile business. But when an interiors magazine asks to photograph Claire's perfect home her rural dream begins to fall apart. The magazine article leads to a series of tragic events that will be the catalyst for Claire to change her life. This is a poignant love story set against the domestic idyll of roses, bunting, fairy cakes and D.I.Y.

For more information about **Kitty Glanville**
and other **Accent Press** titles
please visit

www.accentpress.co.uk

Printed in Great Britain
by Amazon.co.uk, Ltd.,
Marston Gate.